P9-CQE-062

The Crowded Earth

THE CROWDED EARTH

People and the Politics of Population

By PRANAY GUPTE

W · W · NORTON & COMPANY
New York London

Published simultaneously in Canada by Stoddart, a subsidiary of General Publishing Co. Ltd, Don Mills, Ontario.

Printed in the United States of America.

The text of this book is composed in Avanta (more commonly called Electra), with display type set in Clarendon. Composition and manufacturing by Haddon Craftsmen Inc. Book design by Winston Potter.

Portions of this book have appeared, in slightly different form, in the International *Herald Tribune*, the *New York Times Magazine*, the *Atlantic Monthly*, *Forbes* Magazine, and the *Reader's Digest*.

FIRST EDITION

Library of Congress Cataloging in Publication Data

Gupte, Pranay.
The crowded earth.

Bibliography: p.
Includes index.
1. Population. 2. Population policy. 3. Developing countries—Population policy. I. Title.
HB871.G975 1984 304.6'6 84-6145

ISBN 0-393-01927-6

W. W. Norton & Company, Inc., 500 Fifth Avenue, New York, N. Y. 10110

W. W. Norton & Company Ltd., 37 Great Russell Street, London WC1B 3NU

1 2 3 4 5 6 7 8 9 0

This one's for Jayanti—
for her affection, patience, and support;
and for A. M. Rosenthal—
for giving me a start in life.

Bahout mohabbat say—With much love

Contents

Foreword

At the end of the eighteenth century, the Reverend Thomas Malthus rang an alarm bell to warn the world that its population was growing so fast that it would inevitably outrun food supplies. Being a humane man he feared for the poorer people who would suffer hunger and death, and being a man of the cloth he also feared that the resulting turmoil would cause a degradation of social morality. By the last quarter of the twentieth century, an entire carillon of alarms was ringing, warning that the world's annual population growth would inevitably exceed Spaceship Earth's carrying capacity. The language of "population" was often spoken in hyperbole and phrases like "population bomb" and "population explosion" were tossed about like grenades in public debates; new sects calling themselves "populationists," "the population community," and "the population movement" were formed. And since sects promote the formation of counter-sects, groups set themselves up against the "population mafia" denouncing their motives as being anti-life and even genocidal.

In this intellectual climate, the United Nations hosted a first-ever world conference on "population" in 1974 in Bucharest. Some three thousand delegates from one hundred forty countries convened to decide on a World Population Plan of Action, a sort of Magna Carta of fertility. The chief value of this meeting was that it was held at all. Everyone was there—the industrialized Western states of the First World, the Communists of the Second World, and the poor nations of the Third World. Even the Vatican sent an "observer." Some participants at the conference argued that the world's "population problem" was not a matter of the rate of biological reproduction but a question of the rate of resource development and fairer distribution of the gains of economic growth. Some government leaders of countries with vast, still untapped natural resources offered the view that national "greatness" came from a large population. The politicians talked politics and the demographers talked statistics—and neither understood the other.

Ten years have passed and much has changed since Bucharest concerning the world's views and attitudes about "population." The most important change is that there is now a widespread common understanding that "population" is not one "problem" but many, and therefore will not yield to a single solution or a quick fix, such as compulsory sterilization or saturation of a community with contraceptives. It is now understood fairly universally, I think, that there are no "global" solutions because people don't live on the globe but in communities within nations, and each country has its own needs and possibilities. For example, India and China need to reduce the size of the family, while West Germany, France, and Hungary want to increase their numbers and are encouraging their people to do so.

We are now told by the experts that the world's annual population growth is slowing down. But our "population problem" is far from over, because the world is still adding ninety million people each year. Although the brakes have been put on the previously rampant rate of population increase, the developing world is young and fertile—and even if each young couple is persuaded to limit family size to two children, the world's annual addition of people will keep growing every year for the foreseeable future. The real population problem, therefore, is to persuade countries to accept this as an unavoidable reality and to plan for it now. Another vital need is for everyone in the rich and the poor countries to realize that the great issues confronting them—population growth, environmental pollution, urban blight, mass illiteracy, hunger and malnutrition, disease, social unrest, drug abuse, unemployment, bad housing, and transportation—are inseparably intermeshed.

Pranay Gupte's *The Crowded Earth* is a valiant enterprise in relating those seemingly diverse concerns. His book is a population odyssey. As he travels through the five continents, through the corridors of the United Nations, in the chanceries of Europe, the bustees of Bombay and Hyderabad, the favellas of Latin America, the villages of Kenya, Sri Lanka, and Indonesia, talking to government officials, administrators, economists, planners, physicians, agriculturists, ecologists, paramedics, extension workers, and people in the towns and villages whose needs they are expected to serve, Pranay Gupte weaves their varied perceptions of needs, problems, and possibilities into a rich human tapestry.

He takes "population" out of the hands of the demographers and specialists and politicians and gives it back to everyday people.

Varindra Tarzie Vittachi

The Crowded Earth

One

Ten Years after Bucharest
A Journey to People

THE STORY THAT UNFOLDS in this book is a story of many people in many lands all across the globe. It started as a journey begun many years ago when the *New York Times* made me a foreign correspondent and assigned me to Nairobi to cover Africa and report on how the emerging states of that troubled continent coped with their new nationhood, how they struggled to move from economic backwardness to modernity. It was a wondrous experience for a young man on his first posting abroad, especially for a journalist whose reporting until then had been more or less restricted to chasing fires in the South Bronx, monitoring muggings in Brooklyn, and writing about zoning and singles' bars in the New York area suburbs. I felt I was a storyteller in a bazaar, telling the world about itself—wars, warts, and all. They were delightful days: one evening in Teheran, an Iranian family I had interviewed near the grand mosque asked me over for a meal of chelo kebab; not long after that, another Moslem family I met in Baghdad invited me to celebrations in honor of a new-born daughter. In tension-filled Kabul, with Soviet tanks rumbling through the streets of the Afghan capital, a Sikh family that had befriended me took me along to a traditional wedding that lasted three days. In northern Ghana, I was made a blood brother by a local tribe; in neighboring Nigeria, I was made an honorary citizen. Those years as a foreign correspondent brought me a thousand instant friendships and gave me glimpses and insights into strange and sometimes bewildering life styles. There were passionate dialogues over dinners about where the world was going, about what was happening to different societies as they sought to improve their living conditions, about, most of all, how people felt about where their own lives were headed.

A great newspaper such as the *Times* gives its correspondents much flexibility to research and write on economic development and on sociopolitical trends. But ultimately journalism is history in a hurry, and so the correspondent often finds himself having to set aside his thematic research to take off in pursuit of the "hot story," the coups, earthquakes, and natural and man-made disasters that seem to strike the Third World with special frequency. Thus, not long after I had studied how Mauritius was accelerating its female literacy programs and lowering its previously high birthrate, the *Times* packed me off to Iran to cover the Islamic Revolution and the subsequent taking of American hostages by militants. Some months later, I was examining how Malawi had undertaken a strenuous effort to increase its agricultural output when I was pulled away to travel to Afghanistan in the wake of the Soviet invasion. There were many frightening, life-threatening situations: in Iraq, while covering the war between that country and its neighbor, Iran, I was pinned down for hours by Iranian snipers near the town of Khurramshahr, which then had been occupied by the invading Iraqi forces. In Beirut, while reporting on tensions between Moslems and Christians, there were bombs and bullets to be dodged and no clear sense of who was hurling and firing the projectiles. In the West African state of Liberia, arriving in the immediate aftermath of a bloody *coup d'état,* I was very nearly shot by rebel troops, who had no idea that I was a journalist and unarmed. Some months after that, in the East African nation of Uganda, where yet another government had been toppled through violence, I was shot at by soldiers who disliked journalists and knew I was one.

For a young man who always wanted to be where the action was, all this was terribly exciting indeed, although being shot at is not exactly an experience I would recommend. As I flew from place to place, from country to country, and from continent to continent chasing crises, I began to develop the feeling that somehow I was missing the "real story." It was all very well to write about societies under stress, but what about the everyday battles ordinary people fought just to exist? What impact did the great political upheavals have on the daily lives of people? My daily reporting, of course, examined some of these questions, but I was left with the nagging feeling that I needed to find the connections between national crises and individual problems. But where to begin?

I was convinced that the way to understand the daily struggles of people in the world's poorer societies—the societies where I'd spent much of my time as a foreign correspondent—was to focus on a subject that permeated their existence. Would I then write about food and hunger? Or the efforts to obtain decent housing and clean water? Or employment? Or better schooling and health facilities for children? It occurred to me that to focus on any one of these topics would be tackling just a part of the big picture. There was a larger story to be told, and so I resolved that I would write about this overcrowded world of ours, about "population." "Population" is a code word for the study of man and demographics. The popular understanding of "population" unfortunately has been that it is about birth control and family planning. "Population" means much more: it includes topics that determine how people's lives are changed—health care, aging, migration, urbanization, women's education, and social politics. As a journalist, I came across instance after instance of propaganda on the part of governments about how much was being done by them for the welfare of ordinary people. Much of this propaganda was designed to persuade people that their lives were really better than they thought. I thought that "population" provided a sort of umbrella-handle to look into the things affecting developing societies the most: overpopulation, infant mortality, urbanization and migration, the rapidly aging populations of many societies. Somewhere on the road, I had come across an essay penned by Lester R. Brown, a Washington-based thinker and futurologist, in which he said, in part:

> In an increasingly interdependent world the consequences of continuing population growth affect everyone, regardless of where the growth actually occurs. Each person added to the world's population, however poor, exerts an additional claim on the earth's food, energy, and other resources. Expanding food production requires either fossil fuels or animal draft power. It also demands growing quantities of fresh water. Land is required for living space as well as for food production. Even minimal needs for clothing and shelter exert additional claims on the earth's resources. . . . At issue is whether we can create a workable world order for an increasingly interdependent world. The role of population policies in that effort could be decisive.*

*Lester R. Brown, *In the Human Interest* (New York: Norton, 1974), pp. 13–19.

Journalism had given me the unique opportunity to see for myself the miseries wrought by overcrowding. I broached the idea for a book on "population" to Timothy Seldes, my literary agent in New York. He was at once enthusiastic. He and other friends cautioned, however, that I should not attempt to write a book that was weighed down with complex statistics and lengthy demographic analyses. At any event, I wasn't trained as a demographer. What I did possess was a reporter's eye and the experience of more than fifteen years with what is arguably the world's greatest newspaper. I soon discovered that "population" was a field in which hundreds of books and tomes had already been written, but that despite such proliferation of literature the subject of population was little understood by the general public; "population" enjoyed little popularity. I felt that perhaps this was because these books were rarely about people, although their subject matter was people. I resolved that mine would be a book about the impact of population programs and development efforts on the everyday lives of men, women, and children in different parts of the world—about how the lives of these people were being changed; about the fabric of their lives and how it was stretched by their daily struggles to make ends meet; about where the fabric gave; about the hopes, disappointments, aspirations of people; and about how the rends and tears were patched up. I spoke to friends at the United Nations Fund for Population Activities, and they seemed equally enthusiastic about the value of such a project and were forthcoming with a travel grant. They pledged non-interference with my reporting and writing.

And so it was that in the late summer of 1982, armed with a stack of spiral notebooks, a hardy camera, and a hundred rolls of film, I set off on a journey that eventually took me to and through more than fifty countries. The idea was to see for myself whether population programs, on which the United States, other Western nations, and the developing states themselves had spent more than $6 billion since 1974—the year when most nations of the world resolved at a megaconference in Bucharest to commit themselves to a stepped-up global struggle against overpopulation—had really improved the lives of people for whom the projects were intended.

It was not an auspicious time to embark on such a journey. A major controversy was brewing among those associated with global population programs. There were those who held that the vast sums spent on such programs were by and large wasted and that the allocations had been dissipated by widespread mismanagement of resources and by corruption. The United Nations itself was particularly under attack for having funded allegedly questionable population programs in countries such as China, where there were reports of infanticide and forced sterilizations. (Neither the Chinese nor the United Nations condoned such malpractices.) But there were also others who asserted that, of all the categories of expenditures for development purposes by the West, the money that was best spent was on population programs. These supporters, worried that the West was cutting back its financial commitments at a time when more money, not less, was most essential for population projects, stressed that it was the injection of Western funds into population work that had resulted in a dramatic lowering of the world's annual population growth rate. By 1982, the proponents of population programs said, this rate had been lowered within a decade from more than 2 percent to 1.7 percent annually. They said that by the year 2000 the growth rate would fall to 1.5 percent if current population programs were maintained. Roughly translated, what this meant was that in 2000 the world would have 6.1 billion people, not the 7 billion plus that futurologists had feared during the 1970s. Thanks to the Western investment in population activities, the boosters of the programs said, even developing countries long notorious for high birthrates were starting to show significant declines in fertility patterns. I was told that the downward trend in birthrates marked the end of an unchanging pattern that had existed for centuries, since sharply rising population growth rates had been a fact throughout the modern historical era. The population programs that were credited with having brought about this epochal change had emphasized female education and the development of better health care systems, two factors that had received priority financial investment during the 1974–1984 decade.

I set out to obtain a photograph of that decade. What did the falling population growth rate really mean for individuals in different parts of the world? Was the quality of their everyday life improved because of the myriad programs and policies fashioned for them by population experts in and out of government? Did people now live significantly differently from when the global population programs first got started? My approach was that of a journalist; I expected answers but often wound up with more questions. I went where I fancied, including places I had already visited for the *New York Times,* and I decided early on not to confine myself to only the so-called Third World. The world's "population problem," I decided, was of concern to the developing countries and to the industrialized ones as well because of the increasing interrelationships and interdependencies of the modern world. If China suffered from "overpopulation," the problem of West Germany was that it hadn't enough people and so the Germans were forced to import labor from countries such as Turkey and Yugoslavia, with all the resulting problems of implanting aliens in their society.

By the time my travels were completed some fourteen months after I'd started, the world had added another 100 million people to its population. Actually, some 125 million babies were born during the time I was on the road, but about 25 million of them died. They were mostly victims of traditional killers of infants in developing countries such as diarrhea, tetanus, cholera, dehydration, and malnutrition. I was a witness to some of these deaths: in Masai villages in Kenya, a country with the unenviable distinction of having both the world's highest birthrate and the highest infant mortality rate; in urban hovels in Nigeria, which is competing with Kenya to become the world's fastest-growing country in terms of population; in hillside shanties of Brazil, a strange blend of modern cities and communities where medical facilities are primitive. There was little I could do to save those children, and there were times when tears seemed an inadequate response to the conditions I saw. Most of these dying children had already lost their battle of life at the moment they were born because there was absolutely nothing their parents could do to nurse them to good health and well-being. In some instances, the parents didn't want those children to begin with and so they neglected their welfare. I wanted to take some of these children, who were being abused so openly and violently, home with me, but how many kids can you take home to your wife? The world, which responds so mightily to what UNICEF calls the "loud emergencies"—such as famines, droughts, and natural disasters, where infant deaths are particularly high—seems to me to be tardy about assisting the "silent emergencies," in which more than 45,000 children perish every day around the world from preventable causes. The daily tragedies of up to 400 million children who UNICEF says go to bed hungry each night and, if they survive, are impaired mentally and physically for the rest of their short lives and of up to a billion children who are growing up illiterate do not seem to trouble the world's conscience as much as the "emergencies" that grab the headlines. The world's "silent emergencies" are the most underreported stories today.

This book is a personal journey through many lands, a journey in search of everyday people. It is part political travelogue, part contemporary sociology and history, and part demographic observations and in no way does it reflect or endorse the positions held by the United Nations, which funded many of my travels. I have set out to write a book about everyday people for everyday people, and I planned not to weigh this book down with heavy theories and statistics and theorems. I went to villages and spent time with peasants as they worked their land. I visited urban slums and met with the destitute. I sought out young professionals in cities and aged men and women in old folks' homes. I wanted to find out about the hopes, fears, aspirations, concerns, problems, and dreams people have and about how people related to their environment. My theme of "population" gave me the excuse and the license to ask people pretty much about anything.

When I began my journey in the late summer of 1982, in clangorous Mexico—which was then reeling from the devaluation of its currency, the peso, and from the news that its overall debt to foreign banks was nudging the horror figure of $80 billion—I thought I'd concentrate on assessing the impact of birth control programs on countries of the developing world. But I quickly found out that the "population problem" affects us all, not just the poorer countries, and I was persuaded that to write on just birth control would be too restrictive. The months I spent on the road, hopping from hotel to hotel and hovel to hovel, also taught me that "population" did not mean just the numbers game. I found that the issues raised by the interrelationships among population size, the environment, resources, and economic development are complex—but that at the heart of the matter was a simple, central point: the more people we have in the world, the less the earth can adequately support them.

During the course of the fourteen months I spent researching this book, that point cropped up over and over, albeit in varying degrees and different circumstances in (chronologically) Mexico, Britain, Sri Lanka, India, Singapore, the Philippines, Taiwan, Thailand, Indonesia, Malaysia, Australia, Hong Kong, China, Japan, Hawaii, Cuba, Colombia, Panama, Ecuador, Peru, Bolivia, Chile, Brazil, Barbados, Jamaica, France, West Germany, East Germany, Sweden, Switzerland, Kenya, Tunisia, Egypt, Morocco, Saudi Arabia, Norway, Nigeria, and Yugoslavia.

After my travels were over, after the notes were sorted out and the pamphlets and brochures arranged and reviewed, after the interview sessions with hundreds of individuals were transcribed, mountains of statistics studied, and complicated graphs digested—after all this I was convinced that what we had in store was a population explosion that would devour the globe's dwindling resources and render meaningless the gains that were made over the 1974–1984 decade in lowering overall birthrates.

There are those who smugly insist that the "population bomb" has been defused because of the Western world's investment in population programs during this decade. I don't think that the bomb has been defused at all. Its fuse is long, and it is still burning.

As I write this, in early 1984, the world is reported by the United Nations to contain some 4.6 billion people. By this time next year, about 88 million people will have been added to the global population. By the fall of 1999, the overall world population will grow to 6.1 billion, according to estimates by both the United Nations and the World Bank. To look at it another way, so quickly is the world's population growing that in a bit more than two years the new additions will equal the current population of the United States of 242 million. To look at it still another way, the unprecedented numbers by which the human race is expanding are as follows: 150 a minute, 9,000 an hour, 216,000 a day, and roughly 80 million a year. Of the world's current population of 4.6 billion, more than a quarter lives in what the World Bank says are conditions of "absolute poverty." Yet, the fastest population expansion is occurring in the poor, already overcrowded, and less developed nations—the very places where food, housing, sanitation, and economic opportunities are in critically short supply. By the year 2000, 80 percent of the world's people will live there.

The United Nations estimates that the human population of 8000 B.C. was about 5 million, taking perhaps a million years to get there from 2.5 million people. The world's population did not reach 500 million until nearly 10,000 years later, around A.D. 1650. This means that it doubled roughly once every thousand years or so. The global population touched the billion mark around 1850, doubling in some 200 years; it took only 80 years more for the next doubling as the population reached 2 billion in 1930. The doubling time now is about 35 years. If the current population growth rate holds up, and it is likely to, the world will have 9 billion people by the year 2030, 21 billion by 2110, and perhaps 60 million billion people within the next 1,000 years. It is easier to grasp the implications of these increases if they are translated into other terms. For example, the world's labor force will grow from 1.8 billion to 2.6 billion between now and the end of the century. If all these additional workers are to be employed, it will be necessary to create as many jobs between now and the year 2000 as exist today in all the industrialized countries put together. In fact, if the people in the developing countries are to improve their living conditions, the number of jobs to be created will have to exceed the additions to the labor force to take into account the backlog of those already unemployed and underemployed.

These kinds of figures immediately raise the question of what demographers call "carrying capacity," or how many people can ultimately be supported by the global biological and ecological system, and at what level. The Rome-based Food and Agricultural Organization of the United Nations says that at current rates of population growth at least 65 developing countries of the 140 or so states belonging to the so-called Third World will, by the year 2000, find themselves possessing 500 million people whom they won't be able to feed properly. The FAO warns that even if food production were to be doubled by the year 2000 —an unlikely possibility—there would still be at least 50 million in 20 countries whose basic dietary needs would remain unmet. Imbalances between food availability and population growth imply continuing widespread malnourishment in the Third World, and this in turn means high infant mortality rates, shortened life spans for adults, and stepped-up social and political turmoil. The prospects for increased food production to keep up with the needs of a growing global population are not good at all. A case in point is Nigeria, the giant West African country of some 100 million people. In the 1960s, and even in the early 1970s, Nigeria exported food; now it must import more than a billion dollars' worth of grain and food products each year. Nigeria used to be able to afford such a high import bill because its oil exports generated revenues of more than $25 billion each year. But the world's oil glut of the early 1980s meant a sharply reduced oil income for Nigeria—at a time when its population kept exploding in numbers, so that the administration of President Alhaji Shehu Shagari couldn't quite cut back on food imports without risking widespread social unrest.

Here are some "trends" that the United Nations Fund for Population Activities, which is the world's largest source of multilateral assistance for population projects, says can now be discerned:

- In the early 1950s, only one government, that of India, had recognized the importance of a national population policy and had instituted a formal, nationwide population program. Now "population" has achieved a high degree of acceptability, and more than 90 percent of the world's states permit popular access to family-planning programs; in 70 percent of these countries there is official government financial support for such projects. Globally, for every dollar put annually into population projects (the annual aid figure from the West is about $350 million, of which the United States contributes nearly $300 million) by Western countries, the developing countries themselves put in four dollars. This domestic contribution to population programs by the recipient countries themselves is on the increase, while the contributions from the West have been stagnant for the last five years or so, in real terms.

• Current birthrates are considered "too high" by at least 100 countries, and they would like to bring about a dramatic decline in population growth. A recent study by the London-based World Fertility Survey shows that couples in most developing countries wish to have no more than 5 children per family. The survey showed that the average desired family size varies between 3 children per couple in Turkey to 6.8 children in Kenya. But the study by the World Fertility Survey also showed that in twenty-one countries surveyed, the average number of children per couple was uniformly high and ranged between 5.2 children in Indonesia and 8.6 children in Jordan. Moreover, the World Fertility Survey also found that the percentage of women actually using contraception was low: under 20 percent of married women in the fertility age range used contraceptives in Bangladesh, Kenya, Nepal, and Pakistan; between 20 percent and 50 percent in the Dominican Republic, Guyana, Indonesia, Jamaica, Jordan, South Korea, Malaysia, Mexico, Peru, the Philippines, Sri Lanka, and Thailand; and more than 50 percent in only Colombia, Costa Rica, Fiji, Panama, and Turkey. The survey found that there now are some 800 million women in the childbearing ages in developing countries, and about 600 million of them are married. The World Fertility Survey estimates that of these married women only about 26 percent practice some form of contraception, so that close to 500 million married women all over the Third World are in need of family-planning information and services if the global population growth rate is to be further lowered.

• The world's population is now increasing at the rate of about 1.75 percent a year, or a doubling time of a little over thirty years. But the poor countries are increasing their populations at a much faster rate: at 2.5 percent annually, or a doubling time of less than thirty years. The World Bank says that nearly 3.6 billion of the world's 4.6 billion people live in the developing countries.

• Birthrates and death rates vary dramatically around the world. In Kenya, for example, 65 babies per every 1,000 of the population are born each year; by contrast, in most of the West the birthrate is barely 10 babies per 1,000 of the population. The death rate is highest in Chad, with 23.2 people per 1,000 of the population dying annually, while this rate is lowest in Fiji, with 4.2 people per 1,000 dying each year. Most developed countries, according to the United Nations, have an annual death rate of between 8 and 13 per 1,000 of the population. The figures for the average expectancy of life also vary dramatically between the developed and the developing countries: in the developed countries, life expectancy is around seventy-two years; in the Third World it is about fifty-seven years, with the lowest being in Chad—forty years. The annual population growth rate for the developed countries is barely 0.68 percent, and for the Third World the figure is 2.5 percent.

• Africa is likely to continue to be the "trouble spot" in population growth. The current population of 470 million will swell to 853 million by the year 2000. Between 1950 and 1980, the birthrates on this continent did not decrease significantly, changing only from 48 per 1,000 of the population to 46 per 1,000 (the average). A key factor that inhibits the major reduction in birthrates is the high levels of infant and general mortality rates. In fact, the highest death rates anywhere in the world are to be found on the African continent.

• Asia is likely to be the bellwether region for population trends. It is not only the most populous of all regions, Asia is also home for the largest proportion of the world population. From 1.4 billion persons in 1950, the Asian population has continuously climbed to 2.6 billion in 1980 and is expected to rise to 3.6 billion in the year 2000 and to 6 billion by 2100. The most sensational progress in birth control has been in China, where, through a rigidly imposed system of economic and other penalties, the annual natural rate of population increase has been brought down in the last decade from 35 babies per 1,000 of the population to 15 per 1,000. China now has officially adopted a one-child family policy and expects to lower its annual birthrate to 5 per 1,000 by 1986. But Asia also has such population problem cases like Bangladesh, where the annual birthrate is 45 per 1,000 of the population, with no signs of imminent decreases.

• Latin America is the most urbanized of all developing regions, with 65 percent of its population of 365 million now living in urban areas; by the year 2000, 75 percent of the region's population will be residing in cities and towns.

• Aging of populations is likely to emerge in Latin America more rapidly than in other developing regions on account of its low mortality and moderate but declining birthrates. The United Nations estimates that the number of elderly persons in Latin America will increase from 23 million in 1980 to 41 million in 2000 to 93 million in 2025—a fourfold increase in less than fifty years. The increase in overall population during the same period, however, is expected to be a little more than double.

- The decline in birthrates has been most striking in the industrialized countries of the West. From 832 million people in 1950, the population of the developed countries has increased to 1.13 billion in 1980 and is projected to increase to 1.27 billion by the year 2000. This represents an increase of only 23 percent over a hundred-year period.
- The developed regions—which is to say, the countries of Europe, the Soviet Union, the United States and Canada, Australia, New Zealand, and Japan—are experiencing the lowest birthrates ever. Current low fertility in these societies has been linked to such transformed parts of the social fabric as the declining importance of the family, the changing role of women, and the rapid rise of nonfamily households. Consequently, says the United Nations, one important population issue that will confront many of the developed countries relates to the question of how nations will respond to the new prospects of near-zero or even negative natural population increase in the decades ahead.
- One significant demographic manifestation of these developments is the rapid aging of populations especially in the developed countries. The population of the elderly, those sixty-five years of age and above, has increased from about 200 million in 1950 to 375 million in 1975. By the year 2000, this figure will have risen to more than 600 million, and to over 1.1 billion by the year 2025—an increase of more than 225 percent since 1975. Thus, a number of social issues have already grown in importance: the need to shift resources from familiar forms of young-age dependency to welfare systems for the aged; probable needs for changes in political attitudes toward immigration so as to enable certain countries with particularly aging populations to allow more "young" immigrants to enter their societies; and the need for special municipal and health services for the aged.

What is happening in the world today is that, although the overall population growth rate is slowing down, current net additions to many national populations are still higher than, say, thirty years ago. This tendency is likely to accelerate so that by the year 2000 the world in fact will add more people to its rolls each year than it does today, which is to say that the world's annual population increase will be to the order of some 90 million to 100 million, as compared to roughly 80 million in 1983. Thus, whatever the nature of efforts undertaken now to lower the world's annual population growth rate, the numbers of people actually being added to the world's population each year will increase by almost 50 percent by the end of the century. And of this increase of some 2 billion people, more than 90 percent will take place in the impoverished Third World, the United Nations says. Part of the reason that the Third World will experience such a huge increase in numbers is that it already has a large people base to begin with; another is that decreasing mortality rates mean that people live longer and add to this people base. Most of the population in the Third World now consists of children and young people, and nearly 40 percent of the total population of the Third World is now below the age of thirty. Authoritative studies such as the World Fertility Survey have shown that the average number of children born to women in developing countries is 4.64, compared with 2.05 children per woman in the industrialized nations.

An alarming consequence of such population growth will mean that by the end of the century there will be eleven countries with populations of over 100 million each: China, India, the Soviet Union, the United States, Indonesia, Brazil, Pakistan, Bangladesh, Nigeria, Mexico, and Japan. Just thirty years ago, there were only four members of the "Hundred-million-plus Club"—China, India, the Soviet Union, and the United States. Twenty-two nations currently have annual population growth rates in excess of 3 percent, or almost double the world rate, according to the U.S. Census Bureau: Kenya, Saudi Arabia, Syria, Nigeria, Iraq, Rwanda, Malawi, Tanzania, Zambia, Zimbabwe, Ghana, Ivory Coast, Niger, Senegal, Algeria, Ecuador, Venezuela, Bangladesh, Iran, Uganda, Zaire, and Morocco.

I say "alarming" because I don't know where all these people are going to live. In the developing countries themselves, the large cities are already bursting at the seams. Anyone who's been to Lagos or Mexico City or Shanghai or Bombay or Jakarta or Cairo will know what overcrowded cities are all about: filth and crime and chaos and decay and disorder. By the end of this century, more than half of the world's population will live in large cities. In 1950, there were only six cities with populations of 5 million and over, and their combined population was only 42 million. By 1983, the number of the 5 million-plus cities had risen to twenty-six, with a combined population of 252 million. And by the year 2000, says the United Nations, the number of the megacities —those having at least 5 million people each—will climb to sixty, with a combined population of at least 650 million.

The United Nations gave me these projections: by the year 2000, Mexico City's current population of 16 million will swell to 31 million; Tokyo-Yokohama, with nearly 20 million people now, may have 26 million by 2000; greater Cairo will expand from 8 million today to 16 million by the end of the century; Jakarta will increase its population in this period threefold to 16 million.

The commercial metropolis of Bombay, the Indian city where I was born in 1948, serves as a frightening example of the population explosion in Third World cities, which, says the United Nations, have been growing at the rate of 4.1 percent annually. At first sight, Bombay is a lovely city, a collection of seven islands linked by a massive landfill. The city sits by the Arabian Sea and has corniches with beaches and parks: these beaches are always crowded—day and night—not because Indians love the sun and the surf but because for most residents of this city these areas afford the only open spaces to stretch their arms a bit. Debjani Sinha, an urban affairs writer for *Business World*, a fortnightly publication of much influence in the Indian corporate world, told me that according to her estimates more than 10,000 people stream into Bombay every week from different parts of India in search of jobs. They are mostly poor people, and they cannot afford the high rents demanded by landlords; about the only residential buildings going up these days are luxury skyscrapers where one-bedroom apartments are selling for the equivalent of $100,000. So where do the new immigrants go? They squeeze into *chawls*, densely packed tenements, where as many as a dozen people share small, ill-lit rooms and as many as a hundred people share a common latrine. Or the immigrants shack up in shantytowns, in structures fashioned out of tin sheets or in abandoned sewage pipes. I visited one such shantytown in the Bandra neighborhood one afternoon and was taken by a Bombay social worker to meet a "typical family."

This family consisted of an emaciated thirty-year-old widow named Shaila Pyarelal and her eight children. Shaila had probably been quite beautiful once, but childbearing and the travails of life had worn her out. She told me she'd been living in a large drainage pipe for four years; her husband was killed when he slipped from a crowded commuter train as he was traveling to his janitor's job in downtown Bombay. There was, of course, no insurance for his family. How did Shaila make ends meet? She earned some rupees occasionally by working as a maid for middle-class families in a housing development not far away from the shantytown, and sometimes she begged. Even the shantytown Shaila lives in is getting overcrowded, and patrol squads formed by slum residents daily turn away newcomers who demand space in the tin shacks and sewage pipes. "My husband and I came to Bombay from Uttar Pradesh, but had we known things were so bad here we wouldn't have come at all," Shaila said, speaking in her native language of Hindi. "And I wish I had known something about birth control when I got married—I wouldn't have had so many children. They may have been the gift of God, but they have turned out to be the curse of my life."

Halfway around the world from Bombay's slums and the despair of Shaila Pyarelal, I met a woman named Hilda Vasquez. She lives in a dilapidated house on the outskirts of Mexico City, already a metropolis of 16 million mostly poor people. The neighborhood in which Hilda and her four small children reside is called Netzahualcoyotl, an area that forms part of what Mexicans call "Cinturon de Miseria"—Belts of Misery. These are the fastest-growing areas of Mexico City, which is probably the fastest-growing city in the world because of the influx of peasants who flood into the city by the hundreds every day. Hilda Vasquez, a plump woman with a face weighed down by worries, came to Mexico City some years ago because her husband wanted a job in the city and because their tiny farm near Guadalajara did not provide them with sufficient income. Speaking in Spanish, she told me that within days of getting to Mexico City her husband abandoned her and their children. Now she works in a local tortilla factory and earns the equivalent of four dollars a day. Her older children, the two boys who are nine and eight years old, respectively, often bring in additional income through such activities as polishing shoes at stands in downtown Mexico City. Hilda would like to return to her home town, but the family farm is now in the possession of relatives, who, she says, refuse to allow her back. As in Shaila Pyarelal's neighborhood in Bombay, living conditions in Hilda's area are, at best, primitive. Electricity and water supply are sporadic; homes get broken into frequently by neighborhood thugs; the roads are unpaved and dusty; in winter, when it gets very cold in this 7,000-foot-high city, there is no heating available.

"I wish I could tell all those people who keep flocking to Mexico

City not to come, that there aren't any jobs here, that the magic of the city is an illusion," Hilda told me, "but these people keep coming. The city keeps growing. What will happen to us?"

This book is about people like Hilda Vasquez and Shaila Pyarelal, the casualties of modern life and tradition and sometimes even of the ambitious development programs intended for them.

Theirs is not a "new story" because the existence of poverty and the problems of development are not new. But what population growth in the last three decades has done and will continue to do in the foreseeable future is to make these problems more intractable by changing their scale. In fifteen years's time, there will be 5 billion Hilda Vasquezes and Shaila Pyarelals, or more than 80 percent of the world's total population. What then?

I don't think our lawmakers and policy drafters and purse-string holders display sufficient concern about these problems nowadays. When I told a congressman friend of mine in Washington about my book project, he shrugged wearily, then said, "Ah, the population bomb. So what else is new?" Another friend, a newspaper editor, responded pithily with a journalists' shorthand code: "Mego"—My eyes glaze over. These kinds of attitudes translate into an overall public weariness, in the West at least, with population matters; and the weariness in turn translates into diminishing funds for population projects at a time when the need for money is more, not less. The London-based International Institute for Strategic Studies, a prestigious think tank, estimates that nations of the world now spend more than $800 billion each year on defense and on weapons acquisitions and sales. In contrast, says the United Nations, these same nations spend barely $1 billion on population programs. And because of inflation, in truth less and less is being made available to deal with the problem of more and more people.

Appearing before a congressional committee in 1983, Secretary of State George Shultz said that "rampant population growth underlies the Third World's poverty and poses a major long-term threat to political stability and our planet's resource base." There are a few others like Mr. Schultz who have publicly worried that the world is headed toward a new catastrophe, a population explosion of unprecedented dimensions. Robert S. McNamara, who served for fourteen years as president of the World Bank, expressed similar concern in a recent speech: "Short of nuclear war itself, population growth is the gravest issue the world faces over the decade ahead. The threat of unmanageable population pressures is very much like the threat of nuclear war. If we do not act, the problem will be solved by famine, riot, insurrection, war."

Such warnings should not be minimized. For nations of the industrialized West, and especially the United States, the foreign policy costs and the economic consequences of overpopulation in the Third World are not hard to assess: as populations grow beyond the carrying capacity of developing countries and local governments are unable to provide the additional jobs, education, food, and health services needed, political unrest could mount in those nations, bringing new waves of illegal immigrants and new fears of hostile governments close to home. As the domestic problems of developing nations rise, their borrowing from Western institutions could also be expected to increase—but the worldwide recession has cut into the ability of these Western financial institutions to offer affordable loans to the Third World states, whose imports have fallen because they cannot borrow now the foreign exchange they need to pay for these imports from the West. Anthony Solomon, president of the Federal Reserve Bank of New York, said recently that American exports to about thirty troubled debtor nations of the Third World fell by more than $10 billion in 1982, a drop of more than 20 percent from average annual exports to those countries. He said that this cost the United States almost 300,000 jobs and American exporters more than a billion dollars in profit.

Even for a journalist brought up on a diet of nonadvocacy and impartiality, it is hard to report on a subject like population and not come away with the conviction that the world needs to act urgently and forthrightly in dealing with our "population problem."

This book is essentially a reporter's notebook, an account of what I saw and heard in different lands over a period of time. This is a book for the everyday, general audience; where possible, I have dispensed with the heavy jargon that characterizes fields such as demography. It is not my intention to be an alarmist or a doomsayer—but the world's "next explosion," that of population in the Third World, could spell doom for a number of poor societies that already cannot adequately feed, house, and clothe their millions, or provide decent employment.

Yet at the same time this is not merely a reporter's journal. As a journalist, I was trained to visit places and write "objectively" about them. Often this meant raising a wall between one's feelings and perceptions so that the "reader" out there got the story without the reporter's own emotions mixed in. This, or course, is nonsense. Foreign correspondents, particularly, are always being subjective in the choice of their material and in their characterization of the subject. Population is not a story that can be told in a clinical fashion, and I haven't attempted to do so. The blood, gore, tears, laughter, and joy in the following pages are those of the people I met, but also of mine.

Many years ago a writer I admire greatly, Dom Moraes, undertook a journey through several countries that were experimenting with new population programs. He wrote a book titled *A Matter of People,* and there was a section in it that impressed me so much that I would like to share it with you:

> As a writer one wanders the world, and leaves one's books and articles as footprints. Had I come simply as a writer, all the farewells would have been easy. Had I come simply as a writer, I would have interviewed politicians, looked around me, and said to my friends when we parted, "See you sometime, somewhere," and been pleasantly surprised when I next bumped into them in some unexpected corner of the world. Because I had come as a writer on population, I was unable to do this simple thing. I had started to see all the countries that I had visited as scarred, difficult battlefields on which wars nobody else was aware of were being fought. I saw these countries in terms of whether or not they would survive this mysterious and unknown series of wars, and I saw my friends as the possible victims.
>
> If this sounds overstated, I can only say that, covering my first shooting war, before I knew much about what actual war was like, I had feelings that were radically the same. There are, of course, an enormous number of experts behind every war, plotting its course, swinging its armed puppets this way and that. Behind this particular war stood a host of demographers and world agencies, fronted by its opposition. Demographers are fine, world agencies are fine, but in Algeria and Israel, Vietnam and Belfast, and the Indian border, it was always the helpless ones on the torn earth who were the people that mattered.

Ten years ago, scores of men and women from all over the world met for several days in the Romanian capital of Bucharest. They argued fiercely over where the global population growth rate was headed; they debated over what could be done to put the brakes on rampant population increases. At times during that Bucharest session, which was organized by the United Nations, it seemed that no one had a clear idea about what worked in the field of population and what didn't. There was, in fact, considerable uncertainty about the efficacy and efficiency of existing population control programs. It was apparent in Bucharest that the West had misgivings about the Third World's willingness to institute meaningful population programs; and delegates from the developing states were skeptical of the medicine the West was prescribing to solve the world's overpopulation problem.

After much discussion and fractious argument, the delegates who had assembled at the Bucharest conference came out with a "World Population Plan of Action." The plan encouraged governments to acknowledge the relevance of population matters to development planning; it endorsed the usefulness of family-planning programs and the right of couples to determine freely the size of their families; and it stated that each country should determine what remedial approach was most appropriate to its own circumstances.

Ten years after Bucharest, the world's population problem has by no means been resolved. Countries such as Nigeria and Kenya find themselves with exploding populations; infant mortality rates are still high in places like Cambodia, Afghanistan, and Haiti; general health care services are by no means universal in many Third World states.

Yet, it has been demonstrated that "population" can be influenced through concerted governmental commitment; through the infusion of money into specific projects aimed at lowering birthrates and infant mortality rates and at improving general health care; through sustained research programs and better communications; and through increased education and economic opportunities for women: where female literacy has risen, birthrates have fallen. It is possible to show, as I will in this book, that those countries that have steadfastly—and democratically—persisted in their population work have also realized the best gains. The examples are manifold: in five years, Mexico's annual population growth rate dropped one-third, from 3.4 percent to 2.3 percent, the fastest drop of any nation in recent history. Colombia, Tunisia, Costa Rica, Sri Lanka, Thailand, Indonesia, Zimbabwe, and Singapore have similarly experienced dramatic drops in their previously high population growth rates.

And so, ten years after Bucharest, it is possible to say that with the possible exception of the Green Revolution the best investment in development that governments of the West and the Third World have made has been in "population." To put it another way, had they not spent the money things would have been far worse: we would have had more people, more ill health, more babies dying daily, and most certainly more social tensions than already exist in the poor countries of the world.

Two

Africa
"How We Breed Is How We Live"

WITH ITS FORMIDABLE canyons masquerading as potholes, Kugbuyi is the sort of street to be found in virtually every part of Lagos, the sprawling, clangorous capital of the West African nation of Nigeria.

Kugbuyi Street is less than a mile long, but if you are driving through it, or dare to be a mere pedestrian, it seems a much longer thoroughfare because the traffic is suffocatingly thick. The pavements are crowded with makeshift stalls, where it is possible, for a price, to buy a variety of goods—from solid gold Rolex watches that are no doubt stolen to transistor radios to vegetables to strips of fat-heavy meat. Pickpockets flourish here during the day, muggers at night. There are open sewers off Kugbuyi Street, and the offal overflows continuously. The fittings on lampposts are broken. There are violent graffiti on most buildings and refuse and rubbish everywhere. Sanitation workers rarely bother coming around, so when the mounds of trash become mountains, neighborhood residents set fire to them. Little urchins, just a step away from miscreanthood, scurry around peddling candy and cigarettes. Beggars with deformed or amputated limbs cruise the street. Motorists perform mad ballets around the potholes, and sometimes when it rains heavily the cars break down and are abandoned on the road by their drivers—and soon these vehicles are stripped to their shell by local vandals, who then sell their booty on the very street where the goods were obtained. Kugbuyi Street is a microcosm of Lagos.

About midway down this street stands building no. 4, a decaying three-story brick structure whose floors sag and whose ceilings are propped up by frail wooden beams. There is a small grocery store on the ground floor where customers frequently fight over the scarce supply of vegetables, maize, cassava, and rice. There is always the danger of a riot over food. Stabbings occasionally occur. Sometimes the corpse of a mysteriously dead stranger will rot in a nearby alleyway for days until the police carry it away. The electricity in building no. 4 frequently fails. Some of the steps on the narrow staircase are missing. No one remembers when the building was built, and the Lagos municipality doesn't seem to have the relevant records. There are six apartments in this building, and they contain fourteen families, or roughly a hundred men, women, and children, in eighteen rooms, with dozens of "relatives" coming in for extended visits. There is just one lavatory on each floor. Building no. 4 is typical of Kugbuyi Street.

Tokunboh Oladeinde has lived here most of his adult life. Thirty years old, with deepset eyes and a wide forehead that give him the appearance of a professor perpetually pondering, Oladeinde is a civil engineer who also teaches part time at an adult education school. He is married and has four children, and like everyone else in building no. 4, Oladeinde has his dreams.

One dream is to strike it rich: some of his boyhood friends have already done so—in business, in trading, in expediting deals for foreign firms that sought to exploit Nigeria's oil boom economy.

Another dream is that Kugbuyi Street will be repaired one of these days, although Oladeinde thinks that this dream will take longer to come true than the first one.

And still another dream is to move his family out of Kugbuyi Street, perhaps to a quieter neighborhood in the Ikoye section of Lagos, or perhaps to Victoria Island, where there is more space between dwellings and less traffic than in the vicinity of building no. 4.

"Kugbuyi Street is finished, it has nowhere to go," Oladeinde says, guzzling foamy Nigerian beer whose bouquet fills the room. "I can't even pine for the good old days. We never had any good old days here. It was always nasty and crowded. Every day now more and more people squeeze into this building, into this neighborhood, into this crazy city. This country is going to ruin with so many people. When are we going to stop breeding like this? How are we going to feed all these new millions? When are we going to have some sanity in our congested cities?"

The despair on Oladeinde's face suggests that he knows the answers to such questions. His wife practices birth control. But it is a different story with their neighbors. Babies are born every month, it seems, in building no. 4.

I went to visit the owner of the grocery store in the building. A large, chunky man, he told me that he had eleven children.

"Eleven!" I said. "What do they do? How do you take care of them?"

"Ah," Ibrahim Mesahi, the storekeeper, said, "I need all the help I can get. I have ten boys and one girl. They all work with me in the shop. I am proud of it. These days you just cannot trust outsiders. How do I know that if I hire some worker, he won't take off with my goods? As it is the food situation is bad in Nigeria, and people are stealing all the time. With my children, at least I can watch them. They are honest. If my wife could, I would have even more children. They are a blessing, my sons. I save money this way. Look around you!"

His sons were in the shop, big, strapping youths in their teens, and they were working as salesmen, loaders, and accountants.

Nigeria is already, along with Kenya, the fastest growing country on the continent, and Africa is already the fastest growing continent in the world. Africa has the world's highest birthrates and the lowest prevalence of contraception. Most governments south of the Sahara have shown little interest in family-planning programs, little interest in urban planning, and little interest in committing resources for stepped-up food production. Most countries don't even have a reliable idea how many people live within their borders. For example, in Ethiopia I was told by some officials that their country's population was 26 million; other officials said it was 30 million; still other officials used the figure of 35 million; and some United Nations technicians said the real figure was more like 40 million. It is said that Nigeria's population is 90 million. It is also said that Nigeria's population is 100 million. It is even possible that Nigeria's population is 150 million. There hasn't been a published scientific census here since Britain granted Nigeria independence in 1960; in a country where tribal sensitivities can often upset the political balance, discussing how many people each of the 250 ethnic communities has is not a popular pastime with Nigerian leaders. With an annual population growth rate estimated to be nearly 4 percent, Nigeria is adding to its population each year a city the size of New York.

Africa itself, in fact, is growing five times faster than the industrialized countries of Europe and North America, and twice as fast as the world generally. Peasants are abandoning farms to trek to Africa's cities in search of mythical jobs; on the average, says the World Bank, African cities are each adding nearly 3 million to their populations each year. Most of the newcomers squeeze into shantytowns and slums, and the result is not only unemployment and high urban crime but malnutrition and the spreading of communicable diseases. The growth of cities in Africa is faster than in any other region.

The current growth rate suggests that the population of 475 million scattered through fifty African states may double by the end of the century. And since more than half the continent's population is still under the age of fifteen—and therefore about to enter the sexually active and childbearing stage—the likelihood is that the continent's overall population will keep increasing through much of the next century. The United Nations says that by the year 2099 Africa will have some 2.2 billion people. And as black Africans are growing more numerous, they are also becoming poorer and hungrier.

Twenty-two African countries are now facing catastrophic food shortages, according to the Food and Agriculture Organization, a Rome-based arm of the United Nations. Back in 1973, a famine resulted in the deaths of hundreds of thousands of people and millions of cattle along a belt that stretched below the Sahara from Cape Verde, off the coast of Senegal in the West, across the continent to Ethiopia. Most of these same countries are again affected, the United Nations says, along with southern African states that normally have plenty of rain and therefore adequate food, such as Lesotho, Botswana, Swaziland, and Zambia. The crisis, says the FAO's director general, Edouard Saouma of Lebanon, is the result not only of a punishing drought but also of preventable factors such as rapid population growth, nomadic farming, poor food distribution systems, and a shortage of trained people and research services.

In January 1984, the United Nations sponsored a population conference in Arusha, a Tanzanian resort that sits in the shadow of Mount Kilimanjaro. After delegates reconciled themselves to the fact that, despite the great physical beauty of the place, Arusha's hotels lacked adequate running water and sufficient food for everybody, they got around to the business of the conference.

Representatives of forty-four African states spoke of the need to slow down population growth on the continent. Delegate after delegate warned that unless population control measures were stepped up there would be little economic progress in Africa. Several representatives noted that Africa, with a continentwide per capita income of under $800—compared to a world average of $2,755—already was the poorest region in the world and that continued high population growth rates would surely cripple Africa beyond repair. The assembled delegates heard speech after speech from their fellow Africans that Africa was now the fastest growing region in the world, with an annual population growth rate of 3 percent: this upsurge in population growth was occurring at a time when growth rates of all other regions of the world were declining.

What was significant about those speeches in Arusha was not what the delegates said but that they made those speeches at all. Ten years ago at the World Population Conference in Bucharest, African delegates balked at suggestions from the West that something be done urgently to put the brakes on the continent's burgeoning population growth. "Population" was not a particularly popular subject with most African leaders: the emerging nations of the 1960s and early 1970s often equated population growth with national strength. Many top African leaders, especially those who espoused socialism, held that family planning was a conspiracy fashioned by the industrialized nations of the West to sap that strength. Moreover, some of these African leaders subscribed to the Leninist view that the true goals of nations should be class struggle and a fight against imperialism: "population" was thus never a priority for them.

African leaders also felt ten years ago that there wasn't enough demographic evidence to warrant programs to bring down birthrates in their countries. In fact, more than twenty-one African states—out of fifty nations on the continent—had never even conducted censuses then. Some African leaders felt that low densities of population throughout the huge continent (Africa is four times the size of the United States) did not justify costly population control programs.

"But now attitudes are changing in Africa," says Werner H. Fornos, who, as head of the Washington-based Population Institute, a nonprofit organization that is active in promoting population programs and research all over the world, is possibly Washington's most energetic lobbyist for population causes. "Experience over the past decade has caused today's African governments to view the matter from a new and more enlightened perspective. They see that basic services are not accommodating people, mortality and morbidity rates are still unacceptably high, urban areas are deteriorating as the result of massive rural-to-urban migration, and development efforts tend to bog down intolerably. National leaders are recognizing that population growth without adequate resources and services results not in national strength but in national disaster."

In their "Kilimanjaro Declaration," the delegates who had assembled in Arusha urged that "governments should ensure the availability and accessibility of family-planning services to all couples or individuals seeking such services freely or at subsidized prices." The declaration called for a stepped-up drive of population control, where warranted. The Arusha declaration was really nothing short of a major breakthrough because it marked a dramatic shift in African attitudes—from rigid pronatalism to a wider recognition of the urgent need to curb Africa's rampant population growth.

Nigeria is Africa's particular horror story.

One out of every four Africans lives in this country, which is as large as California, New Mexico, and Arizona combined. There are at least 250 tribes in Nigeria, and they speak some 100 languages and dialects. Nigeria's multiethnic cultures date back to antiquity, but the country did not make any significant impact on the modern world community until the early 1970s. That was because Nigeria, a major producer of crude oil, found itself suddenly wealthy from the sale of its crude oil. The price of oil was dramatically increased by the cartel known as OPEC, the Organization of Petroleum Exporting Countries, and Nigeria was now earning annual revenues of almost $30 billion.

It was all very heady for the Nigerian military men then in power, and they went berserk. The junta proceeded to fashion an ambitious development program that called for the spending of $100 billion by 1980—a plan that was nothing short of a masterprint aimed at pulling a primitively tribal and economically backward country into the modern age. Thirteen thousand miles of roads were to be constructed, at a cost of more than $3 billion, with another $3 billion earmarked for streamlining Nigeria's communications system. Steel mills rose, forests fell to feed paper mills, housing complexes went up, and slums were razed in some towns. Western salesmen, offering everything from hairpins to private jets to prefabricated palaces, descended to make astonishingly lucrative deals in Lagos, which quickly resembled an American frontier boom town of the nineteenth century. Hotels sprang up, sometimes without the proper electricity and water connections. (Just off Kugbuyi Street, one such hotel remained unoccupied for months until a group of squatters from western Nigeria moved in and took over the facility for their own accommodation.)

The spending spree continued recklessly, with the Nigerian military government confident that even if it lifted 2 million barrels of crude oil each day—or twice the average daily production—Nigeria's oil reserves would last more than forty years. The rural poor flocked to cities like Lagos, Kaduna, Kano, and Ibadan, drawn by visions of waiting jobs and wealth to be plucked easily off the urban tree. In the early 1970s, Lagos was a modest, swampy, malaria-ridden city of no more than 500,000 people; by 1980, the population of the capital city had shot past 5 million. And as Nigerians abandoned their farms, what was once a food-exporting country soon had to import a billion dollars' worth of food annually.

Even such imports could have been easily afforded by Nigeria had oil revenues stayed at the level of the mid-1970s. But beginning in 1981, world oil prices slumped in the wake of an oil glut, and demand for Nigerian crude started to decrease. By 1983, Nigeria was taking in barely $12 billion. The halcyon years were over, probably never to return, yet the bills kept rolling in. And the population kept increasing.

I first went to Nigeria in 1979, when everybody was still intoxicated with the possibility of transforming the nation into a modern industrial giant. I recall landing at the spanking-new Murtala Mohammed Airport in Lagos—an airport designed along the lines and looks of Amsterdam's Schiphol Airport—and being told by a cocky immigration officer that Nigeria's gross national product was more than half that of the other forty-five black African states combined and that Nigeria was the world's sixth biggest producer of crude oil and the largest supplier of oil, after Saudi Arabia, to the United States.

"Our future is absolutely limitless," the immigration official, Mohammed Sambulakhiah, said to me, as we chatted while my luggage was being brought from the aircraft into the terminal building. Sambulakhiah later invited me for dinner at his home. His wife, Sadia, served us Texas steaks. She was pregnant with their ninth child.

"Where do all of you live?" I asked, looking around the three-room apartment, where there wasn't much room to move.

"I'm not worried—soon we'll move into a big house," Sambulakhiah said.

It turned out that his wife had attended law school and obtained a degree. Didn't she want to work, I asked?

Sadia was about to reply to the question when her husband cut her off.

"In Nigeria, we believe that the role of a woman is to bear many children," he said. "That we have many children is Allah's wish. Besides, I am not worried about the future of my children. This country has so much oil that the next generation is going to have an even better time than us."

It was a time not only of great expectations in Nigeria but also of great hope. Nigerians were about to end thirteen years of military rule and, on October 1, 1979, they would replace dictatorship with an American-style democracy headed by President Alahaji Shehu Shagari. The very first interview that Shagari granted to a foreign correspondent was to me, and the new president impressed me at the time with his sober, thoughtful manner.

"We simply must not bank our future on the fact that we have oil," Shagari, a slim, bespectacled man who always wore the flowing robes of his Moslem north, said to me. "We must restrain our spending and develop our agriculture and our infrastructure. We in Nigeria need to be more self-reliant, to promote small-scale industries. We cannot continue being an importing country forever." Shagari, a poet and former schoolteacher, managed to hold together the political fabric of his vast nation over the next four years but was completely ineffective in managing the economy.

Nigerians continued spending as if there were no tomorrow. Shagari's friends, relatives, and political associates built up formidable —and illegal—bank accounts abroad, and at home they lived like decadent royalty: they raised palatial homes, maintained fleets of luxury cars, acquired the latest in electronics, gave orgiastic parties. Millions of dollars in meat from New Zealand, Australia, and Holland was imported each year for the pantries of these affluent Nigerians. There was a sport lately among men of means in Nigeria, and it was called "keeping up with the Alhajis." It was an indigenous version of the familiar "keeping up with the Joneses," but it did not involve buying that extra dishwasher or that second car or that fancy five-gear lawnmower to match what the neighbors had acquired. "Keeping up with the Alhajis" meant acquiring that Lear jet; or if there already was one in the hangar, then it meant buying that refurbished Boeing 707. I knew of some wealthy Nigerian businessmen who habitually flew for their Friday prayers to the Moslem holy city of Mecca in Saudi Arabia, stopping in London on the way back home to pick up groceries and a copy of the Sunday *Times*. *Alhaji* is ordinarily an honorific used by Moslem males who have made the traditional pilgrimage to Mecca at least once during their lifetime, but in Nigeria the term also came to be used as a metaphor for those close associates and friends of Shagari who had made millions because of their proximity to him and the resulting access to contract giving.

Even as all this was happening, ordinary Nigerians were not only growing more numerous, they were also growing poorer, more malnourished, more sickly, and more resentful of the privileges of the politically well-connected. Even accepting the usual poor bookkeeping in Nigeria, the records concerning the country's oil income seemed to be unusually thin—or even nonexistent. More than 85 percent of the national wealth was reputed to be controlled by the clique around Shagari and by powerful business interests. It was not uncommon for foreign bidders to pay up to 40 percent of a project's already inflated cost in "commissions" to Nigerian expediters, who often were the very politicians in charge of handing out contracts. The average Nigerian earned less than the equivalent of $600 a year. One in every nine Nigerian children died before the age of one through preventable causes like malnutrition, dehydration, diarrhea, and tetanus. Violent crime became rampant in cities like Lagos, as people fought over scarce everyday food supplies. By late 1983, a bag of rice, weighing a kilogram, came to cost more than the equivalent of forty dollars. A yam, a staple food like cassava and maize, cost seven dollars. The new millionaires of Nigeria, of course, didn't much worry about the inflation, which was estimated by Western economists at 40 percent a year. They imported their meat and caviar and fine wines and fruit. Some of the newly wealthy also brought in British butlers and Mediterranean maids. The wealthy sometimes moved around Lagos in helicopters so as to avoid the "go slows"—the notorious traffic jams that plague this capital city. Meanwhile, shantytowns mushroomed. Municipal services, shoddy to start with, broke down entirely. Cities like Lagos were often without power for twenty out of twenty-four hours. Prostitution became widespread, and young men pimped for their sisters. There were riots in some of the northern towns. Unemployment rose to 40 percent, a record for Nigeria.

In August 1983 Nigerians went to the polls, and Shehu Shagari was elected to a second four-year term in the Nigerian presidency, amid charges of fraud and vote rigging.

The country was on the verge of a collapse.

On the morning of Saturday, December 31, soldiers dragged Shagari out of bed, handcuffed him, and led him away to jail. It was a military putsch, the fifth in twenty-three years of independence, and, of course, it ended the Shagari civilian presidency—and with it the hopes for democracy in black Africa's biggest and wealthiest state, and possibly in the rest of this troubled continent as well. Some months after the coup, I was at a development conference in Brioni, Yugoslavia, when I ran into the Nigerian military leader who in 1979 had handed power over to Shagari. The leader, General Olesegun Obasanjo, told me that the putschists wanted him back at the helm but that he turned them down on the grounds that as the "father" of Nigeria's democracy he could now hardly take part in its destruction. "I had such high hopes for democracy in Nigeria," General Obasanjo, who is now a businessman-farmer, said. "I am shattered. I really feel let down."

Perhaps Shagari's cerebral style would have been more suitable for a system that had a prime minister who reported to an executive president —as, say, in France. In other words, Shagari could have functioned better as a technocrat, a man behind the scenes who kept things moving in a quiet, methodical manner. Nigerians traditionally do not respond very well to unassuming leaders; they are more impressed and more swayed by forceful demagogues. For many Nigerians, the abstemious, low-key Shagari came across as a Caspar Milquetoast.

Now many Nigerians are echoing their ruling military junta's contention that with Shagari's downfall the country can get moving again. The breathless news reports by many Western correspondents visiting Nigeria often seem to suggest that ordinary Nigerians are actually welcoming the return of dictatorship. I wonder how many ordinary Nigerians these correspondents actually interview. However slow and ponderous democracy is, it is always better than a dictatorship because ultimately a democratic system is more responsive to the needs of ordinary people. And in Nigeria, dictatorships have had dismal records as far as development is concerned: it was the military that left Shagari's democratically elected government a legacy of rampant population growth, rising infant mortality rates, and increasing morbidity—not to mention useless projects, unpaid bills, and a treasury that was close to empty.

No matter where you look around the world, be it Ferdinand E. Marcos's Philippines or Augusto Pinochet Ugarte's Chile or Haile Mariam Mengistu's Ethiopia, no matter which authoritarian state you examine, what is the evidence that dictatorships are a "better" form of government for development? If anything, dictatorships retard economic development by imposing on the creativity of people. And as far as "population" is concerned, it is plain disaster for governments to force people undemocratically to have smaller families: Prime Minister Indira Gandhi found this out when voters threw her out of office after the 1975–1977 "Emergency" period when she suspended democracy in India. During the "Emergency," Mrs. Gandhi's henchmen allegedly forced thousands of males to get themselves sterilized as a way of bringing down the country's population growth rate.

Shagari had inherited from the military the legacy of neglect of population matters. Nigerian governments traditionally held that the best way to ensure appropriate population growth was to provide better health care services and to fold family-planning services into the country's overall health care system. The problem in Nigeria, however, was that basic health care was so wretchedly inadequate. What Nigeria really needed was a stepped-up drive to expand health care services and also an accelerated program to promote family planning. Shagari himself acknowledged to me that his administration during its first four years in office had failed to pay sufficient attention to social services. He told me that family planning would be a special priority in his second term, and I have no doubt that Shagari would have acted more forthrightly to energize his national population commission. Indeed, Shagari had already put into motion the machinery for a fresh census, the first step for any population-planning program in the country.

The last time I saw Shagari, in November 1983, he was both jubilant over his electoral success and disturbed over the rising social tensions in his country. Despite his reelection, Shagari was not in an enviable position. The country's balance-of-trade deficit had soared past the dread figure of $5 billion, and its American and British bankers were no longer willing to give commercial loans until Nigeria paid off its short-term debts. Shagari had to swallow his pride and go topee in hand to the International Monetary Fund, the lender of the last resort, for a new line of credit of up to $2 billion. The IMF, as it does when nations come a-begging to it, was asking for severe belt tightening on the part of the Nigerians. Shagari was prepared to freeze wages and prices, but he wasn't about to accede to the IMF's insistence that Nigeria devalue its overrated currency, the naira. Devaluation carries with it a certain amount of political risk, and despite his recent triumph at the polls,

Shagari didn't think such a drastic step would go across well with Nigerians.

Shagari told me that he realized one of the main problems Nigerian planners had was that no one knew how many Nigerians there were.

"That's been so disturbing to me," the president said. "We can only plan accurately and meaningfully if we have accurate data. As you know, in Nigeria the question of a census is much too entangled with politics."

That last sentence was an understatement. A great deal of the tensions in Nigeria have traditionally been the result of rivalry among the three major ethnic groups: the Hausa-Fulani of the north, the largest ethnic group; the Yoruba of the southwest, the second largest group; and the Ibo of the southeast. The numerous other minority tribes have long been fearful of domination by the "big three," and they have spiritedly preserved their own languages and traditions and have resisted being absorbed into the cultures of the more powerful tribes. (Among the more prominent of the minority tribes are the Tiv, Kanuri, Igala, Idoma, Igbira, and Nupe in the North, the Ibibio, Efik, Ekoi, and Ijo in the East, and the Edo, Urhobo, Itsekiri, and Ijaw in the West.)

The ethnic population and rivalries are significant in Nigeria because the central government's resources are parceled out on the basis of such considerations. In recent years, there has been clamoring to divide Nigeria up into even more states than the current nineteen. The agitation for more states, which worried Shagari—and which the new military junta will have to contend with—is a direct manifestation of the fact that minority tribes see their own numbers increasing and want therefore to carve out their own territory to reflect their status. At present, the 245 or so minority tribes make up about 30 percent of Nigeria's estimated population, but proof—through a reliable census, for example—that their numbers have increased substantially could have a profound effect on Nigeria's ethnic, and therefore political, structure.

The question of population and politics is especially thorny in Nigeria. In the late 1960s, the Ibos of eastern Nigeria felt that the central military government, which was dominated by northern Moslems and by the western Yorubas, was discriminating against them. The Ibos decided they would break away and form an independent state called Biafra. A horrible civil war ensued, and a million people died before Nigeria was reunified by force. Ethnic strains and stresses have not quite disappeared in Nigeria, however, and in the final months of the Shagari presidency there were disturbing signs that such tensions were increasing in some areas. The Nigerian military regime may soon be facing a new domestic ethnic crisis, perhaps a version of the Biafra situation. It cannot afford to neglect the minority tribes, many of whom feel that in recent years they have been excluded from enjoying the fruits of national development.

The new Nigerian government also will soon have to do something about the country's alarming population explosion. For at least a decade now, the official attitude has been that family size will shrink as modernization takes place and that the country will be able to support its growing population and also raise the standard of living. The officials are wrong. Population pressures are retarding proper economic growth. Unless the government promotes a major family-planning program, the annual rate of population growth will accelerate. More than half of Nigeria's population is under twenty years of age, and when these Nigerians start producing children, which should be very soon, you are quickly going to have a country of thousands of Kugbuyi streets. Nigerian culture, unfortunately, values fertility, and couples are encouraged to have large families.

Successive governments in Nigeria have said that acceptance of birth control is a matter of individual choice. Nigerian leaders have also held that a growing population would be fed by accelerating agricultural production. This sounds good, but it is, of course, nonsense. Nigeria's food demand is growing by more than 5 percent annually, while the current yearly food production growth rate is barely 1 percent. The country now imports 3 millions tons of grain; by 1985, Nigeria will need to import almost 6 million tons of grain. According to government estimates, agricultural production would have to increase by at least 6.5 percent annually to close the gap between demand and output. I just don't see how Nigeria is going to do this, particularly since one of the main causes of agricultural decline—the flight of rural manpower to urban areas—continues unchecked. From 1960 to 1982 the proportion of Nigerians living in urban areas rose from 22 percent to 60 percent. The average age of an agricultural worker is now forty-two, and rising, and mechanization is still a novelty on most Nigerian farms. In addition, productivity on farms continues to be hampered by the lack of good-quality seeds, proper tools, fertilizers, adequate storage, marketing facilities, and water supply, and decent roads into the hinterland. The transportation network is in a shambles.

The country's leaders have long been talking about undertaking a "green revolution." People are to be fed without importing food. Between 1975 and 1979, the military regime then in power allocated barely

2.5 percent of the budget to agricultural promotion. Shagari was talking about spending as much as 15 percent of the budget, or some $5 billion in four years, on agriculture. What he failed to address was how to persuade people who had fled rural areas to return to farming. He would talk about offering private entrepreneurs tax holidays if they went into large-scale farming, but what about ordinary peasants who had abandoned agriculture? Nigeria, which cannot afford to go on importing a billion dollars' worth of food each year as it now does, simply has to revive its languishing agriculture to feed its burgeoning population. Otherwise it can look forward to a plethora of food riots.

* * *

Yusuf Mohammed was one man who decided he would contribute to the country's food production program.

He is a tall, athletic, forty-four-year-old man who was one of Nigeria's best-known architects. I traveled up to Rido Junction, in northern Kaduna State, to visit him, and found Yusuf locked in meetings with his farm manager, production hands, and accountants. I walked around the farm while Yusuf completed his work. His farm covers 2,000 acres of verdant land in Kaduna State, nearly 600 miles from Lagos. The farm is almost completely mechanized and has its own power generator. There are several ranch-style, split-level buildings that Yusuf designed himself. Among the products of Yusuf's farm: corn, maize, cassava, yams, tomatoes, broilers, and more than 35,000 eggs a day.

"Everybody talks about the green revolution—I decided that I would not just talk but do something about it," Yusuf told me in his pleasing British accent. He has a pleasant face and a sturdy build. I had expected an architect to look out of place on a farm, but Yusuf seemed to fit right in, down to his mud-splattered boots and his frayed jeans. "Nigeria's wealth, its true wealth, is in its land. We have to feed ourselves first—and we have the land and the manpower to become a major food producer. We have to contend with the fact that we have all these people to feed."

He told me as we lunched on roasted chicken and a tomato salad—from his farm, of course—that only 82 million of Nigeria's 250 million cultivable acres were actually being used for agriculture. Agriculture was also handicapped by the fact that the average farm was no bigger than two or three acres, if that. This meant that mechanized large-scale farming, which could result in cheaper food production and in cheaper food, was not feasible.

The country's successive governments, military–civilian–military, talked loftily about promoting agriculture, Yusuf said, but did little to ease bureaucratic restrictions and ennui. Despite his own political connections and his national prominence as an architect, it had taken him a year to obtain official approval to buy his land and another year to get a long-term, low-interest loan of $900,000. This loan complemented almost $1 million of his own family money that Yusuf poured into the business to buy thickly forested land from local chiefs. Rido Junction is about as rural a community as you can find in Nigeria, and much of the land around here is carpeted with mango trees and tall grass. This is bush country, made green and lush from the rain that falls gently much of the year. It took Yusuf more than six months to clear the land before it could be tilled. Now he employs more than 100 men and women.

"The need really is for the government to set up more cooperatives, more extension service facilities, more training programs in villages, and better incentives for more people to get into agriculture and stay in it," Yusuf said. "That, I think, is the only way we can stop this rapid flow of people to the already overcrowded cities of our country."

Yusuf no longer practices architecture because he doesn't have the time. Farming brings him joy, and it also brings him new wealth: products from his enterprise are sold not only around Rido Junction but all over Kaduna State. He is quite a sight around Rido Junction as he zooms by in his British sports car from one corral to another, from one broiler pen to another. Yusuf also regularly visits the homes of his employees to ensure that all is well with them. It is not enough, Yusuf told me, to give people jobs; it is also important to get them to adjust their traditional life styles to the modern era. So he emphasizes such things as proper sanitation and sanitary habits, he sees to it that his employees' children are enrolled in school—and he promotes the concept of smaller, healthier families.

It is a difficult task to convince traditional rural Moslems in Nigeria to have small families. One afternoon in Kaduna, a bustling town that reminded me of semirural communities in India where pedestrian traffic is constant and everybody always seems to be shopping at small, brightly lit stores, I was being taken around by a man named Alhaji Coomasie. He is a tough, rugged man who works in Lagos for Mobil Oil as a public relations officer but who travels up to his native Kaduna every weekend to "be with my people," as he puts it. What he really comes to Kaduna for is to relax, for five days a week in Lagos is enough to to drive anyone crazy. I told Coomasie that I wanted to visit ordinary Nigerians to understand their attitudes concerning such matters as development. He suggested I meet with some traditional Moslem peasants.

I went to the home of Mohammed Abusaza. He lived about ten miles outside Kaduna, on a farm where he raised sheep and cassava. He is forty-five years old, a lean, craggy man with teeth stained from chewing tobacco and eyes that shrewdly size you up in seconds. He thought at first that I'd come to buy sheep from him, and he launched into a long recital of the excellent value of his livestock until my translator, a local student named Jennifer, interrupted him and told him the true purpose of my visit. Mohammed seemed disappointed.

"You're a journalist?"

It was not really a question, just a statement.

I nodded.

"You will write about me?"

I nodded again.

"You will write well about Nigeria?"

Another nod from me.

Mohammed perked up. We had been talking so far in a meadow where his sheep were grazing languidly, and now he gestured that we follow him. The herd was left in the charge of a spindly youth, whom I took to be one of Mohammed's sons. Mohammed, a stocky man with large eyes and lips, wanted us to join him for tea in his house.

He lived in a cottage of sorts, with brick walls and a roof that seemed an odd combination of straw and corrugated steel. I could hear the screaming and squealing of children. Mohammed opened an ancient wooden door that creaked so violently I thought a bear was growling somewhere nearby.

The interior was abuzz with children. There were children on the mud floor, there were children on window sills, there were children squalling in the dimly lit kitchen. There even were children trying to climb up to the ceiling by jumping atop a dresser. In the kitchen a woman sat, alternately watching some of the children and keeping an eye on a pot that sat on a stove.

"They're all mine," Mohammed said, with a large smile.

"How many?" I asked.

"Fifteen!" Mohammed said. I swore I could see his chest swell with sexual pride.

"Fifteen! Why do you need so many children?"

"It is God's command. Besides, I need all the help I can get for my farm. And my children will provide for me in my old age."

"How many wives do you have?"

"Four. But I was married six times. Two of the women died after childbirth."

"How many children have you fathered in all?"

"Twenty-one! But six have died. There is much illness around Kaduna. Not enough clinics. Few doctors."

"Are you planning to have more children?" I asked.

"Of course. Three of my wives are at present with child."

"Have you considered family planning?"

"What for? Who am I to refuse Allah's gifts?"

"But what about your children? Are they getting the proper care?"

Mohammed shrugged.

"They eat well. We all eat well. That's what matters."

"Why do you keep producing so many children?"

Mohammed grinned and whispered hoarsely to Jennifer, my translator. She giggled.

"It is a matter of my manhood," was what Mohammed had said.

* * *

Back in Lagos, I went by to chat with my friend Tokunboh Oladeinde and some of his neighbors on Kugbuyi Street. We sat in Oladeinde's small living room early one evening. It was steamy inside, and the tabletop fan could not be made to work because there hadn't been electricity all day. The fumes from cars crawling along Kugbuyi Street drifted into Oladeinde's quarters; my eyes burned. It was getting dark, and the beams of automobile headlights on the street cast weird patterns on Oladeinde's walls. The noises of the human traffic on the pavement below provided a cacophonous soundtrack to our conversation. Somewhere in the building a couple was arguing wildly; babies were crying. Somebody's transistor radio was playing American pop tunes. It was getting very oppressive.

There were five young men in the room, including Oladeinde and myself, and as young men do, we discussed women.

"There is no morality left anymore with Nigerian girls," someone said. "They will do anything to get a job and keep it. And the more women are out there getting jobs, the less employers want to hire men."

"That leaves us men at a disadvantage," someone else said. "There's no way we can match what the girls have to offer."

There were guffaws all around. Of the four Nigerians in that room, only Oladeinde was gainfully employed.

Someone said that Nigeria would have to perform economic miracles merely to keep up with its rapidly increasing numbers of people, especially in the cities.

Someone else said that the population growth didn't really matter because Nigeria had so much land.

Oladeinde snorted.

"And how are you going to persuade people to leave the cities and go to these open areas, eh?" he said. "You guys feel like returning to your villages? Who's going to give you jobs back there?"

That was a very pertinent point. There is no rural repatriation program in Nigeria. People who want to return to the countryside must do so at their own expense. And there are seldom any jobs waiting for them if they do indeed trek back into the rural regions. Moreover, the physical size of Nigeria is misleading. There are areas containing wet rain forests, deserts, and rocky terrain, where agriculture cannot be easily undertaken.

"There are no jobs here in the city, there are no jobs back in the village—what are we to do?" said a man named Ezenekwe. He told me that he had been without a job ever since he arrived in Lagos from his village in eastern Nigeria. He had a bachelor's degree in economics, Ezenekwe said, but for almost a year he hadn't been able to find employment. Meanwhile, he was staying with cousins on Kugbuyi Street—but now the cousins were running out of patience and said they could no longer support him.

"Maybe," Ezenekwe said, wryly, "I will take to pickpocketing. I hear it is a very lucrative business."

As neighborhoods such as Kugbuyi Street get overcrowded, people are being forced to live farther and farther away from the central city. African cities, unlike their counterparts in the West, do not usually have suburban satellites. What happens is that shantytowns keep expanding from the perimeters of the central city. There is no efficient transportation system in most African cities, so those who cannot find housing in convenient downtown neighborhoods that are close to their places of employment must commute for hours to and from work every day. Zahed Baig, a young corporate executive in Lagos, told me that many of his employees commuted as much as three hours each way every day.

"When they fall asleep on the job, you really cannot blame them," he said. "They just are too tired by the time they get to work."

* * *

Musa Mohammed has lived all his forty years on the shores of Lake Victoria, a vast expanse of water that divides Kenya from Uganda and provides livelihood for fishermen from both East African countries.

He has, in fact, not even traveled more than fifty miles away from Sio Port Village, where he was born and where his father and grandfather before him lived and eked out a living from the placid waters of the lake. Like them, Musa is up before the sun has climbed into view every morning, even before the local muezzin has issued his call to prayer. He nudges his boat from its rack on the Kenyan shore, pushes it into the water, then starts up its engine and heads a mile or two away to cast his nets to trap Nile perch and other fish. Like his father and grandfather did before him, Musa is back in his wood shack shortly after midday to eat a meal of boiled maize—called *ugali*—and a spicy fish sauce, after which Musa rests for the rest of the afternoon before joining his friends later in the evening for conversation and a round of moonshine in the time-honored tradition. The routine seldom varies for him, as it probably did not for his father and grandfather, and like them, Musa Mohammed will probably never do anything else but go out in his boat, haul in the catch, and sell it at a local government market, from where the fish will be transported to distant cities like Nairobi. Like his father and grandfather, Musa is tall and has a thick nose, sturdy limbs, and hands that can squeeze the breath out of a python.

Unlike his father and grandfather, each of whom died before his thirty-fifth birthday of typhoid, Musa Mohammed will enjoy a long life span, as will his six sons and seven daughters. That is because modern medical care, sanitation, and education have come to Sio Port Village, brought to this remote, still largely rural and undeveloped region by Hillary and Julia Ojiambo.

The Ojiambos were both born around here, received their primary education in Bucia, then went abroad on scholarships to study cardiology and psychology, respectively. They returned to Kenya to practice social medicine. It has helped that Julia Ojiambo is now a minister in the national cabinet of President Daniel arap Moi, and it has helped, too, that Hillary Ojiambo teaches at medical school in Nairobi and is in a position to ask his students to travel to this area for practical training.

Had it not been for the Ojiambos' ability to raise funds from foreign and domestic sources to get health, education, and family-planning projects going here, Bucia would still be in the dark ages.

To me, the work of Hillary and Julia Ojiambo underscores an important point concerning "development": the total volume of foreign aid for population work and development is actually very marginal relative to what countries and organizations themselves spend on development efforts. Policy makers in the West often assume that Third World states spend very little of their own money for development and instead keep coming back to Western donors for more. The truth is, for every $1 that the West gives to the Third World for population and development programs, the developing countries themselves put in $4 of their own. The Ojiambos have received around $5,000 from organizations such as Boston's Pathfinder Fund; they have raised several times this amount in Kenya itself from domestic sources—and the Ojiambos have put a minor fortune of their own into social programs for Bucia's people.

The true value of the foreign "development dollar" has been that it served as a spur for local development efforts in Bucia. Hillary Ojiambo acknowledges that without the initial seed money from foreign sources, Bucia's programs would never have gotten off the ground. It was the initial infusion of foreign aid that helped start the training programs locally. Now, of course, the Bucia project is self-financed and self-sustaining—an illustration of how Western development dollars can come into a place, establish a working system for local development, and then phase themselves out.

Indeed, I would argue that the whole system of development assistance was never intended to keep foreign aid going but to phase such aid out after establishing a development momentum in an area. Unfortunately, the perception of many influential Western policy makers is that Third World countries really would prefer a permanent dole from the industrialized nations. Such a perception is often based on the strident political rhetoric emanating from some Third World leaders, who talk about a "transfer of technology" and other adjustments to ensure a fairer shake for poor countries.

I was introduced to Hillary Ojiambo by a man named Dieter Erhardt, a huge, bespectacled German who is the Nairobi representative of the United Nations Fund for Population Activities. Erhardt is a nervous man, and part of his tension can be attributed to his genuine concern about the population explosion in Kenya, which—along with Nigeria—now has the world's highest annual population growth rate. This 4 percent annual rate is not something that Kenya, a poor country with few natural resources, can afford. (Nigeria at least has oil, which fetches it billions of dollars in revenues each year.)

At the rate that Kenya is going, its population of some 18 million overwhelmingly impoverished people very likely will double in about a decade. Until recently, the country's leaders and politicians simply have not been very serious about checking rampant population growth, and now it may well be too late to reverse the growth momentum. Erhardt told me that Kenya now received more than $20 million each year from the World Bank, the United Nations, and other Western sources, for its population control projects. Many of these projects appeared to be caught in the bureaucratic logjams characteristic of foreign-sponsored development programs in the Third World. But Hillary and Julia Ojiambo had got going something unusual, Erhardt said to me. They had successfully instituted a grass-roots health care and education program that was run entirely by the locals themselves.

My first impression of Hillary Ojiambo was not particularly warm. Short and solidly built, wearing a garish dashiki shirt and jeans, he seemed stern, a bit too prone to dwell on his health care goals for Bucia. But I later understood that his preoccupation with Bucia and its plight stemmed from genuine feeling for a region where he grew up. All but three of eleven children in his family had died in their infancy because of preventable illnesses like dehydration and diarrhea. We met at Nairobi's Wilson General Aviation Airport early one morning; Dieter Erhardt had hired a small, two-engine plane for the two-hour flight to Bucia. Our plane was piloted by a young Kenyan white, who swaggered to the aircraft, summoned us in, and took off so steeply that his passengers almost fainted. It was a lovely morning to fly. We quickly left Nairobi behind and moved past Mount Kenya, whose peak was not cloud-covered as it usually is. We could see Masai herdsmen and their cattle. Coffee plantations soon came into view. Then the hilly terrain became flat, occasionally pocked by ponds and traversed by streams, as we approached Lake Victoria.

"Bucia should be around here," the pilot said.

But he couldn't get a visual fix on what Professor Ojiambo said was a dirt airstrip at Bucia.

"You're the pilot," Professor Ojiambo said tartly. "I've never had to identify Bucia from the air before."

So we flew around in circles. The pilot said he did not have a very good map. He thought we were now in Ugandan air space, a possibility that alarmed me because I knew how paranoid the Ugandan armed forces were about unidentified aircraft and how quick they were to shoot them down. Then the pilot spotted an airstrip barely visible in the high grass and a cluster of huts down below.

"Let's land and ask those folks the right directions," he said.

It all would have been very comical had it not been for the worrying fact that we were now lost—and out of radio range of the pilot's home base in Nairobi.

We landed—with a crash.

The small plane sank into a crater that the pilot had not seen from the air. The two propellers plunged into the soft, red soil. Our seat belts saved us from being thrown out of the aircraft. We jumped off the plane —only to find ourselves surrounded by machete-wielding youths who had converged on the crashed plane.

Professor Ojiambo took charge. He shouted something in Swahili. Immediately the crowd responded and started moving back. A tall, elderly man came toward us, greeted the professor, then said in English:

"Welcome!"

We had crashed about forty miles from Bucia, in a tiny backwoods place called Sega. The elderly man who welcomed us was a local schoolmaster, and the machete-carrying youths were his students. They had, he said, come to rescue us.

It was obvious that the plane was wrecked. We were told that there was a missionary compound about four miles from where we'd crashed. The schoolmaster said we could radio for help from there. Still somewhat shaken from the shock of our crash, we all of us set off on foot, taking a trail that wound through the bush. It rained as we walked, a soft, velvety rain that felt pleasant. The earth smelled rich and wet. The local youths decided to escort us all the way to the Christian mission, which, it turned out, was run by the Franciscan Sisters of Saint Joseph. We made for a strange procession in the bush—a snakelike stream of humans trampling through the undergrowth without a word. There were moments during the hike when it struck me that this was what it must have been like for those early colonial explorers who traversed Africa. I felt very alone.

The sisters were at once friendly and welcoming. We were given warm buns and hot tea. It felt good to be fussed over. Professor Ojiambo ran to a telephone to call Bucia, where his wife Julia was supposed to be waiting for us at the local airport. The pilot, cool and nonchalant, took his time getting to the mission's radio room to raise Nairobi. I decided I would look around the compound.

The mission consisted of four or five one-story buildings made of bricks. The walls were painted in pastels; some of the buildings had verandahs. Jacaranda and hibiscus were everywhere. Behind the compound was a large field where maize, cassava, and millet were grown. The mission also had a large vegetable patch. I was joined by Sister Isabelle, a young woman who wore a blue habit. She had piercing, expressive eyes, and she gave me a quick rundown on the mission. It was founded thirty years ago, she said, when it was all dense wilderness here.

"We were the first to bring modern health care and modern methods of farming here," Sister Isabelle said. I remarked how courageous those early missionaries must have been and how equally brave their present-day successors. Sister Isabelle beamed.

She showed me around the mission's health clinic, a bright, clean building with beds, examination rooms, and a pharmacy. On this day, there were no in-house patients. I was surprised to see a preponderance of family-planning posters. They seemed out of place in a Catholic mission, especially since Pope John Paul II had come down hard against artificial birth control. I asked Sister Isabelle about this.

She smiled.

"We leave the question of contraception entirely up to the villagers," she said, "but we do strongly recommend that they have small families. The fact is, Kenya's annual population growth rate of 4 percent is the world's highest. We don't have the resources to feed all these people who are being born every minute. We need to take urgent action."

"Who distributes the contraceptives?" I asked.

"Roving doctors who go from village to village do that," Sister Isabelle said. "These doctors come around a couple of times a week. We get the contraceptives free of charge from the government."

Condoms are in demand here, and lately more and more women have been asking for IUDs. But the birthrate hasn't declined appreciably. Perhaps it's too early for such a development.

There was a huge, multicolored poster at the entrance to the mission's health clinic. It showed a happy Kenyan family consisting of a couple and two children (a boy and a girl). The caption on the poster read, in both English and Swahili:

"Family-planning doesn't mean you should not have children. But have only as many children as you can afford—and make sure you space their births."

Julia Ojiambo decided she would drive in her Mercedes sedan and meet us at the mission. She was a small woman, sprightly, full of good cheer. She wore a white turban, a long, one-piece, patterned blue dress, and a red sweater. Even though she was a cabinet minister, there was no air of self-importance about her.

We drove to Bucia, through emerald green countryside. The pilot stayed behind; his air charter company would be sending another plane to transport us back home later in the day. The crashed plane in Sega would probably be stripped to its frame by the locals by the time the air charter company got around to returning for it. The scenery started changing after a dozen miles out of Sega. Here it hadn't rained for weeks, Julia said. The fields and sides of squat hills looked parched. The vegetation was stunted. The cattle grazing on barren meadows looked forlorn, even sickly.

"What you have to understand is that around these parts of Kenya it isn't simply a question of providing more health services to the people," Julia Ojiambo said in her low, measured voice. "It's a matter of changing attitudes. It's a matter of overcoming superstitions and fears. So if you're going to come in and say, 'Hey, let's bring down the birthrate,' you're doomed to failure. You have to come in, settle with these people, work methodically to win their trust—and then you get results."

Our first stop would be Sio Port village, at the edge of Lake Victoria. Again the scenery changed. It became green once more. We drove over hills on a dusty, winding road that jolted the Mercedes and jarred our backs. More than once Hillary Ojiambo had to caution the driver to take it easy, counsel the man did not heed. Africans generally are devilish drivers, particularly when they are behind wheels of a sleek, foreign-made car.

"Stop!" yelled Hillary Ojiambo.

A few more feet and our Mercedes would have plunged into the water. The road had ended abruptly at the edge of a cliff. I could see a cluster of dwellings below us, by the waterside. Fishing boats lazily drifted in the lake. We walked down a dirt path to the homes, where a group of children were playing the flute, shaking tambourines, and banging on tin drums. A tall, big-boned man was playing a harmonica.

The man was Musa Mohammed, and the children were his.

"I am teaching them music—so they will stay out of trouble," he said.

Musa greeted Hillary and Julia Ojiambo warmly, bowing to them in the traditional fashion. It was through their assistance, he told me, that the lives of two of his thirteen children were saved. Hillary Ojiambo had personally treated the children for jaundice and had them taken to a clinic for treatment.

"Why did you have so many children?" I asked.

"What God has given you, you can't throw away," Musa replied. "Some of my children now go to school. With their education, maybe they will help me in my fishing business. Maybe one day I will have a fleet of boats, instead of just one boat now."

Musa's four wives had given him twenty children, of whom thirteen have survived. The infant mortality rate is especially high in this area, Hillary Ojiambo explained; malaria, diarrhea, and tetanus are the main killers. The Ojiambos had initiated a project to educate the residents of Sio Port village about sanitary habits and the importance of boiling water for consumption. Villagers were also being taught to take their children to local health clinics for regular inoculations. But there was still suspicion among some villagers of doctors, particularly of those physicians who administered injections.

Hillary Ojiambo knows that a breakthrough has taken place, nonetheless, in changing local attitudes: not long ago, Musa Mohammed brought his wives and all his children to a local clinic for complete checkups.

I asked Musa about this.

"Allah has brought modern medicine to us in the form of the clinic," he said, pointing to the gray, leaden skies. "Who are we to refuse Him?"

Some miles from Sio Port village is a community called Ageng'a. It is named after a bald-headed hill. The community consists of a couple of dozen sheds, shacks, and modest brick structures, which constitute a health training center that Hillary and Julia Ojiambo founded for Bucia Province. They obtained money from Boston's Pathfinder Fund and some other foreign organizations, but all the technical and medical expertise was indigenous.

"What we resolved right at the start," Hillary Ojiambo said to me as we drove to Ageng'a, "was that if you wanted to motivate backward people, don't get foreigners to help you. Let the locals be the change agents. People in areas such as Bucia are still very suspicious of outsiders. The problems here were of poverty, malnutrition, ignorance, and backwardness. High-tech solutions and massive economic development programs had no room in such a situation. You would just have created a layer of povertycrats here. We thought that the problems of Bucia had to be tackled from the grass roots, by the people of the area themselves. The people of the area had to be their own change agents."

The fact that both Hillary and Julia Ojiambo hailed from Bucia meant that the locals could trust them. This was an important part of their early success. Julia held a series of *barazas*, or meetings, with villagers all over the province to find out more about what their health requirements were. Hillary would ship some of his Nairobi students to Bucia to carry out health surveys and assess the needs of the community. These students also helped select local residents for training programs. The "development dollar" was in the field.

Among the first to sign up for training as a health volunteer was Leonida Barasa. She is a resident of Machange village, which consists of a collection of huts and shops not far from the shores of Lake Victoria. Leonida's husband, Samuel, is a farmer. Five years ago, after she had had her last child, Leonida became a birth control practitioner.

"I never wanted to have five children," she told me, gloomily. "We cannot afford so many children. But in Machange nobody knew anything about family planning—until this health project came along."

Hillary Ojiambo invited me to see Leonida conduct one of her training classes. A dozen men and women, in their late twenties or early thirties, had gathered in a small conference room. Charts displaying local demographic data festooned the walls. Also tacked up were illustrations of the human reproduction system. There were posters exhorting Kenyans to pay more attention to proper health care and nutrition for their children. The subject of this particular seminar was how villagers could grow better vegetables. Leonida Barasa, it seemed, raised the best tomatoes in the area.

With a self-assured manner, Leonida proceeded to talk in Swahili about fertilizers and insecticides, about spraying plants and siphoning water to roots. Then she talked about how it was important to squeeze in the message of family planning even as these men and women were providing instruction to villagers in such subjects as agriculture and horticulture and livestock breeding.

"Remember, everything is interconnected—farming, nutrition, hygiene, family planning," she said. "How we breed is how we live."

A woman named Dinah Makhulo from Buleiri Village broke in. "It's so natural for us to keep having children that we often don't realize the problems," Dinah, the mother of two children, said. "Men want children as insurance against old age. They don't like having daughters, so they keep insisting on children until a son comes along. But no one thinks of the poor wife who has to bear these children. Then when a woman like me says she wants to have no more children and wants to raise vegetables, there is trouble at home."

The Ageng'a center where Leonida Barasa now trains health care workers offers three-month courses for local residents. When I visited the center, I was told that it had 161 such trainees. They were housed in one-story brick dormitories that nestled in the hollows of Ageng'a Hill. It was hard to believe that barely a year ago this area was covered with thorn trees and wild vegetation; now it looked like a campus: Lake Victoria lay in the distance, covered with a thin mist that was floating toward us.

What struck me at the Ageng'a center was the extent of communal participation. None of these people had anything to do with the national government; everyone at the center, from the instructors to the trainees, were local residents of Bucia Province. There was none of the propaganda and rhetoric here about "development" or "family planning." Rather, there was emphasis on the everyday things—like vegetable growing, sanitation, child care—that mattered in people's lives. And the message of family planning was subtly inserted into day-to-day life here so that people came to realize that fewer children meant more happiness and health. I wished fervently that the idea of Ageng'a would catch on in the rest of Kenya, Africa, and the Third World.

* * *

I found myself one warm spring day in Asilah, a Moroccan village of white-walled houses, narrow twisting streets, and bustling bazaars. Its sandy beaches are usually carpeted with fishermen's nets. This is a picturebook community, situated where the Mediterranean meets the Atlantic. Tangiers is a few miles to the north, and across from Tangiers, on the other side of a narrow strait, is Gibraltar. The homes in Asilah all have electricity, the cobbled streets are kept clean by diligent sanitation crews, there is virtually no unemployment and no crime, and Asilah

—unlike many Moroccan villages—rarely runs out of drinking water. Asilah has also become what is perhaps the Third World's leading cultural mecca.

The man who made all this possible in the space of less than five years is Mohammed Benaissa, a young filmmaker who was born in Asilah, left it some years ago in frustration, then decided to return and transform a dusty, poverty-ridden village into a prosperous place. All of a sudden, Asilah finds itself enjoying the status of a "model village," not only in Morocco but by reputation through much of the developing world. In August each year, it hosts the Asilah Cultural Festival, which attracts artists, artisans, singers, sculptors, musicians, poets, writers, politicians, professors, scientists, film producers, economists, and other experts. The festival they gather for celebrates not only the arts but also the whole business of "development."

"I think that what we have shown here in Asilah is that Third World communities don't have to wait for outside financial help to rejuvenate or develop themselves," Benaissa, a slim, good-looking man, says. "It is possible to generate our own self-help ethic, to get development going our own way. Then the whole world will come to you."

With a population now of about 22,500, Asilah is one of hundreds of villages that speckle this land of 21 million mostly poor people. Until its "rebirth," it was a typical village, albeit prettier than most because of its seaside location. Infant mortality was high; the annual population growth rate matched the national figure of 3.25 percent; health care facilities were inadequate, with the nearest hospital in Tangiers, fifty miles to the north; the dirt roads were rutted and impassable during the rains; there was seldom any electricity; and potable water had to be brought from deep wells many miles away. Little economic aid was forthcoming from the administration of King Hassan II, despite repeated pleas from Asilah officials.

Mohammed Benaissa and I talked about Asilah's past in his ancestral home, a house packed away in the village casbah. It had high ceilings, ornate carved furniture, an inner courtyard, and a living room with large stuffed pillows. We were enjoying a hearty meal in typical Moroccan style, which is to say that the dishes were served in the living room on large platters (Moroccan homes do not have conventional dining areas; everyone eats in the living room). There was couscous, there was baked lamb, there were a dozen stewed vegetables, and there was fruit.

"Do you know that you are sitting in a house that was part of

Asilah's Jewish quarter?" Benaissa said. "About twenty-five years ago, there were more than 4,000 Jews in Asilah. We had four synagogues. The Jews all emigrated to Israel. They had been here for 3,500 years. That's how old Asilah is."

We walked around town after the meal. It was a lovely Mediterranean evening, and the sky was shot with stars. It was an evening made lovelier by the presence of Mohammed's teenaged daughter, Shafiah, a graceful, sultry beauty, who seemed very popular with everybody we passed. We walked past Asilah's palace, an ancient crenelated structure that had been restored recently under Benaissa's supervision. It now serves as a sort of dormitory for artists who visit Asilah during the August festival—known locally in Arabic as *moussem*—each year. Some of the buildings suggested Spanish influence. I asked Mohammed about this.

"The Spanish ruled Asilah until 1956—it was a pocket of Morocco that they had seized from the French," Benaissa said. "It was a humiliating period for *zailiches* [as the people of Asilah are called]. The beaches were segregated by the Spaniards; even our local movie house was segregated."

Benaissa fled Morocco to seek his fortune elsewhere. He made documentaries in Britain and in the United States, then worked for the United Nations's Food and Agriculture Organization in Rome. He became a regular on the international diplomatic circuit, a sought-after consultant on Third World affairs. He became possessed, he told me, with a desire to return home. By now, of course, Benaissa was very well off; he had invested in a Rabat newspaper called *Al Mitaq al Watan,* which was prospering.

When Benaissa came back to Asilah, he was even more distressed than when he had left the community. The place was moribund. Residents were morose. Unemployment was increasing. The fishing business, a staple in the area, suffered from a shortage of funds for boats to replace the community's aging fleet. The weaving industry that once had flourished was practically dead. Cobblers had done reasonably well here once, but now there were no cobblers left; they had gone to get jobs in cities like Casablanca and Rabat. But there weren't jobs waiting for them in Casablanca and Rabat either: Morocco, the world's biggest exporter of phosphates (which are used for making fertilizers and whose sale fetches the country more than $1 billion each year) was finding that the slump in world demand was hurting its economy, as was the sputtering war with a Marxist guerrilla group called the Polisario, which claimed the Moroccan possession of the Western Sahara. External debt was now beyond $6 billion, and Morocco's Western bankers were reluctant to lend it any more money. Unemployment and inflation were spiraling.

A local artist named Mohammed el-Mehlek suggested to Benaissa that he contest municipal elections. "We need someone to shake up this place—to get things moving," Mehlek told Benaissa. And so it was that Mohammed Benaissa, one-time international gadfly, became Asilah's mayor.

Not long after his election, Benaissa was walking through Asilah's clamorous bazaar when it occurred to him that his village would be a wonderful site for a cultural festival. Why not invite to Asilah his friends from various cultural communities around the world? He decided to organize a summer music festival and request his fellow villagers to clean up the community in preparation. Perhaps, Benaissa thought, if a sufficient number of big names came, King Hassan's government would sit up and take notice, and maybe it would provide some funds for the revitalization of Asilah. He, meanwhile, would put his own funds into getting Asilah into some sort of shape for the event.

That first festival, in 1976, drew performers like the jazz pianist Keith Jarrett, a couple of members of the Rolling Stones, the Italian writer Alberto Moravia, and artists and authors from twenty Third World countries. Benaissa spent more than $8,000 of his own money and persuaded some of his wealthy Moroccan friends in Rabat and Casablanca to chip in. Most of the guests paid for their own travel; villagers housed the visitors.

"We got local children to paint village walls, local women swept streets, local men hauled off the garbage—by the time the festival started, Asilah sparkled," recalls Benaissa's uncle, Mohammed Andalousi, a tough, gnarled fellow. "The sprucing up was especially good for our children, who got the opportunity of expressing their talents in graffiti on the village walls. The point we got across to their parents was that Asilah need not be shabby and dilapidated, that we may be a poor village but we still could be a clean village, so that the conditions that bred disease were not there."

Moroccan newspapers raved about the week-long festival. Tourists heard and rushed to Asilah, straining its resources. People pitched tents on the beaches; the one hotel in the village had barely a dozen rooms. Then the ultimate accolade arrived—a personal message of congratulations from King Hassan, along with a check for $120,000. The king also asked Benaissa if there was something he could do for Asilah. With great alacrity, Benaissa responded with several suggestions, most having to do with money to improve roads, sanitation, and power in Asilah. Within weeks, aid in the form of government technicians and materiel started to arrive.

But it wasn't just "aid" that Benaissa was interested in. He wanted villagers to have employment, so he organized municipal teams, each with specific functions such as cleaning streets (Asilah now has fourteen full-time garbage collectors, who move about in tiny vans supplied by the West Germans), patrolling neighborhoods and fixing water lines. Asilah's houses were repainted. Youths were encouraged to decorate certain walls with imaginative graffiti, and pedestrian byways were decorated with art reflecting a mix of Asilah's traditional Moslem heritage and contemporary design.

Benaissa tapped sources in the Canadian government, which has long been active in providing development assistance in Third World countries. With the $15,000 the Canadians gave, Benaissa bought etching machines so that local artisans could make ceramics; Iraq sent, at its own expense, sculptors and potters to train Asilah craftsmen to produce goods that could be sold. Within two years of that first culture festival, Asilah had virtually no unemployment: residents found jobs in a new power station the government built; or they were given work at the new telephone exchange; or they obtained employment in the expanded harbor. Or they were hired to work on a construction project for 800 new houses that are being built for *zailiches.*

"We showed the world that you don't need oil wealth to develop your indigenous economy. You need the will, you need imagination, you need good local leadership," says Mustafa Jubed, who runs the Casbah Restaurant, an enterprise that was born in the wake of the first Asilah festival.

I lunched one afternoon at the Casbah Restaurant on a fresh catch of jumbo shrimps, crawfish, and Mediterranean sole. Mustafa, a solicitous host who kept me in a sated state, told me that now 100,000 people came every summer for the Asilah festival. With its choice location facing the beach, the Casbah Restaurant mints money every summer. Mustafa even has gotten into exporting fish these days.

Walking around Asilah later that afternoon, I came across two pharmacies that had opened up after the first culture festival. Behind the sprawling bazaar was an ancient building, freshly painted and patched up in places: it was Asilah's "new" hospital, and it has 140 beds. I met a young physician here named Ahmed Benmalek.

Benmalek, a tall, strapping man with wavy hair, came to Asilah from the town of Oujda, near the Algerian border. He was, like thousands of young Moroccans, drawn to Asilah by the culture festival. Benmalek liked the physical beauty of Asilah so much that he stayed on.

"I was puzzled. Here was a community of thousands, and it had not a single doctor!" Benmalek told me, speaking in French. "This was inconceivable to me. I decided I would move to Asilah to practice my medicine."

It proved to be a more difficult thing to do than Benmalek had envisioned.

"I found *zailiches* had been living in closed isolation—there were a lot of sullen, withdrawn people here who didn't particularly like the idea of a stranger coming and settling down amidst them," the young physician said. "Many of them would prefer to go all the way to Tangiers to see their doctor rather than come and see me here in the village. I had to work hard to get these people to accept me. The more I treated their children, the more they started to trust me."

One of the first things that Benmalek did was to enlist the assistance of the Moroccan Health Ministry in setting up family-planning services in Asilah. The ministry, with help from the U.S. Agency for International Development, has trained more than 500 fieldworkers to visit homes and spread the message of family planning. The project is known as VDMS—an acronym for Visites à Domicile de Motivation Systematique—and the fieldworkers try and persuade women with large families to accept contraception such as the pill or IUD. The fieldworkers also gathered statistical data that was then passed on to national economic planning officials. By 1983, virtually every household in Asilah had been reached by these fieldworkers, and the use of contraception increased from almost zero in 1977 to more than 65 percent. The annual population growth rate fell by 1983 to 2 percent.

A typical visit by a VDMS representative goes something like this. The fieldworker turns up at a home in Asilah, usually one suggested by the village *muquaddam*, a senior citizen who is selected by the local community to be an ad hoc government official. The home selected is one where the mother has at least three children.

"I would like to recommend that you try the pill for two or three months," the female fieldworker tells the woman.

The woman asks questions: How does the pill work? Is it safe? Will it give me any kind of disease? Will it affect my health? What if I miss a day? Suppose I decide to have more children—will the pill give me a deformed child?

The VDMS fieldworker returns to individual homes three to five months after the first visit to inquire about contraceptive use and to replenish the stock of pills. More than 250,000 households all over Morocco have now been reached by such fieldworkers. In addition, the Moroccan Family Planning Association dispatches teams of population aides to persuade families to become birth control acceptors. These teams show films that emphasize the social and economic value of small families. Often, the fieldworkers must set up shop in village mosques because not all rural communities in Morocco have public buildings or health clinics. Some of these makeshift clinics are decorated with family-planning posters. The most frequently displayed poster shows King Hassan urging Moroccans to have smaller families. Another poster carries a quotation from former Prime Minister Ahmed Osman:

"Our galloping demographic increase is a burden on the family and on the state."

Benmalek's priorities also included controlling diarrhea and malnutrition, the two major killers of children in Morocco. This meant that he would have to teach modern methods of sanitation to *zailiches.*

"My work involved getting people to change their habits," Benmalek told me. "It meant getting them to give their children oral rehydration salts, vitamins, and weaning foods. A lot of rural Moroccans still have dietary taboos. For instance, they will not give eggs and brains to their children because they believe, wrongly of course, that these things will damage their children's health."

People like Benmalek and Benaissa capitalized on Asilah's spreading fame as Morocco's "culture center." They persuaded Spanish authorities to donate a fish storage facility. The West Germans came through with a gift of a truck and two tractors so that a local cooperative farm could be expanded.

"What started off as a cultural festival has brought us a whole new lease on life," Abdelsalam Khombleti, the head of Asilah's fishing cooperative, said to me late one afternoon as we stood at Asilah's piers, watching a couple of the cooperative's five new trawlers come in from the Atlantic. "For years we lived in misery. It had simply not occurred to us that our economic plight need not continue, that we need not continue in a state where the general population's health was poor and our children were dying of illnesses that could be prevented."

Mohammed Benaissa acted to expand the scope of the Asilah Festival. It was no longer just music, dancing, singing, and displays of art but also serious seminars on development featuring experts such as

Bradford Morse—head of the United Nations Development Programme—and academicians from the Third World and from the West. Crown Prince Hassan of Jordan has attended the festival, as has Leopold Senghor, former president of Senegal and *éminence grise* among African statesmen. The Asilah Festival—which has now become self-sustaining because of the large participation and the contributions from various cultural organizations and foundations around the world—has become a forum for the exchange of ideas about the direction of economic and political development in the Arab, African, and Third Worlds generally.

"Who would have thought that we'd come this far, that we'd change our lives in just a few short years?" said Abdelaziz Tagnaouti, a local fisherman.

Then he paused.

"Wait, I take that back. Of course, we imagined the change. Where would we be without our imagination and determination? But it all needed a catalyst, and Benaissa was that catalyst."

One evening I chatted with a man named Mohammed Al-Arbi, a local shopkeeper. Before the Asilah Festival got going, he owned just a small stall where he sold candy, toys, and seashells that were bought by occasional tourists as gimcracks. Now Arbi owns a full-fledged supermarket.

"Life has changed for us in Asilah," he said to me over a glass of thick Arabic coffee. "People have become more sociable, more sure of themselves, more certain that their children will have opportunities to make a decent living."

I decided to throw a curve at him.

"How many children do you have?"

"Three sons," Arbi said.

"Are you planning any more?"

"Of course not. My wife practices birth control now. Three children is enough. I want to give them the fullest opportunity to develop themselves, to get a good education, to pursue the careers they want. How can I pay attention to my children properly if I keep fathering more of them?"

"Did you want more children?"

"Yes. And we probably would have had more. That is the tradition in Morocco—to have as many sons as possible. I don't subscribe to the tradition now."

This tradition is a pre-Islamic Berber custom under which a tribe's common land is divided among the male offspring, which meant that families tried to have as many sons as they could in order to obtain larger shares of the communal property. The government, to this day, favors older—and large—families when it comes to distribution of farming lands. Mohammed Arbi owns only a small plot of land, and his three sons are still below the age of ten. His future lies in commerce and trading, he says, not agriculture. He no longer subscribes to the old Berber view concerning children. In his case, there has been an attitudinal change.

Not long ago, Arbi voted to give Mohammed Benaissa yet another term as mayor of Asilah. Benaissa won overwhelmingly.

* * *

Back in New York City, I lunched one day with an old friend, Bradford Morse, who heads the United Nations Development Programme, the world's biggest development assistance agency. Brad, a former congressman from Massachusetts, is "Mr. Development" himself, a tireless campaigner for Third World countries.

I told Brad how impressed I was with what Mohammed Benaissa and his *zailiches* were doing in Asilah, how they were relying primarily on their own imagination and efforts to lift themselves up by the sandalstraps. The *zailiches* were bringing down their infant mortality rate, their birthrate, and their morbidity, on their own—through changes in attitudes and a willingness to work to change their ways. Foreign aid was welcome, of course, but Asilah did not depend for its livelihood on it. I told Brad that I thought the people of Asilah has fashioned their own happiness their own way.

Brad, a large, intense man, stopped poking at his pickled Chinese cabbage.

"You know, many of us in the development business often confuse our ability to donate technique with the capacity to change other people's lives," he said. "That change really has to come from the people themselves, those we'd like to help. Development isn't just about building roads or distributing contraceptives. Development is all about the enlargement of individual human lives. If you aggregate that development, you end up enlarging society."

Three

The Kenyan Experience
Birthrates and Putsches

KENYA IS A PUZZLE, the odd man out in Africa and the world. It has the world's highest annual population growth rate, a staggering 4 percent plus; and at a time when growth rates are declining elsewhere in the world, there are few signs that fertility trends in Kenya are about to follow suit. The infant mortality in this East African state is also horrendously high. In fact, Kenya offers a textbook lesson in how high infant mortality rates often account for high birthrates, because as couples see their children die from diseases—that are often preventable—they keep producing more children as an insurance against old age and as economic assets in rural areas.

But classic textbook solutions of family planning do not appear to be working in Kenya, perhaps because there still is no comprehensive network of family-planning services, perhaps because the vigorous political commitment to reducing fertility that one sees in other African countries like Tunisia and Zimbabwe just isn't there in Kenya. There are few leaders in Kenya bold enough to push through the dramatic population program that the country desperately needs to save itself, and, of course, there are no myrmidons to carry out tough antinatalist policies in this one-party state.

Kenya is a population kaleidoscope. There are several dozen tribes, which rarely get along with one another. And all of them collectively dislike the richest tribe of all, the Asians, who aren't even ethnocentric natives of Kenya. The tensions between indigenous tribes explain the political tenuousness in Kenya today; the fright among the Asians concerning their own precarious status in their land of adoption perhaps foreshadows an even more difficult economic future for this country.

To make sense of Kenya and to grasp the implications of "population," it becomes important to understand the ethnic politics and problems here. So wrapped up is Kenya's leadership in sorting out these problems and in ensuring a smoother ride for Kenya's battered economy that it seems to have very little time or energy left for tackling the one problem that is really holding back the country's social and economic progress—rampant population growth.

There are about 160,000 Masai in Kenya. Two of them, both under the age of two, were dying of diarrhea and dehydration the morning that Michael Meegan and I drove into the tiny hamlet of Ordanyati in Kenya's Rift Valley.

To call Ordanyati a hamlet is taking liberties with the language. There are only five shacks here, each windowless and with gaping holes where doors might fit, each with walls and floors fashioned in typical Masai style with a mixture of mud and manure. Sticks hold up the roofs. The shacks nestle in a natural depression whose rocks form a kind of crenelated compound around the settlement.

Meegan, a sinewy Irish Jesuit, grabbed an ancient medicine bag, leaped out of the battered Peugeot we had driven in, and ran to the spot where a woman named Saosaro was tending to one of the dying children.

I thought for a moment that her child was newborn, or perhaps just a month or two old, but Meegan quickly explained that the boy, Yayou, was actually just under two years of age. Disease and malnutrition had retarded his growth. Yayou was in shock; he didn't emit a sound. His eyes bulged out of their sockets, his throat was red with rashes, his naked torso resembled a bunch of twigs thrown together. His knees were grotesquely deformed, and where his toes should have been there were only open, festering wounds.

A few feet away from Saosaro and her son lay another child, Tajo. No one was tending to him. His mother was said to be lying down inside her shack with a man. Tajo, too, was in some trauma, for he stared without seeing and did not respond as dogs playfully tugged at his bed sheet. Both children had running sores on their bodies. Flies did minuets on the pus. The stench from nearby droppings of human and animal excrement was overpowering.

I was horrified, but Meegan coolly went about examining the children, cleaning their bodies with lotion, listening with a stethoscope, then bandaging their limbs gently. He was no newcomer to such scenes, having worked in the slums of Lima, Mexico City, and Calcutta. There are perhaps 9,000 missionaries in this East African country, but Meegan probably tends to more dying Masai than does any other missionary. He holds a diploma in tropical medicine, and his knowledge and extensive experience are severely tested here. Diarrhea, malnutrition, tonsillar infections, congenital venereal disease, dehydration, and colitis are rapidly taking a toll among the Masai, once fierce warriors, nomads of the plains, slayers of lions, with a culture said to go back hundreds of years. But the tribesmen remain suspicious of outsiders and resist seeking outside medical help. If a baby is ill, more often than not it is daubed with red ocher and its veins pricked by an arrow to exorcise it of the evil spirits that supposedly brought the malady about. Superstition reigns among the Masai, and superstition breeds suspicion of outsiders who don't subscribe to such practices. So Meegan-the-itinerant-physician must become Meegan-the-social-worker to overcome these barriers—and sometimes even physical hostility—before he can practice his medicine among the Masai.

Meegan was sent here by an organization called the International Community for the Relief of Starvation and Suffering.

On the way to Ordanyati, which is about sixty miles out of Nairobi, Meegan showed me photographs he had taken of diseased Masai children in different parts of Kenya. My companion, Kantic Das Gupta, a Nairobi banker interested in social issues, nearly threw up looking at those pictures. They were in living color, and they were gory. After that we drove on in silence through the Kenyan bush. It was a gorgeous day, like most days in this part of the world. The sky was a brilliant blue; the acacia trees were festooned with clusters of tiny white and orange flowers. We passed Masai herdsmen tending their emaciated cattle; the Masai measure their wealth in cattle, which are prized and rarely sold or slaughtered—except when there is a celebration in honor of a marriage. Occasionally, rickety little Masai boys, barely knee-high and clad in shorts and tattered vests, would wave at us and then throw pebbles at our car after we'd driven by. We roared up rolling hills speckled with Masai shacks, known as *bomahs,* and we finally entered the Rift Valley, its fissures and crevices covered with a carpet of green. "If you think you have seen suffering and malnutrition," Meegan said presently, "wait till you see what's happening in Ordanyati."

The moment we arrived, Meegan was besieged with requests by mothers to look at their children. The women clutched at his clothes, jabbering away in the Masai tongue, which Meegan does not speak. He communicated with the women through a strapping teenager named Mariyake, who learned English at a missionary school in the Rift Valley that the Irishman enrolled him in not long ago. Patiently, Meegan explained that the mothers should keep feeding their babies with a dextrose solution that he had distributed, that they should ensure their children were given daily doses of vitamins he had handed out, that all water and milk should be boiled before consumption. There is no running water in Ordanyati, and the Masai must trek five or six miles of rocky terrain to fetch water from a pond or a stream. Sometimes they encounter lions. Almost always they come across snakes. It is the women who do such chores because their menfolk are out wandering or sometimes getting drunk on homemade brew. It is the women who must pick wild fruits and milk their goats. The women are the ones who go and get the firewood for cooking. Therefore it is the women whom Meegan tries to educate first. Saosaro, the mother of Yayou, seemed bewildered when Meegan told her that the boy would soon die.

"I want to save my child," Saosaro shrieked.

"I will try very hard, you know that, but this child should have been shown to me weeks ago. Why did you wait so long?" Meegan said, which seemed to calm the Masai woman a bit.

As he spoke, a group of Masai men ambled over. They wore torn shirts and frayed sandals, and each carried a spear. Some wore their hair in traditional braided style, with ocher splashed on their scalps; two men had on Mickey Mouse caps; a third man wore a T-shirt with an obscene gesture printed on it. Meegan tried to tell the men that they, too, were responsible for the health of their children. The men smiled and nodded, but I wasn't so sure they quite followed what Meegan was saying, or if they even cared. Meegan, in fact, no longer expects that these men will join him in his efforts to improve health and sanitation in their community. What Meegan has done is to train Mariyake and four other male teenagers to diagnose about fifty diseases common among the Masai. The boys receive instruction in basic hygiene, sanitation, nutrition, and maternal and child care; Meegan's Dublin-based organization contributes financially to such training, as do the Kenyan government and the United Nations. Meegan wants Mariyake and his friends first to focus on bringing down the alarming infant mortality rate among the Masai. Of every ten children in developing countries, it is estimated that at least three die before their twelfth month; among the Masai, who live in what are possibly the most primitive and unhygienic conditions anywhere, the infant mortality rate is close to seven of ten. Rather than improve the health standards of their community, the Masai choose to keep producing more children in the hope that at least some will survive and be their insurance against old age. The average Kenyan woman, according to a survey conducted by the United Nations, has 8.1 children; in other parts of Africa, women have been known to have up to 20 kids in the hope that at least some of them will live. The United Nations also says that the infant mortality rate in Africa is 137 deaths per 1,000 live births, or eleven times higher than in the United States. Western Europe has one physician for every 575 persons; Kenya has one doctor for every 30,000 persons; Upper Volta, one of the most miserable countries in black Africa, has one for every 100,000 persons. Even these figures may be on the low side because few reliable statistics are available in African countries, which tend also to fudge figures that cast them in an unfavorable light. Meegan is of the opinion that the actual infant mortality rate among the Masai may be higher than registered deaths.

Mariyake seems enthusiastic about his task. He told me he knows he can spread the new notions of hygiene and nutrition among his people more effectively than could any outsider. Like most young Masai males, Mariyake suffers from syphilis, for which Meegan is now treating him. Not many months ago, Mariyake, the oldest son of Saosaro, ended his seven-year apprenticeship as a *morani*, or fledgling warrior. He was now eligible, among other things, to bed any woman who would sleep with him, but Meegan persuaded Mariyake that first he must cure the syphilis he contracted from a homosexual experience he had had. Homosexuality is common among the young Masai. Mariyake is also assisting Meegan in building additional health clinics for Masai settlements elsewhere in the region. He wants to continue with his formal education at the missionary school. Perhaps one day, Mariyake said, gazing out at the Rift Valley, he might even be able to become a physician like Meegan.

On the drive back to Nairobi, I asked Meegan if there was anything else he could have done to save those two Masai children, such as transporting them to a hospital. No, he said, he had tried, but their parents wouldn't let him. Both children, he said, would probably live for at most another week, and then he would probably be around when the Masai buried them. Meegan goes to several such burials every month, and you would think he'd be inured to such deaths by now, but cloudbursts of tears still flow down his face whenever one of his "patients" has died. I asked him what was it he did initially that made the Masai overcome their traditional distrust of outsiders and allow him to treat them.

He shrugged.

"It is easy to be romantic and poetic about these beautiful, sensitive people," he said. "They are one of the great warrior tribes, more famous than the Zulu, more structured than most other tribes. But their culture is dying. There is no room left for the warriors to wander the plains. Their land has been redistributed. Few are nomadic anymore. They wear Western clothes, they have transistors in their *bomahs* and sometimes battery-operated television sets, too. They are being killed off by venereal disease and other things like poorly done circumcisions and cliterodectomies. There are large numbers of unwanted pregnancies. There are large numbers of sloppy abortions, which result in death for the women. Babies are dying from burst tonsils. There is increasing blindness."

We were approaching the outskirts of Nairobi, and the traffic had thickened. A couple of *matatus,* vans that are used to transport people, almost rammed into us, and Kantic Das Gupta, who was driving, swerved wildly to head off a collision. Meegan was so absorbed in his monologue he didn't even get fazed by the incident. "I never tell the Masai that they should live as we Westerners live," Meegan went on. "The key thing was for me to obtain their acceptance, and I did so by doing the things I do best—saving lives or at least reducing people's suffering. I feel about the Masai as I do about anyone. I hope I could treat a child in Brooklyn with the same love and attention as a Masai baby."

Kantic and I invited Meegan for coffee at the Intercontinental Hotel. The contrast with our earlier surroundings could not have been greater. Here we were, in a restaurant by the swimming pool, liveried waiters gliding to and from our table fulfilling our orders. Western tourists, tanned to a lobster complexion, lounged by the pool, tall drinks in hand. Women in swimsuits that left nothing to the imagination gracefully cut through the water. Ordanyati seemed very far away indeed. I espied a tall Masai walking along the road outside the hotel, carrying a pole, fancy metal loops hanging from his large-lobed ears. Meegan told me that the Kenyan government had made attempts to create jobs in Nairobi for those Masai who wished to work in an urban environment; few accepted such employment, and fewer still stayed in the city more than a day or two after making the transfer from the open plains to the frenetic city. To see a Masai in Nairobi today is an odd sight indeed. An ironical coda to my encounter with Mike Meegan was that a couple of days after the visit to Ordanyati, some American friends insisted on taking me along to a "model" Masai village a dozen or so miles outside of Nairobi. Freshly scrubbed Masai warriors danced for us, then demonstrated their prowess at spear throwing. They flexed their muscles and flashed their genitals. Busloads of foreign tourists had come to this site to marvel at the Masai. We were then taken for a tour of *bomahs.* The "huts" had electricity and neat kitchen furnishings. There was canned food on shelves. Toys were carefully arranged in open closets. Smiling women, wearing only colorful necklaces, cuddled babies. English-speaking Masai teenagers peddled trinkets, haggling with customers with savvy and shrewdness. No deformed limbs here, no burst tonsils, no stench of excrement, no whiff of disease and death, no traumatized babies, no shacks of mud and manure. These were not Mike Meegan's Masai, and the Irishman will never be needed here. I could have been on a movie set, and probably was.

* * *

Nairobi, where I spent three years as Africa correspondent for the *New York Times,* is a pleasantly laid-out city of vast parks, plentiful hibiscus and bougainvillea, luxury hotels with year-round tourist traffic, colonial-style bungalows with large gardens, and modern skyscrapers that are the tallest in black Africa. The city sits on a plateau a mile above the Indian Ocean and a hundred miles south of the Equator and enjoys a wonderfully temperate climate all year along. Its airport is the most modern and efficient in all of Africa, the roads are well paved, and the pavements generally so free of litter that they actually seem to sparkle.

Shortly after daybreak on Sunday, August 1, 1982, the crackling of gunfire and the rumbling of heavy military vehicles echoed through the streets of the Kenyan capital city. A putsch was being carried out, the first major coup attempt since Kenya became independent from Britain in 1963. The putschists were air force personnel, led by a private said to have Marxist leanings, who quickly seized the local radio station and forced a well-known announcer to broadcast a statement declaring that the "corrupt and dictatorial regime" of President Daniel Torotich arap Moi had been overthrown and replaced by a national "People's Redemption Council" of military officers and enlisted men. In the event, the announcement was premature. By midafternoon of that day, army troops loyal to Moi recaptured the radio station and regained control of the capital city—but not before much havoc had been wreaked by the rebels.

In the space of a few hours, most of the commercial section of downtown Nairobi lay devastated. Losses suffered by Nairobi businessmen, particularly those of Asian origin, exceeded $500 million. At least thirty Asian women, including five girls under ten years of age, were reported to have been raped by marauders who roamed Nairobi at will. Some of the putschists and their student supporters tore through affluent residential neighborhoods, waving clenched fists and loaded rifles. "Power!" they shouted, "Power at last!" They raided homes, beat up occupants, and carried off whatever they could find. Stereo sets, television units, video machines, gold watches, and Mercedes and Peugeot cars were especially coveted.

On a visit to Nairobi a year after this putsch attempt, I met with a longtime friend named Geeta Manek. She is a sprightly young businesswoman of Indian origin with an impeccable British education. During my three years in Nairobi, I found Geeta to be one of the few people around who expressed any great optimism for a stable Kenya. This time, I saw a different Geeta, downcast and despondent. I joined her one evening for dinner at her family home, a house within a walled-up compound. "Kenya was always a place of civilized values in a continent of turmoil," Geeta said. "Whether the events of August 1982 will be a scar on our national life or just a scratch—this only time will tell."

The motives and tactics of the putschists are still being debated in Kenya, and President Moi has characterized the rebellion as an "extreme act of hooliganism." But there is ample evidence that support for the putschists, in spirit at least, went well beyond the handful of air force men and their friends who organized the coup attempt. For months, if not years, before the incident, it was clear that widespread dissatisfaction was building up among ordinary Kenyans over Moi's leadership. He was perceived as a man who tolerated corruption and had no real sense of how to manage the economy. By August 1982, once-prosperous Kenya had become a virtual basket case under Moi's dubious helmsmanship. And contributing to the overall malaise was the fact that Kenya's annual population growth rate had edged past 4 percent—the highest in the world and the highest recorded ever for any country. With 18 million people packed into a country the size of California, Kenya had a gloomy demographic future to look forward to: the national population would double in less than eighteen years. Family planning efforts of the government were weak and obviously ineffectual. The World Bank, not normally given to hyperbole, characterized the situation as "explosive."

At any time of day or night in cities like Nairobi and Mombasa, young men who cannot find jobs hang out at street corners cadging cigarettes, sometimes picking pockets and offering to act as dragomen. At night, the unwary tourist can get mugged by these youths, who lately have been known to stab or shoot those who resist them. The young women frequently sell their favors cheaply at sleazy bars where tourists or visiting foreign servicemen gather. Or they work as masseuses at a variety of massage parlors that have sprouted in Nairobi, where sex can be had for the equivalent of five dollars an hour and herpes is on the house. Many of the young men and women, and their parents as well, are not natives of Nairobi. They are emigres from the countryside, where less than 20 percent of the land is of decent agricultural quality. I was told by Julia Ojiambo, a Kenyan cabinet minister, that a decade ago about 300 people lived on every square mile of cultivable land; now the figure is 400 people, and by the end of the decade it will be nearly 600 people per square mile. In the most fertile farming districts around Nairobi and up near Lake Victoria, it is not uncommon to find a population density of almost 1,100 persons per square mile. Peasants are abandoning their farms and trekking to the cities, where the annual population growth rate is twice the national figure of 4 percent. And meanwhile annual food production is growing by just about 1 percent. This means that Kenya, once the breadbasket of East Africa, must import food; I was told by a senior government official in Nairobi that more than 75 percent of the country's annual food requirements are met through imports from the West. This also means that the demand for jobs far exceeds the availability. Kenya, I was told by Julia Ojiambo, has a labor force of almost 9 million people, but there are jobs available for just 1 million people. Moreover, 300,000 people enter the labor force every year, but fewer than 20,000 new jobs are created annually.

All these things have grave implications for President Moi, but also for Kenya's Western patrons such as the United States, which gives this country nearly $100 million a year in economic aid, more than to any other black African state and just a bit less than what it gives to the biggest recipient of American largesse on the African continent, the mostly Arab nation of the Sudan. President Reagan, delighted that any Third World leader should even want to build a politically compatible relationship with Washington, has called Moi a "genuine friend" of the United States, an encomium that was played up in the government-controlled Kenyan press. The United States is very pleased that Moi acceded to its request for "transit facilities"—a euphemism for military bases—in the Indian Ocean port of Mombasa. The Americans are spending more than $20 million to improve facilities in that natural harbor so that huge American aircraft carriers can berth here.

Kenyan government ministers have stepped up their shopping-list visits to Washington and other Western capitals for more economic assistance, more weapons, and more investment by American businessmen. (The assistance and weaponry have flowed from the Reagan people, but American businessmen, who are perhaps a shade more skeptical than government officials, have balked at committing themselves more fully to investment in Kenya. The total American capital invested currently in Kenya is around $500 million.)

However generous and willing foreign donors were, it must have been humiliating for Kenya to go to them begging bowl in hand. For nearly two decades, this East African tropical paradise had been considered by outsiders and by its own rulers as a showcase of Western-style capitalism in a continent of political and economic turbulence. Kenyans had enjoyed a per capita income of $400, which, although low by Western standards, was among the highest in black Africa.

Sharad S. Rao, formerly the country's chief law enforcement official, recalled that Kenya was an enduring favorite of British, West European, and even American businessmen. "What we offered here was stability, a sense that in Kenya we knew how to get things done efficiently, without the kind of bureaucratic delays that plague other African states," Rao, a native Kenyan of Indian origin, said to me as we lunched late one balmy Sunday afternoon at the Nairobi Gymkhana, a sprawling club with well-maintained tennis courts, quaint bungalows, flower-filled gardens, and a luxuriously green field where men in cream-colored flannels were playing cricket. Rao, a dapper man with an engaging manner, waved toward the scene, which was like a picture-postcard English setting—tranquil, leisurely, leafy, genteel. This wasn't Africa at all, at least it did not seem the Africa of revolutions, coups, earthquakes, starvation, and overcrowded shantytowns that I'd known for years.

Under the patronage of Western investors and their Kenyan associates, Kenya became black Africa's leading commercial center. High-rise buildings sprang up. Industries mushroomed. The country's principal exports of tea and coffee were imaginatively marketed around the world; revenues from these exports and from the foreign sale of refined petroleum products (derived from crude oil purchased in the Middle East) and pyrethrum (a natural insecticide) fattened Kenya's hard currency reserves. Responding to advertising and promotional campaigns that played up Kenya's great natural beauty and abundant wildlife, foreigners came here in planeloads. They outfitted themselves in crisp khakis at expensive Nairobi bespoke tailors, then, "Bwana Jim" hats—the ones with decorative, artificial, leopard skin bands around the crown—jauntily perched on their heads and cameras dangling from their necks, these tourists went on safaris in the African bush. Or they lolled on Mombasa beaches, fully naked and oblivious to the crowds of gawking natives, tanning themselves silly.

Planeloads of expatriate Britons also arrived. By 1982, there were more than 50,000 Britons in Kenya, twice the figure at independence in 1963. They worked as technical and industrial "consultants," insurance peddlers, travel agents, bankers, teachers, agribusinessmen, managers of hotels, and, a few of the women among them, entertainers in Kenyan nightclubs. These expatriates quickly created a new colonial society in Nairobi, one that carefully and subtly excluded from its fraternizing most nonwhites. Their favored hangouts were such exclusive preserves as the Muthaiga Club, a formidable estate of pink stucco buildings, a large golf course, and grass tennis courts, and the open-air bar at the Norfolk Hotel in Nairobi. During my years in Nairobi, I found many of these "expats" mean, petty, surprisingly unclassy, and often racist. I was disappointed at how eager many of my white Western journalist colleagues seemed to be accepted by these neocolonialists and how thrilled to get invited to their frequent dinner parties and cocktails.

Although Britain is Kenya's largest trading partner, trade and the obtaining of technical expertise have recently been stepped up with Singapore, India, South Korea, and Brazil. Kenya has had an unusual relationship with Israel, a pariah in most black African states because of the general support African leaders give to the Palestinian liberation movement. Although formal diplomatic ties do not now exist between Israel and Kenya, a healthy informal relationship is indeed there. Israeli commandos help guard Kenyatta International Airport in Nairobi; Israelis train Kenyan military personnel in antiterrorist tactics. There are an estimated 1,000 Israeli technicians and businessmen in Kenya today. Large numbers of Israeli tourists come to Kenya's game sanctuaries and to the beaches of Mombasa. The Israeli national airline, El Al, stops in Nairobi each week on its way to and from South Africa.

As the Kenyan economy prospered, Kenyans grew increasingly mindful of the experiences of their two immediate neighbors, Uganda and Tanzania. In Uganda, the dictator Idi Amin Dada not only indiscriminately slaughtered hundreds of thousands of people, he single-handedly ruined the country's economy through such extreme measures as deporting the entire 75,000-strong Asian mercantile community, neglecting sugar and coffee production, and assigning all trade to illiterate factotums and cronies. Amin was toppled in 1979 by the Tanzanians and now lives comfortably in the Sands Hotel in Jidda, Saudi Arabia, but his country is unlikely to recover fully from his eight-year reign of terror.

The Ugandan capital of Kampala, once even more prosperous than Nairobi, once a gay place of nightclubs and busy shops and thriving commerce, is today a sad, desolate city of empty stores, potholed streets, and high crime. Up until the early 1970s, people from Nairobi would drive for weekends to Kampala to party there or to shop. Now, merely to land and disembark at Kampala's Entebbe Airport (built in the 1970s by the Israelis during a period of warm relations between them and Amin) means putting one's life in danger. Immigration officials and their customs colleagues will put a gun to your head if they feel like it, and if they don't feel too good about you they might even pull the trigger. There is no law and order in Uganda, and the legacy that Amin left for his countrymen is one of anarchy and brigandage. In Tanzania, the "socialist" policies of the government of President Julius K. Nyerere brought the country close to economic ruin.

The economic progress in Kenya, in contrast, brought with it social conditions that were mostly free of the restrictions and restraints prevalent in most other black African states. You could walk into any bookstore in Nairobi and find a remarkably wide variety of works, even volumes on Marxism, an anathema to the Kenyatta and Moi regimes. News kiosks carried the latest European and American publications. Western pornographic magazines sold especially well. President Moi would frequently point out to visitors that there were no political prisoners in his country. Local newspapers often carried articles critical of government policy. Cartoonists gently poked fun at Moi, a member of the Tugen subtribe of the minority Kalenjin community. Unlike a number of African states, Kenya even held regular elections, no matter that only one political party was permitted to contest them, Moi's Kenya African National Union.

By 1981, the economic bubble had burst. High world prices for oil and declining revenues from Kenya's key exports of tea and coffee meant that imports, including food grains, had to be dramatically reduced. The inflation rate rocketed to 25 percent a year. Unemployment rose. College students, chanting Marxist slogans, rioted; they not only questioned Moi's leadership abilities, they also charged that he had turned a blind eye to corruption and nepotism among his closest colleagues and political associates. There was mounting criticism of Moi's relationship with Washington; many student leaders accused the president of having sold out to the Reagan administration by giving the Americans military facilities in the port of Mombasa. Radicals said further that the U.S. Central Intelligence Agency had beefed up its staff and operations in Nairobi and was using Kenya as a listening post for black Africa; there were also accusations that CIA operatives were assisting the Kenyan security agencies in devising ways to clamp down on dissidents within the country. At this point, Moi began losing his nerve. He shut down various universities and ordered the army to transport students back to their villages. Moi aides started "discovering" Marxist revolutionary plots everywhere, but particularly among college students and their faculty members. Charges were bruited about that Libya and even the Soviet Union were financing Marxist cells throughout Kenya.

Adding to Moi's discomfiture was his poor performance as chairman of the Organization of African Unity, the cheerleading fraternity to which all fifty African states belong. Moi had assumed the one-year chairmanship in 1981 after he'd hosted a lavish summit meeting of the OAU in Nairobi, an event that achieved little and cost the Kenyans more than $25 million. Moi flew around Africa trying to resolve a variety of thorny questions, such as the claim to the Moroccan-held Western Sahara by a Marxist guerrilla group calling itself the Polisario. But often the Kenyan president seemed poorly prepared in his meetings; on a couple of occasions, some Western diplomats reported, he even confused Mauritius with Mauritania.

At home, repression increased. Dissidents were locked up. Newspaper editors who questioned Moi's policies were hounded and silenced. Government spokesmen accused the country's intellectuals of causing chaos. The government also said that in the future it would determine what books pupils would read in school. Plays staged by students in schools were subjected to close scrutiny by government censors. In one of the most dramatic incidents of tightening control by the regime, the Moi government sent three truckloads of armed police to the small rural community of Kamirithu to destroy the open-air theater, where a play by the controversial antiestablishment writer Ngugi wa Thiongo was being performed.

There was a man named George Githii, editor of the *Standard*—one of the three English-language dailies in Nairobi and a newspaper owned by a London-based concern called Lonrho—who once was a solid supporter of Moi. Githii was so alarmed by what was happening that he wrote an editorial that was to cost him his job. In it, he said, in part:

> This country has been increasingly gripped with fear, the fear of detention of individuals without trial. . . . It is an important lesson of history that a society which is full of gossip and hearsay and fear about the fate of some of its people soon becomes responsive to undemocratic ideas, and this development can only have rather adverse consequences for the future of our country.

The editorial appeared on July 20, 1982. Within eleven days, the streets of Nairobi were echoing to the sounds of gunfire. The putsch attempt had taken place.

My wife, our infant son, and I lived in Nairobi for three years. I was sent to Kenya by the *New York Times* as the newspaper's Africa correspondent, a job I initially coveted but, as it turned out, did not especially enjoy. During the assignment, which ended at the time of the August 1982 coup attempt, I was always uncomfortable with the reality of being an Indian-born resident of a country whose mostly black population has come to loathe and resent Asians, who are seen as exploiters, or worse. I was not the least bit surprised that the putschists and their supporters directed much of their malice at the Asian mercantile community and wrecked their homes and businesses. President Moi and his associates said they were shocked by the carnage—but Moi, in this case, has been trying to have it both ways. It was he, after all, who launched what was widely perceived as a punitive campaign against Asians when he said in a speech in February 1982 that they had been a disgrace to the nation:

> Instead of Indians using their advanced knowledge in business to improve their profit margin, Asians in this country are ruining the country's economy by smuggling out of this country currency, and even hoarding essential goods and selling them through the back doors. From now on, anybody found hoarding or smuggling will be punished severely. If he is an Asian, he will be deported immediately regardless of whether he is a citizen or not.

Many Asians hold Kenyan citizenship, and the president failed at the time to specify just how he would deport his own citizens. Most Asians felt Moi was making them scapegoats for Kenya's economic deterioration. This perception was later reinforced when Moi sought to dismiss or undercut Asian officials in his government. In August 1982, the virulence and zeal with which the putschists ransacked Asian-owned shops and homes further solidified Asians' feelings that the hatreds harbored by black Kenyans toward them were beyond pacification, and perhaps even beyond control. It was a classic case of a minority under siege.

There can be little doubt that if this minority is driven away from Kenya the country's economic health will be seriously affected. Asians of Indian origin came to this East African state at the turn of the century to help build the Mombasa-to-Kampala railway. They stayed on to prosper as merchants and bureaucrats. The British, who colonized Kenya in the nineteenth century, used these Asians as a buffer between themselves and the black masses. The blacks began to resent the Asians for their wealth and their usually racist attitudes toward the indigenous population. Over the years, and especially since 1981, this resentment deepened because the Asians' prosperity insulated them from the economic problems most other Kenyans had to cope with: the 20 percent-plus inflation; the annual 4 percent population growth rate; and the limited amount of land available for agriculture, which has forced many peasants to trek to the cities for jobs and which has resulted in steadily declining food production. To some extent, the Asians attracted the envy and malevolent attitudes on the part of the blacks. They rarely socialize with the blacks. They live in huge bungalows and drive around in handsome, imported cars. They speak disparagingly of the blacks, often calling them "monkeys." Asian women will rarely date black men, much less marry them; but Asian men frequently go out with black women on the assumption that they are sexually easygoing.

Many Asians have seen the writing on the wall and have been steadily taking their funds and their families out of Kenya. A confidential study prepared in 1982 by the U.S. Department of State said that Kenyan Asians had squirreled away more than $5 billion abroad, mostly through currency smuggling. When Kenya obtained independence from the British in 1963, there were 200,000 Asians in this country; now there are fewer than 65,000. The State Department study also found that Kenyan Asians controlled 90 percent of the country's retail trade and almost 25 percent of Kenya's gross domestic product of $4 billion. I was told reliably that the emigration of Kenyan Asians to Britain, Canada, the United States, and Western European countries is now taking place at the rate of 700 families a year. At this rate, there won't be too many Asians left in Kenya in about five years.

There are influential black Kenyans who suggest that if that happens it will not be necessarily a bad thing for this country. Such Kenyans feel that Asians never have had an emotional stake in this country and that Kenya will survive and prosper even if this entire mercantile community packs up and leaves. I think this view is rubbish, a lot of bravado. The Kenyans who espouse this view seem to have forgotten what happened in neighboring Uganda when Idi Amin tossed his Asians out: the retail economy simply collapsed. I foresee a reprise in Kenya.

I know several Asians who don't visualize a complete evacuation from Kenya of their own. One such person is Nitin Madhvani, a young industrialist with substantial investments in Kenya; he doesn't see himself packing up and leaving for good. Another Asian, Sharad Patel, said I was being excessively pessimistic about the future of Asians. Patel, in fact, has personally done very well by the theme of exoduses: his recent film, *The Rise and Fall of Idi Amin,* made millions of dollars. One evening in Nairobi he invited me to dinner at his new home. Patel had built for himself a virtual palace on a sprawling estate. His home is lavishly stocked with Persian carpets and objets d'art.

"Do I look like someone who sees no future for himself in Kenya?" he asked me, waving around his property.

Another guest, Chenni Singh Vohra—a lawyer and hotel owner—nodded.

"There will always be an Asian presence in Kenya," Vohra said. "Come back in a few years and you will see all of us still here."

I wish these friends well, but I disagree with them. I think their days in Kenya are numbered. And I wish they'd get out while they can, before the fire next time incinerates them.

The Asian "problem" is only one among many political complexities in which President Daniel arap Moi is enmeshed. His own political survival is undoubtedly a preoccupation for him—just as it surely is for Moi's American patrons, who are pouring in not only military assistance but also millions for population programs.

One of the ironies about Kenya is that although it now has the world's highest annual population, it was the first country in sub-Saharan

Africa formally to adopt a national family-planning program. That was back in 1966.

The Kenyan experience points to what happens when there is a lack of strong political commitment to solving a country's population problem in all its dimensions, be it rampant population growth, ethnic tensions, high infant mortality, or poor health care. Jomo Kenyatta, the country's "founding father," never discussed population control publicly because the subject was held to be out of synch with national values concerning fertility and because he was worried that any population control drive might be uncharitably interpreted by Kenya's minority tribes as a Kikuyu plot to thin out other ethnic groups.

But by the time Moi succeeded Kenyatta the political and cultural climate of Kenya had subtly changed, and Kenyans would have responded favorably to a firm presidential initiative on family planning, especially if it had been tied to the overall economic situation. Indeed, early in his presidency Moi had the unique opportunity to take the situation in hand and work forcefully to promote the national population program that was already on the books. He let that opportunity slide, and now it may just be too late.

Four

Middle East Caldron
The Nightmare of Egypt

I HAD SPENT the morning walking through the "City of the Dead," an immense cemetery in the oldest section of Cairo—only to find that there were living creatures here, hundreds of thousands of them, squatters who had illegally occupied, for months and even years, the edifices that Egyptian Moslems traditionally construct over the tombs of their deceased.

There is almost no affordable or new housing available in Cairo for the poor, and these squatters are mostly illiterate peasants who have abandoned their impoverished villages to come to President Hosni Mubarak's capital to find jobs. This influx from the rural areas of Egypt is not new, but now it appears to be accelerating. It is said that the new immigrants are pushing Cairo's annual population growth rate beyond 7 percent. Abutting the "City of the Dead"—I would call it the "City of the Living Dead"—is the dilapidated Khan el Khalili neighborhood, where population density is already a frightening 142,000 per square kilometer, or roughly 1.4 persons to every square foot!

No matter that adequate housing is not available, no matter that water supply and basic sanitation are practically nonexistent, the poor of the countryside keep trekking to Cairo, drawn to this extraordinary metropolis by some perceived promise of a better life. It is almost as if there were satanic magic in Cairo's air, some malevolent force that beckons the poor only to make them poorer.

I went up to a man who sat in front of his "home" smoking a foul cigarette. His name was Mohammed Abu Maguid, and he had come to Cairo from Gheta village in northern Sharkeiya Province. Mohammed was a thin, hollow-cheeked man, and he looked sickly. He coughed horridly as he smoked. Inside his home was his wife, Wafaa. She was cooking on a kerosene stove. Ragged children screamed around her. Back in Gheta, Mohammed worked on a small farm as a soil tiller.

"What hope is there left in my village?" he said in Arabic that was translated for me by a companion. Mohammed and Wafaa decided that they would follow some of their relatives to Cairo to pursue a more lucrative livelihood, better shelter, and perhaps even some schooling for their five children.

So they came here some months ago, excited especially, they said, by the fact that for the first time in a generation their country was at peace with Israel and that the energies of the nation could now be more fully devoted to the business of prosperity for the 45 million overwhelmingly poor people of Egypt. Like many trusting villagers, they had believed Mubarak's slain predecessor, President Anwar el-Sadat, when Sadat, in the wake of signing a peace treaty with Israel, had proclaimed there would be a new era of prosperity for Egyptians. For Maguid, as for thousands of peasants like him who have emigrated to Cairo, any rhetorical reference by Mubarak to "prosperity" is instantly interpreted to mean more jobs, better housing, and cheaper food.

Once Maguid and his family came to Cairo, in an overcrowded bus that broke down frequently, they found this city no different from what it always has been, peace treaty or not—a place of gallimaufry, rambunctious, on the verge of unraveling because of the burgeoning population that is now estimated at more than 8 million, a city of disillusioning contrasts between the ostentatious rich of Sadat's and Mubarak's "New Class"—those who live in the high-rise apartments of the affluent Zamalik or Garden City sections, or in the natty bungalows of the Heliopolis suburbs—and the very poor of the Khan el Khalili slums or the "City of the Dead." Maguid found that Cairo's sewers were overflowing, that its buses and trains were thoroughly unreliable, that telephones seldom worked, that prices of most consumer items grew annually at the rate of 35 percent. Maguid searched for weeks for a job and finally was hired as a sweeper in a mosque in the Khan el Khalili section. He seemed despondent when I met him, for this was not the Cairo he had so naively imagined. Until now, the people of Egypt could be told that a certain amount of distress and suffering was inevitable since the country had a war economy and so sacrifices had to be forthcoming from the civilian population. The capacity and willingness of Egyptians, warm, gentle people like Maguid, to respond to their leaders and adjust to their environment is awesome. But there is a discernible rise in expectations now, and more and more Egyptians, like Maguid, are asking, Will Mubarak be able to deliver on his promises and those of his deceased mentor, Anwar Sadat?

I traveled to Egypt to ask this question myself. There were other related questions: What, realistically, are Mubarak's chances for transforming a backward, still feudal country, where the per capita income is barely $225, into a modern nation? Does Egypt have the will, the institutions, the resources, and the right leadership to achieve such a transformation? Will "peace" mean a qualitative improvement in the lives of everyday Egyptians such as Maguid? How long will it be before the rising restlessness and resentment of the masses explodes? Will Mubarak be able to survive in office if the economy does not improve? In which economic direction is Egypt headed?

It seemed to me, as I roamed through this wondrous land, that the answers to each of these questions would somehow be shaped by one central reality: that Egypt's annual population growth rate was still nearly 3 percent, which meant that more than a million Egyptians were being born each year. If the current growth continues, Egypt's population could easily double within about ten years. And in a country where the majority of people live on barely 4 percent of the land, imagine what the density and congestion will be like then. No matter how sophisticated and how energetic Mubarak's economic development plans, unless there is a stepped-up campaign to lower the annual population growth rate, the Egyptian efforts to provide a better life for people like Maguid are going to be doomed.

It is an ancient land, already "ancient" by the time Herodotus, the great historian of the Greeks, arrived in Egypt in 450 B.C. to record his observations about the descendants of the Pharaohs. Modern historians are uncertain about when specifically the country we now know as Egypt was first settled, and by whom. Some have theorized that Africans moved into the Nile Valley from the south—from Nubia—and others say that it was the Libyans from the west and the tribes from the Arabian desert to the east who initially established outposts of mankind in Egypt. Whatever the origins of the early settlers, there was, by 4000 B.C., a thriving, robust civilization in Egypt, and by 3100 B.C. a king named Menes had formed a monarchical entity that extended from Aswan in the south to the Mediterranean in the north. Recorded Egyptian history starts with Menes, and Pharaonic rule eventually resulted not only in the creation of such massive monuments as the Pyramids of Giza, the Sphinx, and the Colossi of Memmon but also in seminal developments in mathematics and writing. After the Pharaohs it was the Romans who ruled Egypt, and many centuries later it was the Moslems.

Modern Egypt is predominantly Moslem. Following the death of the Prophet Mohammed in A.D. 632, Arab armies swept through what is now known as the Middle East. In less than ten years after the Prophet's death, Egypt had been conquered and an Arab empire established. This empire flourished, and the Mohammedans established such great centers of power and learning as Cairo. The Arabs translated Greek works on philosophy, science, mathematics, and medicine, and they invented trignometry and algebra (a word derived from the Arabic *al-Jabr,* meaning the reunion of broken parts). The Arab empire gave way to conquest by the Seljuk Turks. The Crusaders seized the Holy Land and were driving toward Egypt—but their push was repulsed by a hero of Islam, a Seljuk officer named Salal al-Din, better known as Saladin. After the Seljuk Turks, Egypt came to be dominated by the Ottoman Turks, followed by the French armies of Napoleon. Eventually, a man named Mohammed Ali (1769–1849) founded a dynasty, which lasted until King Farouk, a corrupt man given to depravity, was ousted by a band of young military men led by Gamal Abdel Nasser in 1952.

Then, as now, it was the River Nile that formed the great nourishing spine of Egypt. The country has 400,000 square miles, but more than 95 percent of the land is desert. Just about 4 percent is cultivable, and so the communities of ancient Egypt—and modern Egypt—came to life on the banks of this great river. Mohammed Ali recognized the potential of the Nile, and so he introduced cotton from India, initiated modern irrigation, redistributed land, and started Western-style schools. His grandson, Ismail, presided over the construction of the Suez Canal, which was completed in 1869. That year, too, Cairo was redesigned, the Opera House was opened, and Verdi was commissioned to write *Aida* to celebrate its opening.

If the Nile is the great river and sustainer of life in Egypt, it is also the cause of the country's present-day blight—overpopulation. Cities and towns on the fertile banks are densely packed, and while the country's population of 45 million might not otherwise seem unduly huge on account of the great land space of the country as a whole, the fact of present-day Egypt is that more than 95 percent of its people live in communities straddling the Nile: the fertile belt on either side of the river is often only about between 8 and 9 miles wide. Virtually all of Egypt's agriculture is carried out on the banks of the 960-mile Nile. (The ancient Egyptians described their country as having the shape of a lotus plant: the Nile was akin to the stem, the Fayoum oasis was like the bud, and the Nile delta was like the lotus flower itself.)

Since 1966, the communities right by the river have attracted more and more people from the more remote desert areas. In that year, the High Dam at Aswan was opened, and now the flow of the river is regulated. It used to be that torrential floods terrorized residents of villages along the river's path, but no more. Today, nearly two-thirds of Egyptians are fellahin, or peasants, whose lives are very much tied to the Nile. Despite efforts at introducing modernization through expensive government projects, these fellahin, by and large, still live in primitive conditions—using, for instance, such devices as the *sakiya,* a bucket attached to a wheel driven by circling oxen or camels, to lift water from wells onto the fields. But although the land is very fertile, yielding excellent and world-renowned cotton, maize, wheat, rice, and corn, Egypt must import almost 90 percent of its annual food stock on account of population pressures. The per capita income of Egyptians has, for the last several years, been hovering at around $225, and although the gross national product is said to increase at about 6 percent annually, such growth can barely keep up with the population growth.

One consequence of such horrific population growth is that Egypt is having a harder time each year feeding its people. Not only is less than 4 percent of the country cultivable, but 20,000 acres of that land are said to be lost each year to the urban spread that is the result of the government's policy to create more residential developments for the middle classes and to the unauthorized—but overlooked—takeover of land by squatters. Egypt's population does not eat well despite the large import bill and the billion-dollar food subsidies provided by the Mubarak government. There is a need for more chicken and meat to upgrade the basic Egyptian diet of beans, rice, and bread. Khaled el-Shazly, an agronomist based in Alexandria, has estimated that the average Egyptian consumes less than 22 pounds of meat a year; by contrast, the average American consumes 186 pounds.

Another consequence of the mushrooming population growth, which has made Egypt the most thickly populated country in the Middle East, which has a total population of about 160 million, is that Egypt now has a severe housing shortage. In Cairo alone, more than 2 million housing units are thought to be needed. Meanwhile, people like Maguid and his family must live in primitive conditions. He and his wife, Wafaa, and their five children live in one room, which was never built to house even one person in the "City of the Dead." The gaping holes that constitute windows are covered by torn fabric. There is no electricity or running water, and the floors are made of cold stone. It gets very cold here during the winter, and during summer days the dust that blows in from the nearby desert makes life intolerable. Unless one is very rich, it is virtually impossible to obtain decent housing in Cairo.

Take the example of Osama el-Ansary, a young instructor in the Commerce Department of the University of Cairo. Osama comes from a relatively well-to-do family, as does his bride of five years, Wafaa. Nevertheless, they had to search for more than a year recently to find a home for themselves, as they wished no longer to stay with Osama's parents. A number of rental agents demanded up to $200,000 in "key money," or, in plain language, bribes, for an apartment in such desirable sections of Cairo as Zamalik and Garden City. "Who in the middle class can afford such money?" Osama, a tall, pleasant man, said. Eventually, he and Wafaa were forced to look for a home in the suburbs of Cairo, and they obtained a one-bedroom apartment in Helwan Gardens for the equivalent of $75 a month in rent. But before they could take possession of that apartment, the rental agent asked for, and received from Osama, more than $2,000 in "key money," which meant that Osama had to draw out all his savings. The apartment is on the fourth floor of a housing complex. The bedroom is barely bigger than a closet of an average New York City apartment. The kitchen is the size of a sink. Osama and Wafaa laid out dinner for me on a colorful Cairene carpet, for their living room wasn't large enough to accommodate a dining table. Wafaa had done what she could about decorating the walls, but the paint was peeling: she had put up some wedding photographs and calendar pictures depicting scenic tourist spots in the United States such as the Grand Canyon (where the Ansarys one day hope to go, they said). There were also Arabic inscriptions from the Holy Koran on the walls. Thousands of young professionals like Osama live in apartments like this, with little hope of moving into a larger unit.

Dinner consisted of delicious lamb kebabs and rice and imported Pepsi Cola. Pepsi is a popular drink in Egypt, and its import contributes to the annual $5 billion importation bill Egypt incurs over bringing in not only soda pop but also wheat and Bic ballpoint pens from the United States, butter from Norway, stereo and color television sets from West

Germany, as well as Mercedes cars and chocolate bars from Switzerland and Belgium. Cigarettes and cosmetics also come in from Britain, France, and elsewhere. Such an import bill helps toward maintaining Egypt's annual trade deficit, which is usually around $3 billion.

"We are all hopeful that the burdens of everyday life will ease for us," Osama said, quickly caveating that perhaps his hope was excessive. He pointed out that despite the promise of the later Sadat years—particularly after the peace treaty with Israel was signed and the animosity that cost Egypt 100,000 lives and $25 billion was set aside—the nation's illiteracy rate was still around 70 percent. Unemployment was more than 50 percent among people between twenty and forty years of age, a fact that manifested itself in increasing demonstrations in cities like Cairo, Port Said, and Alexandria and in rising street crime.

Osama insisted on accompanying me back to my downtown hotel because he was concerned I might be mugged. We rode an aging train that, even at that midnight hour, was packed. We rode in a compartment that had wooden seats and that bounced so hard over the rails that I soon stood up. Osama told me that it had been years since the Egyptian railways had got new rolling stock. The authorities generally blame riders for the poor state of the railways: in 1982 alone, according to statistics released by the government, train travelers broke 54,000 panes of glass, stole 53,000 water faucets, and destroyed 36,000 square meters of seat covers.

Osama had spoken vaguely about economic progress, but some of the leading economists I spoke with did not even bother expressing any form of hope.

"I am definitely not an optimist," said Dr. Nazih Deif, who was President Nasser's finance minister and later a governor of the International Monetary Fund in Washington. "There aren't any permanent grounds for hope. We'll have our ups, but mostly our downs. I'm disturbed at the lack of seriousness and focus in our government planning, particularly this go-easy attitude when it comes to pressing problems like population growth, when we are in a race with time. Historically, our targets have rarely been met."

Over and over again, people I met told me that to understand the complexities of Egypt and to assess its development efforts it was necessary to measure the population situation in the country.

The population of ancient Egypt, which is to say in the days of the

Pharaohs, was said to be about 3 million. No one can be quite sure about the accuracy of such historical estimates, just as no one can be quite certain about what standards of precision were used by a French expedition in 1800 to assert that Egypt's population in that year was 2.5 million. It was only in 1822 that the first census was taken, and it showed that Egypt then had 7.8 million people. Subsequent efforts at census taking were weak, and a nationwide mechanism to conduct a census every ten years was set up only in 1900. According to Egypt's Central Agency for Public Mobilization and Statistics (CAPMAS), between 1900 and 1940 the population grew at an average rate of 1.7 percent each year. But between 1945 and 1965 this annual figure rose to 2.8 percent. Egyptian officials attribute this increase, at least partially, to the fact that Egypt's mortality rate was on the decline because of improved health care so that people were living longer. The mortality rate was 31.2 per 1,000 of the population in 1936; by the mid-1960s, the figure had dropped to 15.2 per 1,000 of the population. It is now about 11 per 1,000. These officials also say that infant mortality rates were also falling because of better health care facilities: in the 1940s, the annual infant mortality rate was 150 per 1,000; by 1965, the figure had been brought down to 116 per 1,000. Now it is said to be around 75 per 1,000—still high, but falling nevertheless.

It was only in 1953 that a national population commission was formed. There were some leading social workers who felt that Egypt should have begun a formal family-planning campaign well before then. In Alexandria, a charming city on the Mediterranean, Zahia Marzok, one such prominent social worker, told me that as far back as the early 1930s she had agitated for some sort of comprehensive nationwide family-planning program. "Even back then it was apparent that we were heading toward a population crisis, that we were going to have many more people than we could reasonably support," Mrs. Marzok, a stout, friendly woman said. Her concern went unacknowledged. Then, in 1953, the newly formed population commission started eighteen family-planning clinics. Some years later, the commission came to be called the Egyptian Family Planning Association.

But it wasn't until 1962, or almost a decade after the commission was formed, that a major national figure came out with a policy statement concerning population problems in Egypt. President Gamal Abdel Nasser proposed at that time a national charter that specifically referred to the urgency for checking population growth. A division for population studies and family planning was created within the Ministry of Social

Affairs in 1964, and the next year family-planning services were made available on a limited basis in about forty government health clinics. In 1965, too, the Nasser administration, in an attempt to coordinate various governmental population control efforts, set up the Supreme Council for Family Planning, which by 1973 came to be called the Supreme Council for Population and Family Planning. The agency remains the chief coordinator of Egypt's population control efforts, with its chief enforcement arm being what is known as the Population and Family Planning Board.

I went by to have a chat with the board's head, Dr. Aziz el-Bindary. My friends at the United Nations had urged I spend time with him, assuming he had time to spare, of course, and a number of people around Egypt spoke of him in reverent tones.

He is of middle height, balding, deeply tanned, chain-smoking. The sharp, darting eyes are deceptively hooded by thick lids, and below the eyes are circles of fatigue. He is said to be a voluble man, but he is also quick to smile. He does not, however, inspire familiarity. No one, not even his closest associates, calls him by his first name. It is always "Dr. Bindary." I thought he looked much older than his fifty-seven years, for the years have clearly ravaged his features and furrowed his face. If he gives the impression of being continually under pressure, it is because Dr. Bindary most surely is. As head of the Population and Family Planning Board, he is the one key figure entrusted with ensuring that Egypt's growing population size is stabilized.

Aziz Bindary has his work cut out for him. He admitted to me that at times he feels he is in a goldfish bowl, for when people talk about lowering Egypt's birthrate, they generally mean, "What is Bindary up to these days?" His goal is to bring the birthrate down to 2 per 1,000, a very ambitious task indeed, and to provide efficient health, education, and job opportunities in even the remotest villages. Bindary helped shape the government's policy concerning population to focus on what he calls the "development approach." He defines the policy in terms of four major interrelated aspects: growth, distribution, characteristics, and structures. Translated into layman's language, what Bindary is talking about is providing education that includes family-planning courses, increased participation of women in the labor force, modernization of agriculture so that peasants are encouraged to stay in the rural areas instead of emigrating to the cities, industrialization in the countryside so as to create more jobs there, improved social security through pension and old-age schemes so that people have fewer children as insurance against old age, and reduced infant mortality through improved health care services.

"Of course all this is very ambitious," Bindary said, lighting up yet another American cigarette. "I would like to achieve something ambitious, within a short span of time. I am anxious to correct an image that development is a long-term process. If we put our minds and wills to it, we can achieve something substantial in Egypt. I am aware that everybody in the Arab world and in the Third World is watching what we do here."

We spoke in Bindary's beautifully appointed apartment on the embankment of the Nile, in the Garden City section of Cairo. The wooden floors were partially covered with intricately patterned Persian carpets; books tastefully climbed up portions of walls; indoor plants brought a dash of green to the living room; hidden speakers gently splashed Chopin on my ears; works of art by Egyptian artists were discreetly exhibited; the flavor of the homemade coffee was just right. Below us the Nile, wide and brackish at most times, now shimmered in the light of the setting sun. Bindary was relaxed, unlike the previous times I had seen him at his book-lined, gloomy government office just off Tahrir Square, where all of Cairo's thoroughfares seem to join up. As head of the Population and Family Planning Board, Bindary monitors the dozens of population programs currently operating in Egypt. This is no mean feat, especially in a country where bureaucratic rivalries are traditionally bitter. Moreover, population control projects are administered by several ministries, which frequently do not see eye to eye on many matters. "It's a well-known fact that if you are a trouble-shooter, people try to get you," he said to me. "I think corruption is one of the biggest catastrophes for Egypt."

This is candid talk, and Bindary has sometimes got into trouble with his superiors because of his forthrightness. "But that is the way I am, to be blunt is my nature," he said. Bindary added that if population programs are to succeed in Egypt, some tough talk and tough thinking are required. "What we have in Egypt is a system of technocrats," he went on, in his Cambridge-accented English. "We have to try and induce accountability, which at present is practically nonexistent in government. To have an effective family-planning program, you also have to have an effective economy—where jobs are amply available, where health facilities are adequate. Family planning cannot exist in a vacuum by itself. You can't just distribute contraceptives and tell people to go ahead and start lowering the birthrate." He was now talking about what has become a controversial subject among Egyptian population planners. The debate swirls around this key question: Should Egypt continue to pursue the traditional means of family planning through the distribution of contraceptives—methods that have met the stout resistance of the orthodoxy of the Arab culture? Or should Egypt link population matters to the wider issue of development and concentrate on building its infrastructure and widening social services to the people?

"We are adopting the developmental approach because it has become a must in the Egyptian context," Bindary said. "We want to prove that development in a developing country starts with changing the social system, with the setting up of a new value system. This will change things much more quickly than traditional family planning programs and systems. What we are attempting to do in Egypt now is to reeducate people to entrepreneurship in place of passive attitudes. In our country, there is this unfortunate tendency to rely on government to do everything."

Bindary's agency has helped fashion a number of billboards for busy byways in Cairo and other cities. One poster, for example, is prominently displayed near Tahrir Square and shows a contented two-child family able to afford good clothes, fine coffee, a goat, and a radio set. The caption reads, in Arabic: "The choice is yours." Radio and television commercials broadcast daily the message of family planning. One television cartoon shows a crowing rooster—to remind viewers that the pill must be taken daily. So popular did a radio commercial tune on family planning become not long ago that the song rocketed into a national pop hit! The radio commercials are particularly aimed at village youths, urging them not to flee their rural areas for the attractions of the big city.

"If you can get modernization into the village, if you can close the gap between villages and cities, then you can very quickly change traditional modes of behavior," Bindary told me. "Also, the more women you have working, the more you decrease the chance that they will have big families or have babies early in life."

In place after place during my travels through the Third World, I found that where women were given educational and economic opportunities they invariably chose to have smaller families. When a woman has a job, it impels—not compels—her to limit the size of her family. In Sri Lanka and the southern Indian state of Kerala, for example, as traditional discrimination against women was eliminated and obstacles to their education and employment were removed, women came increasingly and productively into the local mainstream. In these places, there was a noticeable improvement in the content and pace of development. When women became relatively autonomous, their sense of their own worth and value increased, and this without fail was reflected in lowered fertility.

It seemed to me, listening to Aziz Bindary speak, that what the Egyptians really wanted to create in their country was a felt demand by women for family planning, a demand for contraceptives that was the result of a personal conviction that birth control was good for them personally and economically beneficial for their families and community. Unfortunately, the West's "population Mafia" has long emphasized the supply-side system: the assumption here is that if you saturate a place with condoms and contraceptives, birthrates and fertility patterns will soon fall. The question that rarely gets adequately answered is why people should go in for the acceptance of contraceptives at all, especially people in traditional and conservative societies like Egypt.

A more enlightened approach is to make people want to incorporate family-planning practices into their everyday life. One way to do this is to demonstrate to women that if they delayed marriage and had babies later in life rather than earlier they could be more economically productive human beings. This is a slower process than the "supply-side" approach, of course, but perhaps in the longer term it is a surer means of reducing a society's fertility. It appeared to me that Egyptians like Aziz Bindary were trying to popularize this approach and were succeeding.

Not long after my conversation with Aziz Bindary, I found myself driving back to Cairo late one evening with an Egyptian sociologist named Sarah Loza. At the suggestion of her friend Dr. Bindary, Mrs. Loza had taken me earlier in the day to a factory in El Badr village, which was located in the governorate of Tahrir.

What I saw that day was a project in which women in their late teens and early twenties manufactured chemises for Egypt's uniformed services. Started in 1974, this project has been financed mostly by the United Nations Fund for Population Activities, one of the biggest donors to Egypt's population program (the single largest donor is the U.S. Agency for International Development, which gives the Egyptians some $20 million each year for a variety of family-planning projects).

"What we have here is an example that what women do economically can be reflected in fertility," Dr. Loza said to me as she guided me around the cavernous plant with its sewing machines, cutting tables, and warehouses filled with fabrics. Scores of women were busily at work. Dr. Loza, a petite woman impeccably attired in French clothes, went on: "These women are showing that they are perfectly capable of working and earning a living—that they don't have to be an economic burden to their families. And because they demonstrate that they can indeed stand on their own two feet, their families are less insistent on marrying them off early." Dr. Loza supervises the Badr plant and visits here once or twice a week. She introduced me to a nineteen-year-old woman named Wafaa el-Magd. Wafaa was tall, big-boned, dressed in slacks and a sweatshirt. She could have easily found herself a job in New York as a model, I thought, except, of course, that she didn't speak a word of English. Sarah Loza translated.

"I have worked here for a year now," Wafaa said. "My parents wanted to get me married, but I convinced them that if I worked, I could bring home money for everybody. Now I make as much each month as my father does in his job in the fields." (She takes home the equivalent of $25 a month.) "Perhaps soon I will make even more." She said she saved some of her money because she wants to finish high school and maybe go on to college someday.

Wafaa may or may not get that opportunity for further education, and it may well be that by the time what I'm writing gets into print she could be married, with a child. But I sensed in her, and in the other young women I met in Badr that day, a determination not to be maneuvered by traditions and family influences. I think such an attitude can only augur well for population control in Egypt.

A few days after that visit to Badr, I got to see another aspect of population-related development efforts. I was taken to El Fayoum, a governorate southwest of Cairo. Fayoum is known for its extraordinary greenery, even though it sits on desert land, and it is fabled for the poultry raised by its farmers. The Fayoum oasis has been celebrated in Egyptian poetry, and I found out why. The date trees, the acres of fields where vegetables are grown, the narrow winding roads, the roadside kiosks where freshly slaughtered lamb is roasted on spits—all these are the stuff of exotic Arabian fantasies that people have, and in Fayoum it is all before your eyes.

On the way to Fayoum, I stopped briefly in the village of Tobhar to meet the headman, a craggy man named Abd el-Azim el-Lawag. He wanted me first to see his shiny new Indian-made motorcycle, which had been given to him by Bindary's Population and Family Planning Board. "This makes me much more mobile," Lawag said. "Now I can travel far and wide to spread the message of family planning." He is one of dozens of village headmen around the country who have been given motorcycles by the family planning board. Egyptians respond to authority, and so when a village headman promotes birth control, villagers invariably stop and listen. The Egyptian government provides small transistor radio sets to these headmen for distribution in villages to family-planning acceptors. The government also provides assistance to set up chicken-breeding farms and day-care centers in places like Fayoum so that more jobs can be generated locally and mothers can be assured that their young children are taken care of by qualified personnel while they themselves are at work. I could see now the reasons why officials like Bindary are promoting the concept of "development" in conjunction with promoting family planning. Ordinary rural Egyptians worry primarily about food and jobs and health care. The "message" of family planning must be gently squeezed into their consciousness.

One afternoon in Salam village, about sixty-five miles from Cairo, a woman named Horaiya Abdel-Aziz, a farmer's wife and mother of eight children, talked with me about her aspirations. Horaiya, a strong-featured, smiling woman, served me hot biscuits, homemade cheese, and black tea in the living room of her neat, mud-and-brick house. Her farming community's pressing needs were electricity and clean water, and only then could anyone even begin to talk to villagers about family planning, said Horaiya. (In Egypt, married women are allowed to use their maiden names, a small concession to them in an overwhelmingly male-oriented and male chauvinistic society.) Had she known what family planning was all about, Horaiya said, she would never have had eight children. It was a sentiment I heard over and over again not only in Egypt but other parts of the Third World. Like the majority of Egyptians, Horaiya is a Moslem. I asked her if she had run into any Islamic resistance to the idea of family planning, now that she practices birth control. There are some authoritative population planners who believe that one reason the family-planning campaign in Egypt hasn't been as successful as it could—given the fact that hundreds of millions of dollars have been spent by the government and by foreign donors—is that there has been opposition to birth control on religious grounds. Horaiya told me that she saw no active religious resistance in her village but that some fundamentalist Moslem sheikhs, or priests, had murmured something about birth control being part of a Western plot to dilute Islamic values.

There is no doubt in my mind that conservative Moslem leaders, including the so-called fundamentalists who want a return to Islamic law, morals, and ethics for the individual and the state, are opposed to family planning. A report published not long ago by the London-based International Planned Parenthood Federation said that some of these religious figures—among them members of the banned Moslem Brotherhood—are angered by what they consider the post-1973 Western "takeover" of Egypt. The Sadat regime, and to some extent the Mubarak government, were viewed as encouraging what some fanatical Moslem leaders have characterized as the "cultural rape" of Islamic Egypt, according to the IPPF report. The views of these opponents, the report said, reach a wide, receptive section of public opinion. These opponents are confident there is strong and growing opposition to birth control in Egypt —the biggest Arab country in terms of population size—and they hold a deepening conviction that the strength of Islam lies in large families.

Does Islam actually oppose any form of family planning? According to Dr. Saad Gadalla, who has directed a successful family-planning project in Egypt's Menoufia Governorate, the first recorded reference to a "population problem" in Egypt dates back more than 1,300 years. He quotes a man named Amr Ibn el As, a companion of the Prophet Mohammed and the conqueror of Egypt in A.D. 641, who warned in a homily that drudgery, poverty, and humiliation would descend on Egypt if its people wasted their wealth or had "too many children." One of the Prophet's own sayings reads: "The most grueling trial is to have plenty of children with no adequate means." It is indeed true that Islam does encourage the begetting of children, but it also enjoins believers to have only as many children as they can look after. The Koran says: "No person shall be charged beyond his means. A mother shall not be pressed unfairly for her child, nor a father for his child." Shaikh Hasan Ma'mun, rector of the mosque-university of Al-Azhar in Cairo, said in a religious document called a *fatwa* back in 1964:

> The early followers of Islam were few and weak in the midst of a vast majority of aggressive and oppressive people. . . . The good of the Moslems then required that there should be a call for the multiplication of their number, in order that they might be able at the time to fulfill their responsibilities in defending the mission of Islam and protecting the true religion of God against the powerful and multitudinous adversaries threatening it.

> But now we find that conditions have changed. We find that the density of population in the world threatens a serious reduction in the living standards of mankind to the extent that many men of thought have been prompted to seek family planning in every country, so that the resources may not fall short of ensuring a decent living for its people to provide public services for them.
>
> Islam, as the religion of pristine nature, has never been opposed to what is good to man. Indeed it has always been ahead in the effort towards the achievement of this good so long as it is not in conflict with the purposes of God's Law.
>
> I see no objection from the Sharia [Islamic law] point of view to the consideration of family planning as a measure, if there is need for it, and if the consideration is occasioned by the people's own choice and conviction, without constraint or compulsion, in the light of their circumstances, and on condition that the means for effecting this planning is legitimate.

Moslem scholars note that the early Islamic scriptures mentioned the practice of *'azl*, or coitus interruptus. One of the Prophet's companions said: "We used to practice *'azl* during the time of the Prophet. The Prophet came to know about it, but did not forbid us. If this were something to be prohibited, the Koran would have forbidden us to do it."

The grand mufti of Jordan, Shaikh Abdullah Al-Qalqili, issued a *fatwa* in 1964 in which he said: "There is agreement among the exponents of jurisprudence that coitus interruptus, as one of the methods for the prevention of childbearing, is allowed. Doctors of religion inferred from this that it is permissible to take a drug to prevent childbearing, or even to induce abortion. We confidently rule in this *fatwa* that it is permitted to take measures to limit childbearing."

Another Moslem scholar, Dr. Ismail Balogun of Nigeria's University of Ibadan, wrote:

> The question that arises because coitus interruptus was the only contraceptive known by the Prophet's companions, and which practice the Prophet condoned, is this: Can Moslems of today practice any other method? The answer can only be in the affirmative, as long as the other methods are not injurious, either to the man or the woman. The question is tantamount to asking whether a Moslem can today wear clothes different in shape from those worn by the Prophet and his companions during their time.

Scholars at Cairo's ancient Al-Azhar University—widely recognized as the world's leading Islamic educational institution—have also studied the thorny question of abortion. They make a distinction between the two stages of pregnancy: the first 120 days, and the remaining period before childbirth. Most classical Moslem religious scholars opine that it is permissible to have an abortion for valid reasons, mainly medical, during the first stage. As for induced abortion after the first 120 days, virtually every modern Moslem agrees that Islam prohibits abortion except where dire medical emergencies require it to save the mother's life.

One morning at Al-Azhar University, I spoke with a number of young Moslem scholars, none of whom seemed particularly troubled by the promotion of family planning by the government. One scholar quoted from recent writings by a professor of Islamic law at the university. The professor, Dr. Ahmad Sharabassy, wrote:

> Family planning, as understood by Islam, is not opposed to marriage or to the begetting of children, nor does its concept imply disbelief in the doctrine of fate and divine dispensation—for God Almighty has bestowed reason upon man to enable him to distinguish between the useful and the harmful, and to help him follow the path that would assure him happiness in this world as well as in the world to come.

Surrounded by the marble archways and stone lattice-work of the old university, with the muezzin's distant calls summoning the faithful to prayer, it was hard for me to believe that not everything emanating from Al-Azhar was accepted by Moslems as valid—I was, of course, being naive in even beginning to expect that Al-Azhar's interpretation of Islam would be totally accepted—but it seemed to me that the scholars here put in a great deal of effort and thinking and discussion into sensitive issues like family planning. More importantly, I thought, what these scholars were doing was to relate theology and arcane philosophy to modern, pressing concerns of a developing society such as Egypt. They have recognized that religion must be relevant, and in saying that they saw no problem with the acceptance by Moslems of family planning the Al-Azhar scholars have endorsed the position of the Mubarak and Sadat governments that birth control must be considered a vital component of Egypt's developmental strategy.

Many conservative Moslem intellectuals, clerics, and politicians do not share this view, however, and they are puzzled by the interpretations of the Al-Azhar faculty. Some of the more strident among these are even charging that attempts to control family size are an imperialist, Western, or Zionist conspiracy to weaken Egypt and undermine Islam. Pamphlets condemning family planning are circulated in cities like Cairo and in rural communities. Family-planning workers have occasionally been threatened. Officials of Egypt's Ministry of Religious Affairs—known as the Waqf—express concern at this. The ministry's director general for the administration of mosques, Dr. Abdel Rahman el-Naggar, says that he personally has pursued the subject of family planning with religious opponents. One of his arguments is that although birth control programs are directed at individuals, the business of family planning really concerns the welfare of the entire nation. Dr. Naggar gives frequent talks on radio and television on the subject of family planning. But no matter how strenuously people like him work toward convincing critics of birth control, it is unlikely that opposition among conservative Moslem clerics is going to abate. Family planning is an issue these opponents have cleverly tied in with the Mubarak government's overall Western-oriented policies, and it is this tilt toward the West, and specifically the United States, that these conservatives are vehemently against.

The genesis of the current Western orientation of Egypt's economic and development policies was in the perceptions of Anwar Sadat in the early 1970s that Nasser's socialist policies had failed dismally. Not long after the Yom Kippur War of October 1973, President Sadat unveiled what he called his "Open Door" economic policy. It consisted of three major reforms. First, an investment law was passed with the aim of encouraging foreign concerns to set up joint ventures in Egypt. Thus, for example, Colgate-Palmolive agreed to build a factory to manufacture toothpaste, shampoo, and shaving cream in cooperation with Egyptian entrepreneurs. The Xerox Corporation opened an office in Cairo and announced it would invest more than $10 million in the country. The second aspect of the Open Door policy was that Sadat altered Egypt's banking laws so as to encourage foreign banks to open branches in the country. Among those who did so were Citibank and Chase Manhattan, both financial giants in the United States. More than thirty-five foreign banks have opened branches or offices in Egypt now, and these help channel into the country more than $2 billion than Egyptian nationals living and working abroad—mostly in the oil-rich Gulf states—remit to the home country each year. (These remittances are Egypt's biggest source of foreign exchange, followed by the $700 million earned annually from Suez Canal levies and the $500 million obtained from tourism.) The third aspect of the Sadat reforms was that major oil companies were invited to apply for licenses to explore for oil. Egypt is already mostly self-sufficient in crude oil, but now that it has regained possession of the Sinai from the Israelis, the expectation is that new finds will enable it to become perhaps a significant exporter of crude oil. Sadat, a charismatic leader, ordered that the 1978–1982 development plan be revised extensively to increase expenditures to $21 billion, including huge new outlays for the public sector to spur better housing, better transportation, and better communications. (For example, $2 billion is being spent to modernize the current antiquated telephone system and to increase the number of telephone lines from 370,000 to more than a million.) Sadat, and Mubarak after him, vowed to make Egypt agriculturally self-sufficient. Ambitious plans were drawn up to reclaim desert areas and build massive housing complexes on this land.

Just outside of Cairo stands one such complex, known as the Tenth of Ramadan City. It was completed late in 1978, and I decided I would visit and chat with occupants. Few people I met there had anything nice to say about their new homes. The water supply was sporadic, I was told, but not as sporadic as the electricity. The drainage system was a disaster. Window panes frequently just popped out, or they popped into apartments whenever the desert winds grew too strong. The buses supposedly commissioned to transport inhabitants of this complex to work places in Cairo generally broke down. Most apartments were already overcrowded, as occupants brought in unauthorized relatives to live with them, or even sold space illegally and exorbitantly.

Agriculture hasn't done too well either. Driving to Alexandria one morning with my interpreter, Michiel Misdary Sefren, I passed a large oasis in which was located a 4,000-hectare farm. That farm was "presented" some years ago to Egypt by the Soviet Union in the halcyon days of their alliance. The Soviet technicians who helped run that farm are gone now, and much of the dairy machinery lies in disrepair. The technicians went home when Sadat, in a fit of pique, tossed out thousands of Soviet military advisors and intelligence operatives in 1973. That was the year when he formally renounced Nasser's socialism. The farm, once a showcase in dairy production, hasn't been doing too well since—handicapped by a lack of qualified personnel to operate it and by the fact that the farm machinery donated by the Russians has long since broken down. Meanwhile, Egypt must import millions of dollars of food to properly feed its people: a third of Egyptian bread is made from American wheat.

There are some areas where imaginative agricultural efforts are combined with family-planning promotions. In the village of Agameen, in the Fayoum Governorate, I met three extension workers, Zeinab Mohammed Mahmoud, Nadia Omar Abdel Latif, and Amal el-Syaed Nawgoud. They had been sent to this village to train peasants' wives in the use of agricultural machinery so that they could assist their husbands in the field. Then these three women, all Cairenes, decided they would also instruct their charges in contraception. In the event, the women of Agameen seemed to accept the pill best.

Imagination and enterprise are two elements that Hamed Fahmy likes to stress continually. He is the son of former Foreign Minister Ismail Fahmy and has been administrator of the United Nations population program in Egypt. Hamed is a man of medium height, about forty years old, with dark, good looks. Like many Egyptian men, he is a chain-smoker. Over dinner one evening at his elegant Cairo apartment, he told me that recent United Nations efforts have focused on assisting the government's population-related development efforts. One target of this program is ordinary villagers, and in the last three years more than 14 million peasants in 525 villages spread out over twelve governorates have been reached, he said. He thought I should see one such program.

And so I found myself one day in El Qantara. The village is a clangorous community, like most Egyptian rural communities, and it sits in the middle of the sandy wasteland that stretches all the way from Port Said on the Mediterranean to Cairo. There are mud and adobe huts here, and the roads are not paved, and until the United Nations–sponsored health program was set up here recently, there wasn't even a full-time medical clinic around. I was reminded by a local official that in not having basic health care services, the 3,000 residents of Qantara were among the 800 million people of the Third World who the United Nations estimates have little access to essential health facilities. Now there are four small clinics here, with five full-time physicians. Medical vans have been given by the United Nations, which has also set up a family-planning counseling service.

Just off the main road, under a colorful canopy that shakes every time a sharp gust of desert wind comes along, Sabar Taufek Selem operates a kofta booth. The smell of the grilled lamb and fried onions suffuses nearby homes. A group of men, all in dusty *galebeyas,* the long flowing robes Egyptians customarily wear, sat on wooden benches near the kofta booth. They were discussing the new developments in their village with what seemed to me the enthusiasm of boys. Selem, a tall, rotund man and the father of seven boys, said he took his family to be inoculated and then himself signed up for contraceptives. Abdel Qatarh, a farmer and herdsman, said that when he and his wife, who have eight daughters, agreed to practice family planning, they were told they could receive a low-interest loan to develop their tiny farm and perhaps buy better fertilizers. "I don't understand this thing about birthrates and growth rates," Abdel said, cackling, "but I do understand the feel of the Egyptian pound in my hand. Fewer in my family means more from my field."

Five

Asia
Population Laboratory of the World

NOORJAHAN AHMED lives in a *bustee*, a neighborhood of tin-roofed structures and dusty, unpaved streets in Hyderabad, an otherwise graceful southern Indian city of minarets, bungalows, neat parks, cricket fields, and plane trees. She is a small, slim woman who looks as fragile as a sparrow, and although she is no more than twenty-four years of age, her face is that of a much older person. The years have been hard on Noorjahan, partly because her Moslem parents, pleading poverty, married her off when she was fourteen. In her ten years of married life she has produced five children. She herself has fifteen brothers and sisters. Her husband Syed, who is a plumber, makes the equivalent of $70 a month, which is barely sufficient to feed and clothe their children properly and send them to school, much less take them to the circus occasionally or away from the *bustee* on holidays.

Noorjahan is up by dawn every day of the week except Sunday, for her husband must leave home early for work at a factory that is a good hour's labor on his bicycle. She prepares a breakfast of *chappatis*, a pancake-type bread made of unleavened wheat, and minced meat with potatoes and chopped onions, feeds her husband and then the children, and treks to a community well a mile away to fill up two pails of water, which she brings back home. There is no running water in Noorjahan's home, which consists of a small room where everybody sleeps, an adjoining area in which a cooking stove is placed, and a tiny, tiled alcove for washing. There is no latrine, and for anything more than the simplest ablution, family members must go to a communal toilet a hundred yards away from Noorjahan's home. There is, of course, no air conditioning, nor any fittings for ceiling fans, and the stubby tabletop revolving fan that provides some relief during the hot, humid hours also pushes in the stench from a nearby open sewer.

Noorjahan's days are spent cooking, sewing, washing, scrubbing, and taking care of her daughter and four sons; at night, after the children are asleep, and whether she wants to or not, she must service her husband in bed. If she refuses, Syed is liable to slap her, or, if he is drunk, he will likely punch her in the mouth. Several of Noorjahan's teeth have already been knocked out by her spouse.

Hers is not an uncommon story in this overwhelmingly poor land of nearly 800 million people, a country whose annual population growth rate of 2.2 percent will push India's population beyond the 1 billion mark by the end of the century. What is unusual about Noorjahan, however, is that not long ago she decided she would have no more children, despite the desire of her husband and his and her orthodox Sunni Moslem parents. Noorjahan, aware that she was risking the permanent displeasure of her in-laws—and possible eviction from her husband's home—nevertheless pleaded medical necessity, went to a family-planning clinic in the Begumpet section of Hyderabad, and obtained a tubectomy.

Her friends in the *bustee* warned Noorjahan that a sterilization operation would cripple her, possible even kill her, and that evil would befall her family if she went through with it. A group of local eunuchs went up to her and complained that their traditional business of dancing at babies' christening ceremonies would be jeopardized if women started to have fewer babies. Noorjahan went ahead anyway. The sterilization operation guaranteed that she would never again bear children: Noorjahan was one of 4 million men and women who get themselves sterilized each year in India, often against the wishes of their spouses and often to the accompaniment of peer disapproval. The fact that she did not obtain a tubectomy earlier was a reflection of the conservative attitudes of orthodox poor families, both Moslem and Hindu, all across India. In Noorjahan's case, it was also a reflection on the dearth of proper family-planning information and facilities in many parts of India, which in 1952 was the first country in the world to set up a formal national family-planning program and which spends in the vicinity of $175 million each year on various birth control projects.

The fact that Noorjahan Ahmed finally did go to a local family-planning clinic was a tribute not only to her determination and courage but also to the patience and persuasiveness of a young American-educated physician named Pramila David. Mrs. David, a tall, intense woman and mother of two teenagers, runs a nonprofit organization called the Center for Population Concerns. For the last six years, the center has offered comprehensive family-planning services, including a day-care facility for the children of poor women who are employed, and vocational and education classes for adults such as Noorjahan, who is now being trained as a seamstress.

* * *

Hundreds of miles from where Noorjahan Ahmed lives, Dewa Ayue Maday Gria also spends some of her spare time learning how to be a seamstress. She lives in the tiny mountain village of Gunaksha in Bali, a lush and beautiful island in the Indonesian archipelago. Most days she is busy raising pigs and chickens, or tending her patch of pineapple, spinach, eggplant, and cassava. Dewa and her husband built their two-room house with their own hands, chopping wood in a nearby forest and dragging the lumber in by handcart. The walls are a combination of wooden planks and straw matting. Mangy dogs wander around. The fragrance of flowers suffuses the area. Inside the house, the furnishings consist of a couple of credenzas, a rug or two, and a cupboard to store dishes. Clothes hang on pegs. A black-and-white television set sits in one corner of what is the bedroom; there is also a transistor radio and an ancient gramophone.

Tacked on the porch of her small wooden shack is a thumb-sized sign identifying the short, wiry Dewa as a practitioner of family planning. That status gives her access to cheap government loans, and she has used the equivalent of about a thousand dollars over the last seven years to improve her homestead, buy more pigs for breeding, and expand her garden. The thirty-seven-year-old Dewa, a Hindu like most people in Bali, told me she decided eleven years ago to start practicing birth control by using an intrauterine device (an IUD) because "three children is enough."

In Indonesia, a heavily Moslem nation of 154 million people where most families consist of at least five children, that attitude is unusual. Even more unusual is the fact that in a culture that still values sons more than daughters Dewa and her husband, a government employee, made their decision to restrict their family size even though their three children were girls. They would, of course, have liked to have tried again to have a son, Dewa said to me, but it became a matter of simple economics. If they now had a fourth child, Dewa would be required to repay the old loans faster and wouldn't be eligible for new credit she says she needs. She is receiving free instruction in sewing and making clothes at a special government class for women who have agreed to use contraception.

"I have profited by birth control," Dewa told me, offering me a glass of hot milk that had been generously spiced with cinnamon. "Who would not want a son? He would support us in our old age. But the real question for us now is can we support another child?"

Deway Ayue Maday Gria and Noorjahan Ahmed have never met, nor are they likely to. But in their own way they are examples of an emerging trend in Asia and in many other parts of the developing world—a discernible determination by women to reduce their family size by resorting to birth control, often against the wishes of their conservative husbands.

I found during my travels that more and more women also seem to want to get out of their homes to involve themselves in economic activities, a situation that could eventually lead to even more women producing fewer children and thus bringing down Asian nations annual population growth rates. The experience of places such as Bali, Sri Lanka, South Korea, and the southern Indian state of Kerala has shown that, where women were brought into the economic mainstream through increased female education and employment, there was not only an overall decline in the population growth rate but also an improvement in the content and pace of development and in the general quality of life of the entire community.

More than any other continent, Asia is a bellwether region. With a population of some 2.7 billion people, Asia is not only the most crowded continent, it is also home to more than three-fifths of the world's overall population of 4.6 billion. The two most populous nations in the world, China and India, are in Asia, and their combined population by the year 2000 may well exceed the current total population of the entire continent. Of the dozen countries in the world with populations of over 100 million each at the end of the century, six will be in Asia. Of the thirty biggest urban centers in the world by the year 2000, seventeen will be in this continent, each with a population of more than 10 million.

It was an Asian state, India, that first got the whole business of population control going back in 1952. Asian countries like Singapore, South Korea, Thailand, and Sri Lanka have led the way in demonstrating how a mix of political commitment and economic incentives can result in swift decreases in previously galloping population growth rates. Yet, it is in Asia too that states such as Bangladesh, Pakistan, Nepal, and Burma are the cause of serious concern to demographers, who worry that it may already be too late to check these countries' population explosions. The overall Asian population has continuously increased from 1.4 billion people in 1950 to almost 2.7 billion people in 1984; by the year 2000, the figure is expected by the United Nations to climb by another billion people, and by 2025 to perhaps 4.5 billion. And in the year 2025, Asia's population will continue to constitute nearly 60 percent of the total global population.

Experts such as Steven W. Sinding of the U.S. Agency for International Development in Washington say that in view of this large concentration of population in the region, what happens in Asia will largely determine the overall trends in world population. Much, if not most, of the billions of dollars poured by Western nations—and especially by the United States—into population control work over the last decade was in fact channeled into Asian countries.

Sinding, a tall, intense man who has served in AID posts in various parts of Asia, notes that three-fourths of the world's annual population growth—or more than 80 million people—is taking place in Asia. I first met him in Manila as he was about to end a three-year assignment in the Philippines and return to Washington to head AID's entire population division. We spoke in his plant-filled office in the Ramon Magsaysay Building; I could see Manila's teeming crowds push and squeeze through the capital's streets.

"When one talks of the world's population problem, one is really talking about Asia, because this is where most of the world's people live and where the worst population growth is occurring," Sinding said. "Asia has led the way in every aspect of population. It has shown us what works in population control and what doesn't. Moreover, at a time when there is a general slackening of financial commitment on the part of Western donors to population programs, it can be demonstrated that the best dollar-for-dollar investment for development by the West has indeed been in population programs in Asia. What we have learned in Asia is a pretty good indication of what can and cannot work elsewhere. In a sense, Asia continues to be the world's laboratory for population."

When population experts like Steve Sinding talk about Asia, they usually divide the continent into two regions, East Asia and West Asia, which exhibit contrasting demographic phenomena. Broadly speaking, the states of East Asia, such as Japan and China, have engineered dramatic fertility declines. China's population control efforts, which involve pushing couples into accepting the one-child family policy, have resulted in what are probably the world's most sensational results: China halved its birthrate from 34 per 1,000 in 1970 to 18 per 1,000 in 1979 and 16 per 1,000 in 1983. The goal is to bring down the annual birthrate to 5 per 1,000 by 1985. But most countries of West Asia and South Asia, such as Pakistan, Bangladesh, Nepal, and Burma, have annual birthrates of at least 45 per 1,000 of the population. These countries can least afford such population growth.

India's population control record is mottled: thickly populated and rapidly growing provinces such as Bihar and Uttar Pradesh—which have failed to popularize birth control among couples in the twenty-to-twenty-eight age group, the so-called high-fertility group—are the despair of population planners and demographers; but other Indian states, such as Kerala and Maharashtra, have energetically established literacy programs for women, created jobs for them, set up effective contraceptive distribution, and launched maternal and child care clinics by the hundreds. In these states there was a dramatic decline in birthrates, a decline that was preceded by equally important and dramatic declines in infant and general mortality rates. But Kerala and Maharashtra are not the norm in most of Asia or even in India itself, where over the next decade there will be a population increase of more than 220 million, according to the United Nations.

When population experts talk about Asia, they not only despair about the continuing high population growth rates in West and South Asian states, they also worry about high mortality rates in many Asian countries. According to the United Nations, although life expectancy in Asia increased by six years between 1965 and 1980—largely because of reductions in infant and childhood mortality—seven of the thirty-six countries in the Asia–Pacific region had an average life expectancy for their citizens of below fifty years. Moreover, the gap in life expectancy between the many developing states in the region and the few "developed" ones, such as Japan, Taiwan, Singapore, and South Korea, has widened during the last decade. The states of East Asia have the lowest death rates, averaging about 10 per 1,000 of the population, mostly because of the good health care available in these nations. In countries where the mortality rate is brought down, there is almost invariably a simultaneous decline in the birthrate as well. Countries such as Afghanistan, Bhutan, and Nepal continue to experience high mortality rates—at least 20 per 1,000 of the population. In these countries, the health care system has yet to reach citizens widely, and it is not uncommon for residents of some areas to trek dozens, even hundreds of miles to get to the nearest clinic.

I visited an Afghan village called Khwaja Mussahaffir not long after the Soviets invaded Afghanistan in 1979. There were about fifty-five mud-walled homes in this rural community, a school, a warehouse for grain and fruits—the local products—and even a community center where villagers could—but rarely did—go to learn all about Marxism, but there was no health clinic. I asked the village headman, a craggy man named Mohammed Jalali, where the nearest clinic was.

"In Kabul," Jalali said, "more than thirty miles from here. Some of our people die before they reach Kabul. One of my wives gave birth before we reached Kabul, and our child died."

The demography of Asia has generated almost all major population issues: high fertility, high mortality, rapid population growth, expanding numbers of women in the childbearing years, and increasing numbers of elderly people. And, in view of the wide variations that exist in the continent, population problems of all types will continue to exist in Asia and vex demographers and planners for decades to come. Experts say, moreover, that in statistical terms the demography of Asia implies staggering socioeconomic problems by the year 2000.

For example, according to the United Nations Fund for Population Activities, even assuming a continuing trend toward decreased fertility rates, Asia's demography in the year 2000 would involve the need to provide health, educational, and nutritional services to nearly a billion children under the age of fifteen; gainful employment to more than 650 million youths; population and health services, including family-planning services and counseling, to nearly 950 million women; and social, municipal, and economic services to about 650 million persons above the general retirement age of sixty-five years. In addition to these problems are those related to urbanization, internal migration, and population redistribution.

Six of the twenty-first century's ten "supercities"—meaning those with populations of 15 million each or more—will be Asian cities, according to the latest estimates by the United Nations: Shanghai, with 23.7 million people, up 66 percent from its 1980 population; the Tokyo–Yokohama metropolitan region, 23.7 million, up 19 percent from 1980;

Beijing, with 20.9 million, up 83 percent from 1980; Bombay, with 16.8 million, up 102 percent from 1980; Calcutta, at 16.4 million, up 86 percent from 1980; and Jakarta, with a population in the year 2000 of 15.7 million, up 115 percent from its 1980 population.

Viewed against such projections, the current performance of many Asian states concerning population control is discouraging indeed. Only a handful of countries—Singapore, Taiwan, Thailand, Sri Lanka, South Korea, and China—have acted forthrightly to promote birth control programs and committed adequate funds to population projects. Mongolia openly encourages large families; Burma has banned contraceptives; in Pakistan and Bangladesh, no effective family-planning policies can be discerned. In the Philippines what was once regarded as an innovative family-planning program may soon be dismantled because of the Roman Catholic church's opposition to artificial birth control and because of the resistance from influential government officials.

In Malaysia, so worried are family-planning officials about the attitude of Islamic fundamentalists toward birth control that they changed the name of the national Family Planning Board to the Family Development Board. When I visited the agency in Kuala Lumpur, its officials seemed confused about just what their mandate was, and the agency's head, a woman named Datin Noor Laily, threatened to have me deported if I wrote about the family-planning situation in Malaysia—an absurd overreaction on her part, it seemed to me. Equally absurd was the advice of a local representative of the United Nations that I shouldn't even go around interviewing anybody, on population or any other subject, without clearance from Mrs. Laily! Adding to the general uncertainty among population officials was a recent statement by Prime Minister Mohammed Mahathir that Malaysia could easily sustain a fivefold increase in its population of 14 million.

Vietnam, wracked and wrecked by decades of civil war and colonial exploitation, is only now expressing concern about its population growth rate, currently the highest in Asia. The United Nations Fund for Population Activities has only just been invited by the Vietnamese to assist in the creation of a health care and birth control program.

India's family-planning program is still feeling the aftereffects of the time during the mid-1970s when some members of Prime Minister Indira Gandhi's government promoted the forcible sterilization of thousands of males. The alleged atrocities were said to have been perpetrated with the knowledge of Mrs. Gandhi's late son, Sanjay Gandhi, who was instrumental in persuading his mother to declare a state of emergency, suspend the Constitution, and jail thousands of political opponents. The accelerated family-planning campaign of this Emergency period proved to be a major electoral embarrassment in 1977, when Mrs. Gandhi's ruling Congress party was swept out of power. Now Mrs. Gandhi is back in office but has been cautious about taking any bold steps with regard to family planning.

Writing in the *Indian Express,* India's largest English-language daily newspaper in 1983, a New York–based demographer named Moni Nag said that to achieve any major decrease in the country's annual population growth rate India "needs a political will comparable to China's." India's Ministry of Health and Family Welfare, which is in overall charge of all family-planning activities, recently said that by the end of the century the country's annual population growth rate should be brought down from the current 2.2 percent to 1.2 percent.

Nag noted that China was able to slow down its annual population growth rate because a significantly high proportion of its population had accepted modern birth control methods and more women were marrying at a later age. But in India, Nag wrote, only about 23 percent of Indian couples of childbearing age currently practiced birth control (more than 70 percent of Chinese did so, in contrast). Nearly half of India's 120 million married women of childbearing age are still in their teens or in their early twenties, and every year 5 million more women join this childbearing group as the females born in the 1960s become potential mothers in the 1980s. I wasn't very impressed with those Indian family-planning government officials who deigned to talk to me; much of what they said was in the realm of political rhetoric or wishful thinking about what family-planning programs would achieve in India.

One of the few officials who I thought seemed to have clear thoughts on the subject of population was Sat Paul Mittal, a member of India's national parliament and a founder of an organization known as the Asian Forum of Parliamentarians on Population and Development. Mittal, a short, fat man with a ready sense of humor, recognizes that India's daunting population control tasks are not going to be performed by mere rhetoric. He wants more political commitment from India's leaders and a better monitoring of existing government family-planning projects.

"We need a renewed nationwide commitment to population control," Mittal said. "It is not enough to say that the birthrate is falling, that health facilities are getting better. We cannot be complacent about population control. It requires constant effort, more funds, better training for our fieldworkers, and more incentives for them and for family-planning acceptors."

His thoughts are echoed by Dr. Pramila David in Hyderabad, a courageous young physician who has persisted in running a nonprofit family-planning center for the poor despite thin finances, the opposition of some local politicians, and an inexplicable lack of support from the Indian government.

For more than five years, Mrs. David has run the Shilpa Clinic, a warren of clean, well-lit rooms, an operating theater, and a large yard with a garden in the Begumpet section of Hyderabad. She feels that it is not enough for the government merely to sponsor billboard advertising extolling birth control, or even radio and television campaigns that urge people to practice family planning. It is far more important that there be intensified personal contacts between family-planning personnel and potential clients. Dr. David fears that complaints about the way some government-run family-planning clinics are run may produce a backlash against family planning similar to what happened after the "Emergency" period of 1975–1977.

"As it is, people are often afraid to come around and seek family-planning services, even when they need such services desperately," she said. "In India, family-planning services are simply not in the same class as surgical services in hospitals. How can you win the confidence of people that way? In India, a lot of effort is put into providing incentives for people to come and get themselves sterilized, but very little thought is put into making family-planning services more attractive."

A case in point is a government clinic in the rural community of Nandiyal, not far from Hyderabad. It is a sprawling facility meant to offer sterilization services for men and women from the deep rural hinterland. But it is more like a factory than a facility: more than 200 sterilizations are carried out here every day by medical personnel who work with an impersonal attitude freighted with boredom and irritation.

Rows upon rows of stretchers lay on an open, unprotected verandah with still bodies on them—I thought they were corpses until I heard some of the bodies groan. These were women on whom tubectomies had just been performed, and they had been left to rest outside because there was no post-operation room in the Nandiyal facility. It was hectic inside the operating room itself, as patients were being lined up for their sterilization, ordered to undress, scrubbed perfunctorily, put under anesthesia, tubectomized with a laparoscope, then herded out hastily on stretchers. The surgical instruments were "sterilized" for barely three minutes, whereas the standard practice at most hospitals is to sanitize these instruments for at least fifteen minutes before using them again. I felt sorry for the patients because many of them had walked for dozens of miles to come and get themselves sterilized; they had shown faith, they had responded to the government's call for women with more than five children to obtain tubectomies, and in their long journey there was implicit trust that they would be treated well. Yet most cattle in India receive better treatment than these poor women in the Nandiyal clinic, I thought.

I went up to a small group of women who were starting the trek back to their villages. They were shy and tried to hurry away from me.

"How do you feel?" I said to them, through a translator.

When they heard the local Telugu language, the women stopped.

"I wanted to ask the doctor some questions," one woman, who carried two children on her shoulders, said hesitantly.

"What kind of questions?"

"About how this operation would affect my health and the health of my two children," the woman said.

Another woman broke in.

"But no one bothered to listen to us," the second woman said. "They had us remove our sarees, they did the operation, they put us on the floor. And when we woke up, they told us to go back to our village."

Driving back to Hyderabad, I passed billboard after billboard extolling the virtues of small families, some billboards proclaiming that the "best" services available anywhere in the country were at government-run clinics. It seemed such a hoax to me, such an abuse of trust. If the Nandiyal clinic was in any way typical of what the government was offering, then Mrs. Gandhi's administration would inevitably soon face unpleasant popular resistance to its family-planning program.

Pramila David's clinic in Hyderabad offered a refreshing contrast. It is not a birth control clinic in the strictest sense because what Dr. David has set up here are a number of "follow-up" health care services for women who get themselves sterilized. There is a kindergarten school here, as well as adult education courses, which are virtually free. Mrs. David believes in what she calls "total care."

"I don't see how one can talk about family planning and not talk about the care and welfare of children," she told me in her book-filled office at the Shilpa Clinic. "Emotionally, I hate children being neglected and left to be emaciated. What a sheer waste of human effort it is to produce a baby you cannot afford and then put that baby through terrible traumas. A child requires its parents' time and attention for emotional growth. But in large families among the poor, you see the sheer impossibility of giving enough time to kids. They get neglected. And thus the child gets cranky, and the cranky child becomes the cranky adult. It is a vicious circle, and it starts with the irresponsible act of having more kids than you want or can afford."

Dr. David has produced easy-to-understand brochures on family planning. Her staff members journey to poor neighborhoods and try to persuade women to start practicing birth control and also bring their children to the Shilpa Clinic for medical examination. Mrs. David gives out vitamins and tonics for the children, and often for their mothers, too.

One of her complaints is that few physicians in India go into family-planning work as a full-time profession.

"Although family planning is the big cry of the nation, how many doctors do you find in this business? Ten? A dozen? When you are a physician providing family-planning services, as I am, you feel isolated. The practice of family-planning medicine really has to be a full-time preoccupation, if you want to be honest about it. It cannot be simply a matter of prescribing contraceptives, or occasionally performing a sterilization. There isn't money to be made in family-planning medicine. You therefore have to be motivated, you really must want to be of service to the unfortunate."

As she spoke, a nurse slipped into the office to summon Dr. David to meet her next patient. A woman named Patangi Kumari had brought her three-month-old son for examination. Patangi, a bony, high-cheeked woman who on this day wore a fancy silk saree, was twenty-six years old and already had had three other children. Dr. David persuaded her and Patangi's husband, Laxman, a clerk in a local government office, that four children was enough, considering that Laxman's salary of about ninety dollars a month was hardly sufficient to sustain the family's needs. Patangi obtained a tubectomy at the Shilpa Clinic. I asked Patangi whether she had been afraid of getting herself sterilized.

"Of course," she said in her local language of Telugu, which Dr. David translated. "My neighbors told me that I would go blind if I got sterilized. And my husband was afraid that if he got a vasectomy he would become impotent. I decided I would go ahead and get a tubectomy. My fears were overcome by Dr. David and her staff. They told me I had nothing to worry about, and I trusted them. I am fine. No problems whatsoever since my operation. And I don't feel any different as a person."

Patangi then said her self-confidence and self-esteem had actually increased since the sterilization. The fact that she had now fully controlled her fertility had opened doors for her: she would be not just a mother but an economic producer as well, Patangi decided. Availing herself of free cooking classes at the Shilpa Clinic, Patangi is learning how to make savories that she can sell as tea-time snacks in her neighborhood of Phoolbag Colony.

Later that day, I went by to see Pramila David's husband, Lessell David. He, too, is a physician who has specialized in family-planning matters. Lessell David, a tall, handsome man with a deep voice, some years ago started an acclaimed birth control and maternal care clinic in Allahabad, a populous city in India's northern Uttar Pradesh State. Now he teaches population courses at the Administrative Staff College in Hyderabad, India's equivalent of Harvard's advanced management school. He has gained quite a reputation as India's leading "thinker" on population matters. We discussed the "impact" that thirty years of family-planning programs had had in India.

"The main impact is that family planning as a subject is no longer taboo," Lessell David said. "And family planning as a subject seems to have made people aware of what the possibilities for a better economic and even a better family life are. A lobby for family planning has developed. Besides the fact that family planning is good for the country and for the planet, it has been shown to Indians that family planning is also good for the individual."

A few days after my visit to Hyderabad, I happened to be in the capital city of New Delhi chatting with Dr. J. C. Kavoori, president of the Family Planning Foundation of India. Kavoori, a short, thick-set man, was bundled up in sweaters, and on top of these he wore a thick wool jacket. He consumed cup after cup of richly sweet tea to warm him up, for it was winter in the north and his ground-floor office overlooking a park was unheated (most Delhi offices do not have central heating). Kavoori's nonprofit organization supports many family-planning projects around India, including Pramila David's Shilpa Clinic in Hyderabad.

He was critical of the Indian government's emphasis on sterilization and, indeed, of the government's overall reliance on the contraceptive approach to controlling population growth. "There is no emphasis on innovation," Kavoori said in his raspy voice. What the government should be doing, he suggested, was stepping up its education programs, bringing about cultural and attitudinal changes so that people would want smaller families.

"There should be social changes," Kavoori asserted, adding that the current family-planning programs of the government were much too dominated by India's medical hierarchy, which had a vested interest in promoting sterilization because of the money-making opportunities for physicians.

Kavoori also feels that the country's family-planning programs have been managed poorly, mostly because there was no central organization to direct both the government's efforts and those of a host of private agencies. Thumping his chubby hands on a sheaf of papers, Kavoori urged that a central organization, perhaps a sort of population commission, be established as soon as possible.

Moreover, he said, the Indian government had not used foreign assistance "very wisely." Millions of dollars in foreign assistance that could have been put to use never found its way to field projects because of bureaucratic delays. For example, Pramila David's clinic was given a few thousand dollars five years ago by the United Nations Fund for Population Activities to acquire much-needed medical equipment. She has yet to see a penny of that sum. Her "file" is said to be floating around somewhere in New Delhi's Himalayan government bureaucracy. No foreign grants can be received by indigenous organizations without prior approval of the Indian government, which has never been known to act expeditiously.

It seems to me that if the Indians want to rejuvenate their family-planning programs and bring about a drastic nationwide reduction in birthrates, they will need an efficient central mechanism to ride herd. I would suggest an independent quasi-governmental body rather than just another layer of bureaucracy. Around the time I met Kavoori, Prime Minister Indira Gandhi was interviewed by the editor of *People* magazine, the publication of the London-based International Planned Parenthood Federation. The editor, a veteran journalist named John Rowley, asked Mrs. Gandhi whether she favored the idea of a population commission that would coordinate various population control efforts in India.

"I am not too keen on coordinating bodies," the prime minister said.

Rowley persisted: "You have ruled out the idea of a population commission?"

"It is not ruled out," Mrs. Gandhi said. "It is possible to have something of this sort, but how much will it be able to coordinate? Or will it become just one more organization which has to be coordinated with others?"

When people talk about "population," they usually are referring to birthrates and death rates. In India, the world's biggest democracy, a high annual population growth figure is of course a major problem. An equally intractable problem is high unemployment, especially among university graduates. Hundreds of these graduates go abroad each year for higher studies. Many of them do not return home—not because they don't want to but because they cannot find the jobs they desire. Educators, politicians, and industrialists all express concern over the "brain drain." But there has been no serious effort made to attract back to India its skilled sons and daughters who settle overseas. Some of these emigres probably would not want to return home anyway; some have tried to resettle themselves in India but found the bureaucracy too daunting, and they soon fled back to the West. In India, overpopulation translates into a scrambling for too few decent jobs by too many qualified applicants.

Fifteen years ago, a young man named Naresh Trehan decided to leave this scene. Fresh out of medical school, he left his native New Delhi for postgraduate studies in the United States. He became a topflight cardiovascular surgeon in New York, but instead of living happily ever after on his annual six-figure income, Trehan resolved to return home and practice social medicine. Reversing the traditional "brain drain" that has resulted in the emigration of thousands of Indian physicians to a more affluent life in the West, Trehan has already brought back home with him a dozen other doctors who had settled in the United States.

These youthful physicians are starting what is the most comprehensive heart institute in the Third World and one of the most modern hospitals anywhere, a prototype of a medical institution for developing countries that is focusing not only on treating local patients who cannot afford medical care abroad but also on research into the special conditions in poor countries that cause or exacerbate certain kinds of diseases. The New Delhi facility is being called the Escorts Heart Institute—named after the Indian corporation that is giving Trehan millions of dollars to launch the facility—and it represents an unusual arrangement between a Third World institution and one from the West. When Trehan finally leaves New York, he will not sever all ties with his hospital, the New York University Medical Center, but will continue working there and in India, a plan under which staff members from the New Delhi heart center will be able to fly to New York for free training and refresher courses.

Moreover, physicians from the New York hospital, which has one of the best facilities in the world for cardiac surgery, have also agreed to travel to New Delhi to perform surgery at Trehan's new heart center and to instruct medical students. The New Yorkers' efforts are being donated. And each of the Indian physicians whom Trehan brings back home with him is selected on the condition that he will give half his time free to the heart institute. Through such arrangements, the heart institute will be able to provide medical care virtually free of charge to the 50,000 patients who are using its services.

"Most of the Indian doctors I know in the United States would love to return to their homeland if the right opportunity came along," Trehan, a handsome, wiry man with a bushy mustache, told me. "Like myself, most of these doctors have reached a point in their professional lives where they don't have to worry about making a living. They are successful, and they are financially well off. Our concern is more about whether top-rate medical facilities are available in India and whether we can get to practice the kind of medicine we want."

Trehan was approached by several hospitals and medical schools in India to join their staffs.

"I concluded, however, that if one wanted to do anything significant in cardiac medicine in India you'd have to start from scratch," Trehan said. "There's a fifteen- to twenty-year gap between available medical technology in India and the kind of sophisticated medicine I am accustomed to in New York. I felt it would be impossible to bridge this gap if I went to existing institutions. I'd not only need new technology in India, I'd need to foster new institutional discipline. So if I was to make the move back to India and do these things, then why not in a brand-new institution altogether, one that I could shape from the very start?"

The offers to return home also coincided with a time in Trehan's life when he felt his two infant daughters should grow up in their own culture. And as sometimes happens in the case of those who leave poor countries and make good in rich ones, he felt that he owed some sort of debt to the country and culture where he was born. This sentiment gathered strength each time Trehan made a trip to India.

Trehan started visiting India as often as he could. His medical practice in New York, meanwhile, was burgeoning. By 1982, he'd performed more than 3,000 open heart operations, many of them on affluent Indians who would fly over to the United States specially to be treated by Dr. Trehan and who could afford the $30,000 that such surgery cost. He joined hands with his friend Parvez Ahmed, a cardiologist in New York, in exploring the possibility of starting a heart clinic of their own in India. They have worked closely since and will share responsibility for running the facility.

The two young doctors found that India had a comprehensive primary health care network. There were government-sponsored clinics in virtually each of India's 550,000 villages. Very few of these clinics were more than dispensaries, however. Still, it was clear that the millions of dollars that the Indian government had spent since independence from the British in 1947 on health care had resulted in a system where any Indian needing elementary medical attention could be assisted within a few miles of his home.

But that did not mean that sophisticated medicine was widely available. Most of the large hospitals were either run or subsidized by the government; senior physicians drew salaries of at most 3,000 rupees a month, or roughly $300. With no incentives worth mentioning, the government was failing to attract into public service physicians and medical technicians who could conceivably have improved the public health system. There were too few state-of-the art facilities in specialized medicine, Trehan and Ahmed found.

For example, the Indian government had officially determined that cardiac medicine as practiced in the country was not yet up to par with world standards, and so the government allowed anyone wishing to obtain heart surgery legally to take up to $30,000 per person out of the country for medical expenses. Trehan discovered that 2,000 persons availed themselves annually of such an opportunity; thus, through these individuals, India was sending out almost $60 million of its scarce foreign exchange for heart surgery to be performed abroad. In addition to this money was at least as much going out in illegal transactions, as wealthy heart patients bought hard currency at black market rates to ensure their upkeep and other expenses while abroad.

"It was a sad irony—Indians spending vast amounts to travel

abroad to have surgery done on them by other Indians!" Trehan said.

During a professional visit to Greece, he was invited to lecture at a cardiology center in Athens. Trehan was impressed with the fact that the facility was run efficiently by indigenous surgeons and other medical personnel. If it could be done in Greece, he said to himself, why not in India?

So he discussed the idea of a heart hospital with friends and business acquaintances in his native New Delhi. Hari Nanda, chairman of a large corporation called Escorts, offered to donate some of the $20 million that Trehan estimated a new facility would require. Trehan persuaded other businessmen that the private sector should play a key role in introducing sophisticated medical care for India's teeming millions. He argued at scores of meetings with potential donors that heart disease was now 99 percent curable or treatable but that in a country like India, where cardiac facilities were poor, the disease was claiming more lives than it should—and also was affecting economic productivity because heart disease resulted, too, in preventable disabilities and morbidity.

Trehan told these businessmen and industrialists that the private sector could supplement the role of the government in providing medical care; it could finance the purchase of modern equipment; it could subsidize medical facilities so that Indians could avail themselves of sophisticated treatment and not have to pay through the nose. The present system had resulted in gross inequalities, Trehan would tell his audiences, because only the rich could afford to travel abroad for heart surgery, while the majority of Indians with heart problems stayed home, suffered, and sometimes died. In short, Trehan said, here was an opportunity for both philanthropy and public service. He would commit himself to returning to New Delhi to supervise a new heart institute personally, Trehan said.

The funds began to flow in. The Indian government donated a plot of land in New Delhi for the hospital. The New York-based filmmakers Ismail Merchant and James Ivory gave Trehan's project the entire proceeds of a special screening of their 1983 movie, *Heat and Dust,* which was based on Ruth Prawer Jhabvala's novel of India.

Returning home is a courageous move for Trehan. It means shifting homes; it means adjusting to a whole new bureaucratic mind-set; it means saying farewell to American friends and neighbors of more than fifteen years; it means giving up a wonderfully lucrative medical practice. Some of Trehan's Third World acquaintances in New York were surprised when they heard he would be moving back to India. Some of their comments: You could never live in India again after such a comfortable life in America. You will never make as much money in India as you did in New York. You will be worn down by the bureaucratic hassles in your native country.

But Naresh Trehan and his wife Madhu, who is a writer, resolved that nothing would stop them. Perhaps Trehan is being innocently optimistic. But what impressed me about his move was how carefully he'd studied the logistics of the medical and bureaucratic situation in India, how he had plotted every move so as not to be surprised or sabotaged.

Trehan to me is a trailblazer. He is convinced that the sophisticated technology of his heart institute can be tapped by the general medical system in India, that there will soon be numerous spinoffs for various other areas of specialized medicine. Eventually—and within Naresh Trehan's lifetime—what he is doing is bound to have a salutory impact on health care for India's overwhelmingly poor population. One man's dream may be able to accomplish what millions of dollars of government expenditure hasn't.

* * *

Varindra Tarzie Vittachi, the most famous writer and editor that Sri Lanka has produced, is fond of saying that the world's population "problem" will be solved in the human mind and not in the uterus. He tells an anecdote that involved himself and a legendary figure, a population hard hat who for many years was part of the American population-experts scene.

According to Vittachi, this man once told him that the way to solve the overpopulation situation in the Third World was to insert intrauterine devices in 2 billion women.

"But how are you going to get these women to lift their skirts and sarees for you?" Vittachi asked the American expert.

The point that Vittachi was trying to make was that in order to bring about any significant change in the population situation there would first have to be a change in attitudes of people around the world.

"We're talking about a revolution first in the minds of people," Vittachi says. "You have to motivate people. You have to persuade people that if they accept birth control there is a personal profit in it for them."

To persuade people to accept birth control, Sri Lanka embarked on a nationwide scheme to educate its women—not only educate them in the conventional sense through literacy programs but also provide them with information regarding family planning. The Sri Lankans raised the consciousness of their women about having smaller families. It was shown how smaller families meant happier families and healthier families.

This educational effort made Sri Lanka's women want to go and sign up as birth control practitioners. So successful was this effort that other Asian countries started emulating it. One of these countries is Indonesia, an archipelago of more than 13,500 islands and the world's fifth most populous nation. Through the promotion of literacy, a stepped-up system of contraceptive distribution in villages, and the co-opting of traditional village chieftains for the national birth control cause, Indonesia has, in the last ten years, slashed its annual population growth rate from 3.5 percent to 2.1 percent—a remarkable feat for any country, but particularly one as crowded and congested as Indonesia.

* * *

As the huge Garuda Indonesian Airways jet broke through a dense cloud cover and eased down toward Surabaya, what came into view was a vast landscape of paddy fields, coconut groves, and fruit farms. Here and there narrow dirt roads traversed the rich green countryside. Few people seemed to be around and about. The maddeningly crowded capital of Jakarta was 600 miles behind to the west, behind a range of oddly shaped mountains, and here I was in the coastal plains of East Java.

The tranquility was deceptive, as I found out after landing at Surabaya's antiquated airport. This part of the island of East Java is among the most thickly populated areas of this Southeast Asian nation, with a density of 7,000 persons per square kilometer. Surabaya, which seems suddenly to pounce on you as you drive out of the airport, has some 2 million people.

I was received at the airport by two local officials of the Indonesian government's national population agency, the BKKBN, which stands for Badan Koordinasi Keluarga Berencana Nasional. They did not speak much English, but they smiled a lot, and whenever our Nissan land rover passed by a family-planning billboard, one of them would get quite animated.

"Lookee!" one official would say.

"Yes, you lookee! Good!" the other man would add.

There were many such family-planning billboards between the airport and the outskirts of Surabaya. My neck grew stiff from looking. The airport was located in a predominantly rural area, but as we approached Surabaya, the billboards changed character: in the countryside, they were about health care and birth control; near the city they mostly advertised Japanese radios and television sets.

I thought we were headed for a hotel, but the BKKBN officials took me first to their local headquarters, a compact, two-story building, where I was introduced to their boss. He was a short, bald, pot-bellied man who wore a brown safari suit. His trousers were so low-slung, it was a wonder they stayed up. He was, like many Indonesians, a man with a one-word name—in his case, the name was Widjanarko—and he had a two-word title—population chief. His office had an assortment of trophies and medals displayed in glass cabinets; Widjanarko explained that the awards were accumulated by fieldworkers attached to his office.

"Welcome to our humble quarters!" Widjanarko said. "We will now at once show you what life is really like in this part of Indonesia!"

Before I could suggest that I would have preferred first checking into a local hotel, Widjanarko pushed me into a waiting jeep, and we dashed off for a quick tour of the city. Widjanarko talked without pause, even as he drove like a maniac. Surabaya, he said, had lagged behind other parts of Indonesia in population control. This was partly because Indonesia, unlike some Third World states, decided a decade ago that it would first focus on controlling the burgeoning population rate in rural areas, where more than 87 percent of the country's 154 million people live. It was only in recent months that the authorities had stepped up their population control campaign in the nation's major cities, such as Surabaya. Now big billboards urge citizens to have smaller families; buses carry posters concerning family planning; volunteers scurry through neighborhoods and offer counsel on birth control. The local government, through Widjanarko's office, makes available to the populace a variety of contraceptives.

"There is great demand for contraceptives—for condoms and pills and IUDs," Widjanarko said in his nasal accent, which seemed to me a poor imitation of an American twang. As a result, the annual population growth rate in Surabaya had declined from 4.4 percent in 1975 to 2.3 percent in 1983.

"But our death rate is also falling—down to 1.1 percent annually

United Nations, from various Indonesian foundations, and from individual contributions. Patients are not charged fees—they couldn't afford to pay anyway. Particular emphasis is put on inoculating children and on ensuring that their parents give them vitamins and proper nutrition. This clinic, Tiarkoesbandi told me, introduced the concept of postnatal follow-up care to the neighborhood. I walked around the clinic, accompanied by Tiarkoesbandi; my companion Widjanarko was chatting with some pretty nurses. In one ward, a dozen women lay in beds: they had delivered babies, who were in another room.

Tiarkoesbandi took me to the operating room. I was asked to put on a surgical gown. Inside, a woman named Sumiati had just given birth to her second son. I expected her to be groggy, but she seemed surprisingly alert and in good humor.

"Tell the gentleman what you told us earlier," Tiarkoesbandi said to Sumiati.

Sumiati smiled.

"This is my last child," she said. "No more. Two is plenty."

Tiarkoesbandi told me later that Sumiati had asked for advice about sterilization and that she would probably have an operation soon. Sumiati's husband, Masduki, was waiting in an anteroom. He hadn't even seen his newborn son, so we again went into the area where Sumiati lay. Masduki greeted Sumiati in a subdued fashion (I thought that Indonesians were a strangely phlegmatic people; even the birth of a child did not seem to elicit a full flow of sentiment from men!). He held the newborn child.

"What is your name?" Masduki, a thin, hollow-cheeked man, asked me.

I told him.

"Well, then, I will name him after you. This will bring the boy good luck in life."

I was touched. I told Masduki that Sumiati had resolved not to have more children. Did that bother him?

"I am a poor tailor," Masduki said. "I have trouble as it is in providing for my family."

That evening, Widjanarko took me to a *kampong* meeting. A *kampong* is a neighborhood, and the Indonesian government has a program under which the head of the neighborhood council, an official known as the *bupati,* has the responsibility to promote the concept of birth control in his area. Because the *bupati* is usually a man with considerable influence and a good reputation, his suggestions to neighborhood residents serve, in effect, as directives. The Indonesians had pioneered this business of co-opting neighborhood civic leaders in the cause of family planning, and I was curious to see how the system worked.

This *kampong* was called Wonorjo, and it seemed only slightly more prosperous than Rumah. The homes here were mostly one-story cottages. Transistors and radio sets blared music. The roads were rutted. Children scampered across streets. The smells of cooking were in the air.

We stopped at a community center. It consisted of a large hall covered with a corrugated tin roof; inside were dozens of chairs and a wooden table. The walls had the ubiquitous family-planning posters. The *bupati,* a mean-looking man named Llyas Mardiyanto, was haranguing a group of people when we walked in.

"I keep telling you—we cannot let recruitment fall," Mardiyanto was saying, according to Widjanarko, who translated the Indonesian dialect for me. "We are in no position to slacken our efforts. So go out there and give out those condoms and pills."

His audience consisted of local family-planning volunteers. Each week, Mardiyanto gives them pep talks and also a supply of contraceptives for distribution in the neighborhood. Each volunteer gets a quota concerning how many new birth control acceptors he or she should enlist. In 1971, when Mardiyanto started this system in Wonorjo, his volunters signed up 100 such acceptors; in 1983, the target was 500. Nationwide, the Suharto government wants to bring down the annual birthrate to 23 per 1,000 by 1990, compared to 34 per 1,000 now. This means that 68 percent of Indonesian women of married status and in reproductive age need to sign up as birth control practitioners, compared to only 40 percent, or barely 9.5 million women, at the present time. By 1990, the number of married women who are likely to bear children will increase from 23 million to 30 million.

Mardiyanto has three children, and he and his wife have practiced birth control for the last twelve years. He works in the navy yard in Surabaya. Every evening, he told me, he makes the rounds of his neighborhood. This evening, he asked me along.

We walked to the home of a woman named Kasiyatati. She has five children, and her husband, a carpenter, does not want her to practice birth control. Kasiyatati offered us tea as she talked. Her husband was not at home. Her children were playing outside. Home was a one-room cottage, but Kasiyatati had maintained it neatly. There were photographs of her family, and there was a color picture of President Suharto. There was a well-worn sofa at one end of the room and a large bed at the other end. Toys were stacked on a crate.

"Why does your husband object to birth control?" I asked Kasiyatati.

"He feels it will injure my health," she said.

"Do you share that concern?"

"Of course not! I don't want any more children."

Mardiyanto said he would discuss the situation again with her husband, who had made it a practice to disappear conveniently whenever any family-planning volunteer approached his home. I sensed in Mardiyanto a determination to "convert" Kasiyatati. After all, her husband's resistance to birth control constituted a challenge to Mardiyanto's authority as the local *bupati,* did it not?

Six

Sri Lanka
Ethnic Woes and an Endangered Gem

SRI LANKA, a gem of an island in the Indian Ocean, is generally thought of as a model of political development in the Third World. Here is a country that has managed to maintain its democratic structure for almost fifty years. Several peaceful transfers of power have taken place in the aftermath of vigorously fought elections contested by a plethora of parties. Democratic practices have been deeply imbedded in the political climate of the country. In many poverty-ridden states of the Third World there is a tendency for dictatorships to spring up; not so in Sri Lanka.

While Sri Lanka was reinforcing its democratic traditions, Sri Lankans were busy procreating. The island-nation's population growth far outpaced its economic production. Successive governments found themselves spending more and more on free education and free medical care and food subsidies, all of which were guaranteed under Sri Lanka's social services system since independence from the British in 1948. In the early 1960s, the International Monetary Fund, alarmed at Sri Lanka's economic decline, urged the government to discontinue its free education policy (all education is free, even at medical and law schools). Sri Lankan officials refused to acquiesce, saying that the government could not afford not to give free education to all!

Successive Sri Lankan governments were confronted with a growing population problem: the island's population was getting younger and younger, which meant that unless strong family-planning measures and programs were instituted, pressures for more jobs and more education were likely to become intolerable. (Today, for example, there are 1 million unemployed Sri Lankans out of a total national population of 15 million. The social, economic, and political implications of this situation are horrendous.)

Sometime in the mid-1970s, a major change occurred in Sri Lanka: people started having smaller families. Perhaps this was the result of a nationwide family-planning program; perhaps it was because of accelerated literacy drives; perhaps it was because more and more women were being educated and given jobs. Varindra Tarzie Vittachi, Sri Lanka's renowned writer, not long ago took along an American filmmaker friend named Thomas Craven to see why attitudinal changes had occurred to bring about a slowing down of the country's previously high annual population growth rate. The two men traveled to a hamlet called Galnawa, not far from the ancient capital of Anuradhapura.

Galnawa is part of a region called the "H Area," which is part of an ambitious plan to promote agriculture on thousands of acres of land nourished by the new $6 billion Mahaveli River dam project. Where once there was mostly dry land, the area around Galnawa now has richly green vegetation. Local peasants are prospering. Schools, health clinics, family-planning centers, and day-care facilities for children have been built all over the area.

Vittachi and Craven toured the place and one afternoon met a group of farmers in Galnawa's community center, a modest one-story brick building with a garden in front and a playground in the rear.

"Who here has had a vasectomy?" Vittachi asked in Sinhala, the language of Sri Lanka's majority ethnic group, the Sinhalese.

"I have!" said a man who appeared to be about thirty-two years old.

"How many children do you have?"

"My wife and I have three children—two girls and a baby boy."

"When did you get a vasectomy?"

"Soon after the boy was born."

"Weren't you afraid that if the boy died then you'd not have a son left?"

"Oh, but we have—" the peasant said. Then he stopped and looked at Vittachi.

"Oh, I see what you mean, sir," he continued, with a suggestion of a smile. "But that was a problem during my father's time. He was afraid that I, his only son, would die. So he and my mother kept having more and more children. Some of these girls died, so my parents kept producing more children in the hope of having a second son. But you see, in our time I am fairly sure that my children have a very good chance of surviving in good health, especially because of the new health care clinics we have in the area."

"Aren't you sad that you will never be able to produce another child?" Vittachi then asked the peasant.

"No, sir! Each peasant in this area has been given only two and a half acres for cultivation by the government. These acres that I have cannot support more than three children."

"Why didn't you ask your wife to get a tubectomy?" Vittachi said.

"My wife and I discussed this. But we decided that it would be easier for me to get a vasectomy, especially because she is so frail."

Two things are striking about the above exchange. This particular peasant had overcome the "son syndrome" that characterizes many Third World societies, where sons are valued more than daughters. Implicit in this man's comments to Tarzie Vittachi was a recognition that daughters were as economically valuable as male progeny. And the very fact that a Sinhalese man was able to discuss sexual matters with his wife openly was in itself a breakthrough in social relations; in many Third World societies, men and women do not exchange views on sexuality because to do so is considered improper. That the Galnawa peasant was able to talk to his wife openly about a complicated matter such as sterilization was a reflection of the fact that both he and his wife had gone to school and received diplomas. In their case, education—for which they paid nothing—had "liberated" their minds; education had made it possible for both to understand what sterilization was; education had changed their basic attitudes about the economic worth of their children.

Over the years, free education was even more important for Sri Lanka's minority Tamils. Concentrated mostly in the dry zones of northern Sri Lanka, the Tamils had the misfortune to live on land that was the most sparsely vegetated in the country. There were no lucrative tea plantations here, as there were elsewhere on the island; agriculture was negligible because of the poor quality of the soil. The main resource for human growth in most Third World societies is either land or the brain. The land in northern Sri Lanka was an inadequate resources—and so the main resource for the Tamils became the brain.

They educated their children so well that Tamils quickly became dominant in the nation's bureaucracies, in government, in the commercial world, in diplomacy. They also quickly attracted the animosity and resentment of the majority Sinhalese. Responding to Sinhalese calls for some sort of political action to "redress the balance," then Prime Minister Srimavo Bandaranaike instituted an unusual affirmative action program in the nation's institutions of higher learning. What this translated into was a restriction on the numbers of Tamils who could attend Sri Lankan universities; preference was given to Sinhalese applicants. It was a cynical, short-sighted move on Mrs. Bandaranaike's part, and it spawned frightening social tensions in Sri Lanka. Hordes of young Tamils left the country to study and settle in the United States, Canada, and Western Europe, depriving Sri Lanka of a rich source of brain power. Eventually, President Junius Richard Jayewardene rescinded Mrs. Bandaranaike's directive. The affirmative action plan is gone now, but Tamil–Sinhalese tensions remain to haunt this beautiful island state.

Early on the morning of Saturday, July 23, 1983, Lieutenant Waas Gunawardana of the Sri Lankan army gathered fourteen soldiers under his command in the northern town of Thinnaveli, jumped aboard an ancient army truck with them, and set out on a routine patrol. The day was hot and muggy, like most days in this part of the country, and as their vehicle rattled along the rutted roads of Jaffna District the men chatted and joked. Someone asked Lieutenant Gunawardana how soon it would be before he made it onto Sri Lanka's cricket team, for the twenty-two-year-old officer had distinguished himself at Nalanda College in that sport and was thought by many people in his native Colombo as possessing the potential to play for his country.

The truck was suddenly rocked by an explosion. The vehicle toppled over to one side, and before Gunawardana and his men could spring out, armed guerrillas hurled hand grenades at them and opened up with semiautomatic rifles. Within minutes, thirteen Sinhalese soldiers had died. Within hours, responsibility for the attack was claimed by a group calling itself the Tigers of Tamil Eelaam, a terrorist organization that has demanded a separate northern state for Sri Lanka's Tamils, who constitute just under 13 percent of the country's overall population of 15 million. Within days, as the news of the massacre spread, the tiny, pear-shaped, Indian Ocean island-state was convulsed by its worst racial riots.

Hundreds of Tamils and Sinhalese died; property damage amounted to tens of millions of dollars. Tourist traffic, which had flowed to Sri Lanka from Europe and which had been fairly heavy until the July disturbances, came to a halt. Factories stopped production; shops were closed down; curfews were imposed in the capital city of Colombo and elsewhere. Censorship was imposed, too. The democratic government of President Junius Richard Jayewardene—considered by the West and particularly by the Reagan administration as an ally—found itself in a state of siege, with the seventy-seven-year-old Jayewardene's own hard-won popularity in doubt and a big question mark over the future of the country itself. As a result of the carnage and violence, a central question presented itself: In what form would Sri Lanka survive? Jayewardene, a wily and canny politician, spiritedly embarked on a program of national reconciliation and reconstruction, but for months after the events of July 1983 questions and doubts persisted about the country's ability to hold itself together as a viable national entity. There was particular concern among Western leaders like Ronald Reagan, whose administration had given Sri Lanka more economic assistance per person than to any other country in Asia and who had heaped praise on the free market orientation of Jayewardene's development policies.

Those policies had resulted in one of the Third World's few authentic success stories. In less than a decade, Sri Lanka brought down its annual population growth rate from nearly 3 percent to less than 1.7 percent. It lowered its infant mortality rate from 140 babies per 1,000 in 1945 to 38 per 1,000 by 1980. A measure of such an achievement is the fact that Sri Lanka's infant mortality rate is one-third that of Africa's and less than half that of the rest of Asia. (The rate is 20 per 1,000 in Western Europe and North America, 45 in China, 108 in most parts of the Third World. In certain countries like Afghanistan and Cambodia, the annual infant mortality rate is well over 250 per 1,000.) Sri Lanka, under Jayewardene, sustained such an achievement by accelerating the construction of schools and promoting free education, building clinics and hospitals, offering free health care, and embarking on a stepped-up program of training midwives and nurses. It began importing physicians from other developing countries like the Philippines, India, Malaysia, and Bangladesh.

Sri Lanka demonstrated conclusively the connection between population growth and social development. It showed, over the last decade, that even poor and rural populations, traditionally among the most conservative groups, will change their fertility pattern and behavior under the right conditions, which is to say that smaller families are the consequence of a proper level of social development: adequate nutrition, health, education, housing, and employment, particularly jobs for women. Elsewhere in Asia, intense urbanization has been a problem as peasants drift to cities in search of a livelihood; elsewhere in Asia, and indeed in much of the Third World, essential services like schools, good clinics, banks, and proper housing are available mostly in towns and cities, a fact that contributes to the emigration of peasants to urban areas, making such areas disastrously overcrowded. But in Sri Lanka, essential services have been provided in the countryside so that, actually, cities such as the capital of Colombo have been growing smaller rather than bigger. Sri Lankans live longer than most Asians, eat better, seem happier generally. The average Sri Lankan woman now has four children; in neighboring India, women average five births each; in Bangladesh, the figure is six children per woman and seven in Pakistan. A drive has been on to popularize the concept of a two-child family, which seemed to be catching on.

On the surface, then, things seemed to be moving along nicely indeed for Jayewardene. In October 1982, he was reelected to a second six-year term, and his United National party was subsequently given a huge majority in Parliament to August 1989. When I interviewed the president, he appeared ebullient. He had a clear endorsement of his economic policies from the people, who, after years of deprivation under a previous socialist regime, now found their shops stocked with consumer goods, food plentifully available, and wages on the rise. But ethnic tensions among the majority Sinhalese and minority Tamils had been also simmering under the surface, and the ambush on July 23, 1983, brought the tensions to a boil. At the root of the ethnic conflict lay a simple, central point: when a minority community perceives that economic and social development is passing it by, it will agitate. In Sri Lanka, which had been considered a model of economic development, the danger is that such violent agitation will permanently undo the gains of recent years. That is why it is necessary to understand this ethnic conflict. The implications of Sri Lanka's ethnic problems extend beyond this country's borders to other Asian and Third World states: places like Malaysia, Indonesia, Bangladesh, Burma, and India, which have large and traditionally disaffected minorities, could find themselves suffering from identical economic setbacks if the ethnic situation within their own borders worsens. And if Jayewardene, the Sinhalese establishment, and the Tamils are able to fashion some formula through which a lasting amity between the Sinhalese and the Tamils is achieved, then perhaps Sri Lanka's efforts could well serve as a model for other countries. From my many talks with Jayewardene, I came away with the feeling that he would like as his legacy not only social and economic progress for Sri Lankans but a resolution of the country's longstanding ethnic discords.

According to government statistics, Sri Lanka has 7 million Sinhalese, 1.2 million "native" Tamils, 700,000 Moslems, 40,000 Malays and other minor ethnic community persons, and 625,000 Tamils of recent Indian origin, the so-called stateless Indians, who work primarily in the lush tea plantations of central Sri Lanka. The Sinhalese are overwhelmingly Buddhist, while the Tamils are mostly Hindus. The Sinhalese are believed to have migrated to what is now called Sri Lanka more than 2,500 years ago from regions that now are parts of Bihar and West Bengal states in India. Joining them in the journey across the twenty-eight-mile-wide Palk Straits separating India and Sri Lanka were the first Tamil migrants, who settled down in the northern part of the island around what is today Jaffna Province. With the arrival of Buddhism from India around 240 B.C., Sinhalese civilization flowered and Buddhism spread rapidly, but the Tamils clung to their Hinduism. Settlers continued coming from India, bringing with them religious and cultural influences that have deeply affected the island. With such arrivals came discords and internecine conflicts in the north. Successive waves of invaders from India overcame the proud and highly developed cities that thrived in the north, and Sinhalese rule was slowly driven southward. During Roman times, Sri Lanka was known as Taprobane, a name used by Ptolemy—Taprobane from *thambapanni,* meaning copper-colored sand. Local rulers supposedly exchanged envoys with the Caesars. Arab traders and sailors called it Serendib, the root of the English word *serendipity.* The ancient name *Sri Lanka* could not be properly pronounced by the Europeans, who called the island Zeilan and, later, Ceylon. Marco Polo was a visitor in the thirteenth century, and the Moslem traveler Ibn Batuta came here in the fourteenth century. The Chinese monk Fa Hsien found the island so appealing that he stayed for two years. In the early sixteenth century, the Portuguese arrived, attracted by the prospect of a flourishing trade in cinnamon and other spices, and they seized some of the coastal areas. They also introduced Christianity. In 1658, the Portuguese were forced out by the Dutch, who themselves were thrown out by the British in 1796. By 1815, Ceylon was a crown colony.

It was the British who created a plantation economy based on tea, rubber, and coconuts. They opened roads and railways, they introduced the English language, and they created an elite native class that strived to emulate its colonial rulers. In 1931, the British established universal franchise, along with limited self-government, and on February 4, 1948, the island became a fully independent member of the British Commonwealth. Postindependence politics were pretty much dominated by two major parties, the United National party and the leftist-oriented Sri Lanka Freedom party. Sometimes one was in power, sometimes the other. A change in the country's Constitution in 1972 saw Ceylon become Sri Lanka, the ancient Sinhalese name for the island. (Sri Lankan tea, however, continues to be marketed as Ceylon tea in order to preserve consumer identification.)

I first visited Sri Lanka late in 1982 to attend a United Nations conference on Asian population concerns. It was one of those situations where a person living in the neighborhood of the Empire State Building doesn't summon the energy to ride an elevator to its top. Growing up in the Indian metropolis of Bombay—barely two hours by plane from Colombo—I had met several Sri Lankans, mostly merchants and diplomats. Through them, and through books and films, I knew that Sri Lanka was a lovely land, that its people were gentle and hospitable, and that they welcomed visitors.

The first impression a visitor has is how green the whole place is, how very lush with foliage, coconut trees, and miles and miles of rice paddies. Some Indian friends had warned me that Sri Lankans were not particularly well disposed toward Indians because of their conviction that India would like nothing better than for Sri Lanka to be bifurcated, the northern part being given to the Tamil separatists, who have received succor and financial support in the southern Indian state of Tamil Nadu. In the event, such warnings proved unwarranted and gratuitous. I encountered no personal hostility on that first visit, just as my subsequent trips have not turned up personal or ethnic resistance to me. Nonetheless, any visitor who bothers to look around quickly comes to the conclusion that at the heart of the Sri Lankan sensibility is the Tamil question, and to understand what this meant I traveled up north to Jaffna.

I boarded a small, two-engined aircraft operated by Upali Airways. The pilot was a Tamil, and so were the four other passengers. The plane flew so slowly and so low over land that I might as well have been in an automobile. The landscape changed dramatically as we approached Jaffna District, one of twenty-four in Sri Lanka: the lush green fields of southern and central Sri Lanka gave way to arid, desertlike terrain, then once more there appeared dabs of greenery and coconut groves. The lagoons that dot the Jaffna area do not much nourish the land. The beaches here are pebbly, not sandy as in the south, so few tourists come here. Jaffna itself is a languid, leisurely town of some 200,000 people, who fish, trade, and farm for a living. Few Buddhist shrines can be seen here, but ornate Hindu temples are everywhere, their bells incessantly tolling, strong incense wafting from copper containers, bald, pigtailed priests feverishly chanting hymns. On the narrow roads that wind through mango orchards and coconut plantations, bicyclists and motorists perform complicated maneuvers around potholes. Most cars here are jalopies spewing out acrid fumes, which sour the otherwise clean, salty air here.

Sinhalese people are strangers here, and the soldiers one sees—virtually everyone in Sri Lanka's 17,000-man military is Sinhalese—do not mix with the Tamils. Strangers, too, are the Indian "stateless" Tamils who were brought to Sri Lanka by the British to work on tea plantations in the hilly, central part of the island. (These Indian Tamils, who do not enjoy citizenship rights in Sri Lanka, live mostly around Colombo and around Kalutara, Kandy, Matale, Nuwara Eliya, Badulla, Ratnapura, and Kegalle, traditionally areas where tea and rubber are grown and where Sinhalese are in the majority. So far the Indian Tamils haven't agitated for separatism, although their economic plight is considerably worse than that of the better-educated Jaffna Tamils.)

I went to have lunch with Vettilvelu Yogeswaran, a man in his early forties. Until late October 1983, Yogeswaran, a member of a moderate party known as the Tamil United Liberation Front (TULF), was one of twenty-one Tamils elected to Sri Lanka's 168-member national parliament. After the July riots, President Jayewardene's government amended the Constitution to forbid any advocacy of secession, and because the sixteen TULF parliamentarians refused to take an oath against secession, they lost their seats. Despite its radical name, the TULF generally favors not total separatism but some form of regional autonomy for the Tamil areas of Jaffna and the northeastern coast. Yogeswaran, a first-class raconteur who speaks in a sing-song, accented English, made it plain to me that Jaffna Tamils considered themselves second-class citizens of Sri Lanka. He shares the general view here that the economic boom of the Jayewardene years hadn't benefited most Tamils.

"Our basic mistake was not to ask for independence when the British left in 1948," Yogeswaran said, as his wife served us a delicious hot lunch of vegetarian curries and soft, fluffy rice mixed with yogurt. "I feel that it is clear that the union between the Tamil and Sinhalese areas is not working. There is mutual distrust that will not go away. It's too late to bring about any kind of reconciliation now. Can a separatist Tamil state exist? We think so. We are already self-sufficient in food, and we only depend for our electricity on the south. I'm very, very pessimistic for the continuation of this union with the Sinhalese. I am afraid that the violence and instability are going to be so great that Jayewardene's development plans will be torn asunder."

Yogeswaran himself has been a victim of communal violence: some years ago, during friction between local Tamils and Sinhalese soldiers, his house was burned down, as was the Tamil library here, which housed priceless old manuscripts of Tamil history. Jaffna Tamils told me that since Sri Lanka obtained independence from the British in 1948, majority Sinhalese have attacked Tamil communities in 1956 and 1958 and five times since Jayewardene took office in 1977. Of course, both sides blame each other for starting communal disturbances. The Sinhalese say that Tamil terrorists, operating under the direction of five or six guerrilla groups, have killed more than a hundred Sinhalese in the last decade. (The guerrillas appear particularly adept at raiding police stations in the Jaffna area; they usually make off with rifles and ammunition from these buildings. In May this year, the terrorists kidnapped two Americans but released them unharmed after an unsuccessful attempt at extracting a huge ransom from the Jayewardene government.)

Yogeswaran pointed out that although historically the Tamils and Sinhalese always lived in an uneasy peace, what is these days called the "Tamil problem" really started in 1956, when then Prime Minister S.W.R.D. Bandaranaike (husband of future Prime Minister Srimavo Bandaranaike) fulfilled a campaign promise and made Sinhala the official language. When this happened, it was also stipulated that all government job seekers had to be proficient in that language (English had been the main language until then) and those already employed in government and state-run agencies had to learn Sinhala within a certain period. As a result, say Tamil leaders, the Tamils' share of government jobs dropped from more than 40 percent to 10 percent over the next two decades, while in the private sector their share fell from 35 percent to 15 percent. Some Sinhalese argued, however, that the Tamils—perhaps because of their community's traditionally greater literacy rate—held a disproportionate percentage of jobs in relation to their numbers.

To this day, Tamil leaders like Yogeswaran believe firmly that the 1956 decision to make Sinhala the official language not only dramatically reduced economic opportunities for the Tamils, it also reduced their educational opportunities because one consequence of the decision was that more Sinhalese and fewer Tamil students were admitted to Sri Lankan universities. To be sure, on paper at least educational opportunities were there for everybody, Sinhalese and Tamils alike. But the Colombo government's insistence on Sinhala as the official language quickly froze Tamils out of the national mainstream. Bandaranaike's decision was motivated by political opportunism, but it had a long-term impact that perhaps even he could not have foreseen in 1956. The "Tamil problem" thus started as a linguistic issue, but within a few years it was to become a horror story of racial strife. Scores of young Tamils left Sri Lanka to study and stay abroad. Today there are affluent Tamil communities in Britain, West Germany, France, Canada, and the United States. Tamils have made their mark in the sciences and in education in the West.

"Plight" has become a sort of buzzword when a discussion about Sri Lankan Tamils begins these days, especially in the Jaffna area and in foreign communities where Tamils live. The word was much favored and widely used by parochial Indian politicians—particularly those from the heavily Tamil southern Indian state of Tamil Nadu—who wanted Prime Minister Indira Gandhi to invade Sri Lanka in 1983 to protect Tamil communities from alleged Sinhalese atrocities. Perhaps no Tamil leader is more articulate in talking about the "plight" of the Tamils than Appapillai Amirthalingam. He is a pudgy, affable man who wears simple white garments that have become his trademark. Like Yogeswaran, he was a member of parliament until the fall of 1983, when he refused to take an oath disclaiming secession for Jaffna and lost his seat in the national legislature. I met him in Colombo, in a bungalow reserved for out-of-town legislators. The place was heavily guarded; even the sweet, milky tea that Amirthaligam offered me was served by a pistol-toting policeman. Amirthalingam disavowed terrorism—it wouldn't work, he said to me, it would in fact hurt the Tamil cause. Two of his sons have been accused of promoting radical causes: one son, A. Kandeepan, has sought political asylum in Britain; another, A. Bahirdan, a medical student in Madurai, in south India, occasionally participates in anti-Jayewardene rallies.

"The young Tamils have nothing in common with the Sinhalese," Amirthalingam said. "How are they going to hold this union together? There is going to be more and more polarization. Jayewardene says he gets a billion dollars each year in foreign aid. How much of this comes to the Tamil north? Very little. Just a few pennies for family planning given by the Swedes. The practical solution would be to separate: like what Singapore and Malaysia did."

Amirthalingam was on his fifth cup of tea. Could a small state like Sri Lanka really be divided into two and could these two countries then exist as viable entities, I asked?

"Of course. What choice are we left with? We are being heavily discriminated against in the Sinhalese parts of Sri Lanka, and we feel comfortable only in our Tamil areas. So whether Jayewardene wants to admit it or not, we've had an ad hoc partition of the country anyway. Jayewardene's economic policies are designed to help the Sinhalese areas and not the Tamil ones. Now the government has started imitating the Israeli practice of planting outsiders in the West Bank—only here the outsiders are Sinhalese who are being resettled in Tamil areas to 'pacify' us, to provoke us. I think it is too late for any reconciliation."

President Jayewardene thinks people like Amirthalingam are full of beans. During one of our conversations, held in Jaffa itself where Jayewardene was campaigning for reelection in 1982, the president told me he did not think Sri Lanka would ever break off into two countries. "We will never allow a separatist state," he said, his normally soft voice rising. "Our country is too small to contain two independent nations. I think people like Amirthalingam should stop spouting nonsense and come to the negotiating table and start talking some sense." In late 1983, when Jayewardene hosted a special national reconciliation conference, Amirthalingam and his TULF boycotted the event.

In recent years, the Tamil desire for a separate state has found expression in the establishment of several armed terrorist groups. The most active of these groups is one calling itself the Liberation Tigers of Tamil Ealaam, or the Tamil Tigers, as they are generally known. Sri Lanka police officials say the Tigers have no more than 200 "hard-core" members. It was this group that has successfully raided police stations in the north and stolen arms and ammunition. It was the Tigers who said they attacked the Sinhala soldiers last July 23, an incident that provoked reaction from Sinhalese civilians around the country in the form of arson and looting of Tamil enterprises and shops. In the bitter aftermath of the murder of the Sinhalese soldiers, more than 20,000 Tamils in southern and central Sri Lanka fled their homes. Many of these lived for months in refugee camps specially set up for them by the Jayewardene government. Jayewardene has vowed that every last Tamil terrorist will be hunted down and brought to trial. But the incidents of terrorism continue. Jayewardene appears to be under increasing pressures from the Sinhalese extremists in his ruling United National party who seem to believe that there is an international Marxist conspiracy to carve out a Tamil state from Sri Lanka.

As has been the case all too often in Third World countries, development issues such as population, education, employment, and wages of workers have become victims of the politics of discord in Sri Lanka. President Jayewardene is also soon going to have to deal with the thorny question of the tea and rubber plantation "stateless" Tamils, who, like their Jaffna counterparts, also feel discriminated against. If these Tamils start agitating, as is quite possible, Jayewardene could find himself in a hopeless situation. In 1948, nearly a million of these Indian Tamils were disenfranchised. After protracted negotiations between India and Sri Lanka, some 400,000 Indian Tamils were repatriated. But more than 825,000 Tamils remain in the twilight zone of uncertain personal status. I visited one of these workers at a tea plantation not far from Kandy.

He lived in a small shack with his four children. He was a thin, dyspeptic man with a racking cough. He had come from southern India back in 1946, he said, and he had always wanted to go back home. He could never consider Sri Lanka home, even though Jayewardene now has promised him citizenship. Workers like this man have built up Sri Lanka's tea industry to the point where annual exports exceed $350 million. Old, decaying, he did not strike me as militant, nor did his associates who milled around us out of curiosity. But I kept thinking later that if these workers remained "stateless"—because of a lack of agreement between India and Sri Lanka concerning just how many Indian Tamils have left and how many have stayed behind—much longer, they would probably revolt. And if they did, the impact on Sri Lanka's economy would be devastating.

Sri Lanka's ethnic problems, and especially the violence of the recent past, have overshadowed the substantial progress made in such fields as population, health, education, and general social welfare. Until the terrible events of July 1983, Sri Lanka had shown that a developing country could, with a committed government, put in a superb economic performance. Jayewardene had steadily but firmly repudiated the socialist policies of his predecessor, Mrs. Bandaranaike, under whom a massive and costly welfare system had been created, allocating scarce public money to subsidize everything from rice to kerosene. The socialists had restricted foreign travel, clamped down on imports, and imposed an artificially high value on the Sri Lankan rupee. By promoting a free-trade zone, among other things, where Western, Japanese, and Hong Kong companies set up factories to produce shoes, clothes, and electronics, Jayewardene was able to bring down the unemployment rate from 30 percent to 15 percent by 1983. Shops in cities like Colombo were stocked with consumer goods, a contrast to the seven years of austere socialism that preceded the Jayewardene era, when food rationing and acute shortages of daily necessities were common. Electrification of Sri Lanka's 25,000 villages was progressing swiftly, and in Colombo more than 30,000 units of new housing were being built. The annual economic growth was edging past 6 percent, and the per capita income had passed $300. Total economic assistance from the West was around $1 billion a year, a tenth of it from Washington. Western tourists, including Americans, had "discovered" Sri Lanka, whose officials advertised their country as a "land of peace and promise." The tourists brought in well over $100 million a year.

Perhaps in no other field did Sri Lanka make as much progress as in population control and health care. It raised the legal age of marriage, initiated a program of offering cash incentives to men and women who agreed to be sterilized, stepped up projects for educating and employing women, and set up a system under which food stamps were given to two-child families. Programs of expanding disease control and prevention, supply of potable water, and treatment of malnutrition have been instituted with vigor. A national health service was created; malaria, long the main killer-disease in Sri Lanka, was eradicated, and sophisticated health care services were brought to the villages. Assisting in such efforts has been one of the most remarkable men I have met, Ahangamasgan Ariyaratne, the founder in Sri Lanka of an unusual self-help movement known as Sarvodaya.

I first met Ariyaratne at a dinner party in Colombo. He is not a striking man, short in stature, usually clad in a sarong-style wraparound and homespun shirt and wearing sandals with frayed soles. He smiles a lot, and when he does speak there is a quiet authority in his voice. Many years ago, Ariyaratne came under the influence of Mahatma Gandhi's teachings of nonviolence and selfless social service. He decided he would train volunteers, who in turn would train Sri Lankans traditional skills such as agriculture, dairy farming, and knitting and weaving. Ariyaratne's Sarvodaya movement—*sarvodaya* means awakening—is a sort of domestic Peace Corps, and it takes in post–high school and college youths for stints from several months up to a year at a time. In fact, several top government officials once were trainees under Ariyaratne.

Ariyaratne's ideas are simple: "We go to the people, we share their life, work with them, learn to love them and serve them, help them to help themselves. We promote the idea of self-reliance and community action. Development for a country like Sri Lanka must really start at the grass roots. We cannot expect government to do everything for us."

He sets up work camps in rural areas. I went to one such facility not far from Colombo one afternoon. It was sweltering, but a dozen teenaged boys and girls were cheerfully helping villagers dig irrigation ditches. The youths had pledged to spend their weekends with Ariyaratne. He himself often pitches in for such manual labor. The son of a middle-class mining contractor, Ariyaratne seems at ease with everyone he meets and equally at ease in the dining rooms of the wealthy, whom he persuades to donate to his movement, and in hovels, where he helps the deprived. Those who have known Ariyaratne for a long time say his movement is imbued with the traditional Buddhist principles of Sri Lanka, which emphasize a respect for life, joy through service, and selfless dedication to whatever task is at hand.

Another energetic man is Brigadier Dennis Hapugalle. He is the executive director of an organization called Community Development Services, a private group that complements various government family-planning projects. He fashioned a series of colorful posters that promote the two-child family and personally has obtained pledges from more than 30,000 men and women in rural areas that they would get themselves sterilized after their second child. Financed by private donations and through contributions from abroad, Hapugalle's organization also offers villagers incentives such as chicken to supplement their food supply if they enroll in a family-planning program.

Hapugalle stresses that to push family planning by itself would be a fruitless exercise in a society that is still economically backward. "Family planning must form part of a broader development program," he told me one evening at his modest bungalow in Colombo. "When you help improve productivity, when you create jobs, when you assist women in entering the work force, then the birthrate is bound to go down. When you improve health care for children and infants, people will have fewer kids because their children will live longer and be healthier."

He pointed out that, unlike many Asian nations, Sri Lanka had been fortunate in not experiencing severe urbanization. That was because the government has made sure that peasants stayed in rural areas —through subsidies for farmers, the establishment of a reliable bus service in the countryside, the digging of wells that have ensured adequate water supply to most villages, and a special program under which cheap housing and educational facilities have been built in rural areas. Instead of concentrating all industry in urban areas, the Colombo government has encouraged small-scale industries, such as, for example, brush factories, to locate in the countryside, and this has helped create jobs. "The network of health and economic services in the rural areas has definitely helped in bringing down our annual population growth rate," Hapugalle said. "The question now is, How will we sustain our progress?"

It is a question that troubles many Sri Lankans, from Jayewardene on down. And at the heart of any answer to this question lies the ethnic issue.

"In population control as well as development, our problem now is the ethnic issue," says Wickrema S. Weerasooria, a senior government official and a key advisor to President Jayewardene. "If the ethnic issue explodes, we will receive a permanent setback in our development efforts."

Several things are happening that worry Weerasooria, a plump young man who often acts as Jayewardene's personal emissary to trouble spots around the country and to international conferences on development. An insidious campaign seems to have started to persuade the majority Sinhalese to "go slow" in family planning. Pamphlets have been distributed by anonymous persons warning that if the Sinhalese continue to lower their annual population growth rate soon they will be in the minority. Physicians who work in family planning occasionally have gotten threatening letters about dire consequences to their well-being if they persist in promoting birth control among the Sinhalese. That there have been radical, extremist, "Sinhalese only" fringe groups has been known; but in the aftermath of the July 1983 riots, some of these groups have stepped up their activities. Jayewardene, although widely admired as a man with no ethnic prejudices, is also criticized for tolerating racist remarks made by some of his political associates concerning the Tamils. Various Tamil leaders in Jaffna told me that they fear the remarks of such leading Sinhalese politicians as Cyril Matthews do not help the healing process Jayewardene talks about. Those who fear that continued family planning among the Sinhalese will lead to theirs being in a minority in a few years time have really little to worry about. The Tamils of Jaffna also have a low annual population growth rate.

People like Weerasooria point out, however, that among the Sri Lankan minorities only the Moslems don't seem to be taking well to family planning, a phenomenon common in many countries where there is a sizable Islamic population. The Moslems of Sri Lanka are not enthusiastic about the efforts by the government to promote sterilization and to offer cash and other incentives to couples with three or more children to avail themselves of free sterilization services. Somehow, sterilization, for men at least, is still viewed by many Moslems as a blow to their sexuality. But other Sri Lankans, especially poor Sinhalese, seem to be opting more and more for sterilizations: the average monthly rate of such operations now is well over 2,000.

The question of making continued progress in lowering the population growth rate and increasing the economic growth rate is also tied to what happens with an ambitious $3 billion project known as the Mahaweli Hydroelectric, Irrigation and Resettlement Scheme, which was started in 1978. It was initially conceived as a thirty-year undertaking, although now the time span has been collapsed into less than a decade. Four major dams are being built along the Mahaweli River and its tributaries, and a network of downstream irrigation canals is being created, stretching from the mountainous center of the island in a wide diagonal swath northeast to the Trincomalee region. The dams will provide much-needed hydroelectric power, while the new canals will open up dryland areas to intensive agriculture and resettlement of landless peasants. In fact, many of the farmers already settled in the newly irrigated lands have now harvested their first rice crop. Eventually, more than 150,000 peasant families from the southern part of Sri Lanka are expected to resettle here, thus relieving some of the land congestion elsewhere (Sri Lanka, the size of West Virginia, has a population density of 550 persons per square mile, with 75 percent of the overall population of 15 million concentrated on only 35 percent of the land, the so-called wet zone in the southern part of the pear-shaped island). Some 100,000 acres of new cultivable land will be available to these peasants. Although there have been familiar problems, such as cost overruns and waste, the project is well on its way to completion. Jayewardene told me during one of our interviews that when the Mahaweli Scheme is finally in place by the end of this decade it will significantly reduce rural unemployment, help Sri Lanka achieve food self-sufficiency, and treble power-generation capacity. What he didn't say was that if the Mahaweli Scheme turns out to be the success he hopes it will that, perhaps more than anything else, it will be a lasting memorial to his presidency.

The Mahaweli Scheme is actually part of his overall three-project program to create more jobs, better housing, and increased food supply.

The two other components are the "investment promotion scheme," centered in a so-called free-trade zone, which occupies a 500-acre plot of land adjacent to Katunayake International Airport, eighteen miles north of Colombo; and a huge "housing and urban development scheme," under which more than 150,000 new housing units of all grades are being built around the country. The purpose of the free-trade zone is to upgrade local technology and assemble electronics and other goods for re-export; generous tax holidays and other incentives are being given to investors, who include companies from Hong Kong, Singapore, and Japan. The housing units are meant to relieve congestion in urban and semiurban areas and will, in effect, be a series of mini-townships around the country.

When Jayewardene talks about these things, his ascetic, cadaverous face lights up. He speaks so softly that I had to strain to hear what he had to say. He is given to long pauses. One of our conversations took place at his wife's family home at 66 Ward Place in downtown Colombo. Breadfruit and flamboyant trees graced the front and back yards, and a white Pomerarian dog scampered about. The house had simple furnishings, sofas that had seen better, less frayed days, two huge elephant tusks mounted on a pedestal in the foyer, and photographs spanning Jayewardene's fifty-year career in public life. Security seemed at a minimum. Dozens of party workers and other supplicants flowed in and out of his inner office, where aides were apparently hearing complaints and dispensing favors. It was late in the evening, and Jayewardene's face was etched with fatigue. He wanted to talk on this occasion about his economic policies and about development in general.

"I do not believe in ideology," he said. "I have found it far better to think always in practical terms—about how things can be done, about how problems can be solved. One of our banes in the developing world is slogans—and too many of our leaders mouth slogans and shibboleths and wind up doing very little for our people, whose cause these leaders claim to uphold." I thought the reference was clearly to his predecessor, Mrs. Bandaranaike, and I asked Jayewardene why he felt as strongly as he did about her socialist government. He grew quite animated as he responded to that one: "There is no question that her regime was a dictatorship. She gathered powers to herself as Hitler, Stalin, and Mussolini did. From her conduct arose a police state, which victimized the people. People became fearful. All that affected economic development. The Bandaranaike years were years of deprivation."

Those years seemed a receding memory when I visited Sri Lanka in 1982, 1983, and early 1984. The rationing imposed by Mrs. Bandaranaike had been lifted. Consumer goods were plentiful. The Jayewardene government, in an effort to earn foreign exchange, had set up a multistoried, "duty-free" shopping complex in Colombo, where tourists and visitors could buy a wide variety of items. Every day I would drive past this complex and there would be lines of people snaking around the building. Many in the lines appeared to be Indians, excitedly brandishing their blue-faced passports. I was puzzled by this and was told by a friend that indeed Indians were the biggest customers here. Apparently, special daily flights were organized from nearby Indian cities such as Madras and Trivandrum—each about an hour's flying from Colombo—to transport men who were given itemized lists for shopping. They bought color television sets, Rolex and Cartier watches, clothes, stereos, tape recorders, and perfumes, then took evening flights back to India, where "arrangements"—meaning bribes—with local customs officials enabled the travelers to unload their booty with their organizers without any excise duty. This deal doesn't bother the Sri Lankans, of course, who welcome the inflow of hard currency brought by the Indians. The Indians, in turn, sell the foreign-made goods at huge profits.

The fact that Sri Lanka even allows luxury goods made in the West into the country seems to disturb socialism-minded critics, particularly those still favoring Mrs. Bandaranaike. These critics argue that such an infusion of goods inevitably translates into an import of alien and undesirable cultural values. They cite the preponderance of Western-style discotheques and the presence of fast, sporty cars, Western music and movies, and fashions as examples of deterioration of indigenous Sri Lankan culture. One evening I was taken to dinner at the Lanka Oberoi Hotel by my friend Nirmala de Mel. We ate at the rooftop restaurant, where a British singer gave a performance. The meal was expensive, more than fifty dollars per head, for the steaks were Australian and the champagne was French. The restaurant was filled with young Sri Lankans who were dressed very fashionably indeed in styles that seemed right out of couturiers in Paris and New York. Nirmala, a wealthy woman in her own right—she runs the country's largest travel business—but who prefers the simple fabrics of her native country, confirmed this was so. "The sons and daughters of the newly wealthy just throw their money around," she said. "And they are ostentatious."

Most people in Sri Lankan, despite Jayewardene's economic policies of liberalization and increased opportunities, are not in a position to spend much money on themselves, let alone throw it around. In the shadow of the sumptuous Taj Samudra and Lanka Oberoi hotels, for example, you can find vast acres of shanties. The "new economics" of Jayewardene has not relieved their crushing burden of poverty. And the danger inherent in the continued presence and proliferation of such shanties here and elsewhere is that this is where the population growth rate is high and this is where social tensions are exacerbated. Recognizing the danger, a Sri Lankan group called Save the Children has worked in shantytowns to help build new homes and spread literacy and modern sanitary practices. I was taken to one of the group's projects, in a poor neighborhood known as Kirillapone in Colombo. Hundreds of people live here, and until two or three years ago these shanty dwellers had among them only four water faucets, unreliable electricity supply, and unpaved roads that often sank into the marshy area holding up the shanties. Save the Children, a private, nonprofit volunteer group that is financed by contributions from individuals, sent in architects who donated their time and others who built sixty-six houses and a roomy community center in two years' time. The organization trained neighborhood women and unemployed youths as bricklayers. The homes were fashioned out of bricks made in the Kirillapone neighborhood itself. The idea was not to move residents and resettle them in unfamiliar areas but to keep them where they were in a better environment that they themselves had created. A woman named Anuradha, mother of four children and widowed, was among those who learned to be a bricklayer and went on to construct a house.

She is a tiny woman, about thirty-five years old, with the body of a young girl. Her husband died soon after their fourth daughter was born, and Anuradha had to scramble for a job. Relatives supported her family for several months while she sought employment as a maid. She had lived in Kirillapone since she was a child, in a shanty made out of tin and plywood sheets and strips of cardboard. Her children were growing up rickety, as Anuradha did, for the food they consumed was almost wholly devoid of proper nutrition. When the team from Save the Children arrived, Anuradha asked to join and received training as a bricklayer. Now she and her children live in a two-room house that has proper toilet facilities as well as a water supply that comes from a new water system installed during the rebuilding of Kirillapone. "It is hard to recognize this area now, it used to be so filthy," Anuradha said in Sinhala. "And I feel there is a new purpose in my life."

Health workers from government bureaus were sent to educate residents concerning nutrition, and free food supplies were sent to the neighborhood by the United Nations and by Save the Children. Other workers arrived, women trained as family-planning agents, who now assist local residents to plan their families better and who distribute contraceptives as needed. Neighborhood residents like Anuradha are also being trained to promote the concept of small families and to instruct other residents to use contraception.

The day I visited Anuradha, she proudly showed off her oldest daughter's medal, an award the ten-year-old child had won at the neighborhood school for proficiency in painting. "I want my girls all to study and do something with their lives," Anuradha said. "Unlike me, I want them to get a full schooling. And I want them to marry whenever they want to, not when I tell them to. I don't think they should even consider marrying early."

The Sri Lankan government, in fact, is encouraging people to marry later rather than earlier in the expectation that delayed marriages will result in fewer children and more concentration on productive careers. This promotional campaign, to be sure, is directed at the poorer sections of society, where it is common for people to marry in their teens. Among the middle classes of Sri Lanka, there already has been wide acceptance of later marriages. Jayewardene is concerned about a possible new baby boom if Sri Lankans do not put off marriage and childbearing: more than 40 percent of the country's population is under fifteen years of age, and unless this generation fully accepts the notion of birth control and child spacing, there could soon be a dramatic rise in the nation's annual population growth rate.

One afternoon in Colombo, I was introduced to a striking young woman named Kumari Perera. She is nearly thirty years old, unmarried, and runs a thriving photography business. She had wanted to become a writer, but when her father, a noted Colombo photographer named Joe Perera, died of a heart attack, she inherited his business, being his only child. I asked Kumari what was perhaps a male chauvinistic question: Why she had remained unmarried at an age when surely most of her peers had established their own households with children? I was mildly surprised by her answer. More and more, she said, young Sri Lankans were not marrying until their late twenties or even early thirties. With what has been perceived as an economic boom in the country, more and more of her peers were delaying marriage to establish themselves first in professional careers. "It is not that we have renounced the family as a concept, it is only that many of us have decided to first build the economic foundations that are so necessary to have a happy family life," Kumari said.

I was heartened by what Kumari said. When people delay marriages, they remove more years of fertility from their procreative periods, and in country after country it has been shown that, when this is done, you bring down the birthrate.

Seven

China
The Future Is Now

IT WAS one of those magical evenings in Shandong Province.

The breeze brought in the fragrance of jasmine and also nudged my nostrils with reminders that the Yellow Sea was nearby. The sky was streaked with ocher, and I was tucking away one slice after another of juicy watermelon. In front of me, a hundred colorfully clad children were welcoming me in the traditional Chinese way by singing, dancing, and performing calisthenics. I was the guest this evening of the 4,000 residents of Lin Chun Brigade in hilly Wentan County. Lin Chun Brigade, one of 950 communities in this mostly rural area, is what they call a "model zone" in China, which is to say that its agricultural production and the family-planning practices of local residents are deemed to be superlative and therefore fit to be emulated by the other 1 billion Chinese. After the children were led away by their smiling teachers, I was ushered into a conference room in the office of the brigade's headman, a tall, courteous man named Lin Chi Shun.

Like the dozen other men and women in the room, Lin smiled a lot and seemed eager to explain how his brigade had achieved its "model" status. The conference room contained a rough-hewn wooden table and uncomfortable wooden chairs whose backs swayed irritatingly; the walls were festooned with portraits of the late Chairman Mao Zedong and with posters showing numerous happy couples, each with a single child—a boy, of course. Also on the walls were several testimonials that Lin said were laudatory of his brigade's family-planning efforts. More locally grown watermelons were brought in for my consumption.

Hot, very weak tea was passed around. Peaches followed, then another round of watermelon.

"Not one couple in our brigade has had a second child in the last four years," Lin said. "We have been very scrupulous in following the national one-child family policy."

I don't think Lin or the other assembled local officials expected me to have questions on this matter, for they seemed somewhat startled when I interrupted Lin.

"Does that mean that no woman already with a child became pregnant again?" I asked.

Lin quickly consulted with his colleagues. My government translator appeared uneasy.

"Well, there were second pregnancies," Lin said, "but they were terminated."

He said that in 1982 there were seventy-seven first births in Lin Chun Brigade and twenty-eight abortions. Were the abortions voluntary? "Oh yes, of course," the headman said with alacrity, adding that in 1982 three women, each with one child, had voluntarily asked to be sterilized. Lin Chi Shun was getting uncomfortable talking about this, for I don't think he expected to be asked about abortions, and I myself felt a bit awkward persisting with such questions. But I resolved I would bring up the subject of forced abortions because I thought the subject went right to the heart of the Chinese population planning program: When a government asserted that its country already had too many people and that available resources could no longer adequately provide for a burgeoning population, did such a government have the right to assume regulatory power over its citizens' reproductive habits?

Before I arrived in China, I had read up on numerous press accounts of forced abortions and forced sterilizations undertaken at the insistence of overzealous officials in various Chinese provinces. "Yes," Lin Chi Shun said to me, "there have been some of those things happening around here, although not in my brigade. But the culprits were properly punished." He was unable to elaborate on what sort of punishment had been meted out to the culprits, and I was not surprised at his professed ignorance on the matter. His answers to me were to be replicated in subsequent days by headmen of dozens of other communities across China. While few people I met denied the reports of family-planning excesses such as forced abortions and sterilizations, the instances of these abuses were always somewhere else.

The whole business of these abuses had caused quite a stir in the

West prior to my China journey. Human rights organizations were upset over the reports, and a fresh controversy got started in the spring of 1983, when the United Nations announced that its first-ever population award would be shared by Prime Minister Indira Gandhi of India and Qian Xinzhong, China's minister for family planning. The annual award, worth $25,000 was shared between these recipients in September 1983, but not before several articles and editorials appeared in the Western press questioning the award, particularly to Mr. Qian. (Mrs. Gandhi, various editorials claimed, had authorized a program during 1975–1977 under which thousands of males were forcibly sterilized; Mrs. Gandhi herself says that reports of such occurrences were greatly exaggerated, although she has admitted that overzealous family-planning workers in some cases did indeed herd peasants into trucks and take them away to be vasectomized.) The *New York Times,* in an editorial that otherwise praised the United Nations's work in population, said that the world organization had "blundered into" giving Mr. Qian and Mrs. Gandhi the award.

I met Minister Qian in his office in Beijing, and he immediately launched into an appreciation of what the United Nations award meant to him and to the Chinese. The award had, Qian said, put the imprimatur of the world body on China's family-planning efforts, and he also pointed out that China did not condone abuses such as female infanticide and forced abortions. Qian is a white-haired man in his mid-seventies, sprightly and shrewd and unfailingly polite. He kept getting up from his sagging sofa to refill my cup with tea, and every time he did a fresh band of sweat would appear on his forehead and an aide would hand him a wet towel to dab his skin.

"Considering we have a billion people in our country, it is not an easy job to monitor everything," Qian said, speaking in a thin, raspy voice. "But I don't think it is logical for outsiders to criticize China because of just a few cases of induced abortion. We don't advocate abortions, let alone force people to accept this method. The Chinese government will protect all women, including girl babies—not only protect them but also severely punish those who go contrary to the law."

The minister didn't want to discuss specifics concerning what penalties, if any, had been imposed on those who were responsible for horrors such as forced abortions, and the more I tried to draw him out the more he seemed to get irritated. I told Qian that my impression, after more than three weeks of traveling through his country, was that in China's vast countryside there still was a classic battle between what the government urged and what traditions dictated. In other words, I said, I found that there was still a strong desire among many Chinese, both in the countryside as well as in urban areas, to have more than one child, and to have sons more than daughters. In China, as in other Third World countries, sons are still seen as insurance in old age, while daughters are regarded, as one Chinese saying goes, as "spilled water that cannot be retrieved." Chinese parents accept that once their daughter marries her loyalties will shift to her husband's family. Foreign anthropologists visiting China have found that families with only girls seem to have lesser influence in village affairs than those with sons, who are often the sole support of aging parents. In many Chinese villages I was told of such sayings as, "Boys are precious, girls are worthless," and "Many sons mean a happy and prosperous household." Minister Qian didn't seem to think that centuries-old customs were an insurmountable barrier, and he told me that rural brigades were in the process of setting up pension schemes and homes for the aged. "These things, when fully in place, will assist peasants in gradually changing their idea that sons are an insurance policy." He told me that many of China's family-planning posters depicted a happy couple with their only child, a daughter. The caption on such posters reads: "An only child is a happy child."

The only-child poster may show blissful couples proudly showing off their only child, but it is increasingly clear that the government's one-child policy is being questioned, a development noted by several writers, including Richard Bernstein, author of an acclaimed memoir on China and now a reporter with the *New York Times*. Minister Qian, during his September 1983 visit to New York to receive the United Nations award, admitted as much, although not in so many words. Sections of China's peasantry sees the policy as inhibiting them from having more children to work their land. Several peasants told me that the ancient Confucian custom of filial support is still expected of sons, no matter what the government promised in terms of old-age pensions. In their recent book, *One Billion,* Jay and Linda Mathews, an American journalist couple who spent some years in China, reported that in 1983 the official Chinese press admitted to alarming increases in drownings and other murders of infant girls, as the conflict between the one-child policy and the traditional desire for sons shook the countryside. There is no question in my mind that the one-child policy has spawned many abuses. When I was visiting China in July and August of 1983, the *Nanfang Daily* newspaper reported that more than 210 girl babies had been murdered soon after birth in Guangdong Province in 1982 because their parents had wanted their only child to be a son. The *China Youth News* reported similar recent atrocities in parts of Anhui Province, saying that in some areas the killings of female infants were so numerous that three in five surviving infants were boys. The news service went on to say: "If this phenomenon is not stopped quickly, then in twenty years' time a serious social problem will arise, namely that a large number of young men will not be able to find wives."

A telling indication that China's one-child policy has not succeeded and probably is not likely to was supplied by Minister Qian himself in New York recently. He told members of the Population Council, a private scientific group, that in 1981 nearly 6 million babies were born in China to families that already had at least two children. China's birthrate (the number of annual births per 1,000 of the population) rose from 20.9 in 1981 to 21.1 in 1982, a shift from a formerly declining rate, the minister said.

I had always wanted to go to China, not merely as a tourist to an ancient land that still tickles the imagination but as a reporter who could approach ordinary Chinese and ask them questions about themselves. I spoke no Chinese and so was forced to rely on my government-supplied interpreters, who were mostly honorable and helpful and who seemed genuinely concerned at the awesome population numbers of their country. Clearly, it seemed to me, the two interpreters had been selected for their public relations value: Du Xiangjin, deputy chief of the foreign affairs division of the state family planning commission, and Yang Yang, also of the family planning commission, were both fathers of a daughter each, and neither had plans to have a second child. Du appeared a bit overanxious that I not get any criticism of the one-child policy, and wherever possible he would try to steer the conversation away from this subject. Yang seemed more relaxed and more open and did not shy away from discussing what I thought was a central question concerning China's family-planning experience: If the one-child policy isn't working, then what are the Chinese going to do about their staggering population problem?

The United Nations helped China conduct a census in 1982, providing American computers and more than $10 million to train poll takers and other personnel. The preliminary results of that census showed that the mainland population was 1,008,175,288 as of July 1, 1982. This was 5 million more people than expected. (The 1982 census was conducted by more than 5 million enumerators and supervisors and constituted what was probably the biggest social service exercise of its kind ever. China's last census was held in 1964, which showed that the country had 700 million people. Annual tallies between 1964 and 1982 were based on police registration of households.) China thus contained almost a quarter of the world's total population. More disturbing, the trends indicated that the annual population growth rate had started edging back upward from a low of 1.17 percent in 1979 to 1.45 percent in 1982. Between the two censuses, the average annual population growth rate of the country had been about 2.1 percent, although in some years the rate catapulted past 2.3 percent.

One reason China's annual population growth rate is edging upward again is explained by the fact that those born in the baby boom of the 1950s and 1960s—when Mao said China could easily afford to expand its population—are now having their children. Moreover, 15 million young couples will reach the legal marriage age every year between now and the end of the century, a fact that presents and will continue to present "new threats of unchecked population growth," says Niu Tiehang, a demographer. One afternoon in Beijing I was visited by a man named Chen Guo Xiang, a senior official with the state family planning commission. He was a small man who wore a worried expression, and when he started to talk about demographic projections, I thought he would somehow faint. Chen told me that in the next fifteen years some 225 million Chinese women would enter the child-producing period. If each of these women were to produce two children, China would find itself with an additional 450 million people by the end of the century, or almost twice the current population of the United States. "We simply cannot allow two children per family," Chen said, gravely. "How can we carry out our plans for economic development otherwise? The fact remains that the problems of population are very closely related to the standards of living of our people."

We were sitting in my hotel room at the Friendship Guest House, a huge Stalinist structure built in the 1950s to accommodate Soviet technicians and advisors, who then came in hordes to China during the years of cozy cooperation between the two Communist giants. Birds chirped gaily outside my window, and Chen kept on refilling my teacup insistently. Chen is in charge of training family-planning cadres, or teachers and proselytizers, and also helps fashion population curriculums for secondary schools and colleges, where students are now obligated to study elementary demographics and population theory. Even housewives are trained these days by Chen's units, which are installed in each of the mainland's twenty-nine provinces. "Population education and reduction are absolutely necessary for a country such as ours," Chen went on, as Yang Yang translated.

He told me that China wants to limit its population to 1.2 billion by the year 2000, and for this goal to be achieved there could not be a net addition of more than 180 million by the end of the century. However, if current trends hold and the annual population growth rate increases, even slightly, China will have at least 450 million additional people by the year 2000. And with the annual death rate now only 6 per 1,000 of the population—and falling—the net additions to the overall Chinese population could be even higher by the end of this century. Chen suggested that China's efforts to propagate birth control have been hampered by persisting illiteracy. He said the new census showed that 235 million people over twelve years of age were either illiterate or could read and write only a few characters. Of course, Chen quickly added, the government was stepping up its literacy drive, and this was also evident in the new census figures: the 1982 illiteracy rate was 23.5 percent, compared with the 1964 figure of 38.1 percent. Another reason behind the less than desirable rate of birth control acceptance, Chen said, was the continued presence of feudal attitudes. In China, as I was to learn during my travels around the country, the term *feudal attitudes* is a sort of buzz phrase used by officials to explain away a lot of visible problems—such as the obvious economic backwardness of villages in the northern provinces and elsewhere.

Chen had been sent to lay out before me his government's efforts toward keeping the country's population growth rate low. He pointed out, not without discernible pride, that in the last decade China had almost halved its birthrate from 34 per 1,000 in 1970 to 18 in 1979 to 17 in 1980. "A fertility transition of this magnitude is unprecedented for a large developing country," Chen said, "and it could not have been achieved without massive population education and a national network of community-based free contraceptive services." Chen said that more than 120 million couples now used contraceptive methods, and in the four years that the government's one-child policy had been in effect, nearly 15 million couples had formally pledged to have only one child. He said that the post-Mao leadership, headed by Deng Xiaoping, had designated as top priorities four so-called modernizations—in agriculture, industry, defense, and science—and that fundamental to achieving these modernizations was the whole business of population control. Since 1979, when the government introduced the one-child campaign, authorities have held that the suitable population size for China in the next 100 years would be between 650 million and 700 million. The assumption of Chinese officials and demographers is that if the number of one-child families increased by more than 50 percent, China's birthrate would fall from the current 20 plus per 1,000 of the population to less than 14 per 1,000 by 1985, and the annual population growth rate would fall by 1985 from the current figure of 1.2 percent to below 0.7 percent. Mindful that in the last ten years an average of 18 million babies were born every year, the Chinese amended their Constitution in December 1982 to make it obligatory now for all couples to practice birth control.

Borrowing a bit from their ideological opponents, the hated capitalists, the Chinese decided that to make the one-child policy more acceptable they would have to introduce a system of incentives. An American professor at the State University of New York in Albany recently carried out a study of China's population policies and practices and found that, although specific economic incentives for the one-child family varied around the country, the government had put into effect some nationwide practices. The professor, Kuan-I Chen, found that in the cities the usual income supplement was about two dollars per month until the couple's child was sixteen years old. In the countryside, where 85 percent of the country's population lives, Professor Chen found that the additional monthly allowance was often as high as twenty-five dollars. Should the couple have a second child, however, the allowances are ended and the couple is usually asked to repay the accumulated bonuses. Moreover, some Chinese provinces require that a couple's income be reduced by 15 percent if they have a second child after pledging not to do so, 10 percent additionally if they have a third child, and 5 percent for every subsequent child. Professor Chen also found that medical, nursery, and educational fees for the single child are usually waived. The parents receive extra housing allowances and, where possible, larger living quarters. (Space is at a premium, especially in the overgrown, densely packed Chinese cities. In Shanghai, for example, an individual gets an average of thirty square feet, plus kitchen and toilet; in Wuhan, forty square feet; and in Beijing, forty-five square feet. A number of young couples I interviewed in urban areas around the country told me that one of their highest priorities and fondest dreams was to get larger living accommodations.)

Parents of single children now receive priority in jobs, added bonuses, and special pensions when they retire. It used to be that only sons were able to inherit a man's job automatically when he retired; now, to make the birth of a female child more acceptable, the government has decreed that a female is as eligible as a male to move into a vacant slot created by a man. In conjunction with the one-child policy, the government is also encouraging couples to marry later, although the legal marriage age for women is twenty and for men it is twenty-two. In Beijing, for instance, men marrying after the age of twenty-five and women after twenty-three are given an extra week on honeymoon.

One evening in Beijing I was discussing all this with a friend of mine named A. P. Venkateswaran, who happens to be India's ambassador to China. Venkat, as his friends call him, is a great admirer of China's family-planning efforts and says he has no difficulty in reconciling himself to the fact that at times a state must forcibly intervene in the lives of individuals to ensure the public good. "I think the program here is a good blend of education and coercion," he said, over a cup of sweet, milky Indian tea. Then his eyes twinkled and he rose from his Indian-style diwan. "Do you know that I have been given a 'one-child glory certificate'?" Venkat said. He went to to say that when he arrived in Beijing the family-planning minister, Qian Xinzhong, had inquired how many children the ambassador had. Venkat told Qian about his only daughter, Kalpana, who is married to a young American oil executive and now lives in Papua New Guinea. "Then you arc surely eligible for our one-child glory certificate," the minister said to Venkat. So one fine morning the Indian ambassador went to visit Qian and reminded him of their earlier conversation. Qian at once had a certificate issued to the ambassador—a pocket-sized red card with the ambassador's photograph and gold lettering that guarantees him a large, free apartment, free medical and hospital care, special grain allocations every month, and a waiver of all preschool and school expenses. Needless to say, Ambassador Venkateswaran has not yet made use of his privileges.

His point about state intervention in individuals' lives continued to trouble me long after our conversation that balmy evening in Beijing. It was not that Venkat was for authoritarianism or that he applauded totalitarianism. But he said to me that such were the population pressures on China that the government each year had to import between 15 million and 20 million tons of food grain to feed its people. "What do you do when you have too many people?" Venkat asked. There is little doubt that the Chinese government has no option but to step up enforcement of its one-child policy, however unpopular it may be.

Two fundamental questions therefore present themselves. First, to what extent can governments legitimately intrude on the lives of individuals in order to strike a balance between the public good and the private interest? The Chinese authorities say they do not condone such extreme manifestations of state intrusion as forced abortions, but in a country as huge as China it is difficult to see how the central government is going to be able to ensure that the abuses are checked. By its very nature—and by the scale of the overall population problem—China's population control program is one of restricting births, not really "planning" them in the conventional sense. Steven W. Mosher, an American anthropologist who spent more than a year in rural Chinese communities, wrote in a recent book titled *Broken Earth:*

> Alternately threatening and cajoling, persuading and reasoning, the [family-planning] cadres explain over and over again why it is necessary to follow the party line, applying a steady psychological pressure that deadens reason and gradually erodes the will to resist. Experience has taught the Chinese that arguing back at authority will only make matters worse, and so they listen passively and finally come to agree to whatever is being demanded of them. The whole process is reminiscent of the Chinese proverb, "Water drops can pierce a rock."

Mosher, whose research and observations have been attacked by the Chinese government and by some American academicians as being unfair and misleading, says he attended several village meetings where government cadres, or representatives, pretty much bullied women pregnant with a second or third child into agreeing to an abortion.

The second fundamental question flows from the first. At a time when leading nations of the West such as the United States—countries that initiated global population programs and that continue to finance them—have arrived at a rapprochement with Beijing, how do China's birth control policies square with the general Western—and particularly vigorous American—position on human rights? What if Third World states that are friendly to the West and especially to the Americans and that receive large doses of economic aid, such as Kenya (which has the world's highest population growth rate, 4 percent annually), begin emulating China? Implicit in the Chinese experience are grave foreign policy concerns for the West, particularly now that the Chinese are wooing the Western industrialized countries for financial assistance for a variety of projects, including population programs.

That China expects such aid was made clear to me in Beijing by Zhang Xianwu, deputy director of the Department of International

Relations in the Ministry of Foreign Economic Relations and Trade. A tall, thin man who received me in his mightily air-conditioned office on a muggy summer afternoon, Zhang noted that for many years about the only outside source of assistance for China's family-planning program had been the United Nations Fund for Population Activities whose involvement in the Chinese population program is being increasingly criticized by right-wing groups in the United States. Now, he said, some of the Nordic countries had expressed interest in accelerating economic cooperation with China. He pointed out that no American financial assistance came to China because of a congressional restriction against providing aid to Communist countries. "But obviously we would like to have economic cooperation with any country, including the United States, on the basis of mutual respect of sovereignty," Zhang said, speaking in a mix of Chinese and English. "We would like to see stronger technical cooperation with Western countries, including in the field of population." He added that among the areas where China saw increased investment from the West was the production of contraceptives. "China is backward in its economic development, and our gross national product is still relatively small, but we have ambitious plans for development, and so we seek outside assistance," Zhang said.

My interpreters, Du and Yang Yang, had asked that I specify the areas of China I wanted to visit. Naturally, I said Tibet, which was the remotest province I could think of and where I wanted to see for myself what the Beijing government was doing about development and about the question of population control among minority communities. Du went off to consult with his superiors, but he seemed dubious that a trip could be arranged at short notice. He was right. So Tibet was out, but Inner Mongolia was in. In the event, I found out that no writer had recently been to this distant northwestern province on the Soviet border to report on population matters. I was privileged to be the first, a distinction that was noted in toast after toast to me at a succession of banquets given by provincial officials in my honor.

* * *

We left Beijing late one afternoon by plane. We nearly missed our flight because of the traffic jam; it was the bicyclists who held us up, not motorists, and even the normally cool Yang Yang lost his temper at one point and shouted at some men and women unhurriedly pedaling along the birch-lined road to the airport. The plane we boarded was a Soviet-made aircraft with propellers, and the seats were so uncomfortable that I developed a rare backache. It took two hours to fly to the capital of Inner Mongolia, a city called Hohhot. The terrain changed dramatically as we flew somewhat low over land. Around Beijing it was hilly, and we could see the fabled Great Wall of China crawling northward. Then the hills yielded to great plains, and soon the steppes of Mongolia came into view. It was all very green, a strange yellow-green that did not dazzle the eyes. Waiting at the Hohhot airport shed were two local family-planning officials, who, after a warm handshake, demanded from Du and Yang Yang my travel papers. Every foreigner, and for that matter every Chinese who wants to travel by air, must be in possession of such papers, which are issued for the duration of one trip at a time. (Later in our travels, Yang Yang lost his travel documents in his native Shanghai and had a terrific argument with airport officials who wanted to refuse him permission to board a flight to Beijing. They relented after Du intervened and after Yang Yang had offered the appropriate apologies.) The two local officials, Yin Rei, a Mongol, and Fan Jun-Zhi, a Han Chinese, spoke no English other than "Welcome!"—a word they used in almost every sentence.

Inner Mongolia is the land of the legendary Genghis Khan, the Mongol warrior whose hordes set off from the vast grasslands here and swept across much of the rest of Asia. There once was a flourishing empire here, it is said, and it is also said that once this city of Hohhot was a center for spirited trade and commerce, where merchants of the world gathered to drink, carouse, wench, drive hard bargains, and amass huge fortunes.

All that is gone now, and the Mongol empire lives only in legend. This is now a drab, dull place, and it is difficult for a visitor who has read up on local history to believe the legends. Where once there were colorful bazaars there now are lifeless stalls offering stale vegetables and shoddy consumer goods produced in faraway Beijing or Shanghai. No caravans flounce through Hohhot, and the traffic mostly consists of sturdy military vehicles transporting recruits to nearby camps or striplings to the Soviet border of Soviet-dominated Outer Mongolia not far away and government-owned taxis that rattle more than they run. There still are camels around, but they no longer transport visiting merchants from afar as much as they carry agricultural machinery to farms on the outskirts of Hohhot. Most buildings are aging one-story structures whose paint is peeling. The streets are dusty. Sidewalks are often unpaved. Surprisingly, the local museum has a first-rate collection of dinosaur fossils found nearby and a display of Mongol costumes and tents, along with an informative section on military campaigns waged by local Mongol chieftains in eras gone by.

Whatever the legend, this is not really an exotic place. But Inner Mongolia is a place of great strategic significance for the Beijing government, not only because of the close proximity to the Soviet Union, China's hated northern neighbor and former Marxist mentor. Inner Mongolia is also becoming a sort of test case for China's dubious national minorities policy, which, government officials tell visitors like me, represents a program for coping with racial differences and tensions that is far superior to comparable programs anywhere else in the world. Du and Yang Yang provided the translation for what numerous officials in Hohhot told me was the "correct" interpretation of the national minorities policy: minorities in China are allowed the freedom to maintain or transform their customs or habits or traditions. Minorities, I was told, are also permitted to use whatever language they preferred as the medium of communication in their areas.

According to the Beijing government, there are fifty-five officially designated minorities in China, with a total population of about 65 million, or roughly 6 percent of the country's overall population. The government classifies as minorities all people whose racial origin is not ethnic Chinese, or Han, as the preferred official term for the majority group is these days. It just so happens that China's minority areas, officially known as autonomous regions, are situated in geopolitically strategic places: Inner Mongolia is just south of Soviet-controlled Mongolia; Tibet is near India; Guangxi is north of Vietnam, and Xingjiang is beside the Soviet Union. The phrase *autonomous regions* remains just that, a phrase; in reality, the minority areas are very closely monitored and controlled by the Beijing government. In Inner Mongolia, for example, you can see the People's Army everywhere. Wandering through the streets and byways of Hohhot one afternoon, I could swear I saw more green-uniformed soldiers of the army than I did civilians. They were mostly youths, and they were very curious about my camera. They all seemed Han Chinese, as did most of the folks I was eventually to meet in Hohhot and other areas of Inner Mongolia. I recalled what my friend Chris Wren of the *New York Times* had told me in Beijing—that the government had resettled thousands of Han over the years in minority areas, perhaps as a way to "pacify" the local population. Whether this has been so or not, any visit to Inner Mongolia raises questions about whether the real purpose of China's national minorities policy is to absorb the minority cultures and integrate them into the Han ethnic mainstream rather than, as the Beijing government insists, to let these minority nationalities continue unfettered with their traditional cultures, however quaint.

My translator Du told me that the one-child policy did not apply to China's minorities, who, he said, were "free to multiply as they wished." I didn't think that this was to be taken literally, and some days later a woman named Dr. Sking, the deputy director of the Inner Mongolia Regional Family-Planning Commission, confirmed what I had suspected: that the natives of the province were being persuaded, as much as anyone else in China, to accept family-planning measures. "While the national policy is to allow minorities to have as many children as they want, we in Inner Mongolia think it is time that Mongolians should plan their family size—otherwise we will have grave economic and other difficulties," Dr. Sking, an ethnic Mongol, told me at a fifteen-course dinner her office had arranged in my honor.

A physician herself, Dr. Sking has trained more than 5,000 workers to spread the message of small families. Some of these family-planning workers are attached to local hospitals; some roam the province in vans and seek out shepherds in the steppes. Dr. Sking, a large woman with an engaging manner, was adept at ensuring that my dinner plate was kept full with spicy chopped chicken and stewed cucumbers and boiled beef and a dozen other delicacies. "You see," she went on, sipping from a tumbler of locally made red wine, "the reason why the leniency was applied to Mongol minorities concerning population matters was that until our liberation in 1949 the birthrate here had been going perilously down. Diseases such as cholera and venereal disease were killing off our population. People led miserable lives. The Chinese Communist party decided that to keep such a vast province economically viable there must be growth in cattle and people. But we are living in different times now. Traditional diseases have been wiped out. People are healthier. Now they need to plan their numbers better."

Their numbers are spread out over a province that occupies almost 13 percent of China's territory. There are just about 3.4 million Mongols here, out of a total population in Inner Mongolia of almost 20 million: the rest of the people of the province are mostly Han Chinese. There are also 38 million head of cattle, or three times the figure of prerevolutionary China. Before the Communist takeover of 1949, the entire province had only one hospital, Dr. Sking told me, and now Inner Mongolia has 4,460 hospitals and clinics, 118 maternal and child care centers, and 14 medical schools to train physicians and the so-called barefoot doctors, or paramedical personnel, who travel to remote rural areas. Sking seemed very much at home rattling out statistics, and she had more to give me: the province has 80,000 medical personnel of whom 21,000 were Western-style physicians and 40,000 were barefoot doctors. The infant mortality rate used to be more than 200 per every 1,000 children, and now it had been brought down to less than 20, Sking said. Chinese officials all over the country shower visitors with these sort of figures, for no activity in China can be said to be entirely legitimate unless it can be quantified. After a while, I found these figures to be meaningless, and I said so to Dr. Sking.

"Ah, but these figures reflect day-to-day life in our province," she protested. "You will see what these figures are all about when you go out and meet our people."

The first stop was the tomb of a legendary figure named Wang Zhao Xuan. I was taken to this hilltop monument about twenty miles outside of Hohhot because, Fan Jun-Zhi, the local family-planning official told me, I couldn't begin to understand the nature of the relationship between the Han Chinese and the Mongolians until I had understood what Wang's life had been all about. Wang was a princess of the West Han dynasty who was born around 33 B.C. It was a time of much conflict between local Mongol tribes and the Han, explained Liu Yin Ying, a winsome guide at the monument. To bring about peace, Princess Wang decided she would marry the local Mongol chieftain, and it was this union that brought about an era of peace and prosperity for Inner Mongolia. An epic poem commemorating Princess Wang is included in all primary school textbooks in the province, Liu said, and dance troupes often enacted the story of her life. "Her life showed how we could enjoy good relations between Mongols and the Han," Liu said, taking me around a mini-museum at the bottom of the hill on which the Wang monument is built.

Hundreds of people were at the site this morning, and as far as I could tell they were either Red Army soldiers or ethnic Han Chinese. When I asked Yin Rei, the Mongol family-planning official, whether my observation was correct, he said that most Mongols lived in the deep hinterland and did not often come to visit Wang's tomb. From the hilltop, on a clear day, you can see for miles into the horizon. Hohhot itself looks flatteringly neat. Also visible is a complex of textile plants, and it was to this place that I was taken next.

The Third Textile Factory of Inner Mongolia turned out to be a sprawling affair, with some 2,150 workers, of whom fewer than 300 were Mongols. Various sheds and edifices housing miles of machinery were all drab, the only bit of color provided by a bed of flowers near the office of the deputy director, a fat, jolly man named Xi Zhen Guo. Because fully a half of his workers were women, Xi said, it was necessary that the factory have a comprehensive family-planning program. The average age of female workers was thirty-one, which meant that most were still in their "marriage and high fertility period." I was introduced to Xiang Hong, a twenty-six-year-old woman who is chief of one of the factory's production sections. She told me that the dozen or so production units such as the one she controls together produced nearly 2 million meters of fabrics and textiles each year. "You can imagine how this work keeps us all busy," Xiang said, "and none of us women can manage more than one child each." Six days a week Xiang and her husband, Wang Gan —a technician at another textile factory in the Hohhot area—deposit their six-year-old daughter Wang Xiao Bo at a kindergarten in the mornings and collect the girl on their way home at night. This is a pattern followed by most workers at the Third Textile Factory. Three times a week, groups of women get together and discuss their contraceptive practices, Xiang told me, and each woman also pledges to spread the message of the one-child family in her neighborhood. The purpose of these meetings is not merely to exchange notes concerning the desirability of family planning. It is a way by which the authorities monitor the reproduction cycles of every woman in the factory. If a woman misses her period, for example, her peers know this at once and the authorities are soon involved in urging her to reconsider giving birth if this is her second child. No one escapes the scrutiny of the authorities here. As I left the factory, my eyes fell on a rather colorful poster raised near one of the production sheds. It said, in Chinese: "Family planning is a glorious task." Below it were names of all the factory workers who had formally pledged themselves to having no more than one child per family. There were also names of those who hadn't so pledged.

As we drove out of the factory in a battered Chinese sedan, I saw a young man walking near the main gate leading a little girl by hand. I asked to talk with him. The man was Wu Chen Fen, thirty-seven years old, and he was taking his eight-year-old daughter Wu Hai Yin to the home of relatives for a feast celebrating her birthday. Did he have any other children and did he want any more, I asked. "It's not necessary to have more than one child," Wu replied. "Who can afford it? I would obviously have liked to have had a boy, but now it makes no difference to me that we have a daughter instead. A child is a child, and having a daughter instead of a son doesn't make parents' responsibility any less."

Wu told me he was a recipient of the one-child "glory certificate." Dr. Sking had earlier informed me that in 1982 alone nearly 220,000 people had received such certificates in Inner Mongolia and that the family-planning acceptance rate now was 88.2 percent. I thought this was an extraordinarily high figure. Did it include Mongols on steppes deep in the province? "Of course," Dr. Sking said. "See for yourself."

So off I went, in an old Toyota van made available by the local family-planning office. I was accompanied by my ubiquitous translators, Du and Yang Yang, and by Yin Rei and Fan Jun-Zhi, the local officials. They had brought oranges for the journey into the grasslands and Chinese cookies, and we kept eating all the way to our first destination, a dreadful town called Chi Za Wang Qi. It was very warm, and the myth that all flies had been eradicated from China was demolished in my view the moment I stepped into a local hotel, where a sixteen-course meal had been prepared for us. There were more flies than people, and the flies helped us eat our food.

For dessert I was offered fresh watermelon and peaches, grown locally, and an hour's worth of statistics and propaganda about how well family planning was doing in this part of northern Inner Mongolia. I suppose I must have shown my irritation, or perhaps I was simply too tired to pay much attention, because what was to have been a two-hour session with local officials was abruptly ended after an hour, and we were soon off from this regional headquarters. But not before I was taken to a local maternity center, where medical personnel in orange smocks and white caps feverishly explained to me how many women availed themselves of family-planning services, how many healthy children there were in the municipality, and how enthusiastic the family-planning fieldworkers were about their tasks, even though these workers sometimes put in as many as a hundred miles on the road daily.

Finally, the rough road again. The fields of corn and maize that had surrounded Chi Za Wang Qi slowly gave way to uncultivated grasslands, where camels and cattle grazed and sheep were being herded along by Mongols. The bone structure of Mongols is very pronounced: their cheeks are high, their skin red and raw, their teeth uneven but strong. They are not a particularly friendly people, and the women especially are shy. Three hours out of Chi Za Wang Qi, and we were not far from the Soviet border. Occasionally military trucks rumbled along the dirt road, and when we passed them the soldiers would wave, more in reflex than in cheerfulness, I thought. Then we were upon a collection of gaily colored tents. It was Baying Hoso, or Brigade Number Two, and I was ceremoniously received by Dorji, the deputy chief of the local municipality. At first look, Dorji gave the impression of being a thug. He had small, shifty eyes and a nervous laugh. His hands could strangle an ox, I was sure. I was ushered into a large communal tent, where I sat cross-legged for three hours while Dorji and his associates told me about Baying Hoso.

It was a typical Mongol settlement, consisting of about 375 people, 11,000 cattle, and 300 horses. Baying Hoso had 130 tents plus some other permanent brick structures that served as offices for local officials. Comely maidens served me milky tea and savories while Dorji talked, and a photographer kept taking pictures. Outside the tent, children gathered to witness the spectacle. I was on show.

The Mongols of Baying Hoso are all shepherds. The wool of their sheep goes to a state organization, which then pays them through barter of supplies for everyday living; some cash is put into state-owned banks in escrow for the Mongols. Meat produced here must also be sold to the state organization. This is not a poor community. Every tent has a television set, and every Mongol has a radio. The Soviet Union broadcasts vile propaganda, Dorji said, but this was countered either by jamming the airwaves or by "more effective" Chinese programs. At least a quarter of the brigade's population was not Mongol, however, it was Han Chinese. During my three-day stay at Baying Hoso, I wasn't introduced to a single Han, but I was walked into a brick building and asked to speak to some ethnic Chinese people. My interpreters were a bit embarrassed, it seemed to me, but they complied with my request. A young Han couple I met told me they came to Baying Hoso from Beijing, their birthplace, to teach local children. There is a communal outhouse, located about 200 yards from the grouping of tents. The routine of everyday life is unchanged much of the year: the herds are taken to pasture early in the morning and brought back by midday. The evening meal is the big one of the day, and it consists mostly of meat dishes.

Peng Sige, head of this brigade's production units, spoke in a Mongol dialect, which was then translated into Chinese, which was then translated into English for me. "You see, we Mongols eat nothing but meat; the Han Chinese like vegetables, which we don't particularly. We like sweet milky tea, the Han prefer weak tea that is really nothing but hot water with a few tea leaves. You see, there are these cultural differences among us."

Whatever the cultural differences, there are no two ways about family planning. The sex lives of occupants of every Mongol tent are closely monitored by family-planning cadres, who incessantly preach about the value and usefulness of a one-child family. I accompanied a senior family-planning official named Jing Hua, a Han Chinese, on her rounds of Mongol tents in and around Baying Hoso. Jing had brought along her infant son, who proved as much as an attraction as she herself did. We went in a Chinese-made jeep to the tent of Khe Junje, a twenty-nine-year-old woman with three children. Khe received us warmly and offered us milky tea in her tent, which was about ten feet in diameter and was covered with thick, colorfully patterned rugs. The conical roof of the tent was held up by a red bamboo rod, and the walls, whose interiors were made of animal skins, were propped up by criss-crossed bamboo sticks. On top of a waist-high cupboard were knick-knacks, a powder box, photographs of Khe's three daughters, Sariampat, Urkhan, and Paratapamquay, and, strangely enough, a calendar showing Santa Claus, circa 1970. Khe's husband, a shepherd named Tarji, had wanted another child—a son; but Jing Hua was able to convince Khe to get a tubal ligation.

"I don't want another child. Three is enough," Khe said, now bringing out a whole midmorning meal consisting of noodles, semolina, steamed bread dumplings, and more milky tea. Mongols drink tea by itself and also then pour semolina into it, along with heavy butter, and eat the mixture as a soup. "I don't know why my husband wanted a son," Khe continued. "Our daughters are as strong and help out in tending our flocks of sheep."

Khe's neighbor, Borna, was our next stop. "Neighbor" meant just that she lived closest to Khe's tent, or a distance of ten miles. Borna's tent was not unlike Khe's, except that hers contained an old faded picture of Mao Zedong. Borna is twenty-seven years old and the mother of Chaketo, a five-year-old boy. Jing Hua had tried to get her tubes ligated also, but Borna preferred that an intrauterine device be inserted instead. Jing and Borna then proceeded to discuss Borna's menstrual cycle and the business of her periodic pains quite matter-of-factly, as Yang Yang translated. I was a bit surprised at the casualness with which the most intimate sexual things are openly discussed by the Chinese, but I was to find later in my travels that one consequence of the country's family-planning campaign has been that sex is "desexed" in China. Only

I as an outsider seemed in any way embarrassed. Borna was born a few miles away from where she lives now and told me that it was quite possible that she would have another child. "Not for the moment, however," she said. "At the moment we are poor because it hasn't rained and the pasture is poor for our sheep and cattle."

The problems of Baying Hoso have more to do with the weather and its effect on herds than with overpopulation, I discovered. The Mongols aren't going to overbreed because the Beijing government won't allow that to happen. The more immediate problems have to do with declining pasture area, the result of a severe drought that has hit this part of Inner Mongolia for three years running. Kinh Jutaii, a physician, told me that the area's other problem is that of rats, which eat grain. Ordinarily, these rats are destroyed by birds, but because of the drought the birds have gone elsewhere and back here the rats reign. Still another problem for the Mongols, the doctor said, was their diet. Heavy meat eating had led to dangerously high cholesterol levels in the local population's blood. Many Mongols, he said, suffered from chronic high blood pressure and hypertension. "The only way to improve the Mongols' diet is to increase their vegetable consumption, but this means getting them to increase cultivation of vegetables and get more into agriculture—this means transforming, at least partially, a nomadic community into an agricultural one," Kinh said. "This will be a long-term task."

* * *

A long-term problem for the Beijing authorities is going to be the fact that China's efforts to persuade couples to have only one child have already created an unintended side effect—the spoiled brat. Not long after my return to Beijing from Inner Mongolia, I went to see Professor Shun Chieu Hua of the Population Research Institution at the People's National University. A tall, thin, cordial man, he received me in an office that was right out of an Ivy League university in the United States—book-filled, with a comfortable sofa, a rug, the smell of pipe tobacco, even a fireplace. We went through the customary rituals of discussing the purpose of my trip, while Professor Shun kept pouring hot tea from a thermos flask. "Ah, the only child," he said, presently, "now that is indeed something else, isn't it?" Shun said that although the government had been promoting its one-child policy since 1979, no specific study had been done on the effects of this policy on families.

"I personally feel that there is bound to be great impact on our social system," the professor said. "The policy has the potential of having both negative and positive effects." He admitted that already the only child in a society where children generally are valued and pampered "has the tendency to be overspoiled." Also, Shun went on, "that child may grow up lonely—this business of not having any siblings is a new experience in our society." He pointed out that the Chinese were traditionally accustomed to having large, extended families in which uncles, aunts, cousins, and older brothers and sisters all contributed toward teaching a child how to behave. Now, he said, it was already apparent that some only children were becoming pouty, willful, rude, inconsiderate, and egocentric. A letter to the *Worker's Daily* newspaper not long ago complained that children without siblings often refused to stand in line for inoculations at some hospitals but rushed ahead. The English-language *China Daily* newspaper said, "Because they have no brothers and sisters, some only children never learn to care for others. When in kindergarten, they quarrel with their friends and refuse to share their toys."

The newspaper cited a survey undertaken in Beijing of 1,741 children between the ages of three and five that said that nearly 30 percent of the only children had become fussy eaters. One of those who helped conduct the Beijing survey told the *China Daily* that parents should be better disciplinarians. "The point is to make parents stop doting on their little darlings," the official, Tang Hua, was quoted as saying. The Beijing survey also found, however, that only children were "cleverer, more imaginative, more creative, more inquisitive, and healthier," possibly because they received more attention. My translator, Yang Yang, told me, for example, that he and his wife, a physician, spent far more time with their only child, a girl, than their own parents ever did with either of them.

Yang Yang informed me that since 1980 nearly forty books had been published offering advice on how to bring up only children. More than 5 million copies of these books were in circulation, Yang Yang said. I saw one of these books in Shanghai, at the home of Chang Yi Shu, a thirty-year-old woman who lives in the densely populated Nanshe neighborhood, where there are 80,000 persons per square kilometer. It was really a sort of A-to-Z primer on child rearing, with many illustrations of bonny babies and several sections on the need for disciplining kids. Published by a state agency, the book was distributed free to all new mothers, which Chang was. Her daughter, Chan Yei, was born in February 1983, and, of course, Chang said that one child was enough for her and her husband, Chao, an administrator in a Shanghai handicrafts factory. Already, Chang, a schoolteacher, pointed out, only children accounted for more than half the kindergarten enrollments in big cities such as Shanghai and Beijing.

Chang and Chao live in a compact four-room apartment on the third floor of a postrevolutionary building. In their neighborhood there are other buildings by the score like theirs, four- or five-story, no elevators, two apartments to a floor, with a small playground shared by two or three buildings. There are also a number of older buildings, more ornate, with walls around them and gardens in the back yard. These latter once belonged to the wealthy mandarins of Shanghai, the merchants and traders who made this into a great, bustling, cosmopolitan city. Many of the once fashionable villas are now occupied by Party functionaries. Chang's father recalled for me the years before the revolution, when Shanghai was both a venal and a wonderful place. "It is a different city now, more quiet, more sedate," he said. It is also a bigger city than ever before, with almost 10 million people, and still growing.

I had been invited by Chang and Chao to celebrate the five-month anniversary of the birth of their child. The young couple were friends of Yang Yang, who hails from Shanghai, and the invitation had been relayed through him. On the morning Yang Yang and I arrived at their apartment, the couple was also being visited by a woman named Shui Chien Ying. Shui is the local family-planning activist—I wondered about the coincidence of our mutual arrivals—who goes from apartment to apartment in the neighborhood to inquire about the birth control situation in households. Shui looked much younger than her fifty-nine years, and Chang's father, Cheng Ching Tse, who was visiting her from his home in Quingdao, seemed to take an immediate liking for her, chatting her up with vigor. Shui, a petite woman with twinkling eyes, fussed over Chang's baby. Later, she told me that she makes it her business not only to supply government-provided pills and contraceptives but also advice to young mothers like Chang on how to bring up a baby.

"I'm a kind of social worker for this area," Shui said, "and my business is to offer not just technical but timely advice." She said that many young mothers seemed concerned at bringing up an only child, a "natural worry." Shui added: "But I tell them, 'Look, think of how much more economical it will be for you to have an only child, think of how much more productive you will be at work, and think of how much more time you will be able to spend with your child.' "

Chang, for her part, seemed a bit nervous about motherhood. The baby's cradle was located in her bedroom, and toys littered not only that room but also the small living room. Chang kept asking Shui a succession of questions about why the baby kept getting up at odd hours of the night and what to do about such ailments as colic. It was, I thought, a scene like any other in India or the West—an anxious mother with her first child.

I was curious how ordinary Chinese accepted the inquiries about their sex lives from family-planning agents like Shui. Chang told me she didn't mind Shui's questions at all, particularly since she already had accepted Shui's advice that Chang and Chao have only one child. I had the feeling that one reason Shui was accepted so warmly by Chang was because the former was a sort of mother-figure for her. In fact, virtually all of the family-planning agents I met in Chinese cities—the women who went from door to door and kept abreast of people's birth control practices—happened to be in the fifty to sixty-five age range. A woman named Wan Yei, the chief family-planning "cadre" in Chang's neighborhood, told me later that same morning that because the Chinese traditionally respect elders it was easier for women like Shui to ask people delicate questions concerning their sexuality. The responses agents like Shui elicit no doubt are immediately conveyed to the local family-planning committee, whose officials prevail upon a woman pregnant with her second child and urge her to abort the birth. Agents like Shui also assist in resolving family conflicts, Wan told me.

Wan proved among the most forthcoming of officials I met in Shanghai. Her office, a modest two-room suite, was located in the compound of a housing development called Tian Shang. In this development, Wan said, there were 12,700 households, or 49,900 people in all, many of them workers in nearby textile factories and chemical plants. Wan herself was thirty-four years old and the mother of a seventeen-month-old boy. Her husband, Shu Yeu Ha, was employed in a local factory, and the couple had committed themselves to having only one child, which meant they received extra food rations, a bit more money every month, and additional health and medical facilities for themselves and their son, Cho Yan Lei. Wan said she was worried that because those born during the baby-boom years of the 1950s and 1960s were now in their marriage and reproduction period, the outlook was for an increase in Shanghai's population growth rate. The statistics were disturbing: in 1979, 458 couples got married; in 1982, the figure was 1,200; in 1983, 1,306 couples tied the knot. The marriages were reflected in the numbers of babies born in the development: in 1981, there were 597 births; in 1982, 763; and in 1983, 900.

Once a week, Wan presides over a meeting to which family-planning activists who report to her are invited, as are residents of the Tian Shang complex, who are required to turn up in rotation. I went to one such meeting. It was a warm, humid evening, and as I rode my taxi to Tian Shang I could see a sea of people on the pavements. Men wore thin vests or were bare torsoed, and the older among them were decked out on canvas chairs in front of their houses. Everywhere there were children being given watermelon slices by their parents and grandparents, or bits of candy. The squeals of these kids was louder than the screeching of my taxi's tires, as we frequently braked to avoid swerving cyclists. There were nearly a thousand people at Wan's meeting, and she started off with a slide show of statistics that, I felt, was more for my benefit than theirs. One statistic that stood out: in Tian Shang in 1983, 98 percent of the couples who got married during the year committed themselves to having only one child. Afterward, Wan solicited questions, and most of these had to do with why it was necessary that couples have only one child. Wan's replies were standard: because the economic development of post–Gang of Four China depended heavily on lowering the national annual population growth rate. Shanghai in particular, Wan said as her audience murmured in agreement, suffered heavily during the reign of the Gang, when family planning was not emphasized. Later Wan said to me of that period: "We were all very much depressed during that terrible time. The Gang of Four very nearly ruined China."

The Gang of Four has become a metaphor in China these days for all that has gone wrong. The reference is to something called the Great Proletarian Cultural Revolution, which lasted a decade, from 1966 to 1976, when China was in effect in a civil war of sorts. Thousands were killed by Communist fanatics calling themselves the Red Guards, who attempted nothing less than a complete destruction of China's cultural heritage. Led by Mao's wife, Jiang Qing, the Gang of Four ruled China unchallenged and egged the Red Guards on. So wrapped up were they in demolishing political and cultural icons and in destroying their enemies that such crucial matters as birth control campaigns were largely forgotten. Wan said all this with a special sadness: the Gang of Four were Shanghailanders.

The neglect concerning population matters during the reign of the Gang may seem dramatic in retrospect, but Chinese history has other such instances and periods as well. China's population was already some 60 million when Christ was born; by the twelfth century, when the Sung dynasty was in power, the population figure had climbed to 110 million; the figure then doubled during the sixteenth century, when the Ming dynasty ruled. And by the time the Ching dynasty assumed power in the nineteenth century, the country's population had doubled again. Steven Mosher, the American anthropologist, writes that in the century preceding the Communist takeover of the mainland in 1949, the Malthusian checks of war, famine, and disease kept the death rate hovering near the birthrate, and the population figure stayed at around 500 million.

But after the 1949 Communist conquest of the mainland, the annual population growth rate kept rising: nearly 20 million Chinese were added every year for the next ten years. Chairman Mao refused even to acknowledge that China had a population problem. In one of his more celebrated early speeches, Mao said: "The absurd theory that increases in food cannot catch up with increases in population, put forth by such Western bourgeois economists as Malthus and company, has not only been refuted by Marxists in theory, but has also been overthrown in practice in the postrevolutionary Soviet Union and in the liberated China." Mao rejected outright arguments that population growth would outstrip production; he maintained that "revolution plus production" would solve the problem of feeding and employing China's people: "A country with vast land areas and plentiful material resources need not fear population growth."

Mosher's analysis is that what gave Mao confidence was the fact that what had been a disorganized capitalist society was now replaced by a smoothly regimented socialist one in which people could be directed to do whatever their leaders wanted. Malthus had argued that a country's growing population constantly tended to exceed the food supply, but Mao held that a large and growing population was actually an asset. "Every stomach comes with two hands attached," Mao would say—his way of saying that he saw the Chinese primarily as producers, not as consumers of diminishing resources. Indeed, there were some close associates of Mao who viewed birth control as genocide. In 1952, for example, the *People's Daily* newspaper came down hard against birth control, which, it said in an editorial, was "a way of slaughtering the Chinese people without drawing blood." People, the editorial went on to say, were "the most precious of all categories of capital."

They held a census in China the next year, and the 1953 figures showed that now there were more than 600 million Chinese. Suddenly, members of the ruling elite were concerned. Speeches were made, articles were written in the state-controlled press, and in 1956–57 a birth control campaign was initiated in urban areas. This campaign ignored the fact that then, as now, more than 80 percent of China's population lived in rural areas and that any birth control campaign, to be meaningful, had to focus on peasants, who were breeding rapidly. Instead, what was emphasized in the countryside was collectivization. But again ideology intervened, and proponents of family planning were denounced as rightists and were purged from the Party. In the late 1950s and early 1960s, millions died in China because of famine and disease, and it was then that Chairman Mao stepped in more forcefully to institute birth control as government policy. The national campaign was gathering momentum, and then the reign of the Gang of Four began, and once more it was back to square one. It was not until 1979 that the Deng Xiaoping regime firmly recommitted China to a nationwide family-planning campaign and put into effect the one-child policy. By then, however, many communities were already bursting at the seams. One such community was Fung Tao Brigade, which nestles in a mountainous part of Shandong Province.

To get to this brigade, one has to drive through thick corn fields and dense woods. It takes maybe five hours to reach Fung Tao from the provincial capital of Quingdao, which sits by the Yellow Sea. Shandong is now what the Chinese call a "model province," and visiting journalists are urged to travel around at will. I asked to see a brigade that had really suffered from overpopulation, and local officials in Quingdao suggested Fung Tao Brigade. It was difficult to find this brigade, for it is built into hillsides, and we passed the place once before discovering our error. Chieu Fa, the brigade chief, heaved a sigh of relief when he saw us: nearly 200 tiny tots belonging to the brigade had been lined up in the brigade square to greet me, and they had been kept waiting for more than an hour. Chinese children must be the most patient and the best disciplined ones in the world. These kids stood there not complaining or whimpering, and I wished I had candy to give them. As soon as I got down from the van we rode in, the children clapped in unison, then proceeded to sing for ten minutes, after which they marched around me and were led away by their group leader, a seven-year-old boy named Hua. Their day had not ended, however: the children had another two hours of calisthenics and music lessons before they would be sent home.

Chieu Fa, a craggy man who wore a Mao-style cap even indoors, had arranged a "high tea," Chinese style, in my honor. In attendance were local family-planning officials, whose function seemed to be to nod in agreement at everything Chieu said. I was told that since 1979 there have been no third and second children in the 820 households that form this village. Production of wheat, corn, and potatoes was steadily rising each year, and the per capita income in 1982 was the equivalent of $500, fairly high for a rural community. It used to be that the village had no electricity, no hospital, no nursery schools, and no tractors, until the mid-1970s. There were not even brick houses here, although what is today called Fung Tao had been in existence for nearly 200 years as a backwater village. The infant mortality rate was high, and villagers kept producing more and more children to ensure that at least some survived. During the Cultural Revolution, Chieu said, even talk of birth control was forbidden. "It was all chaos here," he declared. "Every month babies were being born, while our agricultural production declined. No outside expertise was available to us for teaching us how to grow our crops better. It was all politics, politics, politics. It is all different now."

From the photographs I was shown, Fung Tao before 1979 must have been a filthy, overcrowded hovel of a place. The roads were unpaved. Homes consisted mostly of mud and straw structures. Now Fung Tao is something else. The houses here are neat, one-story structures, with a common courtyard for every two homes. The village is built in a gridiron pattern, with a square at the center and a kindergarten school abutting this area. There are playgrounds, a couple of small parks, and a recreation area for older residents. Virtually every house has a television set. A street set apart from the residential area contains community stores, such as groceries. It is a brigade layout typical of Shandong Province. I visited Chiang Huong, a thirty-year-old woman, and her husband, Chien Che, thirty-three years old.

Their house consisted of three rooms plus a kitchen, a toilet, and a small patio. The living room had a television set and a large transistor radio. There were pictures of their eight-year-old daughter Yaya and of parents on both sides. Chien told me he was one of seven children; Chiang, short and sturdy like her husband, was one of eight children. "As children we would complain a lot about the food given to us and about old clothes that were really rags," Chien said. The couple signed up for the one-child certificate, and Chian, who uses an IUD, says she is considering sterilization. Chien showed me around his three-acre plot, which also contains sheds where he raises chickens and pigs. Sometimes, he told me, when the work gets heavy in his field, he wishes he had a son to help him out. But he quickly pushes away that thought. For him, at least, there is now no reneging on the one-child pledge: his village peers won't let that happen.

And that, really, was the heart of it all. So minutely is Chinese socialist society organized that no aspect of an individual's life goes unobserved, especially in rural brigades and communes. Pressure is applied on couples to restrict themselves to only one child not only through family-planning cadres in neighborhoods but also through the work units of both husband and wife. When Chien Che tells me that he will not renege on his commitment to have only one child, at the back of his mind surely is the knowledge that if he and his wife were to have a second child the family income would automatically be deducted through a 10 percent penalty. If Chian were to get pregnant, peer pressures on her to get an abortion would be instant, enormous, and irresistible. In the final analysis, it does not matter how many children Chinese like Chiang and Chien want—they will be allowed no more than one child.

To an outsider like me, all this seemed very drastic indeed. After all, in the West we are brought up to believe that reproduction is an unquestioned human right. When Prime Minister Indira Gandhi instituted forcible sterilizations as a means to lowering India's population growth rate in the mid-1970s, my colleagues in journalism and I were duly chagrined. A few years ago, the then head of China's Family-Planning Ministry, a woman named Chen Muhua, made it plain that the state was going to assume regulatory power over individual reproduction habits. Few journalists in the West protested then, when she said: "Socialism should make it possible to regulate the reproduction of human beings so that population growth keeps in step with the growth of material production."

There are those in China, like Jiang Xing Quan, who believe that eventually the national family-planning policy is going to have to be modified. Jiang is a physician and serves as deputy director of the Shanghai Health Bureau. He is a short, dapper man, about fifty-five years of age, and over dinner one evening at the Meixin Restaurant in Shanghai he told me that however unpopular the one-child policy was, it was necessary for China at the present time. "The one-child policy is not a permanent thing," Jiang said to me. "We will change the policy as our demographic characteristics change." China's demographic characteristics suggest that the government is going to have to stick to its one-child policy at least through the end of the century, and possibly beyond.

Whether 100 percent enforcement of the policy is going to be truly possible is another matter.

On my penultimate day in China, I went by to see several foreign diplomats to discuss some of my reservations concerning the country's population program. One diplomat, an Egyptian who was about to leave Beijing after nearly a decade, said something that stayed with me for months afterward: "Remember, the problem in China these days is not people having more kids but more people having kids." Because of the baby-boom years of the late 1950s and 1960s, China now is going to have to contend with the fact that between now and the end of the century the annual population growth rate may well continue to decrease while more people will be added to the overall population. The government says that 70 percent of Chinese couples of childbearing age currently practice birth control of some sort, but to persuade the remaining 30 percent may well be much more difficult.

Several senior foreign diplomats whom I met in Beijing seem unconvinced that the Chinese have adequate data on which to base meaningful, long-term population policies. China did not even have demographic research facilities until the United Nations Fund for Population Activities was invited in six years ago to provide seed money to establish a demography center in Beijing.

"What China needs is a structural buildup," one top Western diplomat said to me. "China lacks basic data, despite the new census, and it lacks the indigenous capacity to properly develop and analyze demographic data."

Three weeks in China convinced me that the Chinese experience points up in a most dramatic way the dilemma that rapid population growth is posing not only for the Chinese themselves but also traditional Western liberal values.

The Chinese have quite clearly decided that their population problem is so enormous that its solution justifies the severe restriction of individual liberties for the general good of the community. And, of course, world attention focuses on China because one-quarter of mankind lives here. But China is only the most dramatic example of a country taking strong steps to curb individual freedoms for the common good: Singapore long ago made it socially and economically unfashionable for a couple to have more than two children; it continues to impose economic penalties on families that violate the government two-child policy directive. The ill-designed actions of Prime Minister Indira

Gandhi during the 1975–1977 Emergency period, when thousands of men were forcibly sterilized because voluntary family-planning acceptance was not comprehensive enough, were a manifestation of a very powerful feeling among many leaders in the Third World that their countries' "population problem" had simply gone way beyond the question of individual liberties. It was apparent to me during my travels that more and more leaders of developing states feel—without necessarily saying so in public, for fear that their Western benefactors will retaliate by cutting off aid—that the restriction of procreative freedom is required to satisfy the larger social good and goals of the community.

It seems to me that China is only the first of what promises to be a parade of countries in the Third World that will also find ways of further restricting the procreative freedoms of individual couples. The near certainty that this kind of a thing will continue poses a real problem for Western donor agencies, which will have to be guided by the prevailing democratic values of the societies they represent. In particular, it is unlikely that American public opinion will support the sort of measures the Chinese have taken to slow down population growth. Moreover, such measures are out of bounds as far as Congress is concerned: even if the traditional abhorrence of giving economic aid to Communist states were overcome, I do not see a China population aid bill being approved by the U.S. Congress in the light of what is happening in China at present.

The philosophical centerpiece of American and, indeed, most Western assistance for population projects is voluntarism and individual freedom so that enlightened self-interest will coincide with the public interest. Many Americans and Westerners hold that well-run voluntary family programs—such as those sponsored by the London-based International Planned Parenthood Federation—will bring about sufficient fertility declines so that there will be no need for strong and punitive measures. Yet we are starting to see country after country, such as Bangladesh, Pakistan, and El Salvador, coming to grips with what to do when voluntary family planning is just not enough. The Chinese experience points to what many Third World countries may well be forced to do pretty soon.

Most Americans and their lawmakers consider reproductive freedom inviolate, whereas they do not bat an eyelid when it comes to acquiescing to other individual freedoms—such as property ownership or even sometimes speech—being occasionally curbed for the sake of the common good as determined by their government. And their mechanical reaction to what is happening on the population front in China is often one of horror and condemnation. But such a reaction ignores the demographic reality of this overcrowded country.

My own view is this: I do not endorse the measures being instituted by the Chinese. But I have also seen that the future is already upon China—and it is a nightmare. If it takes a radical program involving curbing personal freedoms to ameliorate the situation, then let the Chinese bear the responsibility. After all, it is the Chinese who are going to have to live in their space, not we in the West.

Eight

Skeptics and True Believers

Dr. Billings & Co.

THE BOGEYMAN of the population business is a man named John J. Billings.

Everywhere I traveled, people wanted to know if I had met him. It seemed that I was following in his trail, for everywhere I went he had already been there. Billings is even more peripatetic than Rafael M. Salas, head of the United Nations Fund for Population Activities: Salas is on the road several months a year; Billings is away from his Melbourne, Australia, office several days each month. I was intrigued. Why were birth control workers in many parts of the world so scared of this man? Even officials at the United Nations seemed to be in awe of him. I tried repeatedly to reach him by telephone, but he always seemed to be away —if it wasn't Papua New Guinea, then it was Bamako, Mali, or Jacho, Ecuador, or the Fiji Islands.

One afternoon in Manila, a young physician who was treating a sprain in my foot asked me if during my travels for the population book I had encountered Billings. "He's a charming fellow," she said, bandaging my foot with strength surprising for a woman so slender. "I met him once at a seminar in South Korea. I wouldn't be surprised if he persuades governments of the world to make a bonfire of condoms. He's a very persuasive man. John Billings devoutly believes that the time is long overdue for all artificial birth control programs to be abolished."

He also argues that the pill and the intrauterine device (IUD) should be outlawed. He says international birth control projects such as those financed by the United States and the United Nations have caused great traumas in the Third World and have amounted to coercion against poor people to reduce their family size. Overpopulation is not an immediate problem for mankind, and the earth could support ten times as many people if 25 percent of its arable land could be cultivated, Billings asserts.

Is he a crank?

A neurologist by profession, Billings has emerged in the last decade as the world's most influential spokesman against artificial birth control programs. There are those in the population business—which includes demographers, fieldworkers, fund-raisers, and lobbyists, as well as officials of international agencies that support family-planning programs—who fear that by his constant criticisms of conventional birth control programs and his attacks on agencies that sustain such projects Billings will eventually succeed in turning governments against supporting population programs. At a time when the world economy is still reeling from recession and governments are already cutting back on social programs, Billings's worldwide anti–birth control campaign could well play a key role in eventually dismantling global population projects.

If this is endowing him with too much power, consider the fact that Billings is enthusiastically supported by the hierarchy of the Roman Catholic church. Pope John Paul II meets with Billings regularly and has praised his position. The Australian physician has won the ear of key members of President Reagan's administration and of the U.S. Congress, some of whom are increasingly expressing opposition to current international efforts in birth control. As a practicing Catholic, Billings endorses his church's position that the only acceptable birth control method is the so-called natural method, which relies on a woman's biological clock to assess her fertility.

Dr. Billings and his wife Evelyn, also a physician, have devised a variation of the Church-approved natural birth control system that they call the Billings Method. Rather than rely on body temperature—as most "natural" methods call for—it requires the woman to study her vaginal mucus, since the presence of a certain type of mucus is the "only reliable" way to assess female fertility. The method calls for sexual abstinence when this mucus is present.

I finally reached Billings by telephone at his office in Melbourne. He was at once welcoming. Plane schedules being what they generally are, it took me two days to route myself from Manila via Singapore to Melbourne. The woman in the seat next to me on the Qantas flight from

Singapore happened to be a gynecologist. I casually asked her about the "Billings Method."

"It's a fraud, an absolute fraud," she said, startling a steward who happened to be passing by.

"His so-called method presupposes that most women have vaginal mucus and that it is regular enough to sustain conclusions on whether or not she is fertile that particular day," the Australian physician said. "A lot of doctors like me are persuaded that the scientific basis for the Billings Method is quite shaky—and rocky."

In Melbourne, as it turned out, I had a couple of days to myself before the meeting with Dr. Billings. I looked up a woman named Katherine Betts, who I had been told was prominent among academicians opposed to John Billings and his movement. She is a lecturer of anthropology at Monash University, just outside Melbourne, and since the academic term happened to be in recess she invited me for a chat at her home in suburban Mount Waverly.

It took me more than an hour by taxi from my hotel in the center of Melbourne to Mount Waverly. It was not that traffic was particularly thick; it was simply that Melbourne is a sprawling city—not especially densely populated, just spread out—with a strangely disorganized street system. We drove past cricket fields where on this Sunday men in flannels were batting it out; we passed pleasant parks filled with impressive chestnut trees, acacia, silver poplar, eucalyptus, and Chinese elms. Melbourne appeared graceful, it had a quiet elegance. We passed large mansions that reminded me of English manors.

The outskirts of Melbourne resembled the outer boroughs of New York or London. Small, wood-framed, one-story homes dotted the landscape. Men mowed their lawns; children played in back yards. Ice cream trucks cruised tree-edged streets. Boys kicked soccer balls in open fields. Katherine Betts lived in a neat house with a picture window. It was an academician's home, papers strewn about, books all over the place, a rocking chair. Mrs. Betts was tall, about forty years old, and ascetic-looking. Without much ado she launched into Billings.

"Billings strikes fear into people's hearts about other family-planning methods," she said, with a slight hint of shyness. "People are frightened enough as it is of the aftereffects of such things as the pill and the IUD. There is something fraudulent and sinister about some of Billings's tactics—he tells people that if his 'method' fails, it is the user's fault. He leaves people with a terrific sense of guilt about their sex habits. A Polish friend of mine, who has six children and who is now again pregnant despite using the 'Billings Method' was told by one of Billings's chief associates that she was being punished for her sins!

"An alarming situation in the field of family planning has arisen in Australia in recent years," Mrs. Betts went on. "Government funds and facilities have been misused to promote Billings's ovulation method, which is scientifically unproven. Contrary to accepted family-planning practice, the method is presented in isolation from other methods and without giving accurate information about its effectiveness. It is presented in a context of fear of the social and physical consequences of other forms of contraception, while the attitude taken to procreation discounts failures as the patient's fault. Billings is having his cake and eating it, too!"

Around the time I was in Australia to see Dr. Billings, Pope John Paul II issued his Bill of Rights of the Family. The Pope, more conservative in his views on birth control than most of his predecessors in this century, was said to be concerned that the Roman Catholic church's ban on artificial contraception was mostly ignored by Catholics, especially in Western countries. In the United States, for instance, bishops cited figures showing that nearly 80 percent of American Catholic women used contraceptives; moreover, the bishops also cited surveys that showed that only 29 percent of Catholic priests in the United States believed that artificial birth control was intrinsically immoral.

The Pope came down hard against all forms of artificial birth control.

"We simply cannot accept the contemporary pursuit of exaggerated convenience and comfort," he told a group of American bishops who met with him at the Vatican just before the Bill of Rights of the Family was released. On a number of occasions since then, he has strongly condemned artificial birth control as immoral.

Pope John Paul II called on bishops everywhere to promote "natural" family planning to help needy people determine "the spacings of births and the size of their family." This means, the Pope said, a "broader, more decisive, and more systematic effort to make the natural methods of regulating fertility known, respected, and applied."

The Pope added: "The number of couples successfully using the natural methods is constantly growing." Once again condemning abortion, the Pope said that couples "must be urged to avoid any action that threatens a life already conceived, that denies or frustrates their procreative power, or violates the integrity of the marriage act."

John Billings could derive much satisfaction from what his Pope said, for the papal statements amounted to a vindication—and even an endorsement—of the Billings movement.

I was more eager than ever to meet Dr. Billings. On the appointed day, I arrived at his office on a quiet, nondescript street in Melbourne. From his small waiting room I could see an inner courtyard that had a Japanese-style garden. Secretaries busily typed on IBM electric machines. Several harmless women's magazines lay on a coffee table. It was like any other doctor's office.

Dr. Billings was tall, immaculately attired in what was obviously a custom-tailored gray suit. He was right out of central casting, the perfect distinguished physician. If Hollywood needed someone for a doctor's role, here was the ideal candidate, I thought. Even Billings's voice had just that right tone of reassurance. He was very charming indeed.

He seemed flattered that I had come all the way to Australia to interview him. And he was prepared for our meeting: I was given a stack of his speeches, his bio data, and a copy of his wife's controversial book. I told Billings that the book I had in mind would, among other things, assess whether the money spent on population programs between 1974 and 1984 had really improved the lives of those for whom the expenditures were intended.

"The population 'decade' has achieved absolutely nothing," Billings responded. "These international programs, particularly those funded by the United Nations and the United States, have instead produced great harm and resentment. They have been racist programs, intended to maintain the status quo of the Western countries. There has been applied coercion against poor people to reduce the size of their families. These international population programs have been nothing short of degradation, humiliation, and exploitation of the poor people of the Third World."

It was a strong first salvo. Billings did not stop.

"It is not up to a government or anyone else to impose on people how many children they should have," Billings said. "I am appalled by the fact that so often Third World countries are given aid by the West on the basis of accepting sinister birth control programs. In my travels throughout the developing world I find these programs really do have contempt for people who are poor, illiterate, black, with Oriental eyes, or whatever."

Billings was intrigued by the fact that I had been given an endowment by the United Nations Fund for Population Activities. Salas's agency is a special bête noire for Billings, as are two other organizations heavily involved in promoting population programs around the world: the U.S. Agency for International Development and the International Planned Parenthood Federation.

"The money is used extensively to mold people's way of thinking. I have talked with people in universities who say they've been offered substantial rewards if they were to support birth control programs and concepts," Billings said. "I am aware, of course, that a good deal has been achieved in the field of health—such as the eradication of smallpox, improvements in maternal and child care, et cetera. But people who organize these massive birth control programs are often deceitful—to some extent they are concealing the truth about the 'success' of their programs. Statistics are often falsified. I have met with the UNFPA people in New York—they know their programs are not the success they would like it to be. I just get these vibrations.

"Let no one be deceived: support for these birth control programs betokens an attitude of resentment and contempt toward the underprivileged—the poor, the illiterate, the colored races—resentment that they should be consuming the world's resources, mixed with the fear that by numbers alone they may come to reverse the present inequality of economic status," Billings continued, speaking in a quiet, controlled fashion.

The U.S. government's Agency for International Development, he said, had through its financing of birth control programs brought not encomiums but criticisms on the United States.

"The use of United States government funds for abortion is explicitly prohibited," Billings went on, in the manner of a university professor who has delivered the same lecture dozens of time before. "However, U.S. AID has consistently been the main source of money for such organizations as the United Nations Fund for Population Activities, Planned Parenthood Federation of America, the IPPF in London, the Pathfinder Fund, and so on—and in this way has financed massive birth control programs in which abortion figures very prominently. This is shocking."

He told me that countries of the Third World were often given economic assistance by industrialized states on the basis of their agreeing to institute birth control programs. "This is offensive," Billings said.

"There is a social sickness in the Western world today which has assumed epidemic proportions, a sickness of the mind that is highly contagious," he went on. "This sickness is an obsession about birth control. It both begins and ends in a devaluation of human life and a debasement of human sexuality. It causes people to believe that fertility is a burden, pregnancy a disease, and the birth of a child a misfortune. The psychological invalidism it produces can be found amongst all classes of individuals. Those who promote 'contraception' find in the end that they are reluctant to entrust fecundity to ordinary people and seek to remove from them the ability and responsibility of increasing the size of their family at any time they choose. Though representing themselves as champions of human freedom, they often act to coerce, even by degraded means, men and women to accept sterilizing operations which render them permanently incapable of begetting more children. And many show themselves ready to deny the most fundamental of human rights, that of an innocent, helpless child in the womb to go on living."

Dr. Billings seems to be acquiring more and more followers in Australia, the United States, and many countries of the Third World. His foundation has set up headquarters in Los Angeles and has branches in several countries. He is often invited to give testimony before congressional committees in Washington and also is consulted by government officials in many Western countries. Some state governments in India are encouraging clinics to adopt the "Billings Method" as the exclusive means of birth control. In the West, Dr. Billings appears to have locked on to the women's movement, some of whose influential members would like women to have greater control over their bodies and over pharmaceutical systems catering to women's needs. He also draws support from people who are into natural foods and the health movement.

Evelyn Billings's recent book on the "Billings Method" sold more copies than any previous Australian book on health-related matters. Billings told me during our conversations in Melbourne that one reason his wife's book had done well was that it suggested a simple, inexpensive way by which people could regulate their family size. "It is the only

reliable way to determine fertility," Billings asserted, dismissing the objections of critics like Katherine Betts as "irrelevant and anti-Catholic."

"The use of the natural method really brings out in a husband and wife virtues that help a marriage," Billings said. "This means the wife has to communicate with her husband about her feelings, her fertility, and her sexuality. The husband in turn respects his wife, and the couple abstains from sex when the woman is in her fertile state."

He recalled an incident in the Fiji Islands. A woman with twelve children told him that one reason she'd had so many children was that her husband, a drunkard, would force himself on her. Finally, after consulting with a local "Billings Method" social worker, this woman took to leaving her home on those nights when she knew she was fertile; she would spend these nights with her parents, Billings said. The woman was thus able to avoid pregnancy, Billings said, and her husband gave up drinking to ensure that his wife did not leave their home any time of the month.

"We are not telling people not to have more kids," Billings said to me. "That's up to them. But in most developing countries you need more people, not less. I look at children as a pair of hands, not more mouths to feed. I believe population pressures stimulate economic development. I've seen authoritative studies that showed that the earth's agricultural resources are capable of feeding 40 billion people, almost ten times the world's current population."

This is an argument also used by other well-known figures who are in some way connected with the population business. Professor Julian L. Simon of the University of Illinois calls people "the ultimate resource," which also happens to be the title of a book he recently wrote. In that book, Professor Simon says:

> The standard of living has risen along with the size of the world's population since the beginning of recorded time. And with increases in income and population have come less severe shortages, lower costs, and an increased availability of resources, including a cleaner environment and greater access to natural recreation areas. And there is no convincing reason why these trends toward a better life and toward lower prices for materials (including food and energy) should not continue indefinitely. Contrary to common rhetoric, there are no meaningful limits to the continuation of this process. . . . There is no physical or economic reason why human

resourcefulness and enterprise cannot forever continue to respond to impending shortages and existing problems with new expedients that, after an adjustment period, leave us better off than before the problem arose.

Dr. Billings is an admirer of Professor Simon.

"Perhaps the greatest fallacy of all, one which has deceived many people, is that which would have us believe that the socioeconomic problems of the world, and even the political problems, cannot be solved without a massive reduction in the birthrate," Billings said to me. "The mischief created by this opinion is compounded by the additional delusion that, insofar as a prudent regulation of births is required, this can be achieved only by methods which would attack life at its source, or even worse, would destroy life after it has begun—in other words, by programs of contraception, sterilization, and abortion.

"The prosperity of a country will not be determined by how many people it has—this so-called overpopulation nonsense—but by the application of modern technologies in the agricultural and veterinary sciences to food production and the establishment of educational programs which are adequate to ensure a supply of the skills necessary to sustain secondary industries sufficient to guarantee a basic level of independence," Billings said. "Irrational fear has led to an obsessional prejudice against children, such as to obscure the fact that the vitality of a country is to a large extent provided by its young people. To have a sufficient number of young people there must be babies."

The argument that the best way to ensure a manageable population growth rate is through a faster economic development rate is being debated by demographers. The Brandt Commission Report, a milestone in development economics and politics, argues that although "expanded and more efficient family-planning services are needed," such services, in order to be effective, must be accompanied by general economic and social progress. "In the final analysis, it is development itself that will provide the most propitious environment for stabilizing the world's population at tolerable levels," the Brandt Report says.

But Steven W. Sinding of the U.S. Agency for International Development objects: "We have learned that in many settings enhanced family-planning services have made significant difference concerning birthrates."

Dr. Billings believes that, under pressure from the pharmaceutical industry and from Western agencies with vested interests, the emphasis

in developing countries has been far too much on restricting population growth and not enough on promoting economic growth. The controversy, in which he is playing a major role, is likely to go on for a long time. Meanwhile, Dr. Billings and the position taken by the Catholic church are starting to have a noticeable impact on policy makers in Western countries that traditionally give money for population programs in the developing world. The financial commitment of the West to population programs is now stagnant, or even declining, largely because of the world recession—but also because of the perception of influential Western policy makers that a lot of birth control programs are questionable in their value and are inefficiently managed.

Proponents of artificial birth control methods are worried that as populations all over the Third World increase, there may now not be enough funds for family-planning programs. This prospect delights Billings.

"Propagandists for the pharmaceutical industries have cleverly persuaded many people that opposition to their programs represents an attempt by a minority group to impose their morality upon the world," he told me. "It is of course exactly the other way about. The persons who stand to receive financial gain from the birth control programs are seeking to impose their perverted morality upon the rest of the world."

Steven Sinding, director of the Office of Population at AID and formerly with AID in Manila, gets very upset whenever I mention Billings's name. As the key American official in charge of "population," it is Sinding who frequently must respond to John Billings's charges that AID twists arms in developing countries to get leaders to accept coercive family-planning programs if they wished to receive U.S. economic assistance.

"Show us the evidence!" Sinding said to me one evening as we chatted in his office in Arlington, Virginia.

"Billings claims that there's an evil intent on the part of the West as far as population programs are concerned," Sinding continued, "and that American motives in family planning are racist. There is absolutely no basis for these charges. Where is the documentary evidence? It's infuriating to me that Billings and his cohorts perpetuate this myth. And it's equally demoralizing that Billings's outrageous statements are taken at face value by many journalists."

John Billings aside, there can be no question that the blush is off the population rose. The concern that seemed to stimulate great deal of public attention in the early 1970s and the resulting financial support

throughout the 1970s has diminished as people's attention turned to other problems: first the energy crunch brought on by soaring world oil prices; and more recently, the nuclear disarmament movement. Robert S. McNamara, former president of the World Bank, warned that apart from threat of nuclear annihilation, the only "real" and continuing problem facing mankind was overpopulation. His warning doesn't convince Billings and others who influence Western politicians who hold purse strings in countries like the United States that traditionally have given funds for family-planning programs.

In a world and society that have a relatively short attention span when it comes to identification and resolution of problems, we have difficulty maintaining attention to our "population problem," which requires not just rhetorical recognition but sustained long-term effort—through the rest of this century, and the next. The percentage of development assistance going to population has declined since the mid-1970s. The volume of money available has declined in real terms. This is a reflection of the leveling off of political interest.

Steven Sinding says he sees "further signs" that the population movement may be losing momentum. He notes that articles on the world population problem appear less frequently in major newspapers and magazines today than they did in the late 1960s and early 1970s, when the warnings of people like Ehrlich generated considerable public discussion of the world's "population problem."

"To some extent this decline in media interest in and, perhaps, public support for population programs is a consequence of the fact that programs in many countries are beginning to succeed and fertility is beginning to decline," Sinding says. "If this is true, that the very success of some programs and the recent decline in global fertility have brought with them a certain sense of satisfaction in the United States and other industrialized countries, then it's time to turn up the volume on the population crisis record again. Because the population crisis has not been overcome. Instead, we are just beginning to discover that it may be soluble, but only if developing countries continue to build on the policies and programs they have recently established and only if donor countries and agencies stay the course with the developing countries, providing the funds and technology that will be required at least through the end of the century. The irony of the present situation is that interest and support in the West may be at a plateau or in decline precisely at the time that the Third World has begun to commit itself to solving the problem. This means that just when the demand for resources is at its peak, the supply has begun to dry up."

As Sinding said these things, it occurred to me how very extraordinary it was that a key Western aid official should be speaking in such a fashion: we are all accustomed to Third World types making impassioned pleas for more economic assistance, but here was an official of the world's biggest aid-giving country, the United States, who was saying on the record that it was time the more fortunate nations did more for the less fortunate ones.

Back in 1968, social scientists such as Professor Paul R. Ehrlich of Stanford University shook the world with warnings that a "population bomb" was about to explode. Citing the world's annual population growth rate of 2 percent plus, they predicted that by 1980 the global population would easily double and that by the end of the century the world could contain as many as 10 billion people. They drew frightening scenarios of worldwide famine, riots, and misery; they warned that most of the runaway population growth would occur in the world's poor countries, which could afford such growth the least. And they warned that if something drastic wasn't done to curb the world's mushrooming population, violence would spread like wildfire as more and more people fought for access to declining resources.

Few of those dire predictions have been borne out. By 1983, or three years after the doomsday deadline, the world's annual population growth rate in fact had slowed down to 1.7 percent. The predictions now were that by the end of the century the current global population of 4.6 billion would rise not to 8 or 10 billion but to about 6.1 billion. The fact that the earlier doomsday scenarios haven't quite worked out represents an achievement for the mostly unheralded men and women of the "population business," those fieldworkers, demographers, scientists, family-planning counselors, physicians, and population fund-raisers who in country after country of the developing world worked quietly but energetically to persuade people to keep their family size small.

And a central figure among them for more than a decade now has been Rafael M. Salas of the Philippines. The Harvard-educated Salas is officially an under secretary general of the United Nations and executive director of its Fund for Population Activities. Unofficially, he is known all over the world as "Mr. Population." Salas is unquestionably a towering figure in global population work and the world's leading spokesman for population causes.

Through an unusual combination of political skill and managerial savvy, Salas has persuaded Third World governments to incorporate population programs into their overall development plans. He has convinced leaders that they must match their political rhetoric in support of population work with funds for specific projects aimed at bringing down birthrates where necessary, improving health care, increasing literacy—especially among women—and controlling that scourge of the Third World, infant mortality. He has coaxed Western governments, and especially the United States, to pump billions of dollars into population programs all over the world since 1974, the year when most nations of the world formally endorsed the concept of family planning at a megaconference in Bucharest. Moreover, he has popularized "population" without upsetting cultural values in various countries: he does not, for example, advocate abortion, which is repugnant not only to the Roman Catholic church but also in many traditional societies; Salas's agency does not fund abortion programs of any kind.

Salas has taken the terror out of the word *population*. He has done so by making it acceptable around the world and by convincing governments that it was indeed possible to regulate a nation's demographic trends, however daunting they might be. Salas's success has not only been the overwhelming governmental support he has elicited for population programs in different parts of the world; just as strikingly, he has been able to get governments in a wide variety of countries—Catholic, Moslem, Marxist, democratic, authoritarian—to institute population programs without offending their particular cultural sensitivities. In such Catholic states as Ecuador, Colombia, and Costa Rica, for example, he would underscore the fact that his agency—known all over the world mostly by its acronym, UNFPA—did not support abortion programs and that if the Catholic church was opposed to artificial birth control, then UNFPA would give funds for programs advocating the so-called natural birth control method, which relies on a woman's biological cycle and which is favored by the Church. In heavily Moslem states, such as the ones in the Persian Gulf region, where there has been some religious resistance to the idea of family planning and where in some cases the problem was not of overpopulation but of underpopulation, Salas offered support for health programs that emphasized child and maternal care. In the states of black Africa the need was to conduct first-ever censuses, and so that is what Salas gave money for. The leaders of China asked for, and received, computers to conduct a comprehensive census in 1982. In every case, involving some 5,000 projects in 140 countries in the last decade, Salas left it to the leaders of individual countries to decide for themselves what sort of population program they wanted. And now, because of Rafael Salas's unceasing efforts, every one of the world's developing states has some sort of population policy and program.

"When we deal with population, we are dealing with what is probably the most sensitive aspect of people's daily existence—their sex lives," Salas says. "The question before us was: How do you tell people how many children they should have—and yet not invade people's privacy or upset their personal values? The real message of 'population' is this, I think: Population programs aren't simply a matter of promoting smaller families. Population also means guaranteeing that our children are given the fullest opportunities to be educated, to get good health care, to have access to the jobs and careers they eventually want. It is really a matter of increasing the value of every birth, of expanding the potential of every child born to the fullest, of improving the quality of life of a community."

When asked in what sense does the United Nations really "help" these countries, Salas does not hesitate: "We now feel that the countries themselves are able to undertake the implementation of many of these projects. Our population programs have generated a unique self-help ethic among these countries. Consider the fact that for every dollar they now receive from us in assistance, they themselves put in an additional four dollars. In the initial phase of our work, we created an awareness. There was a time, for instance, when the word *population* itself was not acceptable even in the United Nations. A few ambassadors refused to speak to me if I mentioned 'population.' It was not until the late 1960s that the first resolution was formulated on population assistance to countries in need. But we persisted. What most people don't realize is that the United Nations is engaged in a wide range of activities to solve the problems of development, the problems of population, the problems of resources, and the interrelationships between all of these."

It is not that Salas invented "population." What he did was to put it all together under one rubric: demographers had long warned about the world's exponential growth in population; a few private family-planning organizations had worked zealously in high-growth states such as India to persuade people to use contraceptives; and governments would occasionally fund a project for population "control" in the Third World. But until Salas came along and started the UNFPA, there had been no global program of assistance to countries for population work.

His achievement has been in organizing such a program—so that now the UNFPA is the world's biggest source of multilateral funds for population to developing nations.

The "population business" is a fascinating collection of agencies and individuals. The UNFPA is perhaps the most glamorous single entity because of its multinational composition and because of Salas's peripatetic wooing of world statesmen. But long before the UNFPA was formed, institutions like the London-based International Planned Parenthood Federation (known generally as the IPPF) and New York's Population Council were working mightily to alleviate the world's population problems. By its very nature, "population" does not possess the same allure for the media as do, say, nuclear and environmental issues, and so the men and women of the "population business" usually do not command much ink. I thought that I would sketch thumbnail portraits here of some of the leading institutional and individual dramatis personae, present and past, in this field.

In a book that received much attention in the population business, *Bitter Pills: Population Policies and their Implementation in Eight Developing Countries*, author Donald P. Warwick said:

> International donors have had an incalculable effect on the origin, shape, and direction of population programs in the developing countries. Of all the spheres of national development, population has been the most donor driven. Governments do not usually have to be prodded hard to grow more food or to build more roads, but many had to be persuaded to act on population control. Toward that end, dozens of donors stepped in with grants, loans, scholarships, advisers, exhortations, backstage deals, and even clandestine interventions.
>
> If one had to pick the donor agency with the strongest total impact on population programs in the developing countries, the choice would be AID [the U.S. Agency for International Development]."

The United Nations Fund for Population Activities may now be the world's biggest source of multilateral assistance for population programs, but AID has been the biggest donor, period. Steven W. Sinding, who now heads AID's Office of Population, reports that since 1965 the agency has provided more than $2 billion for "population" in the form of technical assistance and commodities to developing states. In contrast, the UNFPA has given $1 billion since it was formed in 1969, and the next biggest donor, the International Bank for Reconstruction and Development—more commonly known as the World Bank—has given just under $1 billion. Moreover, about 30 percent of UNFPA's budget consists of AID money—so the overall AID contribution to population programs has been quite handsome.

Close to a third of AID's annual population budget of $240 million goes into bilateral assistance to nations whose population increase poses threats for the world as a whole (countries such as Pakistan, Bangladesh, Egypt, Thailand, Indonesia, Kenya, Colombia, and Morocco). Most of the budget, however, goes to assisting other population agencies such as the UNFPA, the IPPF, the Population Council, the Boston-based Pathfinder Fund, Family Planning International Assistance, and the Association for Voluntary Sterilization. AID also supports various projects involving contraceptive, demographic and biomedical research.

The basic philosophy guiding AID over the years has been, as Margaret Wolfson has written in *Changing Approaches to Population Problems* that "there exists in developing countries a large unsatisfied demand for family planning. The focus of the Agency's population assistance, therefore, has largely taken the form of efforts to improve the supply and the delivery of contraceptive services to the rural and urban poor."

The one key figure identified with this underlying philosophy was a man named Reimert T. Ravenholt, who headed AID's Office of Population through most of the 1970s. He was a tough, energetic individual obsessed with what seemed a single mission: to bring down population growth rates in the world's overpopulated poor countries. He believed that population growth could indeed be brought down by voluntary means but that needy countries should be saturated with contraceptives and family-planning services. The issue for Ravenholt was not one of forcing solutions down people's throats but in fact of answering what he perceived to be unmet birth control needs in the Third World. To this end, he professionalized AID's Office of Population, expanding the staff and the budget.

It was Ravenholt who helped establish, along with the United Nations Fund for Population Activities, the World Fertility Survey. The survey became the biggest social science project ever, with projects assessing people's reproductive patterns carried out in forty developing states and twenty industrialized countries. Ravenholt stimulated the development of the laparoscope, the so-called belly button device now widely used for female sterilizations (sterilizations have now become the single biggest means of birth control around the world).

But Ravenholt had his enemies. Many Third World leaders felt he typified the "ugly American" who wanted to impose his own credo on aid-receiving countries. In particular, many black African leaders felt that Ravenholt tried to force-feed family planning on the continent. His personal view that population programs, in order to be successful, must have abortion components was vigorously opposed in Congress by those with so-called right-to-life sympathies. Ravenholt's opponents included such formidable figures as Representative Clement Zablocki, Democrat of Wisconsin and chairman of the House Foreign Affairs Committee. And within AID, too, Ravenholt had his detractors: there were those who felt his approach to family planning was too much tunnel vision and not sufficiently broad in scope. There are officials at AID who feel now that Ravenholt became too powerful a figure within the agency and that his sails needed to be trimmed. By 1979, Ravenholt had been demoted; in late 1980, he quit AID.

Ravenholt's fundamental credo about population assistance remains at the core of AID's family-planning program: that there is a great deal of unmet demand for birth control and that by providing family-planning services the world's population growth can be significantly diminished. But under Ravenholt's successors, this credo has been expanded to include the position that the simple provision of family-planning services in the absence of accompanying social and economic changes will not result in fertility decline. AID no longer argues as it did during Ravenholt's halcyon days that there is a uniform and unquenchable thirst for family-planning services; the position now is that demand for family-planning services is variable and that, indeed, the extent of demand is a function of a country's social and economic atmosphere.

AID now seems to have become far more sophisticated than during Ravenholt's time about what works and what doesn't in the field of family-planning assistance. Take the case of Bangladesh. It used to be that virtually all U.S. assistance for Bangladesh's population programs was given to the government. The government ran some of the worst-managed population projects in the Third World. Now 60 percent of the $26 million currently allocated to Bangladesh is given to nongovernmental organizations engaged in population work. These organizations have demonstrated that they can manage foreign aid better than most government agencies.

It seems to me that AID, under the helmsmanship of its Reagan-appointed administrator, M. Peter McPherson, is showing the kind of flexibility and constant attention to cost-effectiveness that it sorely lacked during Ravenholt's time—when, in fact, AID had more money available than it knew what to do with. AID's longtime special donor relationship with private voluntary organizations dates back to this era, when Ravenholt had ample funds available and made sure he gave the money to private agencies like the International Planned Parenthood Federation. AID officials believe that it is this special relationship with efficient private organizations that explains why so many AID-financed projects in places like Colombia, South Korea, Taiwan, Thailand, and Costa Rica have been successes.

There is general agreement among people in the population business that another impressive aspect of AID's current-day operations is its decentrallized functioning. Steve Sinding runs the main Office of Population in Roslyn Plaza, Virginia, but there are also five regional offices in Asia, Africa, Latin America, and the Middle East. The regional offices have a reasonable amount of autonomy and discretion to channel and control population assistance funds locally.

It may not be fashionable to say it in this day and age of disclosures of government bureaucratic bumbling and bungling, but here is an agency that seems to work very well indeed.

* * *

One of AID's great allies in the population business is the International Planned Parenthood Federation, which has its headquarters in an unprepossessing building on Lower Regent Street, just off the clangor of Picadilly in London. This year, IPPF will receive some $11 million from AID, representing roughly a fifth of the worldwide voluntary agency's budget (which will nevertheless contain a deficit of almost $2 million). The IPPF has now become, after the International Red Cross, the world's biggest nongovernmental organization. AID officials speak highly of IPPF because it has historically been the organization that can take the greatest amount of credit for legitimizing family planning all over the world.

It has done so through a vigorous network of more than 110 national family-planning associations all around the world, from Afghanistan to Zambia. These associations, although funded primarily by IPPF headquarters in London, are autonomous and not necessarily always acquiescent to policy suggestions from headquarters.

But the value of the national family-planning associations, such as the ones in India or Sri Lanka or Egypt, is that they have shown the way: they started birth control clinics when it was not necessarily popular to do so. These associations, in conjunction with London headquarters, also established the basic principle of voluntarism and choice. In India I met a remarkable woman named Avabai Wadia (who has for many years headed the Family Planning Association of India and who now is also the worldwide president of IPPF), who slogged for many years in remote parts of the Subcontinent to put into place a network of voluntary family-planning clinics. Mrs. Wadia's efforts led to the fashioning of a corps of dedicated birth control volunteers—and to rising awareness among Indian government officials concerning the urgency of controlling rampant population growth.

It was in India, in fact, that the International Planned Parenthood Federation was formally founded in 1952 (although an organizational meeting was held four years earlier at Cheltenham, England). The founding members were the family-planning associations of eight states: Holland, Hong Kong, India, Singapore, Sweden, Britian, West Germany, and the United States. Two extraordinarily determined women, Margaret Sanger (who had led the birth control movement in the United States) and Lady Dhanvanti Rama Rau of India, became the copresidents of IPPF.

In many respects, 1952 was a critical year for the international birth control movement. That was the year that a multinational conference organized specifically for the purpose of considering family-planning endeavors was held in Bombay. That was also the year when India became the first country in the world formally to establish a national population policy. And 1952 was the year when the invaluable research organization, the New York–based Population Council, was formed, headed by the philanthropist John D. Rockefeller III.

The energizing forces that were put into motion in 1952 are still very much around. Each year since then, some government or other in a Third World country has announced a national population policy or program. Nearly a half of the United Nations 158 member-states now have a declared policy of reducing population growth.

Because more and more governments are directly getting involved in the population business, organizations such as the IPPF and the national family-planning associations find their thunder frequently stolen. In country after country of Asia, for example, I found that the role of the voluntary, private associations had become less visible, while that of governmental agencies was enhanced. (In black Africa and Latin America, however, IPPF units still are functioning vigorously.) The world recession has also hit voluntary family-planning agencies. Some critics of the population business say that the leadership of IPPF itself has now become old and tired and that the world organization has lost its pioneering spirit.

As a writer and journalist, I am particularly impressed by at least one aspect of IPPF's activities. The organization publishes a quarterly magazine called *People*, an imaginatively produced journal that is among the best in the magazine world. Its editor is a man named John Rowley, a former newspaper reporter and editor, who commissions writers to travel throughout the Third World to report on developments concerning not just family planning but a broad range of development topics such as women's education, maternal and child care, aging societies, and youth employment. *People* has often served as an early-warning mechanism concerning such matters as the world's food production and primary health care. I think the magazine's center section, "Earthwatch," is one of the most superbly presented pieces of journalism around.

Rowley, a silver-haired man with a pleasing manner, has been fortunate in possessing a stable of gifted writers he can count on to produce his copy: Paul Harrison, Jeremy Hamand, and Rami Chhabra, among others. Rowley himself is on the road frequently. When I visited the *People* office in London, I was mildly surprised to see how small a staff Rowley actually has. His stewardship at *People* and the fine product he comes out with year after year should be a model for other magazines, especially those dreadful—and much costlier—publications put out by so many multilateral "development" agencies.

* * *

Dr. Billings had said to me in Melbourne that he did not view overpopulation as a problem for the Third World. Indeed, he had asserted, developing countries in fact needed more people to help build the economy. More kids in poor families were not really more mouths but more hands available for work. I decided to test this thesis out among poor people in and around Bombay, the vast Indian metropolis where I grew up.

Bombay assaults the senses. On this particular visit, I landed at the new international airport just after a violent rainstorm. The monsoon season was in full swing. From the air, the concrete tenements around the airport looked like concrete cenotaphs rising out of a watery graveyard. Here and there one could see specks of color—tattered clothes hanging out of windows to dry. The airport was like a bazaar, with hundreds of passengers squeezed into a customs enclosure manned by only a handful of officials. In India, every incoming passenger is automatically assumed to be—and treated as—a contraband runner, unless he is a VIP (who bring in the biggest caches of dutiable luxury items but who get away levy-less because of their status). I suppose every customs inspection all over the world can be a humiliating experience, but this is especially so in India. The brown-uniformed man who opened my bags wanted to assess a stiff penalty on my dozen rolls of color film.

"But I am a journalist. These films aren't for sale in Bombay, they are for pictures I'll be taking for my work," I protested.

"Ah, everybody is a journalist these days," the official said, somewhat mysteriously, and then waved me on.

Outside the airport building, it was total pandemonium. Rickety men, weighing less than my portable typewriter, demanded that I hire them as porters. Unsavory characters thrust themselves upon me to offer taxi rides. It had started to rain, heavy, unpleasant rain accompanied by sharp gusts. Beggars, many of them maimed, sought shelter under the building's awnings and were relentlessly chased away by policemen. I waited for friends who'd promised to collect me; they were an hour late.

It had been a year since I last came to Bombay, and it at once seemed to me that the place had deteriorated further. Located on the Arabian Sea, it is both a beautiful and an ugly city; its affluent center is surrounded by a sea of slums. This time the traffic was denser, the roads more potholed than ever before, and everywhere there were beggars. This is India's great commercial city, the capital of its thriving movie industry, and more than 10,000 people from rural areas are said to emigrate to Bombay every week in search of jobs and a better life. There are few jobs available, of course, and fewer decent housing units, so the shantytowns keep spreading.

The merciless growth of these poor communities means that the birthrates in slums soar year by year. The government inundates these slums with birth control propaganda, but to little avail. My mother, Charusheela Gupte, who is a social worker, professor, and writer, said to me once that the high birthrates in India's slums would only start going down if jobs were made available and women were given education opportunities. But no one in the government talks of jobs and education opportunities.

I went to a semirural settlement in a suburb of Bombay called Kalyan. *Kalyan* means "blessing" in Sanskrit, the ancient Indian language, and it is understood colloquially also to mean a "good thing." But in real life Kalyan was a miniature version of Bombay, a mess. One- and two-story houses had been built haphazardly; there were ungainly apartment buildings, short, squat structures that looked ready to implode. People who lived here either worked at local factories that produced such things as soap and textiles or they commuted for two hours by train to Bombay. The Family Planning Association of India, run under the stewardship of a feisty, capable woman named Avabai Wadia, has established birth control clinics in most outlying areas of Bombay, such as Kalyan. I had come to Kalyan, in fact, at the suggestion of one of Mrs. Wadia's friends. But I decided at the last moment that instead of visiting yet another family-planning service center I would wander around Kalyan and see what was happening in neighborhoods where there weren't birth control enthusiasts.

I stopped at the home of Pandurang Vengurlekar. In India, as in most Third World countries, it is easy to pop into most people's homes: welcoming guests, even strangers, and offering hospitality to them, is a well-followed custom. Pandurang owns a bicycle repair shop, which consists of a small yard behind his two-room cottage. He is fifty years old and has five children. It was around the lunch hour when I visited him, and Pandurang's wife, Sakhoobai, invited me to join the family for a meal consisting of dry potato curry, unleavened bread called bhakri, and a lentil gravy. It was a simple, delicious meal, and it made me want to take a nap.

Pandurang told me that his two daughters were now married. They lived near Belgaum, the town in Maharashtra State—of which Bombay is the capital—where Pandurang's family had its roots.

"To have a daughter is expensive in India," Pandurang said, speaking in the local language of Marathi, which was his mother tongue and mine. "I had to pay for the wedding festivities. I had to hand over a dowry. It will take me another two years to earn back what I have paid for my two daughters' marriages."

He had spent the equivalent of $700—7,000 rupees—on those weddings, a fortune for someone of Pandurang's economic class.

I asked him about his sons.

"They have no interest in helping me with my shop," the short, cadaverous Pandurang said, somewhat bitterly. "All three boys work as clerks in Bombay. They want to go to the cinemas. They want to buy clothes. They will not provide any of their earnings for this household. Of course, I cannot ask them to move out. Where will they go? There is no housing in Bombay. Now each wants to get married. This means that daughters-in-law will also live with us. Then there will be children, which I will welcome, of course. But what it means is that I must earn and earn to keep providing for my growing family. At my age I am entitled to some rest and consideration."

I asked Pandurang why he and Sakhoobai had five children.

"What choice did we have? Nowadays all these family-planning workers come around in their fancy vans and offer birth control advice. There was nothing of this when we got married."

He was eighteen when his parents arranged Pandurang's marriage with Sakhoobai, who was fifteen. I decided to test out John Billings's "more hands, not more mouths" theory with Pandurang.

"There are some foreign experts who say that large families are good for people of poor countries," I said.

"Foreign experts!" Pandurang cleared his throat and spat out into his yard. "Foreign experts! What do they know about how we poor people really live? Who are these foreign experts, anyway?"

Nine

El Dorado
Men, Money, and Manpower in the Gulf

NOT LONG AGO, the crew of an American cargo ship spotted a trawler adrift in the choppy Arabian Sea off the southeast shore of Saudi Arabia. A launch was sent to investigate the situation, and the Americans found that there were fifty dead men aboard the vessel and thirty others on the verge of death.

They were all Pakistanis, and they had set off clandestinely from their native land for the golden shores of Saudi Arabia. They had each paid the equivalent of a hundred dollars for the journey, at the end of which, the men had been told by organizers near the Pakistani port of Karachi, lucrative jobs awaited them. The men were to leave their families behind, of course, and eventually the womenfolk and children, too, would be able to join them in Arabia. The men who boarded the trawler were mostly carpenters and plumbers, and they each carried with them just a sack or two with the most basic of wardrobes and personal supplies and pictures of their families. They were trusting men, not versed in the ways of the outside world, and it had not occurred to them that there was something wrong with the entire operation. It had also not occurred to them that the "organizers" hadn't even asked the men to bring along their passports, for none of these villagers knew what a passport was. Two days after their trawler slipped out of a small pier not far from Karachi, a storm broke out and lashed the vessel. Two crew members were swept overboard; food supplies were lost. One by one, as the trawler drifted in the open seas, the passengers started to die of starvation and dehydration. By the time the American ship rescued them, the Pakistanis had been at sea for nearly three weeks.

Kuwait, Libya, Oman, Qatar, Saudi Arabia, and the United Arab Emirates—would rise from 44 percent in 1975 to more than 60 percent by 1985. The World Bank projected that these oil-producing states could expect to host well over 4.5 million "guest workers" by next year. In effect, these migrant workers who have come to the El Dorado of the Middle East have created a nation without boundaries. But they are nationals without rights, they are subject to abuse and exploitation, and they have no recourse—because the merest squeak of a complaint can mean instant deportation back to the venal poverty of their native homelands.

* * *

Yanbu used to be a mere dot of a village on the landfilled shores of the Red Sea, a few dozen miles north of the bustling city of Jidda in Saudi Arabia. It is now a mere dot no more. The Saudis, flushed with wealth from the daily sale of the black gold buried under the sandy wastes of their sun-baked country, are raising a $50 billion industrial city here. It will soon house more than 135,000 people; it will contain a vast complex of refineries, petrochemical plants, and oil storage tanks; its piers will accommodate supertankers that will carry away for export some of the crude oil produced in Saudi Arabia's eastern province nearly a thousand miles away and transported here by a transpeninsular pipeline.

Just north of that oil-producing region on the Persian Gulf, where much of this unique kingdom's annual income of $120 billion is generated, another industrial city is also being fashioned. It is called Al-Jubail, and it is a clone of Yanbu. Within a few years, the mess of pipes, fittings, bulldozers, and trenches that is Jubail today will be one of the world's most modern communities, with a population of 300,000, a soccer stadium, tennis courts and an indoor skating rink, parks, mosques, sewage disposal plants, factories, and air-conditioned shopping malls.

If you travel up to Yanbu or Jubail most any day of the week—even on Friday, the Islamic Sabbath—you will see thousands of workers toiling away in the desert heat. Their energy and efficiency seem amazing, especially in view of the temperatures that often soar past 100 degrees in the shade. Everything appears well ordered here. The work proceeds with clockwork precision. When the laborers are done with their day's work—a full nine hours each, no less—they methodically hop aboard trucks that take them to barracks-style dormitories or, in the case of Yanbu, to two barges that serve as hostels.

This is an unusual story, to be sure, for not everybody who head
for the promised riches of the Gulf countries of the Arabian Peninsul
meets with the same fate as the Pakistanis. But the fact remains tha
one of the most massive voluntary migrations in modern times is sti
taking place in the world's most volatile region, the Middle East, a
hundreds of thousands of workers from poor countries head for oil-ric
Arab states in search of jobs and a better life. This influx poses a grav
threat to the continued political stability of some of these oil-rich state
which are ruled by "royal" families whose foundations are, at best, shak
Yet, these oil-producing Arab states cannot possibly hope to achiev
modernization without importing cheap labor from overseas; and i
some cases, these states must factor in a permanent foreign presence fo
continued economic development because their own domestic popul
tion growth rate cannot provide the additional manpower that is neede

There are an estimated 4 million such foreign workers in the o
producing states of the Arabian Peninsula and in other Arab oil-ric
nations such as Libya—fully a fifth of the entire world's migrant lab
force. In some cases, the foreign presence is larger than the "nativ
population of the countries: more than 85 percent of the 1.1 millio
residents of the United Arab Emirates are foreigners, according
estimates by the Geneva-based International Labor Organization;
Qatar, which has a total population of 300,000, more than 80 perce
of the residents are aliens; in tiny Bahrain, located just across the stra
gic Strait of Hormuz from revolutionary Iran—a waterway throu
which 80 percent of the Western world's daily supply of crude oi
transported by tankers—more than 35 percent of the 350,000 inha
tants are foreign, including many Iranian Shia Moslems said to
sympathetic toward Iran's Ayatollah Khomeini and his brand of fur
mentalist Islam, which has been violently opposed to the kind of m
ernization undertaken by many oil-rich Gulf states. And in Kuv
second only to Saudi Arabia in its oil wealth, nearly 65 percent of
country's population of 1.4 million is foreign. The single biggest et
group among these foreigners in Kuwait is Palestinian, a disposs
nationality widely perceived as having the potential for causing u
and political chaos.

In country after country in the Gulf region, I was told by pla
and senior officials that the size and growth of the foreign labor
is one of the most critical problems facing the Gulf states in the
The World Bank said in a recent study that by 1985 the foreign c
nent of the labor force in seven Arab labor-importing states—Ba

If you wander around the construction sites at Yanbu and Jubail, you will be struck by the fact that there aren't too many native Saudis around in the open. Of the 25,000 workers slogging in Yanbu, and of the 35,000 assigned to Jubail, maybe a handful are Saudi—and these don't dig ditches. Rather, the Saudis are the hidden financiers, the bankrollers who parcel out the drudgery to the eager minions from South Korea, the Philippines, Pakistan, India, Thailand, Bangladesh, Sri Lanka, and poor Arab states like Egypt, Syria, Morocco, Tunisia, Jordan, and the two Yemens. Large numbers of the aliens will be required to stay on for years to run and maintain the new giant industrial complexes that the Saudis hope will propel their still primitive desert nation into the modern age.

For a society that clings zealously to its fundamental Islamic values and traditions and whose religious leaders propagandize against encroaching Westernization, the implications of this permanent foreign presence are profound and disturbing. Sheikh Abdul-Aziz bin Baz, Saudi Arabia's religious leader, told me he is worried that whatever the benefits accruing from the presence of large numbers of foreign—and often non-Islamic—workers, what is ultimately at stake is whether the basic, purist tenets of Islamic Saudi society will remain unaffected by alien influences. I visited Sheikh bin Baz at his modest office in Riyadh. Now seventy-one years old and blind since he was nineteen, the sheikh heads the Ulema, the council of Islamic scholars responsible for decisions on matters of faith. (A notable example of such decision making was the authorization that the late King Khalid obtained in November 1979 from the Ulema to send troops to recapture the Grand Mosque in Mecca—Islam's holiest shrine—from armed Islamic zealots.) "It is the duty of our society to hold strongly to our Islamic teachings and values and to repel dangerous ideas that may spoil or adversely affect the serene and tranquil life here," the sheikh told me, speaking in Arabic.

Then he quoted from a poem he once wrote:

"If nations lose their values and morals, they lose themselves."

Even youthful, Western-educated Saudis echo such concerns. "We are a deeply religious society, and although we want to develop ourselves into a fully modern nation, we don't want to lose our basic identity," says Dr. Mahmoud M. Safar, the Saudi deputy minister for higher education. "Cities like Jidda have become melting pots of different cultures and customs, and no doubt all of us can benefit from this exposure to foreign cultures. Yet, we are a society that is fundamentally Islamic—and we want to keep it that way. Perhaps we started off too fast on the track of modernization. Perhaps we committed ourselves to too much industrialization. And perhaps we unwittingly brought in too many foreigners."

Of Saudi Arabia's overall population of some 9 million, nearly a third is said to be foreign. Estimates by the United Nations say that there are today in the kingdom 700,000 Pakistanis, 100,000 Indians, 100,000 South Koreans, 75,000 Thais, 35,000 Bangladeshis, 35,000 Sri Lankans, and more than 200,000 Filipinos. There are also tens of thousands of Egyptians, Syrians, Jordanians, Palestinians, Moroccans, Tunisians, Lebanese, and Yemenis. There are also 50,000 Americans, about 35,000 Britons, and perhaps another 20,000 Western Europeans.

* * *

In many of the countries that export personnel to the oil-rich Gulf states, there is now a dramatic shortage of skilled labor. When I visited places like Jordan, Syria, and Egypt, people would tell me how difficult it had become to find good plumbers or house painters or tile layers. In Damascus, Arpy Kevorkian, who operated a bookstore at the Sheraton Hotel, complained about the fact that she couldn't get an electrician to work on fixtures at her apartment.

"Every electrician in town seems to have gone off to Riyadh or Libya or Abu Dhabi," Miss Kevorkian said to me. "Those who remain are asking fancy fees. I've had to book an electrician weeks in advance—only to have him call at the last minute canceling the appointment because he was off to Saudi Arabia."

While I was once waiting at the Royal Palace in Amman for an interview with King Hussein, I happened to observe some whites pottering about the corridors. They wore overalls and carried tool boxes, and if I recall correctly they were Britons. An aide to the Jordanian monarch later told me that they were electricians. "Our own skilled electricians are all off in other countries making money," the aide said.

But no Arab country has exported as many of its citizens to the oil-flushed Gulf states as has Egypt. There are more than 2 million Egyptians in Saudi Arabia, the United Arab Emirates, Kuwait, Bahrain, Iraq, and Libya. Iraq's strongman, Saddam Hussein, has even instituted a scheme under which Egyptian farmers are being wooed to his country, given parcels of land, and offered economic incentives to engage in food growing. In Libya, virtually all architects, engineers, schoolteachers, and technicians are Egyptians—even though the political relations between

Libyan leader Muammar el-Qaddafi and Egypt's President Hosni Mubarak are extremely strained. The Libyan Supreme Court's chief judge, in fact, is an Egyptian!

Not long ago, a friend of mine named Roushdi el-Heneidi was visiting his mother in the Egyptian capital of Cairo. Roushdi is an Egyptian who has worked for more than a decade with the United Nations in New York. His mother lives in the fashionable Agouza section of Cairo, in an apartment that sits on the banks of the Nile. One evening, the toilet flush broke down, and Mrs. Heneidi telephoned for a plumber. The plumber arrived a couple of hours later and fixed the flush in about ten minutes.

"How much do we owe you?" Roushdi el-Heneidi asked the man.

"Fifty pounds," the plumber said. The sum was equivalent to fifty American dollars.

"Fifty pounds!" Roushdi said. "Why, I could have gotten a doctor to pay a house call for much less."

"Then why didn't you ask a doctor to come and fix your toilet?" the plumber, a young man, said insolently.

Roushdi later told me that he could remember the days when plumbers charged no more than the equivalent of two dollars for minor repairs. Roushdi also made the point that even if he knew a doctor who could fix a toilet flush, he probably wouldn't be able to find one easily available in present-day Cairo. Egyptian physicians are rushing to the Gulf in droves. There are eleven universities, which turn out doctors by the score each year—yet there are fewer physicians in the country today than there were five years ago.

As the oil-rich Arab states import more and more foreign labor, they in fact are creating more and more problems for themselves in both the short and the long run. The cities of the Gulf states are growing rapidly, and the pressures to provide proper municipal services for the migrants is increasing. (The urban centers of the Gulf states are growing at the rate of more than 6 percent annually; city-states like Kuwait and Qatar are growing at between 10 and 15 percent each year. The United Nations estimates that Kuwait and Doha will double their populations in less than ten years. Such growth is unguided, uncontrolled, and potentially explosive.)

Adding to the inherent economic and social tensions is the fact that in most of the oil-rich states the native population is very small indeed. For example, 600,000 of Abu Dhabi's 800,000 people are foreigners. Foreigners also heavily outnumber the indigenous population in Kuwait.

However, foreigners are enjoined from acquiring citizenship in these Gulf states; Kuwait and Saudi Arabia have laws prohibiting foreigners from marrying native women. Because the oil-rich states have small indigenous populations (and a high proportion of the population is below fifteen years of age) and therefore a small labor force (a fact that is exacerbated by the low participation of women in gainful employment: the United Nations estimates that less than 8 percent of the Arab world's labor force consists of women, compared with 36 percent in Japan), they have had to import foreign workers to help with their ambitious development plans. Yet none of these Gulf states is really giving the foreigners a personal stake in the economic future of the oil-rich countries.

While the wealthy oil-producing states suffer from underpopulation, most of the other Arab countries of the Middle East, ironically enough, suffer from overpopulation and limited availability of resources. Such states include Algeria, Egypt, Jordan, Lebanon, Morocco, Southern Yemen, Syria, Tunisia, and Yemen. In fact, says the United Nations, the Arab world as a whole now has an annual population growth rate of 3.13 percent, compared with 2.3 percent for the Third World as a whole and 1.7 percent for the globe. At this rate, the Arab world will double its population in about twenty-five years. It is the overpopulation in the poorer countries of the Arab world that explains why so many people are migrating to the underpopulated and richer Arab states.

One evening in Algiers, I was being taken around the old Casbah by Jose-Luis Vidal, then the Algeria correspondent for the Spanish News Agency. Jose-Luis and I had worked together during the hostage crisis in Iran, and we had also covered the Iraq–Iran war for our respective news organizations. The Casbah is a romantic place; its inclines are steep, its passageways narrow. The white-facaded structures with their *mashrabia* windows—heavily latticed windows behind which women can sit and stare at passers-by without themselves being seen—are on the verge of collapse, and the United Nations in fact is carrying out a project to restore this old section of Algiers. The smells of cooking wafted through the alleys of the Casbah. This was the Casbah of the *Battle of Algiers,* the epic movie that documented the Algerian struggle for independence. Jose-Luis spotted an Algerian acquaintance, a thirtyish man who was playing with his seven children.

We stopped to chat with this man, with Jose-Luis, who spoke both French and Arabic—the two main languages of Algeria, a former French colony—doing the interpreting. He told us that he'd been married at the age of seventeen; his wife was fifteen at the time.

"Did you want a large family?" I asked the Algerian, who worked as a clerk in the Algiers post office.

"My people have always had many children," he replied.

"Can you afford so many children?"

"There's always a way to provide for them," the man said. "For us Arabs, children are always welcome. They are an asset."

It is not uncommon for women in this part of the Arab world to have between six and eight children, according to the World Fertility Survey, a project supported jointly by the United Nations Fund for Population Activities and the U.S. Agency for International Development. The global average is four children per woman; in the industrialized countries of the West, women have an average of two children each. Nafis Sadik of the UNFPA, a Pakistani physician who has written a book on the subject, says that high fertility among Arabs is a function of early age at marriage, universality of marriage, pronatalist cultural attitudes, and the fact that the more children men and women produce, the more enhanced their status in the general community.

Saudi Arabia pays its white expatriates much better than it does its hordes of Arab and Asian laborers. Tax-free salaries of $150,000 a year are not uncommon among whites. Whites are hired as bankers, managers in local outlets of Western-based corporations, technical consultants, physicians, university professors, and schoolteachers. The biggest employer of white expatriates, of course, continues to be the Arabian-American Oil Company in Dhahran, better known by its acronym, Aramco. Asians and Arabs generally are brought in as construction workers, drivers, maids, manservants, cooks, and ditch diggers. The kingdom's new Third Five-Year Plan aims at, among other things, reducing the foreign worker presence through enhanced training programs for native Saudis to operate the country's burgeoning industries and businesses and to look after such facilities as huge new airports in Jidda, Riyadh, and Dhahran. But these aims are predicated on getting more Saudis to accept these relatively low-paying jobs, a daunting task indeed in a country where any Saudi who can read or write can easily expect to start his career near the top of a corporation or business. And in the long run, the hope for getting more native Saudis to manage the levers and lathes of the economy rests with getting the country's annual population growth rate to increase. (The government therefore has supported a pronatalist policy, and large families get special financial awards.)

"Meanwhile, we find ourselves handicapped by a severe manpower shortage," says Dr. Fouad Al-Farsy, the Saudi deputy minister of industry.

It is a shortage that Saudi Arabia and other Persian Gulf states will continue experiencing as long as their development plans remain ambitious. Neighboring Iraq, for example, has imported nearly 2 million foreign workers to help attain its goals of a modern industrial system and infrastructure. But already Arab planners have started saying that the influx of such large numbers of workers from alien cultures has posed the risk that the national identity of the labor-importing states will be diluted as their indigenous populations get swamped by foreign workers. The Baghdad-based Arab Labour Office said recently that its studies showed that racial tensions in some of the oil-producing Gulf states were being exacerbated by the presence of the foreign workers.

In some countries, there have been sinister campaigns against the foreign workers. A newspaper in the United Arab Emirates, *Al-Khaleej*, published a ridiculous editorial not long ago saying, in part: "The increased number of Asians forms a hidden reservoir for the United States and Israel. They are those coherent and militarily trained groups who live in camps and are brought into the country by foreign companies." A Kuwaiti trade union publication characterized Asian workers as a "fifth column that serves imperialist interests." The allusion, of course, was to workers from South Korea and the Philippines, both political and military allies of the United States. In both instances, the governments of these countries tightly supervise the export of labor to the Gulf states. Koreans wishing to work overseas must register with the Korean Overseas Development Corporation, an agency through which the government knows exactly who works abroad and under what terms. Because Koreans in particular are tightly organized and disciplined, their work cadres abroad sometimes give the impression of being paramilitary units. I wouldn't be surprised if indeed covert agreements exist between some of the Gulf states and the South Korean governments under which military-trained workers are shipped to the Middle East as a kind of last-resort protection for the rulers.

There seems to be an increasing perception among the natives of Gulf states, however, that foreigners who work amid them are somehow a threat. A study by Dr. Ahmad Jamal al-Thahir and Dr. Faisal al-Salem of Kuwait University in 1982 found that almost 45 percent of 22,883 persons polled in the Gulf felt that expatriates "threatened their economic well-being." While 87 percent of the respondents acknowledged that their own economic circumstances were better than those of these expatriates and that they were "aware that they enjoyed more rights and privileges" than these foreigners, most wanted the status quo maintained. A majority of those polled by the Kuwaiti professors said that expatriates shouldn't have equal rights along with Gulf natives, and some of the respondents even called for a ban on foreigners residing in the same localities as natives.

* * *

There is no bigger El Dorado than Saudi Arabia. Its mystique and attraction for foreign workers stems from the fact that its proven oil reserves are put at 180 billion barrels, or one-fourth of the world total. According to Aramco, which lifts all the crude oil in Saudi Arabia, the kingdom has sufficient oil to last more than seventy years at the current rate of production of around 5 million barrels a day. Saudi Arabia's foreign exchange reserves are around $150 billion, and the country earns more than $110 billion a year from the sale of its crude oil. (It is the biggest supplier of oil to many Western nations, including the United States.) With an area of 2.2 million square kilometers and occupying most of the Arabian Peninsula, Saudi Arabia is six times as large as the British Isles and four times the size of France. It is a harsh land of deserts, rocky shores, and barren mountains. It is also the spiritual home for Moslems all over the world, millions of whom make an annual pilgrimage to the Grand Mosque in the holy city of Mecca, not far from Jidda. Saudi Arabia's constitution and laws are derived from Islam. Bedouin tribes roam the land, and, indeed, no one really knows just how many of these nomads there are.

Saudi Arabia was transformed by the discovery of oil in 1933. The previous year, a desert brigand named Abdul Aziz ibn Abdur-Rahman al faisal al Saud proclaimed himself "king" of all Arabia. To achieve harmony with the myriad fractious brigand tribes of his "kingdom," he married into many of these groups and eventually took some 300 wives, who bore him forty-one legal royal heirs. Four of these heirs have succeeded him to the throne: King Saud, who reigned from 1953 to 1964; King Faisal, 1964–1975; King Khalid, 1975–1982; and King Fahd, who became monarch when Khalid died of heart disease.

By the time Khalid died in 1982, Saudi Arabia was a major power because of its oil wealth. Its annual expenditures on development would be around $100 billion; the Saudis would give millions in foreign aid to poor Islamic countries, money that was earned as income from investment of foreign exchange reserves of $150 billion. But despite its extraordinary development plans and the frenetic speed with which Saudi Arabia sought to modernize itself, it remained nevertheless a conservative Islamic state. Alcohol was banned. Public theaters do not exist. Women are required to be veiled when in public, and they are not allowed to drive. A concession to growing wealth and the ensuing technological advance, however, was the provision made for young Saudi schoolgirls to receive lessons from male tutors on closed-circuit television. By 1983, 42 percent of Saudi Arabia's 1.5 million students were women; and women accounted for 30 percent of the 55,000 students in higher education. There is some expectation, at least among these educated women, that they will be allowed increased participation in economic production—perhaps as part of an effort to reduce dependence on hired labor from abroad. The Saudi planning minister, Hisham Nazer, has said: "The question now is what sort of jobs you are going to allow women to take rather than whether or not they are going to work."

It was inevitable that Saudi Arabia import labor to service its ambitious development projects. Today, these foreigners are everywhere.

In Jidda, for example, there are entire neighborhoods occupied mainly by one nationality or another. The Rowaice section of this old Red Sea port is now called "Somalitown" on account of the thousands of Somali citizens who live there. Abutting Somalitown is Bangladeshtown, and adjacent to Bangladeshtown is an area where predominantly Pakistanis are to be found. These ethnic areas function as enclaves, and there is very little mixing among various groups. Each neighborhood seems to have developed a reputation for something or the other. If you want to eat a good dish of curried fish, then you go to Bangladeshtown and look up a dingy restaurant off a narrow, unlit street, where a woman named Shamina Chowdhury will cook up a magnificent meal for the equivalent of a dollar. If you desire a hearty dinner of spiced lamb, then Pakistantown is the place to go. If you want sex, try Somalitown, where one afternoon I was approached several times by men who offered female company for any kind of entertainment I chose.

You would think that with such large numbers of foreigners from poor countires there would be crime on the streets of Saudi cities. Not so. Saudi streets, and indeed those in virtually all oil-rich Gulf states, are the safest in the world. That is because the penalties for all kinds of crime are very heavy. Murderers are executed. Thieves lose their limbs. Adulterers are stoned to death. One Friday, shortly after the midday prayers in the Grand Mosque in Riyadh, my friend William Stewart of *Time* magazine and I witnessed executions in the main square outside the mosque. A man and a woman were shot to death: the man had been found guilty of murder, the woman of adultery. The crowd roared with delight when the bullets were fired. I was certain that the victims had been drugged. Each was led from a police van without protest to a spot in front of the mosque, made to kneel, and shot separately. The bodies were then left for public view for nearly an hour before an ambulance removed them. Such drastic punishment is a major deterrent to crime in the Gulf states, particularly in Saudi Arabia.

The ethnic enclaves in places like Jidda contain foreigners who work mostly as houseboys, maids, and drivers or in assorted menial jobs in cities. These foreigners are here on a long-term basis, many with no plans to return to their homelands. In Jidda's Somalitown, I visited a man named Mohammed Sayed, who is employed as a handyman in a local sheet metal shop.

Mohammed is forty years old and has two wives and six children. All live in a ground-floor tenement in the Rowaice section of Jidda; there are only two rooms for the nine of them. The children go to a school in the neighborhood. Mohammed earns the equivalent of $500 a month, or ten times what he would be making in his hometown of Mogadishu. He has been in Saudi Arabia for seven years.

Will he return to Somalia?

"Never!" Mohammed said, emphatically. "What is there back in Somalia for us?"

Not all foreign workers live in ethnic neighborhoods such as Rowaice. There are well-organized "labor camps" near major construction sites in Yanbu and Jubail where male workers without families are given housing for the one or two years that they have contracted to spend in Saudi Arabia.

Late one afternoon in Yanbu, I met with a group of Filipinos and South Koreans whose "home" was aboard two rusting barges moored in the Red Sea. The barges were dilapidated and clearly not seaworthy. Each housed about 600 men, with 4 or 5 men sharing a room. The rooms all had bunk beds, and there was barely space to stand. Some of the rooms were decorated with posters of American film stars or with pictures of nude women. This afternoon, the Filipinos were celebrating Gene Matiling's thirtieth birthday. His wife and three children were back home in Manila, but they had sent him a birthday card. One of his kids had scrawled on the card: "Come home soon, Daddy!"

Matiling, a short, slim man who works as an electrician, pondered that plea.

"I would run home tonight, if I could," he said, presently. "But I make almost a thousand dollars a week here. Where would I make that kind of money in the Philippines? I've been here for nearly a year, and I've just signed up for another two years. It's a personal sacrifice for me to be apart from my wife and children. But here I'm earning enough money that will keep us in comfort at home for a long, long time."

Money was also what brought Arthur Pestano to Saudi Arabia from his native Philippines. Pestano is a physician assigned to the two residential barges. His annual salary is about $80,000. By the time he returns home to his wife and four sons in four years' time, Pestano will have built up quite a nest egg.

What is his nepenthe?

"Work," Pestano said, "and jogging."

The Filipinos do not get along with the Koreans, who are seen as bullies. Dr. Pestano told me that occasionally fights break out between members of the two ethnic groups. On the day I visited his barge, he was treating a fellow Filipino named Renato Sambilay, whose face was swollen after a fist fight with two Koreans. Renato, a tall, sturdy plumber, told me the Koreans had tried to muscle him and another Filipino out of a recreation room where they'd been playing ping-pong.

"This happens all the time," Renato said, grimacing in pain as Dr. Pestano dabbed soothing lotion on his face. "Those Koreans are good fighters, too. They drink, and they come looking for fights."

The Koreans I later spoke with suggested it was the Filipinos who were the raucous type. A Korean steward named Woo Dong Chul told me that for the most part Korean workers kept to themselves and did not mix with other nationalities. Most Korean workers who were brought to Saudi Arabia, he said, spoke no language other than Korean, which made it difficult for them to communicate with non-Koreans.

The occasional antagonism between various ethnic groups can take bizarre turns. Some months ago, five Pakistani workers had an argument with Korean colleagues near Jubail. They were then hacked to death by the Koreans, who stuffed the mutilated limbs into a freezer in the workers' dining hall. An unsuspecting chef later retrieved the flesh from the freezer, made a stew, and served the dish to some Filipinos, who became severely ill.

None of these migrant workers has any great loyalty or liking for Saudi Arabia. Few wind up with any attachment to the Saudis, who are perceived as rude, arrogant people with no sensitivity for anyone else other than themselves.

"They still have sand between their toes," an Indian engineer said of his Saudi employers. "They began as illiterate Bedouins, they will always remain that way. I may make my fortune off them, but there is no way I can get to love them."

A Pakistani named Mohammed Kamal Butt, who works as a chauffeur for an automobile rental company in Jidda, put it this way: "Let's face it—we are here only for the money, and not much else."

For single men like Butt and the Indian engineer, life in the big city can be lonely. Each has a video player in his apartment, but how many movies can one keep watching? Since mingling between unmarried men and women is discouraged in Saudi Arabia, dating is out of the question for such men. They are not encouraged to bring their families here, and returning home even for short visits can be a very expensive proposition.

The restrictive aspects of everyday life in Saudi Arabia are felt perhaps even more severely by the single women who are hired by Saudia Airlines, the country's national carrier. Since Saudi women are forbidden from working in jobs that involve public mixing with males, the airline must recruit women from abroad to work as stewardesses. These women are recruited in forty countries, including Egypt, Morocco, Jordan, Syria, Pakistan, India, Thailand, the Philippines, Indonesia, and Sri Lanka. There even are women from the United States. Whenever the women find themselves in the airline's home base of Jidda, they are required to live in a tightly guarded compound not far from the American Embassy on Palestine Street. No male visitors are permitted here, but the women are allowed to go out—as long as they're back in the Saudia compound by midnight.

Of course, since all rules are meant to be broken, this last one is most certainly broken all the time by some of the Saudia women who have rich and powerful local patrons. Saudia stewardesses are popular guests at parties given by wealthy young Saudi men. An Indian stewardess told me quite candidly that in her first year with Saudia she acquired cash and gifts totaling $200,000 from her Saudi male friends. In exchange, she attended "parties" where she would participate in, among other things, cocaine snorting and group sex.

If there are truly "privileged" foreign workers in Saudi Arabia, it is the expatriates hired by Aramco. The oil company, which is government-owned now and which produces all the crude oil in Saudi Arabia, has built a compound for its American workers in Dhahran that is a city by itself. It is, in fact, virtually a township right out of Southern California. The asphalted roads are wide and edged with palm trees. Homes have neat drives and back yards with barbecue pits. There are swimming pools and baseball fields and football grounds. There is even a stadium with American-style bleachers. American-made yellow schoolbuses ply the streets. There are hamburger stands and ice cream parlors and churches with tall steeples. There even are movie theaters where the latest American films are exhibited—an unusual thing in Saudi Arabia, where no public entertainment is permitted because it is considered un-Islamic. And the law in Saudi Arabia that women cannot drive is not applied inside the vast Aramco compound. Aramco also maintains special beaches where mixed bathing is allowed, and women do indeed cavort in skimpy swimsuits.

Nearly 5,000 Americans work for Aramco, of whom about 3,000 live in this compound. Other residents include some of the 3,000 Britons also engaged by Aramco. I spoke one morning with a lithe young Englishwoman named Brenda Maloney, who had come to Dhahran initially to work for a year as a secretary but then, swayed by her $35,000 tax-free annual salary, decided she'd stay on indefinitely. Miss Maloney, like most of the single women in the Aramco compound, has a social calendar that is booked months in a row. And whenever she gets bored, of course, Aramco provides free transportation to her native England and back for a short breather.

There is no reason why her job should not be held by a Saudi woman. But that will not happen because of the traditional restrictions on Saudi females. Saudi Arabia's recently unveiled Third Five-Year Plan calls for the participation of women in the development of the country, although few details are offered concerning this. With education increasing among Saudi women, who constitute more than 50 percent of the native Saudi population, the increased employment of women would surely help in making Saudi Arabia more self-sufficient and less reliant on imported foreign labor.

Women traditionally have been employed in such areas as teaching or nursing, but only a handful, of course, and only in situations where there was no direct contact with men in work situations. But it seems that as more women get higher education and as more of them travel abroad with their families and are exposed to the ways of Western women, there is a growing feeling among them that they should be contributing more to the economic development of the country. I met one day with Fatimah Khalil Deffaa, a Yemeni woman who is in charge of the women's banking center at the Saudi-American Bank—formerly Citibank—in Riyadh. She told me that when her banking center opened for business in 1980, she was flooded with applications from Saudi women who wanted jobs. Miss Deffaa has hired nearly fifty Saudi women, who work in a strictly segregated environment. One of these women is Wasila Hakim, a twenty-three-year-old who recently returned to Riyadh after obtaining a high school diploma in Britain. She now works as a teller in the women's section of the Saudi-American Bank. Wasila is driven to work every day in a chauffeured family Rolls-Royce and taken home in the late afternoon by her father, a wealthy businessman. When in public, Wasila wears a veil; inside the bank, she doffs the veil. When I talked with her, she had on a pleasing burgundy-colored, one-piece pants outfit. She purchased her clothes in Paris, Wasila said.

Wasila expressed concern about the Westernization of Saudi society and particularly over Saudi Arabia's reliance on imported labor to keep the economic machinery running. "People of my generation think a lot about what this Westernization process is doing to us," she said in her British accent. "When we go abroad for education and come back, it doesn't mean we are Westernized. A taste for Western clothes doesn't also mean we have sold out. People like me obtain Western education to develop ourselves and for the ultimate benefit of our country—that doesn't mean we forget our culture. Our concern about Westernization stems from the fact that we have developed in a rush. We took development in stride as best as we could. We needed foreign labor, so we imported it. Now there is a new generation of Saudis coming up, and the task is to make sure they are sufficiently steeped in our traditional culture."

Wasila seemed extraordinarily thoughtful and reflective for a person her age. But after an afternoon's conversation with her at the Saudi-American Bank, I could not help feeling that within her there was a spirit yearning to break out of the shell into which she'd been stuffed. I felt that women like Wasila were being forced to toe the line back at home in order not to antagonize the traditionalists who supported them. Wasila suggested that there wasn't much she or any Saudi woman could do by way of being rebellious or spurning family traditions; indeed, few Saudi women I met seemed prepared to go and strike out on their own. But then, of course, even if they were so prepared, where would they go?

Beyond the overall, inchoate government policy of encouraging female literacy and education, no one in government will make commitments to career-aspiring Saudi women about employment opportunities. A government commission is said to be examining what areas of work can be officially approved for women. Those few women who have ventured—with the assistance of their husbands—to start enterprises such as boutiques and beauty parlors still run the risk of having their businesses closed down, even if temporarily, by the *mutawaheen*, the so-called religious police, or by members of the Society for the Containment of Vice and the Encouragement of Virtue.

The outlook is for more foreign workers, not less. Michael A. Callen, formerly Citibank's chief representative in Saudi Arabia, told me one evening that with the basic infrastructure now in place here, the emphasis of future economic activity would increasingly be on maintenance and operations, tasks for which the need would be for more foreign technical expertise. There simply aren't enough Saudi nationals available for such tasks. Saudis who return home after being educated abroad are immediately offered high-paying management and entrepreneurial jobs. (There are 25,000 Saudis now enrolled in American colleges and universities and about 15,000 in Western European educational institutions.) Saudis who travel overseas on government scholarships are required to return home after obtaining their degrees and to work with government agencies for a specified number of years. Because government jobs typically offer annual salaries (for Saudis) upward of $75,000, many young Saudis opt to stay on in the public sector.

There is also the matter of tradition.

"Nobody can deny that working with their hands is not acceptable to most Saudis," says Dr. Mahmoud Safar, the Saudi deputy minister for higher education. "It is not easy to persuade our youths to become technicians. They all want to be executives."

But executives need minions and manual workers, and what the Saudis are doing is in effect making certain that their economy will always be dependent on the import of foreign labor. Short of drastically curtailing their development schemes, I don't know what the Saudis can do to be more self-sufficient in labor. And as long as the heavily populated states of the Arab world have a high annual population growth rate, as long as there is an income gap between the poor and wealthy countries of the Third World, the labor migration to the oil-rich Arab states will continue. At the same time, fluctuations in the world oil prices that result in diminished revenues for the oil-producing states are also likely to hurt the poor countries supplying cheap labor. Already, for example, Pakistan's economic development plans have had to be modified because of reduced remittances from Pakistani migrant workers in the Gulf states, which cut back on importing unskilled laborers in the wake of falling oil income.

Some years ago, a Washington-based writer named Kathleen Newland said in an essay titled "International Migration: The Search for Work" that appeared in *Worldwatch Paper,* published by the Worldwatch Institute, Washington, D.C., that "the real solutions" to the problem of international migration for employment "lie in labor-intensive development in the source countries, a restructuring of labor markets in the host countries, and egalitarian income distribution both within and among countries."

Kathleen Newland wrote those words in 1979, and now, five years later, they are no less valid.

Ten

The West
"Migrants, Go Home!"

ONE AFTERNOON in West Berlin, I was wandering through the bustling Turkish bazaar inside the old S-Bahn station at Bulowstrasse when I spotted Ehmet Tutkoli at his shoeshine booth.

He was a short, broad-jawed man, about forty years old, with deep dark eyes and a formidable mustache. He wore a green knitted sweater, a tweed jacket whose buttons were missing, baggy trousers, and an absurd wool cap that kept slipping off his thickly haired head. Ehmet owned one of those antique shoeshine stands with lots of brass trimmings and wooden carvings and mother-of-pearl handles, and, with a gap-toothed smile, he offered to transform the appearance of my frayed shoes for the equivalent of fifty cents. It was an offer I couldn't refuse, and as Ehmet stroked his brushes and snapped his chamois-leather cloth on my shoes, we got around to talking. He spoke in a mixture of English, German, and Turkish, and he punctuated his speech with pantomime. Sometimes Ehmet had to shout so I could hear him over the loud Oriental music that emanated from a dozen stores selling cassettes. The aroma of strong coffee blended with the redolence of freshly made baklava, which was displayed in neon-lit glass cases of bakeries. The columns and pillars of the covered bazaar were festooned with colorful movie posters depicting buxom females and heroic men. Children darted about, occasionally chased by their irate mothers—large women wearing patterned scarves—or yelled at by their fathers, who otherwise languidly played chess or checkers in garish coffee stalls.

He was soon going home to Ankara, Ehmet said, because the West Germans didn't want people like him around anymore. The government of Chancellor Helmut Kohl was offering foreign workers without valid jobs—and shining shoes did not come under the "valid" category—up to $5,000 per family to leave the country and not return. Ehmet said he had lost his job as a mechanic in a local factory as the worldwide recession hit once-booming West Germany. A fellow Turk gave him his spare shoeshine stand, and Ehmet set up shop at the Bulowstrasse station, where the S-Bahn, or commuter trains have long ceased to run. Ehmet starts to work in the late morning at the station, after he has already put in a couple of hours shoe-shining on the Kurfurstendamm, West Berlin's main thoroughfare. His work space at the Bulowstrasse station doesn't cost him anything, but Ehmet, out of appreciation, gives money from time to time to the friend who donated him his shoeshine stand. All told, Ehmet Tutkoli takes home the equivalent of $400 each month. He cannot enroll for welfare benefits—which could bring him food subsidies and health allowances—because of the possibility that someone will report him to the police, who in turn are likely to start deportation proceedings against him and the Tutkoli family. Ehmet's wife, Tasleem, brings in another $300 worth of Deutschemarks from her job as a cleaning woman in a West Berlin hotel. With this money, they must not only raise five children but also provide for the security of Ehmet's aged parents back in Ankara. As a mechanic, Ehmet had earned six times his current income.

"We were invited in by these Germans when they had a need for us," Ehmet said bitterly. "They made full use of us to build their economy, and now they want to kick us out. They are making life extremely unpleasant for us here. There are anti-Turkish marches, our women are molested, our children are abused and beaten up. What kind of a life is this for us?"

Ehmet Tutkoli is one of 1.6 million Turks in West Germany, which has nearly 5 million foreign guest workers—known as the *Gastarbeiter*—in all, or 7.5 percent of the overall population. Government statistics show that 22 percent of the *Gastarbeiter* work in the metallurgy industry—mostly in welding, which is considered the most demanding aspect of metallurgy; about 16 percent in civil engineering; 22.1 percent in the hotel and restaurant business; and almost 20 percent in the textile industry. Few foreigners hold top-paying jobs; most are menial or manual workers, in positions that Germans ordinarily would shun.

In a country where the unemployment figure reached some 3 million by the end of 1983, these foreigners have become natural targets of unemployed Germans, who feel that the foreigners are competing with them for public housing, welfare benefits, and jobs. (A tenth of the foreigners are said to be unemployed, and more than 125,000 of these are Turks.) Ehmet is also one of 125,000 Turks in West Berlin, which has fewer than 2 million residents; like him, many Turks are packing up and returning home rather than face a life of continued uncertainty here. In 1983, more than 70,000 Turks went home.

"For these unfortunates, the party is over," Klaus Stiebler, the respected foreign affairs analyst at West German Radio in Cologne, said to me. "There is a new ugly mood in Germany, and the foreign 'guest' workers seem to be the victims. Germany invited them over when there was a real shortage of manpower in our burgeoning industries. There were plenty of jobs to go around then—I'm speaking of fifteen, twenty years ago, and even as recently as ten years back. But these are different times. Germany, like many other countries of the West, is in economic difficulties. These Turks and other foreign workers who came here are really guests who didn't go home. And Germans are beginning to say that these people have overstayed their welcome. It's a dismaying situation and potentially explosive indeed."

In addition to perceived fears among white Germans about jobs and welfare benefits the Turks might wrest from them, there is another key point that frightens them: while the white population of West Germany is experiencing zero growth, or even negative growth, the Turks—in particular—are overbreeding. Authorities in the capital city of Bonn estimate that the foreign population of 5 million in 1983 will be doubled by the end of this decade if current high birthrates among Turks, Yugoslavs, Moroccans, and other foreign communities continue. What many social commentators worry about, then, is that the fundamental racial and cultural character of Germany would unalterably change.

I traveled to West Germany late in 1983 and again in March 1984—fully 300 years after the army of Karl von Lothringen defeated the Turks outside the gates of Vienna, effectively ending a military threat that had loomed over Europe for 150 years—because what was happening there to the foreign workers was a microcosm of the situation all over Europe. And I was convinced that how the West Germans handled their *Gastarbeiter* problem would set the pattern for the rest of Europe, which had actively recruited the migrant workers to build roads and houses, work in restaurants and hotels, toil in factories that turned out automobiles and electronics, haul out the garbage, and keep the streets clean. Europe used these migrant workers to reconstruct itself after the devastation of World War II, and now that Western European states had remodernized themselves, they wanted their foreign minions to go back home again.

In Britain, France, Belgium, Sweden, and Switzerland, governments are making it extremely difficult for guest workers to stay on and settle—if they so wished. Foreign workers have sometimes been subjected to considerable nastiness. In West Berlin not long ago, thousands of white German youths marched through Kreutzberg, a predominantly Turkish ghetto in the shadow of the infamous Berlin Wall, smashing shop windows and taunting the locals. "Send them back home and give their jobs to unemployed Germans" was a theme sounded disturbingly often during West Germany's election campaign in 1983. Newspapers and television shows endlessly highlight the problem of what to do with guest workers. If Turks are the main targets in West Germany, in neighboring France it is the 5 million plus Moroccans, Algerians, and Tunisians, who constitute almost 10 percent of France's overall population. In Britain, domestic resentment has built up against black West Indians and immigrants from Pakistan, Bangladesh, and India; racial riots have taken place even in usually sedate British communities. There has been discrimination against workers who came to Holland from the former Dutch colonies of Surinam and Indonesia. In Sweden, social resentment has been directed at Yugoslav guest workers and, of course, against the Turks.

When I went to Bonn, a sleepy little town on the Rhine that serves as West Germany's capital, friends in the Bundestag, the national parliament, gave me a recent study by an organization known as the Zentrale fuer Politische Bildung, or the Center for Political Education. The document had caused quite a stir in the country.

The study asserted that West Germany, far from being hurt by the continued presence of its guest workers, in fact could no longer survive without its foreign labor. The study said that one miner out of four in the country was a foreigner, as were 35 percent of high-skill workers in the automobile industry, and one physician out of every seven in the nation's hospitals.

The center's document was widely circulated among West Germany's top government officials, parliamentarians, industrialists, journalists, and academicians. It warned of "mounting racism in West Germany, based on prejudices and a profound ignorance of the importance of foreign workers to the national economy." And to dramatize what could happen if all guest workers left because of harassment and persecution, the authors of the study drew up a "scenario":

If all 5 million foreigners left West Germany overnight, there would be total chaos. West Berlin would lose 13 percent of its population, Bad-Wuertemberg 10 percent, Northern Rhineland 8 percent. Railway traffic would be paralyzed on all major lines, and the Deutsche Bundesbahn, the West Germany railway company, would lose 16,700 of its 342,000 employees.

Power would fail because coal production would fall by 30 percent, said the Zentrale fuer Politische Bildung. In the Ford automobile plants, and at Volkswagen, the cars would come off the production lines only half completed. In schools, half of the students would be absent in some elementary classes, and total panic would reign in hotels and restaurants because there no longer would be Conchita to make the beds and Carlos to bake the pizzas.

To this "scenario" I would add: Who will clean the toilets at West German airports, train stations, and bus terminals? Who will shine shoes of office-goers, and who will scrub pavements and sweep the streets? Who will clear out the garbage? Who will plow the snow? Who will deliver the bread and the milk?

Soon after Helmut Kohl came to power in 1982, he formed a commission to give clarity and definition to what he called a "humane immigration policy." The chancellor said that such a policy should be based on the integration of foreigners into German society, a limit on how many foreigners would be admitted to settle down in West Germany, and the provision of economic incentives for those guest workers and their families who sought to return to their homelands.

Kohl's commission consisted of officials from the agencies most directly involved with the *Gastarbeiter,* the Federal Ministries of Education, the Interior, and Labor; the panel also included representatives from West Germany's ten federal states. The commission's 200-page report, which was unveiled on March 2, 1983, endorsed all of Kohl's initial objectives for a new immigration policy. But the panel then went on to recommend a set of stricter regulations involving the hiring by German companies of foreigners and the inflow of guest workers' families and a firm position against "extremist" groups composed of foreigners (government estimates suggest that more than 125,000 of West Germany's Turks, Yugoslavs, Portuguese, Spaniards, Tunisians, and Moroccans may belong to groups espousing radical politics, the politics usually having to do with issues back home, and not with West Germany). Kohl's commission, whose recommendations were put into effect late in 1983, said that before foreigners were given permanent residence in West Germany the authorities should ensure that these aliens had legitimate jobs and were fluent in German; that the foreigners had proper housing that could accommodate not only the breadwinner but also his immediate family; that proper educational facilities had been arranged for the children of these aliens; and that the foreigners were not fugitives from the law in their native countries.

One question on which members of Chancellor Kohl's immigration commission failed to agree was the reunification of guest workers' families. This is a sensitive issue in West Germany, just as it is elsewhere in West Europe, because of a wide perception that guest workers not only brought over their wives and children but also their extended families. The Christian Democrats want to prohibit foreign workers from bringing over children above the age of six on the grounds that past this age most kids are not able to assimilate in a foreign culture and that they tend to become misfits; these misfits, according to the prevailing argument, later in life have problems finding employment and become burdens on the state's social welfare system. The Christian Democrats who espouse such a view have been bitterly criticized by members of the opposition parties and by the Liberals, who believe it violates human rights. These critics do not want to see a change in the present legislation, which allows foreign workers to bring into West Germany their children up to the age of sixteen.

The ongoing debate over the question of how many children foreign workers should be allowed to bring with them and up to what age will continue in view of West Germany's own dramatically falling birthrate, which has resulted in fewer and fewer German children in schools each year for more than a decade now. Hermann Schubnell, a respected professor of demography at the University of Mainz—and a former director of the Federal Institute of Population Research—points out that for a variety of reasons millions and millions of couples in Western Europe decided in the mid-1960s to have fewer children and that this tendency was most marked in West Germany. In this country, the annual number of births fell by half from more than 1 million in the mid-1960s to fewer than 500,000 by the mid-1970s. By 1982, fewer than 100 children were born by every 100 marriages, and now more than two-thirds of all families have only one or two children. Moreover, the number of marriages each year in West Germany is also declining, with fewer than 300,000 in 1982, as compared to nearly 450,000 in 1970. Professor Schubnell and other demographic authorities say that if the current trend in declining birthrates continues West Germany's net population—meaning native Germans and excluding foreigners—of 55 million in 1983 will fall to 52.2 million by the year 2000, 46.3 million by 2015, and 39.4 million by 2030. In contrast, the foreign population—despite the move homeward of many Turks—is expected to continue edging upward because of high birthrates. Most of the migrants are still in their early to mid-child-producing years and come from countries, such as Turkey, where traditions call for large families. Thus, in West Berlin, the numbers of babies born each year to Turkish, Yugoslav, and Greek migrant workers are higher than those born cumulatively to all German West Berliners. The federal government has stated that the current level of fertility of Germans is too low, but no measures have been suggested or undertaken to encourage Germans to have more children.

Right-wing critics are particularly alarmed. In West Berlin, for example, I found out that one out of every three school pupils was a Turk. In the state of Rhineland-Pfalz, which borders on Belgium, Luxembourg, and France, and whose overall population is 3.6 million, one out of every seven school students is a foreigner. Within the last ten years, according to government statistics, the number of foreign students in West German schools increased from 159,000 to almost 700,000. And, the government figures show, almost 60 percent of these students are Moslem.

The critics are saying that it is not only their religion, racial differentness, and native language that set the Turks apart from other students in German schools. They cite government-sponsored studies that show that more than 60 percent of non-German students drop out of school before obtaining a diploma, compared to less than 10 percent among the West Germans. German parents write to government officials and to newspaper editors complaining that because of the presence of non-German students the standard and quality of education in schools is rapidly declining.

Moreover, the critics contend, their very differentness isolates the non-German students from the general social and educational culture in schools, spawning bewilderment and bitterness and then reinforcing a siege mentality among them.

A particularly vocal critic of Turks and foreigners has been Heinrich Lummer, West Berlin's deputy mayor and the city government's chief official—or senator—in charge of the interior. I went to see him at his office in the John F. Kennedy Platz, in an eerily cavernous building that escaped destruction during the war and whose corridors and passageways seem to echo with ghosts of another era. Lummer is not popular with Berlin's Turks, who correctly perceive him as a man who would be delighted to see them all go home. He is a small, stocky man, with beady blue eyes and a sort of perpetually mocking air. He fiddled with a pencil and occasionally tapped it on his mahogany desk as he spoke with me.

"Look, there's no question in my mind at all that our main problem in West Berlin is the large number of foreigners. Of the city's population, 250,000, or 12 percent, are foreigners, mostly Turks," Lummer said, in neatly phrased English. "These foreigners are not ready to integrate or become Germans. We simply must find ways to limit their numbers."

Lummer has all kinds of proposals to restrict the numbers of Turks coming into West Germany, but the recommendation that has attracted the most controversy concerns his call to deny admission to all dependent children of *Gasterbeiter* above the age of six. Lummer feels that children above this age generally cannot adjust to a new cultural environment without trauma and that by this age their basic values have already been formed. Lummer told me he was concerned that the differentness of the Turks was creating a situation where there was a distinct possibility of major cultural and social conflicts in the not-so-distant future. "It will be good to have fewer foreigners," Lummer said. "We made a big mistake in the past of not defining a time limit on how long foreign guest workers could stay."

As the debate over the presence of foreign workers heightens, foreigners are being accused of a variety of abuses. Lummer himself told me that much of the drug smuggling from East Berlin into West Berlin is undertaken by Sri Lankans and Turks, some of whom ask for political asylum once in West Germany. Lummer was hard pressed to supply me statistics on drug arrests, but he said flat out that if the flow of foreigners from East Berlin into his part of the city were to be restricted, the mushrooming drug problem in West Germany would also be controlled. Under Senator Lummer's supervision, the West Berlin police have stepped up their scrutiny of foreigners in West Berlin.

In a book titled *Migrant Workers in Western Europe and the United States,* Jonathan Power, an editorial page columnist for the *International Herald Tribune,* wrote:

> Perhaps the most intractable problem posed by the new migrant settlement patterns is the arrival on the labor market (and in the unemployment queues) of the second generation of immigrant children, who were either born in the host country, or arrived at an early age. Youngsters seeking work tend to get a raw deal both from their inexperience and from their foreignness (even those born in the country). Yet at the same time, they tend to assimilate the rising expectations of the country's own youth and refuse to do the type of work which first attracted their parents' generation.
>
> This conflict between rising expectations and diminishing opportunities is generally recognized, in every country with a sizable "foreign" population, as one of the most acute social, political, and economic significance for the future.

In West Germany, this future has already arrived and has brought with it social tensions that worry officials, planners, and social thinkers.

"We now have to do everything possible to increase our population," says Peter Petersen, a member of the Bundestag, noting that in next-door East Germany a working woman who has a second child gets such benefits as a full year's paid holiday. (East Germany, a Communist state, has a population of some 16 million and has one of the worst labor shortages of the East European states in the Soviet bloc. Since 1961, when the Berlin Wall went up, more than 3 million East Germans have fled their country for the West, thereby exacerbating the basic worker-shortage problem in what is nevertheless the most industrialized of the East European countries.) Petersen is among those who favor not only increasing the basic German population of the country but also assisting the foreign permanent residents to adjust better to German life. He is especially critical of young Germans who seek to exclude young immigrants from the basic cultural and social life of the nation.

One afternoon I went by to swim in the health club of the Steigenberger Hotel on Rankestrasse and soon found myself chatting with Kristina Mueller, a winsome young masseuse. She is engaged to a man who serves in the West Berlin police force, a man, Kristina said, who would like "nothing better than to bash in a few Turkish heads." Why? Because of his belief that a lot of young Turks were aimless and directionless and not motivated to put in a hard day's work. Her fiancé believed, too, that these young, unemployed Turks contributed significantly to the growing street-crime problem in West Berlin.

That evening, Kristina took me to meet some of her friends, who, like her fiancé, seemed to hold that West Berlin—and, indeed, all of West Germany—would be much better off without the Turks. Her policeman-fiancé was working that evening, but Kristina's male and female friends insisted on going to a nightclub featuring nude disco dancers.

"They come here in pursuit of the good life, but if they like it so much why don't they become good Germans like all of us?" said Hans Otte, a thick-set blond who is a truck driver.

"Yes, why do they live differently?" piped in Karen Steiner, a secretary in a bank. "Why do they insist on eating, breathing, speaking differently? Why don't they blend in? If they are still so attached to Turkey, maybe they should go back, no?"

These were some of the milder comments. As the evening wore on and these young men and women shed their inhibitions, racial epithets were hurled against Turks. Kristina Mueller, who had brought me along with her, seemed embarrassed. "I wish I could say these kind of remarks are the exception among our youth today," she said. "But unfortunately, you will hear such talk wherever you go these days in Germany. The Turks are simply no longer welcomed and wanted."

The next morning, I walked through the Kreutzberg neighborhood, where many Turkish immigrants live. It was a gray day, with promise of rain in the clouds. I walked along the Berlin Wall, a monstrous snakelike structure, fangs, venom, and all, which divides Berlin into two. With me was a friend named Bhaskar Kotian, a young Indian immigrant fluent in several languages, who translated some of the slogans and graffiti on the wall. The neighborhoods near it, like Kreutzberg, are occupied by poor immigrants, like the Turks, Yugoslavs, Greeks, Algerians, Moroccans, Tunisians, and Portuguese. Approaching Kreutzberg on foot, you can see how abruptly the Cold War graffiti changes ideology and orientation. In German, slogans urge the Turks to go home. "Germany for Germans!" reads a particularly noticeable phrase, daubed in red on the Wall. The graffiti soon metamorphose into Turkish messages. Bhaskar shrugged when I asked him to translate some of these slogans. "Ah," he said, "they're about Turkish politics. You know, down with the military, down with the Greeks—that sort of thing." We couldn't find any graffiti that answered back those German exhortations that the Turks leave Germany forthwith.

Kreutzberg is a sad, decaying neighborhood. Its buildings are depressing and poorly maintained. Some of the buildings, especially those constructed before 1945, were long ago scheduled for demolition, but then the migrant workers arrived and there was a housing shortage in West Berlin and the authorities let these structures stand so that the Turks could move in, paying little or no rent. The streets are littered with garbage. Only the wash hanging on clotheslines and movie posters lend color to the scene. There are a myriad of Turkish coffee shops here, packed with unshaven Turks engaged in loud conversation or playing checkers, and there are several shabby restaurants featuring lamb kebabs whose aroma wafts out into the streets. Youths hang out at street corners, cadging cigarettes from foreigners like me. Brawny cats scamper around. Scrawny children run after them. The few cars that are to be seen are of 1960s vintage, dented and in need of fresh paint. Kreutzberg is a down-and-out place, possibly the worst area in West Berlin to live, but for Moustapha Arsat it represented the end of the rainbow when he used to scrounge for a living fifteen years ago on his family farm in Vaan, in eastern Turkey.

Moustapha came to West Berlin the wrong way, which is to say that he smuggled himself via East Berlin in those long-gone days when it was possible to take a cheap Interflug flight into East Germany, then walk into West Berlin at Checkpoint Charlie with relative ease. Since then, of course, the West Germans have required visas of virtually every visitor, most especially of those with Turkish passports. Moustapha's uncle, Echmat Ali, had already established himself in West Berlin as a part-time coffee shop owner in Kreutzberg and as a full-time janitor in a commercial building on the Potsdamstrasse. Echmat would write glorious letters home, boasting of how much money he made and how well his wife and three children lived in a flat in Kreutzberg for which they paid a pittance in rent. A decade in West Berlin, Echmat would say, and he would have stashed away enough money to set him up for life back home in Turkey. So why didn't Moustapaha hurry over, and he, Echmat, Moustapha's mother's older brother, would make sure that his nephew made money. In the event, Moustapha couldn't find a sponsor for a job, and then, not wishing to be involved in lengthy and possibly futile encounters with West German immigration officials at the airport, he traveled to East Berlin and hurried across the East German border to West Berlin (a group of good Samaritans waiting on the West Berlin side of Checkpoint Charlie thought he was a political refugee from the East and lavishly welcomed Moustapha; when it was discovered three hours later that the Turk was not an East German, Moustapha was tossed back into the streets—but not before he had had a wonderful meal and fine wines). Echmat put him to work first as a waiter in his coffee shop in Kreutzberg and then as a sweeper in a bank on Potsdamstrasse.

It is now a dozen years since Moustapha Arsat journeyed to West Berlin. He hasn't gone back to Vaan, fearing that he wouldn't be allowed back into West Germany if he left this country. It is an irrational fear, for he has a valid visa. He has just turned forty; his sons, who are in their early teens, and his wife are with him in Kreutzberg. The uncle, Echmat Ali, returned to Turkey a couple of years ago, bought himself a small hotel in Istanbul with his savings from West Germany, and reports that he is doing fine, thank you. Moustapha has taken over Echmat's coffee shop in Kreutzberg, and he is not so sure he wants to go back home to Turkey again.

It is not that Moustapha isn't concerned about the rising antiforeigner sentiments in West Germany. It is simply that, a dozen years after coming here, he has decided that he couldn't possibly make a decent enough living back on the family farm in Vaan. His annual income in West Germany exceeds $20,000 now. "What future do I have back in Turkey?" he asks. Implicit in his question is a recognition that the Turkish economy is doing poorly. Nearly 40 percent of Turkey's labor force is unemployed, and the country's foreign debts are well over $10 billion. West Germany may want its Turkish guest workers to return home, but Turkey doesn't especially want them back: these workers each year send home more than $2 billion in much-needed foreign exchange. The *Wall Street Journal* recently quoted an unidentified Turkish cabinet minister who said: "Foreign remittances come to our aid like a lottery, a godsend."

Moustapha's life in Kreutzberg is well ordered. His wife prepares the snacks that the Arsats sell in their coffee shop. The two Arsat boys, Selim and Mehmet, help out after school. The boys also attend Koran classes at a neighborhood mosque. The Arsats have a video-cassette recorder at home on which they see the latest Turkish movies. Turkish friends come over frequently for huge meals of feta cheese, lamb kebabs, lentils, sheep liver, thick yogurt, and, of course, the ubiquitous baklava. The Arsats' socializing is confined to Kreutzberg, and they have no wish to move out: after all, where else in West Berlin, a city already short of decent, affordable housing, can you find a five-room apartment that costs less than $100 a month in rent? Moustapha and his family all speak good

German. He thinks that one day soon he will become a full-fledged West German citizen. He hopes his sons will live as adults in West Germany, although, of course, in a better neighborhood than Kreutzberg.

What about Chancellor Kohl's offer for Turks to be given nearly $5,000 to go back home?

Moustapha snorts.

"What kind of offer is that?" he says. "Do you think it is enough money for us to go back home and make a fresh start?"

Spokesmen for immigrant organizations have expressed concern that the Kohl plan could be the beginning of a forced repatriation program. This is vehemently denied by Norbert Blum, the federal labor minister, who says that the government "will never deviate from the principle of free choice."

Still, there can be little doubt that Blum and Kohl and the whole lot want large numbers of Turks and other *Auslanders* to depart. Blum's calculations show that some 85,000 of the 300,000 or so unemployed foreigners will qualify for the government scheme, which runs through June 1984. If everybody who qualifies does indeed accept, it will cost the West German government about $110 million to pay off the departing guest workers and their families. Blum acknowledges that the scheme would save the government almost $50 million in unemployment pay and child welfare benefits. West Germany's antiquated social security system also will benefit from the exodus: employers' contributions—amounting to more than $270 million—do not have to be paid out to the departing workers, although the workers can take with them their own contributions (immediately in the case of the Turks and the Portuguese, and for the rest after two years).

Norbert Blum contends that if the unemployed *Gastarbeiter* leave, it will make assimilation easier for those of their brethren left behind. But there has been little serious discussion in West Germany about what sort of changes the country's class structure would undergo as the immigrants assimilate—as the "guest workers" become plain "workers."

Assimilation is easier for some nationalities than it is for others. On the whole, the Turks—perhaps because of their native language, their Moslem religion, and their traditional tendency to live only among their own—do not integrate easily. Turkish guest workers also generally tend to be lower-class immigrants who hold menial jobs in West Germany. Immigrants from Asian states like India, Pakistan, the Philippines, South Korea, and Sri Lanka usually are better educated and more skilled; many of them work in West Germany as physicians, nurses, dentists, and other professions in the health care sector, where there is an acute shortage of personnel. (Including families, there are in West Germany today 25,000 Indians, 22,000 Pakistanis, 12,000 Filipinos, 8,000 South Koreans, and about 10,000 Sri Lankans.)

The federal government of West Germany has shown some concern about assimilation problems of foreigners, and in 1981 it supported the West Berlin administration's decision to form a special agency for the welfare of foreigners, an organization known as the Auslanderbeauftragte des Senats von Berlin. I met with the agency's head, an amiable woman named Barbara John. Her office is in a brightly decorated suite on the Potsdamer Strasse, not far from the heart of downtown Berlin. The walls are festooned with posters depicting blond Germans happily playing or communicating with obviously Turkish people. The function of her agency, Miss John told me, was to ensure that there was harmony between native Germans and foreigners: she often plays the role of peacemaker in disputes between Germans and Turks. She also helps Turks and others find jobs, or assists them to get wages commensurate with their skills.

"We have to give these foreigners the security that they are truly wanted in our society," Miss John, a large woman with tired eyes, said to me. "We try to get across the message that in this office there are people who care about the plight and welfare of foreigners. We are aware that many foreigners have problems integrating into German society, and we are aware that many of these foreigners suffer discrimination in employment, housing, sometimes even in recreation. I see my role as that of someone who makes the integration process smoother—and in the process lessens social tensions here."

A typical week for Barbara John includes not only meeting with dozens of foreigners in her office but also visiting their homes. She is sometimes accompanied by a sprightly young Turkish woman whom she employs, Selver Mengusoglu. Another regular companion is Cemalettin Cetin, an intense Turk who came to West Berlin on assignment for his Istanbul newspaper nearly twenty years ago and stayed on to start a community welfare organization that is currently supported by Miss John's agency. Escorted by Miss Mengusoglu, I visited Mr. Cetin in his office on Fennstrasse, a sausage's throw from the Wall. It was the end of a day during which he had met with nearly fifty Turks, and he was plainly fatigued. But Turks do not refuse visitors, and Cetin not only talked at length with me, he also stuffed me with rich honey cake and endless cups of strong Turkish coffee.

"I am a worried man these days," Cetin said, speaking in a mix of Turkish and German, which Selver Mengusoglu translated for me. "The climate is getting stickier for Turks, and although the vast majority of Germans favor harmonious relations with Turks, there will always be minorities who do evil things. I am concerned with this minority of people, who have the capacity to do mischief. All we Turks want is to live in peace, with good jobs, proper education for our children. We are willing to integrate in every way, but we also want to hold on to our culture."

Later that evening, Cetin took Selver and I to the home of Mehmet and Seriban Erki, a young Turkish couple who live on the Grunewaldstrasse, in an old, high-ceilinged building with sturdy walls and massive doors. This was not a Turkish neighborhood, but several Turks lived in the area. Selver pointed to some signs daubed on the street entrance to the Erki building. The signs said: "Turks, go home!"

Mehmet, who works for the West German telephone company, and Seriban, a cleaning worker in a government office, turned out to be a pleasant couple. They have two sons and two daughters, all born in West Berlin. They have no intention of returning to Turkey.

"Everyone talks about how difficult it is to integrate into German society," Mehmet Erki said, in between offering me coffee and snacks. "But there really aren't such differences between people that they cannot integrate. We are told that we Turks are different because of our mosques. Well, in our case, the real mosque is in our hearts. The important thing is that Germany is home for us."

His fourteen-year-old daughter Hanim joined us at this point. She was a tall, lovely girl, with a radiant smile. I asked her if she felt "different" in Germany, at her school, for instance.

"I am German," Hanim replied, "why should I feel 'different'?"

The Erkis were visited that evening by a neighbor named Ilse Vorpagel, a plump German woman with buffed hair and a blue dress. I asked her what she thought about Germany's "Turkish problem."

"I have no such problem," Ilse, who is in her sixties, said tartly. "None of us in Germany should have any such problem. What is wrong with cultural diversity? I knew nothing about Turkey when Mehmet and Seriban moved in here. Now I cannot stay away from their songs, their kitchen. It's one world, after all."

The Erki family is unusual in the sense that they do not feel beleaguered in Germany. They appear to have adjusted well. They are a minority within a minority.

My friend Bhaskar Kotian came to West Berlin ten years ago as a student from his native Kerala State in India, then decided he would stay on. He met an Indian nurse named Attamma, who had also traveled to West Germany to work, wooed and married her, and now they have two sons. The Kotians say they have few integration problems, and in their view they have made the transition from being immigrants to being a part of everyday German society. It is not just social habits that constitute this transition; in large measure the transition consists of a change in the Kotians' self-image. Slim, handsome, and not yet thirty years old, Bhaskar works as a free-lance translator for the Indian Consulate and other diplomatic establishments in West Berlin.

"It helps that my wife and I speak German," Bhaskar says. "It helps that we both attend classes at a neighborhood community center, where we learn about German history and culture. This is how I feel: if you are going to live in a foreign country, then you have to be 80 percent like one of them and only 20 percent like what you were in your original culture. I look forward to the day I can vote in Germany."

* * *

"Am I British? Do I feel British? Just look around you."

The speaker is Brijmohan Gupta, and the location is London's Southall district, known among immigrants to Britain as "Mini-Asia." Tens of thousands of Britain's one million plus immigrants from India, Pakistan, and Bangladesh live in this neighborhood, a cricket ball's throw from Heathrow International Airport. You can drive for blocks around Southall and not see a single white face. The stores here offer Indian and Pakistani delicacies and condiments. The theaters run Indian movies. Shops offer silk sarees. The area is suffused with aromas of Asian cooking. Sitar music drifts down the streets, which are thronged with turbaned Sikhs and women ambling along in a variety of traditional wear from the Indian subcontinent.

All roads, of course, lead to Brijmohan Gupta's emporium of food and the fine things of life, like jewelry and watches and video-cassette recorders and stereo sets. Brijmohan is a success story, a man who arrived in London twenty years ago from his home town of New Delhi with five dollars in his pocket and parlayed that sum into a business that makes him millions each year. Britain has been good to Brijmohan Gupta, but not the British. Envious white competitors have called in health inspectors to close down his restaurants, Brijmohan says, and his children have been reviled by white youngsters. Brijmohan himself has more than once been pushed and shoved by young white hooligans for no reason other than that he was an Indian.

It's hard to believe now, but not long ago, in the summer of 1981, the streets of Southall were the scene of some of the worst racial riots in Britain. On the night of July 2, a public bar on the outskirts of Southall had invited a flagrantly racist rock group calling itself "The 4 Skins" to give a musical presentation. The group's songs were bawdy and mocked Asians and were inciting enough for some of the youthful audience of raucous whites to roar out into the streets of Southall. The miscreants smashed windows, looted stores, dragged Asian women out of their homes, and sexually fondled them. Asian males retaliated. Forming defense brigades, they fought back with fury. The pub where "The 4 Skins" had performed was burned down. Someone called in the police. Pandemonium reigned. By sunrise on July 3, more than a hundred policemen had been injured trying to protect the young whites who started the disturbances. The "skinheads"—the young whites who profess fascism and whose colleagues elsewhere in Britain have openly called for an expulsion of all Asians and blacks—had fled, but not before causing property damage of millions of dollars.

By a strange coincidence, the events in Southall were part of a wider racial turmoil elsewhere in London and in many other British communities that warm July weekend and in the days to follow.

Liverpool had its racial disturbances in a long-depressed district called Toxteth. There was much looting there, and for the first time ever in Britain, tear gas was fired at rioters. Manchester had its riots, too, in the Moss Side district, where, as in London's Southall and Brixton and in Liverpool's Toxteth, thousands of Asian and West Indian immigrants live. There were outbreaks of violence in the Handsworth district of Birmingham, the home of Britain's second-largest concentration of blacks (in Britain, these days, the term *blacks* is used to denote immigrants from both the West Indies and Asian countries). Over the weekend of July 10 to July 12, riots occurred in virtually every English city that had an immigrant population. In addition to London, Birmingham, Liverpool, and Manchester, racial trouble was reported in Blackburn, Bradford, Derby, Leeds, Leicester, and Wolverhampton. Gasoline bombs were thrown in the Welsh mining valleys. There were street fights in Market Harborough. In London's economically backward district of Brixton, where there had been racial riots earlier that year in April, there were more clashes between the police and blacks.

The unprecedented violence that summer was shocking because it seemed so out of character for Britain. The belief of the British in their own traditionally peaceful life style was rudely shaken. *The Economist,* a London-based weekly that I think is the world's best news magazine, later offered an analysis of the racial riots in Britain's cities that summer. The magazine suggested that each local riot had its own local causes—it would be absurd to offer any single explanation for the troubles. However, there were some common factors:

- Economic recession, becoming rapidly worse at the end of the 1970s, harshly affected young people, and especially those with little education.
- The decline of the inner cities, brought about by industrial change and by government policies to disperse employment, had left the low-paid and the unemployed concentrated in run-down districts near the centers of many large towns.
- Immigration into Britain in the years of relative prosperity from the 1950s to the 1970s attracted a significant number of nonwhite people from former imperial territories. They took jobs that the British-born preferred not to, and settled in the outworn urban areas where British-born people preferred not to live.
- Racial prejudice combined with educational disadvantage kept the black immigrants, and their British-born black children, out of the better jobs and better homes. Verbal and physical abuse of black people heightened their discontent.
- Crime, particularly crime involving personal violence, increased in the inner cities. The crime-control methods of the police focused particularly on young black people, and offended all black people, including the law-abiding majority.

Perhaps more than any Western country with the exception of the United States, Britain has become a multiethnic and multiracial nation. But it hasn't voluntarily become so. There are still large numbers of white Britons who believe that "one day" the 2 million plus blacks will be sent home—as if "home" for these blacks were anywhere else but in Britain.

After the first Brixton riots, in April 1981, the government of Prime Minister Margaret Thatcher asked Lord Scarman "to inquire urgently into" the racial disturbances. In the event, Lord Scarman drew heavily on U.S. race-relations precedents and came up with recommendations on social policy. There was little imagination in what the Scarman Report said. It called for stepped-up recruitment of blacks by the police. It suggested that education for black children must be improved. It stated the obvious in saying that there was high unemployment among young blacks.

But Lord Scarman also urged the government to undertake a direct assault on the whole business of racial disadvantage. This, he wrote, "inevitably means that the ethnic minorities will enjoy for a time a positive discrimination in their favor. . . . Good policing will be of no avail, unless we also tackle and eliminate basic flaws in our society. And, if we succeed in eliminating racial prejudice from our society, it will not be difficult to achieve good policing."

Lord Scarman, perhaps not wishing to antagonize Mrs. Thatcher in the expectation of some future assignment, made no recommendations concerning new government expenditures for improving the condition of blacks. Critics of his report, like Usha Prashar, director of London's Runnymede Trust—a nonprofit organization that espouses, among other things, the cause of a better life for immigrants—note with dismay that having discharged its moral obligation by commissioning Lord Scarman to "study" the racial riots, the Thatcher government proceeded to do nothing by way of follow-up. The basic causes of the 1981 racial riots—high unemployment among blacks and the decay of Britain's inner cities—remain, no doubt to explode again.

I traveled to Britain in the summer of 1983, two years after the race riots, to see for myself what was happening concerning immigrants and immigration. Extreme right-wing organizations like one calling itself the National Front had been active in calling for a complete end to all immigration and even an expulsion of blacks from Britain. A friend of mine named Jack Gwynn, an Englishman who works in the Merton district of London as a caseworker for immigrants, told me that racial harassment was dramatically on the increase nationally. The brand-new building on Colliers Wood Street of his agency, the Merton Community Relations Council, had been vandalized by right-wing whites, who had warned the caseworkers against cooperating with blacks. Asian men and women moving about in London sometimes were accosted by aggressive young whites who abused them verbally, or even manhandled them, at times violently.

Ugly confrontations between whites and blacks are relatively new.

Britain's population of 54 million in 1983 included just over 2 million people who could be classifed as nonwhites, or about 4 percent of the total. In 1951, when the country's total population was 49 million, there were 75,000 nonwhites, or 0.2 percent of the population. By the year 2000, Britain's total population is still likely to be 54 million. But there is now some controversy over how many nonwhites there will be by that year.

Right-wingers are saying that the West Indian blacks and the Asian communities will grow to between 5 and 7 million by the end of the century. But a study carried out in 1982 by Professor William Brass, a noted demographer at the London School of Tropical Medicine, showed a sharp drop in black and Asian birthrates, from four to two births for an average West Indian woman and from six to about four births per female for those from the Indian subcontinent. Professor Brass, who undertook his research for the government-financed Center for Population Studies, estimated that Britain's nonwhite population will increase from about 2 million now to around 3.3 million by the year 2000. In a conversation at his office, Professor Brass told me that the West Indian birthrate in Britain was "hardly, if at all, above replacement level." Still, the perception persists among many whites, especially working-class whites who have lost their jobs because of the recession, that blacks are breeding like rabbits. This is the common recourse to the numbers-game hysteria manipulated by right-wing groups.

"The racial problem in Britain is connected with unemployment," says Jack Gwynn. "And it is going to continue as long as you have very large numbers of restless young blacks who have been brought up to believe they were British but who then find that they are not regarded as equals with their white peers. A new generation of British-born blacks is growing up confused and resentful." This employment crisis among young blacks coincides with a situation in the rest of Europe, where the labor market is being flooded by the largest-ever generation of school graduates. Statistics gathered by the United Nations show that in every major Western European country the number of children born each year rose between 1955 and 1964. But from 1964 onward, with the exception of France and Ireland, the births in all these European states declined, sometimes dramatically, as in the case of West Germany. And by 1982 the number of teenagers looking for their first jobs was at an all-time high. In Britain, according to the United Nations, about 60,000 black children were born in 1982—nearly 9 percent of total births, although only 4 percent of the country's overall population of 54 million is black. The children of black immigrants, says the United Nations, form a growing proportion of all children born in Britain each year. And the teenaged population has grown fastest in the inner cities, where most of the immigrant population is concentrated.

Merton, where Jack Gwynn works, is a borough that encompasses Wimbledon, the site of the world's most prestigious tennis championship tournament. It has some very exclusive residential neighborhoods, with houses whose walls are covered with ivy and whose back yards consist of flower-filled gardens and immaculate lawns. Located in southwest London, Merton has traditionally been a conservative district, and its borough council reflects this conservatism. Merton has sprawling working-class areas as well. And now 11 percent of the borough's overall population of 160,000 consists of people from Commonwealth countries and Pakistan.

Gwynn, a slim, pleasant man who recently graduated from Cambridge University with the highest honors, explains that the deprived areas of Merton have been receiving fewer and fewer services. The seven municipally supported youth clubs, for example, happen to be located in Merton's better-off areas. Blacks live in the older housing stock, where often there is poor heating in winter and sporadic water supply many months of the year. Few blacks work in municipal jobs, and fewer in the police force—reflecting a nationwide pattern where British bureaucracies and law enforcement agencies simply haven't hired blacks in significant numbers. In London, for example, at the time of the Brixton riots of April 1981, the metropolitan police had some 24,000 officers. Of them, only 110 were black. Jack Gwynn points out that black youths are twice as unlikely as their white schoolfellows to find jobs because of racial discrimination.

"What we're really talking about, then, is comprehensive reform of British institutions," Gwynn said. "Blacks are becoming more organized in Britain, and these institutions—like the civil service and the uniformed public services—will have to change to accommodate more blacks. It is no longer good enough to say that if immigrants live in Britain long enough they will assimilate. We have to get away from this business of emphasizing cultural assimilation toward a much more clearly defined economic opportunity for blacks, one with legal foundation making it difficult for employers to discriminate."

At the Merton Community Relations Council, workers like Gwynn liaison with local employers and others suggesting ways they can modify their relations with poor immigrants. Gwynn's agency is a local manifestation of the Commission for Racial Equality, which was established under the 1976 Race Relations Act. The 1976 act said that the Commission for Racial Equality (known widely as CRE) should play "a major strategic role in enforcing the law in the public interest." The commission was empowered to hold inquiries into reported racial discrimination and to ask the courts to remedy the situation, where needed. But the CRE, which took over a network of what are now 105 community relations councils in various parts of Britain, was also intended to be a sort of social service mechanism for the welfare of immigrants in depressed neighborhoods.

"The real problem is the perception many whites have about blacks," says Gwynn, who is white himself. Bluntly put, the perception is that blacks simply aren't as good as whites in job performance, a perception that has been discredited in study after study but that lives on nonetheless to affect employers attitudes and actions in hiring. Racism in Britain has contributed to the underachievement of black people in virtually every category of opportunity, from education to housing to employment.

Jack Gwynn, who is as idealistic a person as you are likely to meet anywhere, feels strongly that institutional commitments are necessary to give blacks more and better employment; and, he argues, white Britons, particularly in professional service agencies, should receive the sort of racism-awareness training that was pioneered in the United States. "We have got to develop an awareness in this society as to what multiracialism means," he said.

But this will take a very long time to happen. Mrs. Thatcher and Company show few signs of acting to alleviate the immigrants' situation. There are no nationwide job programs for blacks: the political backlash from unemployed whites would probably be too much for the Conservatives to take. There is little commitment to changing school curriculums to take into account Britain's repressive colonial history.

In short, the lessons of the summer of 1981, haven't been learned, and they haven't been forgotten.

The poor men of Britain's former tropical empire first started coming here in significant numbers in the early 1950s, when many British employers recruited them with zest in anticipation of a rapidly expanding postwar economy. They were followed by their wives and families. The cause of international migration to Britain, as to other European states, was rapid economic development and modernization there and the resulting huge discrepancies in wealth between these industrialized states and the tropical countries, many of them former colonies of the European powers. The large waves of West Indians stopped after the passage of the Commonwealth Immigrants Act of 1962, which imposed strict controls. Thereafter, only a trickle of immigrants from the Caribbean states came into Britain, mostly immediate family members. In 1981, for example, just 250 male West Indians, 360 women, and 280 children migrated to this country to settle down.

It was a bit of a different situation with the Asians. Their migration momentum did not get going fully until the early 1960s. British employers in the textile and metalworking industries somehow seemed to keep wanting more Asian workers, who were generally thought to be diligent, honest, and hardworking. Hindus came, and Moslems, and Sikhs, and they brought their wives and dozens of children, and they brought their wives' families.

They came from exotic places with mellifluous names—Jullunder and Amritsar and Ahmedabad and Ludhiana and Lukhnow and Lahore and Karachi and Peshawar. Among them were thousands of Punjabi farmers who had lost their lands to salt. Enormous tracts of arable land had undergone an ecological disaster: more than 20 million acres of irrigated land had become salinated. The farmers sought refuge in Britain.

They came to Britain, too, from her former East African possessions of Uganda and Kenya; and after the mad Ugandan dictator Idi Amin Dada expelled more than 75,000 Asians in 1972, nearly half of those dispossessed men, women, and children—many of them British passport holders—were generously allowed in by the British government to settle here and make a fresh start. (About 4,500 of these African-Asians are still allowed in each year; several thousands of the Asians, who technically are British subjects, are languishing in India and other countries, waiting for Britain to let them in. They may have a very long wait. Total immigration into Britain in 1983 was around 12,000, the lowest figure in a very long time.)

The Asians, traditionally accustomed to living among their own in closely knit fashion, soon developed their particular ghettoes. Most ghettoes are built from the inside: they are cultural fortresses within which communities can speak their own language, eat their own special foods, listen to their own music, wear their own attire. Cultural ghettoes are, most of all, comforting, a refuge from the alien environment of a newly adopted world.

Southall, in London, is perhaps the best known of these myriad Asian ghettoes. I was driven there one balmy afternoon by a cheerful Sikh named Anoop Singh Vohra. He is a tall, relaxed man, and nothing seems to bother him. He and his brothers own several classy hotels in London and Kenya, and Vohra's prosperity is reflected in his tailored clothes and in his Mercedes. We had first met in Kenya, where I'd been posted by the *New York Times* as its Africa correspondent—and I had instantly warmed up to him. As we neared Southall, Vohra explained that the Asians who settled in Southall were, for the most part, working-class people. You can find many of the men and women who clean toilets at Heathrow Airport or who sweep the streets of London living in Southall. It is not an attractive neighborhood. The one- and two-story houses have seen better days. There are far too many dying elms and maples. There are numerous empty lots that serve as makeshift garbage dumps. But when you talk to Southall residents you quickly detect in them not the indifference of renters but the pride of proprietorship: more than 85 percent of the homes in Southall are occupied by the Asian families who bought the dwellings. (The garbage and the trash-littered streets of Southall reflect a traditional Asian practice: Asians keep their own homes immaculately clean and simply toss the junk and kelter out of their windows for someone else to clean up! It is so in Secunderabad and in Sialkot, and it is so in Southall.)

When you talk with these residents of Southall, you nowadays sense in them a new pride, a new element of self-esteem. I mentioned this to my friend Swraj Paul, an industrialist based in London, he launched into a long assessment of the situation. Paul himself is an Asian success story, having arrived penniless in Britain fifteen years ago and having subsequently constructed a business empire that now is spread throughout Britain, and also reaches to the Middle East, India, Western Europe and the United States. The tall, portly Paul, of course, is not a Southall "type"—he lives in the more fashionable Portland Square, hobnobs with royalty and Britain's political bluebloods, and frequently entertains the likes of Prime Ministers Margaret Thatcher of Britain and Indira Gandhi of India, both of whom he considers as friends; Paul's wealth and his social connections have created for him a special status within the Asian community. Paul's feeling is that the riots of 1981 brought about a sea-change in self-perception for Asians. "The young ones, in particular, saw that there was no need to be timid, no need to be constantly self-effacing as many of their parents' generation were," Paul said. "People have now been coming up to me and saying how proud they are to be Indian—and the younger ones are saying how they consider themselves Britons with an Indian flavor." In the wake of the racial riots, Swraj Paul arranged several meetings between Asian community leaders and the police, who he said were simply not aware of the extent to which there were racial tensions in British society.

What a young man named Joginder Singh said to me is typical of the new sentiments of Southallites.

He is a burly Punjabi, about twenty-three years old. He fought off the "skinheads" in the summer of 1981 and has formed what he says are Asian "self-defense" patrols in Southall. Joginder's family owns a saree shop, where he also sells video-cassette recorders and other electronic goods. He was born in Britain, and although everything about him suggests an Indian life style, Joginder considers himself British: his passport is British, his accent is British.

He offered me rich, milky tea in a mug that was filled with so much sugar that I had difficulty stirring the spoon. Some of Joginder's friends joined us—tall, strapping Asian youths who all seemed clones of one another: they wore leather jackets and tight jeans and boots with studded toecaps and high heels. Like Joginder, these youths looked tough. Some were in their late teens, others in their early twenties. They all expressed confidence that racist groups like the "skinheads" would never again foray into Southall. The Asians, they told me, had taught the "skinheads" a lesson they were not likely to forget for a long time.

"No more Paki-bashing here, no more beating up or bullying of Asians by third-rate white riff-raff," Joginder Singh said, violently. "We are part of this country now, and we will not be frightened off so easily."

The second generation of Asians in Britain has finally "arrived."

Eleven

Villages and Grass Roots
How to Be Where Needed

In Bangkok, I was taken to a soiree by a friend named Shyamala Cowsik, an Indian diplomat with features so dazzling that people kept turning around to stare at her. But Shyamala was upstaged that evening by a slim young Thai named Mechai Viravaidya. Mechai walked into the room and started working the crowd, as would an American politician on the hustings. He kept handling out his calling card to everybody. At one point Mechai approached a group of Vietnamese envoys who were chatting to one another and sipping champagne.

"How do you do?" Mechai asked in French, a language widely spoken in Vietnam.

The diplomats bowed and smiled in typical Vietnamese fashion. Before they could say anything, Mechai thrust his business cards in their hands. To each card was attached a brightly hued condom.

"What is this?" one of the Vietnamese diplomats asked hesitantly.

"It is a contraceptive," Mechai replied.

The Vietnamese—whose country's annual population growth rate is the highest in Asia—seemed confused.

"All of us Asians need to understand that our biggest problem is sitting right here between our legs. We just need to bend down and look," Mechai said. "We worry about bombs and communism and capitalism. We should really start worrying more about overpopulation."

It was a typical Mechai Viravaidya performance.

So identified is Mechai with Thailand's family-planning effort that he is no longer just a household word in this country. The forty-three-year-old economist-turned-birth-control-crusader has become a bedroom word: condoms all over Thailand are now commonly called "Mechais." Working under the aegis of a private, nonprofit organization, Viravaidya has distributed contraceptives by the millions and persuaded men to have vasectomies and women to accept sterilization in order to slow down population growth. The organization he started, Community-Based Family Planning Services (CBFPS) is active in 158 districts, encompassing 16,236 villages—18 million people, or about 33 percent of Thailand's population.

The family-planning program in Thailand is an Asian success story. Mechai's key contribution has been to publicize the urgency of population control and set into motion a unique contraceptive distribution system under which, among other things, vendors get bonuses for increased sales and rural Thais get financial benefits if they use contraception. By showing to peasants the economic benefits of family planning, Mechai—perhaps more than any other individual in the field I encountered anywhere—is bringing about gradual but sustained changes in traditional thinking. His work is an outstanding example of how the West's development dollars are put to use at the grass roots and how these dollars can generate an unusual self-help ethic among the recipients.

Bangkok is a mean, murderous city of some 6 million mostly poor people. It is fifty-one times bigger than Thailand's second largest urban center, Chieng Mai. It contains almost three-fifths of the country's entire urban population, and has eight out of every ten physicians in Thailand—despite the fact that 78 percent of the country's population still lives in rural areas. Thailand's overall population growth rate has fallen in the last decade from more than 3 percent annually to a bit less than 2 percent, but Bangkok keeps growing at almost 5 percent each year. Of Bangkok's 6 million residents, nearly 2 million are said to be living in the city's 400 identifiable slums. Prostitution, street crimes such as muggings, and robberies and homicide are rampant. More than 2 million people living in the city are said to be unemployed; many of Thailand's estimated 400,000 "special service girls"—or prostitutes—live and ply their trade in this capital city.

I don't know how people live here. The climate is hot, and the humidity is high. The air is unbreathable. Environmental studies by Mahidol University have shown that half of Bangkok's official water supply is lost through broken pipes, and more than half of the city's burgeoning population depends on pumps that bring up contaminated water. Bangkok has no sewage disposal system. Its 10,000 large factories and hundreds of small workshops inject tons of deadly cadmium, lead, and mercury wastes into Chao Phraya River, which carries these elements into the Gulf of Thailand—the main source of fish for this area's population.

Air pollution in Bangkok is so bad that studies by scientists at Mahidol University have shown that traffic police have lead levels in their blood more than twice that of ordinary police who aren't exposed continuously to vehicular traffic. The motorized tricycles, known popularly as "tuc-tuc" taxis, contribute so heavily to the noise pollution that nearly all the 10,000 men employed as taxi drivers have been found to suffer from hearing loss. There are some 550,000 registered automobiles in Bangkok, and by the end of the century this figure is expected to climb beyond one million.

The taxi driver who took me from Bangkok's airport to the Dusit Thani Hotel was a young man who'd emigrated to the city from the northern region. He said his name was Somm.

"You will need these for protection," Somm said to me, brandishing a brightly colored packet. "Only one dollar."

He was offering me condoms. Single men who land at Bangkok's airport are generally assumed by taxi drivers to have come to Thailand in search of easy sex.

"How come you are selling these?" I asked Somm.

"Mechai's program," he said, taking it for granted that I knew who he was referring to. "When I have sold a certain number of these packets, Mechai's organization pays for my taxi insurance for a whole year."

Mechai's presence is everywhere in Bangkok. At the airport itself, he operates a booth that dispenses condoms. There are similar booths at bus terminals around the city. Department stores carry T-shirts and bikini panties bearing Mechai's slogan: "Too Many Children Make You Poor." He admits that he has borrowed liberally from Madison Avenue's manual of publicity. He has appeared on television programs and filled up condoms as one would balloons. He has unabashedly exploited his ties —by marriage—with Thailand's King Bhumibol and invoked royal blessings on his birth control campaigns. One campaign involves mass vasectomies in Bangkok on the king's birthday each year. In 1983, for example, 3,000 men participated in Bangkok's vasectomy drive on the royal birthday. Mechai, the product of Thai-Scottish parents, has also skillfully brought influential Buddhist priests into the birth control movement: local priests in Thai communities sprinkle "holy water" as blessings on new crates of condoms.

Mechai signs off his nightly radio broadcast with the phrase: "Don't forget your pill!"

His office is in a particularly dilapidated part of Bangkok. It is located in a compound consisting of several two-story buildings, a schoolhouse, a playground, and a small car-park. Open gutters outside the compound form a moat around it; sharks and deadly piranha wouldn't survive in the gutters because of the excrement and offal. The stench is overpowering.

I walked up a flight of stairs to Mechai's office. Outside his door was a large imitation painting of the Mona Lisa—except that this Mona Lisa was holding a packet of birth control pills in her hand. Attractive young women, whom I took to be staff workers, scurried around purposefully; they all wore colorful T-shirts emblazoned with a drawing of three inflated condoms.

One particularly well-endowed woman had on a T-shirt whose legend read: "A Condom a Day Keeps the Doctor Away."

None of the women appeared embarrassed at this display of open sexuality. It turned out that not all of these workers were family-planning experts. I met a young American named Jonathan Hayssen, a native of Wisconsin, who decided he'd come to Thailand after receiving a business degree from Stanford University to assist Mechai in his rural development programs. There were four other youthful Americans with master's degrees in health care. There were also young Thais who had specialized in preventive medicine, paramedical education, crop improvement, pest control, and rural finance. Everywhere there were photographs of Mechai handing out contraceptives, or Mechai helping peasants dig ditches, or Mechai addressing rallies. And everywhere in the office there were slogans about birth control.

Mechai was involved in a meeting with visiting American officials, so one of his assistants invited me to watch a film on a video machine. The title of the thirty-minute film was "The Cheerful Revolution." The whole point about the film was that since sex was fun, birth control should be as well. If Mechai has a guiding philosophy, that is it. Lest Mechai be thought of as no more than a frivolous family-planning dilettante, let me also add that he believes that birth control works best when it is tied in with development efforts. This dual approach has worked remarkably well wherever Mechai has launched grass-roots projects in Thailand.

Earlier that day I had visited a man named David A. Oot. A tall, sandy-haired man, Oot was the director of the population program of the U.S. Agency for International Development. He spoke enthusiastically of Mechai. Mechai Viravaidya is only one part of Thailand's extraordinary population effort, of course. Government-sponsored (and American- and United Nations–supported) family-planning programs have also been inventive and energetic. As a result, the annual population growth rate has fallen from more than 3 percent a decade ago to a bit less than 2 percent now. The goal is 1.5 percent by 1986, which David Oot believed the Thais would meet.

Oot told me that Thailand was recruiting a million new family-planning acceptors each year, a startlingly high figure by any standards (and comparable to Indonesia, which has almost four times as many people as Thailand does and where a massive birth control effort is being promoted by the government of General Suharto).

But what was also truly commendable about the Thai family-planning experience, Oot said, was the fact that this country had gotten virtually every kind of contraceptive into the field: The pill, the IUD (intrauterine device), injectibles like depo-provera (initially supplied by Belgium and now locally manufactured), and laparoscopic sterilizations for females. (The laparoscope is a so-called belly-button device with which an incision is made to reach the female Fallopian tubes, which are then clipped. The Fallopian tubes are the conduit through which the female egg passes from the ovary to the uterus.) Not many countries in Asia manage to get all kinds of contraceptives into general use. India, for example, has concentrated on promoting sterilizations and the IUD as the main means of birth control, and only recently started pushing the pill. No injectables are used in the Philippines. Indonesia does not favor sterilizations.

I found out from Oot that more than 80 percent of contraceptive users in Thailand received their supplies and birth control information from the government, although there were some 700 private organizations—including Mechai's agency—that actively engaged in family-planning work around the Texas-sized country.

"Family planning gets a lot of attention in this country," Oot said.

I asked Oot what he thought accounted for Thailand's evident "success" in population control. Why were Thais accepting family-planning programs so enthusiastically?

His answer was immediate: it wasn't just the relatively efficient contraceptive-distribution system. There has been imaginative use of aid from foreign donors like the United States, Canada, Australia, Norway, and the United Nations Fund for Population Activities. High literacy has helped, as has the fact that women in Thailand traditionally have enjoyed higher status than in many other Third World states; Thai women are generally not as intimidated by their menfolk as elsewhere in the developing world. There is wide cultural acceptance of family planning and no serious opposition to it. Moreover, the predominant Theravada Buddhist religion is not an inhibiting factor when it comes to birth control practices.

Thailand is also at a stage of economic development where it suffers from no special shortage of physicians to travel to remote rural areas to promote family planning. The country's medical schools are turning out graduates by the scores every year. In contrast, in neighboring Nepal, where there is an acute need for family-planning services, only a handful of physicians are available for rural duty. Because infant mortality is lower in Thailand than in many other developing states, couples are seeing their children survive and do not feel—as couples do, say, in nearby Bangladesh—that an additional child is an economic asset and a guarantee of security in old age.

I finally met with Mechai. He turned out to be a nonstop smoker and a nonstop talker. It was an anecdote a minute. It occurred to me that here was a supreme showman, a Thai version of P. T. Barnum, complete with his own contraceptives circus. Mechai's gimmickry clearly was working in Thailand. But how long could he continue emphasizing birth control?

"Not much longer," Mechai said. "Most developing countries have separate fertility and development programs. But if you couple them, the chances are greater that you will have increased economic growth and decreased population growth. One just has to link population control with development. My focus is increasingly on this link."

Mechai has established such a link at the grass roots in a number of places around Thailand. I saw a program in Mahasarakham, one of the country's poorest provinces. Mechai and a group of young workers—mostly students on leave from schools and colleges in Bangkok—helped peasants build irrigation canals, water storage tanks, and breeding farms for chickens and pigs. Mechai persuaded local government officials to authorize low-interest loans and personally pledged technical assistance to those peasants who committed themselves to birth control. The idea is to link economic benefits with family planning.

"We do not believe in coercion," Mechai told me. "Not in Mahasarakham, not anywhere else. It is just that if you agree to practice family planning, you get the first crack at low-interest loans and technical expertise from us. We want people to achieve the twin goals of a better life and reduced population growth in their area. In a poor country such as ours, we don't have the resources to get development going first and then wait for fertility to decline."

Mechai's family planning and development "message" is everywhere in Mahasarakham: water buffaloes had birth control exhortations painted on their sides. Local taxis had such signs on their doors. Bus tickets had various family-planning appeals printed on them. Mechai has instituted what he calls the "supermarket approach" to development here: a peasant need go to only one local building to collect contraceptives, consult with a technical expert concerning agriculture, and cash in a low-interest loan. The idea is to simplify development; elsewhere in the Third World, the tendency is to make life even more baffling and cumbersome, in the name of progress.

I asked a peasant named Thanat what he thought of Mechai's incentive program.

Thanat smiled broadly, his sun-baked face creasing into a thousand lines. His two children, cheerful boys of ten and twelve, were helping him heave fertilizer bags onto a small wheelbarrow.

"Easy to understand," Thanat said. "I put on condom, I get a loan to improve my farm and buy more pigs. If I don't use condom and my wife gets pregnant again, then no new loan for long time."

Mechai's view is that birth control should be open, lighthearted, and relaxed for everybody. He has stressed the bonus approach, rather than the penalty approach employed by, say, Singapore (which frowns on couples having more than two children and makes it financially costlier for people to have a third child). From what I saw of Mechai's grass-roots work in Thailand, here is a marvelous example for the rest of the Third World. Mechai just goes out there and makes it worthwhile for people to sign up as birth control acceptors. And because a taxi driver can get his insurance paid if he sells enough condoms and uses them himself as well, because a peasant in a remote rural area can buy an extra pig with a cheap loan he received by agreeing to limit the size of his family, because a teacher in Bangkok can get financial assistance to buy an apartment if she signs up as a birth control practitioner—because of all these things, people have found out time after time that family planning can indeed be relevant to their needs. It can lead to specific improvements in people's lives.

* * *

Late one afternoon, in the tiny town of Concepcion in the Philippines, Federico Dizon was discussing with me the population growth of his island-nation. Over soft beverages and curried savories, he stated that when Admiral George Dewey's U.S. fleet steamed into Manila Harbor in 1896, the Philippines had 7 million people. By 1965, the figure had climbed to 33 million. Now there are at least 53 million Filipinos, and the country has one of the highest population densities in Southeast Asia—with the ugly prospect of the population doubling in less than about two decades.

"How are we going to feed all these mouths?" Dizon asked. "How are we going to educate them? And what about jobs? Just imagine—85,000 new mouths to feed breakfast here in Concepcion alone within a few years! Whether we like it or not, we are going to have to dramatically control our population growth. And which method to use? That is entirely up to couples. It's their choice. I don't condemn them for whatever form of contraception they use. If they want abortion, it's their choice—there's no baby there."

His manner is that of a family doctor—easy, pleasant, comforting. But he is no physician. Federico Dizon is a Roman Catholic priest who, in this overwhelmingly Catholic country, dares to say publicly that if the only birth control method approved by the Church—the rhythm method—is not satisfactory to individuals, they should choose another method. Father Dizon says he knows he is contravening the Pope's directives against artificial birth control. But he also points out that this country has the highest annual population growth in Asia after Vietnam and that the Philippines desperately needs to curtail this growth rate sharply. Father Dizon, a popular parish priest in this community about 100 miles north of Manila, advocates a sustained, effective, national family-planning program.

"In a poor country such as ours, night is always longer than day in the barrios, the slums," Father Dizon said to me. "So sex is recreation, often the only affordable entertainment for people. Should we penalize them for this? Shouldn't we instead be giving them the means to limit their families, to let the parents be wise enough to learn that it's stupid to produce kids you cannot support properly?"

What seems to be happening in the Philippines these days, unfortunately, is precisely the opposite of what people like Father Dizon say is needed. The country's birth control program, once highly regarded, is in danger of being dismantled. The head of the nation's population agency was dismissed abruptly because of his opposition to fund cutbacks (although early in 1984 the official, Antonio de los Reyes, won reinstatement after a civil service tribunal ruled he'd been unfairly sacked). The new five-year plan barely mentions family planning and, unlike previous development blueprints, sets no specific demographic targets. Aid from Western agencies and from the United States for population projects has often been held up inexplicably by Filipino officials, prompting several donors to trim their contributions to this country.

Indeed, if powerful officials close to President Ferdinand E. Marcos have their way, there may well be no family-planning program in the Philippines at all. Some of these officials devoutly believe that a large population is a nation's best resource; some of these same officials are members of Opus Dei, an arch conservative Catholic organization that fiercely opposes birth control measures other than the Church-approved "natural" rhythm method.

It is still unclear whether President Marcos, who is preoccupied with serious economic, political, and personal health problems, is fully aware of the implications of current and forthcoming aid cutbacks from the Western countries, many of which have made it plain that economic assistance to the Philippines must be linked to a decline in fertility rates. Marcos has made it one of the cornerstones of his political strategy not to provoke the Church into political opposition and criticism (although he gets such criticism anyway!). And it could also well be that, at a time when many Church leaders have complained about the poor human rights record of his regime, the wily president does not wish to anger the Church by renewing his earlier commitment on population control.

But the Church has been fairly muted about the Philippines' birth control program. Manila's influential Jaime Cardinal Sin has been known to say privately that a lower population growth rate (the current annual rate is around 2.7 percent) would undoubtedly be good for the country.

* * *

During my travels for this book, I sometimes came across critics of population control who warned about the consequences of extreme birth control. They spoke about joyless societies where there were few children and where the adult population was aging to the point where, as in Sweden and Japan, there was mounting concern about the implications for future economic productivity. John J. Billings, the Australian physician, spoke of Third World societies where there simply wouldn't be sufficient hands to work in fields and factories. In West Germany, where the annual population growth has fallen to below zero, representatives of the toy industry say that if current trends continue there may well not be a flourishing toy-manufacturing sector in their country by the end of this century.

"The effects of aging of populations raise the question of how these societies will provide social services for them," says Rafael M. Salas, executive director of the United Nations Fund for Population Activities (who, of course, is not a population control critic). "The aging of populations also has implications for the role and functions of the institution of the family. Throughout the world, families are becoming smaller, structurally more diverse, and independent of extended kin relationships. Some of the responsibilities for providing income and social security to the elderly have shifted from families to governments."

The United Nations says that in 1950 there were about 200 million persons above the age of sixty throughout the world. By 1975, that figure had climbed to 350 million. There now are more than 450 million "aged" persons on earth; this figure will reach 600 million by the year 2000, or nearly 10 percent of the world's projected population then. United Nations estimates say, morever, that by the year 2025 the world will have 1.1 billion persons above the age of sixty—an increase of 224 percent since 1975.

Leon Tabah, formerly of the United Nations Population Division, one of the most respected academicians in the field, points out that in 1975 the sixty-years-plus population constituted 15 percent of the population of the developed countries; this figure will go up to 18 percent by the year 2000, or some 230 million people. In the developing states, older people constituted 6 percent of the population in 1975; by the end of the century, their numbers will rise to 360 million, or 7 percent of the Third World's projected population in the year 2000.

I don't think the question of providing for the elderly is going to be as much of a problem in the Third World as it will in the West, however. In the poor countries of the world, it is the tradition to have extended families, where grandparents share the same roof with grandchildren. Even small family incomes are resourcefully utilized so that everyone, young and old, is taken care of; there are few old folks' homes in the Third World because it is just not the custom or the practice to load old people into old people's homes. (There are exceptions, of course. One day in the Malaysian capital of Kuala Lumpur I was taken by a local journalist named M.G.G. Pillai to a "death house." It was really a nursing home for the aged, for those who had no relatives. Admission criteria were strict: entrants had to be pretty close to expected demise, and they had to be the abandoned elderly. It was saddening for me to see old people just lounging around, waiting to die.) People who abandon their aged ones to third-party care open themselves up to social censure; in spite of all the physical impediments in the Third World, such as poverty, people do indeed stretch their own resources to maintain contact and filial links with their elders.

But the Third World countries are finding that with better health care now available people are living longer, a fact that is compounding developing countries "population problem" because the population base keeps increasing, even as the annual birth rate decreases. The question in my mind then is whether Third World traditions of caring for the elderly at home will survive, whether indeed the exigencies of economics will force people to shunt their aged into communal nursing homes that will have to be paid for by their governments. Life expectancy at birth for the world population rose from forty-seven years in 1950–1955 to 57.5 years in 1975–1980, says the United Nations. During the same period, life expectancy rose from sixty-five years to seventy-two years for people in the industrialized countries, while the increase was from forty-two years to fifty-seven years for the population of the developing countries.

In the West, longevity no longer means respectability; as people live longer, it certainly doesn't translate into fruitful economic life for most "senior citizens." The problem is that the conventional retirement age in much of the West is still predicated on a life expectancy at birth of three score and ten years—except that now life expectancy is touching three score and twenty. Many of the West's social services policies are predicated on a chronological cut-off point that is unrealistic now. Thus, people are chronologically old but often physically fit enough to have regular jobs—except that there are few jobs available for senior citizens, and only relatively meager social services and related benefits. As the populations of the West age—which is to say that a larger percentage is sixty years plus—senior citizens must be brought back into the economic mainstream so that social productivity does not decline.

Perhaps in no country is the question of the implications of aging unfolding more dramatically than in Japan.

One afternoon in Tokyo I went to meet a man named Toshio Kuroda. He is a small, thin man with wispy white hair, and he heads Nihon University's Population Research Institute, Japan's most prestigious demographic center. I was late for my appointment with him, mostly because I had miscalculated how long it would take a taxi to move through Tokyo's dreadfully thick traffic. To keep an elderly, aristocratic Japanese gentleman waiting was not the thing to have done, and I apologized profusely. Professor Kuroda seemed a tolerant man, however, and after showing me around his department building he proceeded to outline some of his newest research.

"We have a major problem on our hands," Professor Kuroda said. "Our projections suggest that Japan's pension system will be bankrupt by the time the next century comes around—unless we pay less in old-age insurance or reduce current benefits for our older citizens."

Nihon University's projections indicate that the number of older persons is expected to increase from around 17 million in 1984 to more than 26 million by the year 2000—and to 33 million by 2025. As a percentage of the total population (which is currently 120 million) this figure, said Professor Kuroda, implies a sharp increase in the number of aged persons from about 13 percent in 1980 to almost 21 percent by the year 2000 to nearly 26 percent by 2025! Moreover, fertility trends suggest that Japan's birthrate will keep falling (it is currently about 13 per 1,000, and the annual population growth rate is 0.7 percent; in 1947–1949, in the immediate aftermath of World War II, Japan's annual birthrate was 35 per 1,000); not only is contraceptive use widely prevalent, but legal abortions are being registered at the rate of 700,000 a year.

Males generally are already experiencing a life expectancy at birth of seventy-five years, the professor said, while the female life expectancy was eighty years. Later I wondered about what would happen to Japan's vaunted economic productivity if its people kept producing fewer and fewer children and themselves grew older and older and perhaps increasingly incapable of assembly-line work that results in Japan's present-day automobile and electronics dominance in the world markets.

The problem of aging is being felt severely in Japan's rural areas. Many young educated men and women journey to cities looking for work, leaving behind aging parents. Old-age homes are not at all popular in still traditional Japan, and so a growing number of homes in the countryside are headed by older citizens.

I spoke with a twenty-eight-year-old research assistant at Nihon University named Yasuhito Saito. He had come to Tokyo recently after completing his university education near his family home in Fukushima, he said, and his parents had not been too thrilled when Yasuhito told them that he wanted to live and work in Tokyo. As an only son, his presence was being sorely missed, he told me.

"Why did you come to Tokyo and not find a job back home?" I asked Yasuhito, a pleasant bespectacled man.

"The opportunities here are greater."

"What about tradition? Didn't you feel that you had to stay close to your parents?"

"Traditions change, they evolve," Yasuhito said. "Or at least they should."

Professor Kuroda broke in: "It is the traditions of old-age care that are melting away."

The retirement age in most Japanese companies is fifty-five, although the government has now recommended that it be raised to sixty. Professor Kuroda feels that the retirement age should in fact be raised to sixty-five or even seventy.

"The difference between Japan and the West is that here retirees actually wish to work longer," he said. "There should be some sort of adequate mechanism for this. Perhaps we should have a new economic substructure that employs mostly older citizens?"

I asked Professor Kuroda whether his children lived with him.

He smiled.

"Well, I don't mind that my daughter lives far away from my wife and me," he said. "But my wife wishes she lived closer. You know how it is."

* * *

She was tall, regal, with a serene manner, and she wore clothes that were modestly fashionable. She lived alone in an old-people's home in Kista, a neat suburb of Stockholm. She told me that no relatives visited her, for she had no close kin, and her contemporaries were dying one by one.

Every day was like the previous one, and the next day would be the same for Gerda Sjostrom. She was eighty years old but had no infirmities or illnesses, and so she looked twenty years younger.

It was a subdued summer afternoon when I took a train from the Swedish capital out to Kista. Earlier that day I had met with a woman named Mari Anne Olsson, who helps manage Sweden's social service programs for the elderly under the auspices of the Ministry of Health and Social Affairs. She told me that 17 percent of Sweden's 8.3 million people were above the age of sixty-five, or nearly 1.4 million men and women. The number of people above the age of sixty-five will keep growing, and by the year 2000 the number of people above the age of eighty (who now number about 300,000) could double. The government would find itself with more and more responsibility for old-age care with every year.

There was no special effort to integrate these elderly people into Sweden's economic mainstream, Miss Olsson said, and now the country was increasingly facing the problem of a segregation of its population.

"I look around and already I see young people talking disparagingly about 'them'—about our old people," Miss Olsson, whose bleached blond hair matched her crisp one-piece outfit, said in her tiny office at Jacobsgatan 26, an area where many government agencies can be found housed in formidable, ornate buildings whose baroque style has been repudiated by contemporary Swedish architecture. "I worry about this treatment of our old people. I don't think such attitudes are quite right. In Sweden, unfortunately, there is no tradition of respect for the elderly, as there is in India, for instance."

And with a continued decline in Sweden's annual birthrate, it quickly becomes apparent how few children there really are in this Scandinavian state. Mari Anne Olsson told me that recently she'd returned for a visit to her birthplace of Goteborg and that she found it a place "where there are practically no kids at all."

"What kind of society are we becoming?" she said. "No patter of tiny feet, people increasingly isolating themselves into their own watertight social groups, a society where the old are being slowly but surely segregated? These are worrying questions for our social and economic planners."

I reflected on such questions as I rode the train to suburban Kista. The ride lasted an hour; there were no children or youths in my carriage, just gray-faced and gray-flanneled commuters—the early phalanx of the late afternoon office crowd. One day, I thought, there'd be no more commuting for them, and then they'd all be faced with the decision as to where to live: alone in apartments and houses, as most of Sweden's old people still do, or in communal colonies like Kista.

Kista turned out to be a quiet community of stubby apartment blocks and one-story homes, with leafy parks stretched over gently graded hummocks. The general architecture was typically modern Scandinavian: clean lines, functional, a minimum of exterior decoration. The light was weakening, which made the scene seem depressing. Everywhere there were elderly people strolling singly, or in pairs, or with pet dogs. I went to the Kista Service Center, a state-subsidized facility that I was told was Sweden's largest residential complex for old people.

The center consisted of three five-story buildings, with 300 apartments in which 400 elderly people lived. The average age of residents was eighty years, according to Christine Pederson, a jolly, plump woman who was the center's manager. Residents paid the equivalent of between $200 and $300 a month for one-room or two-room apartments, each of which came equipped with a kitchen. The average monthly pension of residents here was roughly three times what each paid in rent, Mrs. Pederson said.

"But they are very lonely people," she said of those who lived in these apartments. "Most stay by themselves. Of the 400 people here, I would say that maybe only about 50 mix socially with one another. I suppose that in a society like what we have in Sweden, if you're lonely all your adult life, then you're lonely also in your old age."

Mrs. Pederson did not think it was such a good idea for so many old people to live together under one roof. There was no vitality to their lives as a result, she said, nothing really except the dull, deadening routine of the service center: meals, perhaps an hour or two of television, a walk in the area, perhaps a game of bridge, or a bit of table tennis, then refuge in sleep that did not come easily in old age.

We took an elevator to the fourth-floor apartment of Gerda Sjostrom. She used to live in Stockholm once. "But I became very lonely there, even though I was right in the middle of the city," she said, speaking in Swedish that Christine Pederson translated for me into English. She'd worked for more than forty-five years as a maid in the home of an aristocratic Swedish family; she never married.

A lifetime had come down to this: a one-room apartment in a suburb. There were a couple of rugs on the floor of Miss Sjostrom's "home." There was a painting or two. There was a worn green sofa and a credenza on which were framed photographs of Gerda in her youth.

"Isn't it lonely here too?" I asked.

"I suppose I am," she said. "But I read a lot, and I go out for walks, and I chat with Christine here. I've never been sick in all my life, which is a blessing, particularly when one has just turned eighty!"

What did she miss most about her youth?

"The fact that I could travel abroad for holidays."

Does she now wish she'd married?

"Sometimes. Especially when it is my birthday. If I had children and grandchildren, at least I'd get some birthday cards. Or perhaps flowers from them occasionally. I wish I could baby-sit for someone. But there is no work around here for old people, and in any case there aren't any children around."

* * *

For many years now I have known a man named Ajay Mody. He is a pilot with Air India, and during my travels in Africa and the Middle East for the *New York Times* I sometimes would find myself in planes flown by Captain Mody. Each time we met, Ajay would urge me to go and visit his wife Aruna's brother, Daleep Mukarji.

"He is a very idealistic young man," Ajay would say to me. "He could have been a very successful, very rich doctor in Bombay or any of the large Indian cities. Instead, Daleep chose to go and live in one of India's most backward districts and practice his medicine there. He is a very unusual young man—there just aren't too many people like him around, and one wishes there were."

I finally caught up with Dr. Daleep S. Mukarji early in 1984. He is a tall, rather plump man, with a wide forehead, gray eyes, and an engaging manner. From Captain Mody's earlier characterizations, I had expected to meet an intense, wound-up man—for many of the "committed" development specialists one encounters in the field sometimes are afflicted with a zealousness that to an outsider can seem absurd. But Dr. Mukarji turned out to be a jolly sort of fellow, with a puckish sense of humor, a man who savored his occasional Scotch on the rocks.

He lives in a village called Palyakrishnapuram, located in the North Arcot District of India's southern Tamil Nadu State. About a thousand people live in Palyakrishnapuram, which is part of a rural "block" of eighty-five villages. Dr. Mukarji heads a medical team that looks after 100,000 people in this "block," which is known as Kilvayattanankuppam (many people abbreviate this name to K. V. Kuppam). This area is about as rural a region there is in India. There is no organized industry of any kind here. Dirt roads criss-cross the area; water must be lifted from community wells. Electricity is only now being introduced in the region. Virtually everybody lives below the poverty line, which is to say that the average villager earns less than the equivalent of $100 a year. Most people eke out a livelihood from agriculture—from cultivating rice, bananas, sugar cane, peanuts, and mulberries. Most people work as landless laborers in the agricultural sector. There are two or three small factories, which produce *beedis,* strong, foul-smelling cigarettes favored by villagers all over India.

Most houses have thatched roofs. The walls of these homes are fashioned from mud and bricks. At first sight, the area looks somewhat parched and, for otherwise lush southern India, surprisingly bereft of trees. I learned that until a decade or so ago, this area actually was renowned for its tamarind, gulmohur, drumstick, and peepal trees. But villagers foraged heavily for firewood, and they indiscriminately tore down trees. There are very few trees left in Kilvayattanankuppam today, and the saplings that have been planted by Dr. Mukarji and his associates will take many years to mature.

Daleep Mukarji and his wife Azra, who is a native of Hyderabad, came here in 1977. Dr. Mukarji had earlier obtained his medical degree from the Christian Medical College in Vellore in southern India and then received a diploma in public health from the London School of Hygiene and Tropical Medicine. While in London, where many Indians traditionally have studied because of the colonial links between India and Britain, Dr. Mukarji also received a degree in rural planning. Why did he chose to spurn offers he'd received to practice medicine in some of India's wealthy urban neighborhoods?

"I believe it is possible to change India," Dr. Mukarji said to me. "Unless we work at the grass roots, where people matter, unless we work for some meaningful change in rural areas, where 80 percent of India's population lives—unless we do these things urgently, I don't see a viable future for our people. Our villagers have been hearing too many official statements about what is being done for them. It is only when you come to places like Kilvayattanankuppam that you realize how little of this political rhetoric gets translated into action at the grass roots.

"I felt I had to go beyond the textbook," he continued. "I felt I had to bring about measurable changes in village health care. I wanted to demonstrate that we could indeed devise low-cost, feasible medical, family-planning, and development schemes that were relevant to our country."

Dr. Mukarji came to Kilvayattanankuppam under the auspices of the Rural Unit for Health and Social Affairs of the Christian Medical College in Vellore. The college receives some financial assistance from its affiliations in the United States. He brought with him seven other physicians and three veterinarians, mostly young men and women who had just graduated from medical school and who were assigned by their institutions to Kilvayattanankuppam for practical training. In addition, there were about 200 fieldworkers, whom he assigned to the eighty-five villages of Kilvayattanankuppam. "We quickly found that there were practically no health services in this area," Dr. Mukarji recalled. So clinics were set up, as were centers to train more fieldworkers.

Kilvayattanankuppam was a horror story, a microcosm of many isolated regions of rural India. This area was an ongoing example of what many delegates at a world parley in Alma Ata, in the Soviet Union, had warned about back in 1978. They had lauded the parley's initiation of a campaign to achieve "Health for All" by the year 2000; but some of the delegates said that conditions were so bad in many rural areas around the world that unless there was a major infusion of money and medical manpower in those areas the conference's goal of primary health care for all would surely never be met. In Kilvayattanankuppam, Dr. Mukarji found that the infant mortality rate was 117 per every 1,000 live births. Malnutrition was rampant. The local people suffered from respiratory diseases. The incidence of tuberculosis and measles was high. Children were dying from diarrhea and dehydration. Superstitious traditions persisted.

One afternoon, a woman brought her emaciated one-year-old boy to Dr. Mukarji's clinic. The child had contracted diarrhea and now was dying of dehydration.

"Why haven't you given the child any water?" Dr. Mukarji asked.

"Why should I?" the woman said. "He is passing so much water with his stools. If I give more water, he will only pass it out."

Dr. Mukarji patiently explained to this woman that the child needed to replace the fluids he was losing. He administered a glucose solution to the child and asked the woman to bring the child back for further examination in a day or so. He gave her packets of a special solution to be fed to the child. To no avail: the boy died. The woman's in-laws had refused to let her carry out the physician's directives.

On another occasion, a youthful peasant couple visited Dr. Mukarji at his modest, one-story house in Palyakrishnapuram. They were the parents of a two-year-old girl. Two previous children had died. The peasants had come to consult Dr. Mukarji not about their daughter but about the family cow.

"Why haven't you brought your daughter over for the second round of inoculations, as I had asked you to?" Dr. Mukarji said, sternly.

"We are more concerned about our cow right now," the peasant said in the local Tamil language. "Our cow is a valuable asset. She is dying. Can you send someone to look at the cow and give medicine?"

"Are you saying that the cow is more important than your own child?" Dr. Mukarji asked.

The peasant couple looked uncomfortable.

"Well, you see, if our child dies we can always produce another one. We are still young and capable of having many more children," the peasant said, presently. "But if our cow dies, we will not be able to afford another animal."

I found this exchange extraordinary. Later, Dr. Mukarji explained that it was not as though the Kilvayattanankuppam peasants were being callous about the welfare of their child. But the fact was, the cow—which the peasants milked for revenues—was the only source of subsistence for this couple. They simply could not afford to lose the animal.

"When I first came to Kilvayattanankuppam, I found these attitudes quite shocking," Dr. Mukarji said. "I quickly found that you cannot be effective if you used conventional health approaches. You had to be both physician and sociologist, both physician and psychologist. Health is really a behavioral matter. Being a doctor here is not good enough—you have to get people to change their life style. You have to study local customs and traditions."

In places like Kilvayattanankuppam and other backward rural areas of the Third World, one also has to take into account the fact that the high illiteracy rate creates a situation where local people simply do not follow or understand the directions given to them by outside doctors. One afternoon, a woman named Laxmi came to see Dr. Mukarji. She complained of a severe earache. Dr. Mukarji gave her some aspirin tablets—which Laxmi immediately proceeded to insert in her ears!

One of the major problems that Daleep Mukarji encountered when he came to Kilvayattanankuppam was that there simply was no such thing as a "community." All the development textbooks talk about the need to develop the "community" and to foster a "community spirit," but in many Third World societies local areas are characterized by factions, castes, and tribal groupings. In Kilvayatanankuppam, Dr. Mukarji had to contend with the fact that neighboring villages sometimes lived in disharmony with one another. Some of the animosity dated back dozens of years to some dimly remembered altercation over cows or perhaps brides. At any event, the Mukarji medical team found itself also having to play the role of peacekeepers. This was done by frequent visits to homes and by frequent group meetings to which villagers from all over Kilvayattanankuppam would be invited.

"We all need to join hands to improve our living conditions," Dr. Mukarji would say during a typical meeting. "In our fight against disease, there can be no room for personal hostilities."

An initial priority was bringing down the frightening infant mortality rate in Kilvayattanankuppam. Over the years, there had been a perceptible shift from breast-feeding to bottle-feeding of infants. Dr. Mukarji saw that because bottles were not properly sanitized and because water in which the baby formula was mixed wasn't usually boiled, babies got infected. Moreover, the quality of local cow's milk was inferior, contributing to malnutrition among infants. Dr. Mukarji explained to local women that because of bottle-feeding, infants lost the colostrum in the early milk produced by mothers. Colostrum transfers from mother to child a fair amount of natural immunity and resistance to disease.

"Part of the problem in Kilvayattanankuppam was that people traditionally thought of a doctor as someone who could cure anything," Daleep Mukarji said. "The fault also lay with doctors who'd treat these people in the past. They kept giving medicines—but the local people kept returning to their normal unhealthy environment. It became a sort of game: someone would fall ill, go to a doctor, get medicine, get well, then fall ill again back in the same unhygienic environment. So we decided early on that we'd work to change the local environment. We started teaching people about balanced diets, and vitamins, and tonics, and proper domestic and personal hygiene. And then we quietly introduced family planning as well."

The infant mortality rate in Kilvayattanankuppam was brought down through such measures from 117 per every 1,000 live births to 47. Mortality rates for children between the ages of one and five years dropped from 24 percent to 11 percent.

The drops in infant and child mortality over the last six years have led to a decrease in Kilvayattanankuppam's annual birthrate—from 36 per 1,000 of the population to 24 per 1,000. The area's peasants, like their counterparts in many other rural parts of the Third World, traditionally viewed more children as assets. When children kept dying through disease, these peasants kept having more kids as an insurance against old age: there is no old-age social security system in Kilvayattanankuppam.

"People here don't understand such concepts as doubling of population and limitations to the area's carrying capacity," Dr. Mukarji said to me. "You have to just go ahead and make sure that their kids live and then start persuading them that smaller families are happier, even more productive families."

What struck me as significant about Daleep Mukarji's efforts was his integrated approach—his attention not only to health care and family planning but also to economic activity in Kilvayattanankuppam. He and his associates have started a dairy farm in the area; there now are workshops where villagers can learn about water pump maintenance and bicycle repair work. Women are being taught how to weave. The Mukarji team also has set up thirty dairy cooperatives and three sheep cooperatives. A new development is an enterprise where villagers are being instructed in how to raise broiler chickens.

The other significant thing here is that Daleep Mukarji no longer performs charity work in Kilvayattanankuppam. When he and his associates from the Christian Medical College first came here, everything they did for villagers was for free; not a rupee was charged for medical services and supplies.

"Now the area is somewhat better off economically, and our feeling is that if you charge even a nominal amount for services rendered, you actually increase the self-esteem of local people," Dr. Mukarji said. "No one likes handouts."

Daleep Mukarji and his wife are so committed to Kilvayattanankuppam that they adopted a local child; they have two other children of their own. One day, of course, the Mukarjis will move on and go someplace else where they are also needed. I bet it will be to another destitute area. Kilvayattanankuppam will miss them, but the work that Daleep Mukarji has performed will be his lasting legacy here.

* * *

Kilvayattanankuppam is near the eastern coast of India. Kolaba District is on the western coast. In Kilvayattanankuppam, the main language is

Tamil; in Kolaba, it is Marathi. In Kilvayattanankuppam, almost everybody is Hindu; in Kolaba, Hindus are in the majority, but there are also enclaves of Moslems, traditionally bitter foes of Hindus. I went to Kolaba District, which is about sixty miles away from Bombay, at the suggestion of Asha Puthli, a longtime friend.

Asha, an eclectic character if ever I knew one, is a jazz singer and actress who now lives in New York. She grew up in Bombay and in Kolaba District, where her parents long ago bought a farm in a small, quaint village called Tara. It was Asha's father, Umanath Puthli, who pioneered health care and family planning in the area. He went where he was needed, and even though he has been dead for six years now, Umanath Puthli's social service for the deprived of Kolaba lives on in the improved quality of their lives, in the better health care that is available for them, and in the enhanced economic opportunities for the region.

To get to Kolaba from Bombay one must drive. Once the densely populated tenements of Bombay are left behind, you would expect the scenery to change quickly, to become greener, cleaner. That doesn't happen because of the suburban sprawl. The fumes fifty miles out of Bombay are as noxious as they are downtown. One knows, of course, that Bombay has technically been left behind because there are more cows and goats on the road, motorists who speed like maniacs without regard to which animal they hit, and occasional farmland that comes right up to the two-lane highway.

Tara village, where the Puthli family has a farm, consists of about eighty huts. Next to Tara are four other villages: Barapada, Kalai, Dolghar, and Bandhanwadi. The local people here are mostly Hindus, but there are also some Moslems; and there are the Adhivasis, or tribal folk who came to the coast from the nearby Karnala *ghats,* or hills. The road from Bombay to the southern Indian resort of Goa (once a Portuguese enclave) cuts right through these five villages. They are villages like any other to be found in rural India: mud-splattered children flounce about; peasants toil in fields; women carry buckets of water atop their heads and gracefully head home from the community well; cows graze languidly; chickens flutter around; mangy dogs yelp. It is quite possible that the motorist will give this scene no more than a glance or perhaps even fail to notice these villages at all.

But no motorist will fail to spot the Yusouf Meherally Center, a squat, cheerful structure that sits by the Bombay–Goa road, across from the Puthli farm.

The center was Umanath Puthli's gift to the area. It is a full-fledged health care and family-planning clinic. There is a surgical theater in the center and a lie-in ward. People come here daily not only from the five-village area but from hamlets as far away as a hundred miles. Signs painted in English and the local language of Marathi welcome patients. There is a neat garden all around the center, which is named after a legendary figure who participated in India's independence struggle against British colonial rulers; Yusouf Meherally was a friend and contemporary of Umanath Puthli. Smartly uniformed nurses work in the facility. Local villagers contribute *shramdhan*—or free labor—and assist in the cleaning and maintenance work.

Asha Puthli remembers the days when all Tara village had by way of a clinic was a corner in her parents' farmhouse.

"One weekend, my father suggested that I instruct local women about birth control," Asha said to me. "He was concerned about the high birthrate in these villages."

At first Asha thought of distributing contraceptives, but that would have meant first putting in place some sort of paramedical system. Then she saw that a popular local gadget was the abacus, an instrument villagers used for making calculations by sliding beads along rods or grooves. Why not use the abacus to instruct women in "natural birth control"—or the rhythm method, under which a woman abstains from intercourse during her fertile period?

So Asha got together a group of local women and told them all about fertile periods and infertile periods. She told them that each evening they should slide one bead from right to left: the beads marking infertile days—and therefore days when sexual intercourse was not likely to result in pregnancy—were colored black; the beads marking fertile days were red. When each woman came to the first red bead, she should abstain from intercourse until the fertile period was over, Asha told the villagers. They all nodded and went home with their abacuses.

Some weeks later, Asha found that virtually every woman who'd used the abacus had become pregnant. She began investigating the situation.

"Haven't you been using the abacus the way I showed you?" Asha asked one woman.

"Yes," the woman said, bashfully. "But it is difficult for me to see the color of the beads in the darkness."

In those days, of course, there was no electricity in Tara village.

Once it became dark, it was pitch dark—most villagers couldn't even afford kerosene for lamps.

It is very different here now. All homes have electric power. Umanath Puthli, who had made his fortune as a businessman in Bombay, made certain of that. A paper factory was set up by some of his industrialist friends, and jobs were thus created. A school was started. Hybrid seeds were introduced so that rice cultivation and fruit production could be stepped up. Avabai Wadia's Family Planning Association of India helped train local people to start birth control facilities. Some of Umanath Puthli's physician friends from Bombay would come and spend weekends at his farmhouse and treat patients from the villages around here.

Virtually every home has a family-planning acceptor now. Children are no longer rickety; tuberculosis has been eliminated. Agriculture is flourishing. It was all done not through any massive infusion of foreign development aid but because one man decided he would devote all his resources to being where he was needed—at the grass roots. Well before the development experts started talking about the need to "integrate" economic development efforts with family planning and health care, Umanath Puthli and his friends showed here that when you improve the living standards—however slightly and tentatively—of poor people, "development" does indeed act as the best contraceptive.

I asked a woman named Lalitha what she thought were the most dramatic changes in Tara village. Lalitha is a short, thin woman and a mother of three children. Her husband grows a variety of high-yield rice that Umanath Puthli introduced in the area. Lalitha helps out in the Meherally health clinic. She also has learned to read and write.

"The most important change for us has been that we now know that it is possible to improve our lives," she said in Marathi. "Before there used to be despair here. Now we have some hope."

What about family planning, I asked. Were villagers now enthusiastic about having smaller families?

Lalitha told me that she'd undergone a tubectomy and that her husband had also gone and gotten himself sterilized. No coercion was applied by anybody, Lalitha said. They decided to have sterilization operations after careful consideration.

"No one wants big families these days," she said. "What use are big families?"

* * *

When development writers talk about "grass roots," they generally refer to everyday situations in poor countries. But what about "grass roots" in the United States—the 240 million Americans who over the years have financed and given moral support for population programs all over the world? Who lobbies them? Who goads them into prodding their congressmen and local legislators to be more supportive of "population"? Who convinces them that taxpayers' money that finances global population projects has been instrumental not only in ameliorating living conditions in poor countries but also in significantly winning good will for the United States in the Third World?

Over the last decade, several grass-roots organizations have been working quietly and methodically to solicit financial and political support from everyday Americans; these bodies have also been effective lobbyists for the population "cause" in Congress, particularly in the House of Representatives, which has traditionally been dominated by Democrats, who traditionally have been sympathetic to U.S.-financed population programs in the Third World. (This is not to say that the Senate has shown any less interest in "population": people like Charles Percy of Illinois, Charles Mathias of Maryland, Robert Packwood of Oregon, Claiborne Pell of Rhode Island, and Daniel Inouye of Hawaii have been especially vocal and consistent supporters of the population "cause." The eloquent letters of support written by these senators and others to the Washington-based Population Institute, for example, are voluminous and could even form a book by themselves. Their actions on the floor of the Senate have been decisive.) Indeed, there is no doubt in my mind that had it not been for the constant efforts of grass-roots organizations such as the Population Institute and the Population Crisis Committee and their vigilance in monitoring political developments in Washington, American population assistance would have been lower than it is today.

The population "lobby" in Washington isn't a lobby in the classical mold of, say, the National Rifle Association, or the petroleum industry lobby, or gas interests. It is far more altruistic, and far less sinister. Its leaders do not ask for funds or concessions for their own organizations but for causes abroad. And the lobby's aim is as much to promote an understanding of "population" among legislators and the executive branch as it is to ensure that American money continues to be given to population programs. The lobby consists mainly of two nonprofit organizations, the Population Institute and the Population Crisis Committee, both of which are privately funded; in addition, there are a number of other groups—all of which form what many legislators in Washington call the "working coalition" for population. This coalition consists of men and women from different social, political, and intellectual backgrounds; they do not necessarily march in lockstep, as the monied special interests lobby people seem to do.

The Population Crisis Commitee is a sort of blue chip organization, which brings together retired diplomats such as former Ambassadors Marshall Green and Edwin Martin, former lawmakers such as Senators Joseph Tydings and Robert Taft, and former soldiers such as Generals Maxwell Taylor and William Westmoreland. One of its earliest powerhorses was the late, legendary General William Draper, who galvanized the U.S. Congress and administration into making a moral and monetary commitment to "population." The organization's roster reads like a social register, with top Washingtonians and others committed to its cause. Directed by Fred Pinkham, a former president of Rippon College in Wisconsin and a former supervisor of American humanitarian and population assistance funds, the Population Crisis Committee has traditionally used the access privileges of its supporters to lobby key senators, congressmen and administration members in Washington.

One of the reasons that organizations like the Population Crisis Committee and the Population Institute—through its legislative arm, the Population Action Council—focus their efforts primarily on Congress is that American lawmakers have long been the real impetus behind population assistance. The executive branch is often constrained to trim population assistance allocations because of budgetary pressures and a demand for more military and security expenditures. In recent years, too, there has been mounting concern within the administration over the growing deficit in the federal budget.

And for quite some time now, the administration has been vigorously lobbied by such archconservative groups as the United States Coalition for Life and Americans United for Life to suspend all U.S. funds for family-planning programs. Even though U.S. funds do not support population programs containing abortion projects, the New Right critics contend that the pill and the IUD—which are among the contraceptives distributed by the U.S. Agency for International Development—are in effect abortifacient.

Critics of population programs contend, moreover, that family-planning programs by definition tend to be coercive in most Third World states and that they violate the sanctity of the family. Members of the Moral Majority, for instance, have charged that U.S.-financed population control programs overseas are nothing short of "international genocide." These critics conveniently fail to note that American population assistance is given only to those countries that specifically request it—and that the Congress emphatically prohibits the funding of any coercive population programs. But regrettably, some senior members of the administration seem swayed by the outrageous arguments of population critics.

In recent years, serious cuts proposed by the administration in the U.S. population aid program were not only resisted and restored by Congress but lawmakers also increased U.S. allocations to population programs.

In December 1982, for example, David Stockman, head of the Office of Management and Budget, proposed the elimination of every penny of population assistance from the 1983 AID budget. Had this proposal gone through, family-planning programs in many Third World states would have collapsed. Within hours of Stockman's announcement, the population "working coalition" went to work in high gear. Its workers appealed directly to key administration members and congressional power brokers. They produced dramatic charts and graphs illustrating what would happen if U.S. support for population programs were to end. They mobilized thousands of ordinary Americans from all across the United States to telephone their legislators or send cables urging that population assistance not be discontinued. Within a week, President Reagan decided to rescind the Stockman proposal.

For the 1984 AID budget, the Reagan administration had proposed increasing population assistance money by barely $1 million to $212 million. It was Congress, egged on by the population "working coalition," that successfully raised the overall figure to $240 million.

Says Representative William H. Gray III, Democrat of Pennsylvania: "One of the most important foreign assistance advances for which the Ninety-eighth Congress can take credit is the increase of international population funding. Although it will take many more dollars, and more importantly vastly increased awareness and understanding before we can accomplish global population stabilization, I believe we are on our way." And Representative Joel Pritchard, Republican of Washington, says that it is largely because of the educational and communication efforts of the population "working coalition" that there are "more of us in Congress who think about world population, understand the necessity to keep population in balance with our resources, and know that through extensive, sound, and well-managed family-planning programs the world population problem can be solved."

One individual in Washington who specializes in cultivating congressmen and in constantly driving home to them the consequences of overpopulation in the Third World is Werner H. Fornos. Fornos is truly a "grass-roots" man. His work illustrates how aggressive and adept Washington's population organizations need to be to win U.S. dollars for global population programs—and how tenuous each "victory" is.

He is of medium height, stocky, even chunky, with a balding pate, a rebellious waistline, narrow, shrewd eyes, and a tanned face that nevertheless betrays accumulated fatigue from thousands of miles of population-related travel each year. Born in Leipzig in what is now East Germany, Fornos emigrated to the United States as a youth, but you'd never know it from his Americanized accent.

I first met Fornos in New York City in 1982 and found his constant talk about "population" a bit wearisome, even irritating. Fornos, in fact, rarely talks about anything other than this subject. As I became better acquainted with him over the months, however, it struck me that his was the passion of the totally committed. Fornos, who is fifty, lives and breathes "population." But I found out that unlike a great many grim, humorless "true believers" of the population business, Fornos is also a risible character who enjoys a good joke as well as a hearty meal.

He has built his Population Institute into the country's largest public interest network for population matters, with affiliations in each of America's 435 congressional districts. He has skillfully raised funds at the grass roots from thousands of individuals, as well as from foundations and the United Nations, so that in the last four years his agency's annual budget increased from $75,000 to $1.2 million.

He has attracted to his organization skilled professionals like David Poindexter, a former Methodist minister, who promotes innovative communications projects to further the cause of family planning in the Third World. (It is Poindexter along with the Mexicans themselves who has helped shape and produce many of the soap operas on family planning that have been such a hit on Mexican television; India has asked for such programs, too.) Fornos distributes regular newsletters, organizes conferences on population issues in different parts of the world, and presents special awards to newspapers and magazines that work particularly hard to promote the population cause. Dozens of college students are taken on each semester as "population interns," an experience these youths find incalculably valuable in understanding the subject and also the ways and byways of byzantine Washington.

One arm of his Population Institute is the Population Action Council, which vigorously works to build support among congressmen for population programs. Were it not for Fornos's aggressive lobbying efforts on Capitol Hill, for example, U.S. contributions to the United Nations Fund for Population Activities would have been far less than the current annual 30 percent of the UNFPA budget, or around $40 million. Fornos knows this, the UNFPA leadership knows this, and influential congressmen know this.

Fornos, in fact, had once wanted to be a congressman himself. Back in 1972, he was nominated by Maryland Democrats to run for Congress; Fornos lost that race. Earlier he had served in the Maryland State Legislature and also held a number of positions in state government. In addition to such experience, which has served him well in his lobbying of congressmen, Fornos has profited from the fact that he once was part of the Kennedy and Johnson administrations. His insider's knowledge of government has been a boon in campaigning for population causes: it is easy to get lost in Washington's vast bureaucratic maze, and it is easy to find one's causes ending up in political cul-de-sacs. For Fornos, political maneuvering and bureaucratic calibrating are an exact science —no room for mistakes here.

It is not surprising, therefore, that Fornos has his critics in other population organizations such as the Population Crisis Committee, some of whose blue-blood members regard him as an *arriviste.* (He was once referred to by some critics as "The Strident One.") There are those who contend that Fornos is to population lobbying what Jimmy Connors is to tennis: a slugger who never stops charging, whom you either like or don't. Fornos's response to criticism of his style: "We have to keep plugging away."

Although Fornos is accomplished at adjusting his rhetoric to the occasion, I have the sense that he is truly moved by the human suffering he sees in overcrowded parts of the world.

"The critical issue today, even more than the threat of nuclear war, is the creeping population explosion that is taking place. With regard to the nuclear issue, you can get a handful of fusty old men in a room and get them to hammer out an arms control agreement—at least this can be done more readily than solving the world's population-bomb threat. It's because population matters involve a wider range of people threat. It's because population matters involve a wider range of people and leaders, and because the resources just aren't there today to summon up a concerted worldwide campaign."

Fornos makes no bones about his central belief that rapid population growth lies at the heart of many of the Third World's major crises. Around the time we spoke, the newspapers were prominently featuring articles about food riots in Morocco and Tunisia and about the deteriorating political situation in El Salvador—countries that all suffer from intensifying demographic pressures.

Fornos also makes no bones about his belief that an additional million of American money here or an additional million there isn't really going to make a significant difference to the population scene around the world. He notes that by the year 2000 the world will be growing by 100 million a year and that more than 75 percent of such growth will be in eighteen poor countries that already are staggering under the pressures of overpopulation. (These countries, according to the United Nations, are China, India, Brazil, Indonesia, Nigeria, Bangladesh, Pakistan, Mexico, the Philippines, Thailand, Vietnam, Turkey, Iran, Egypt, Ethiopia, South Korea, Kenya, and Zaire.)

What Fornos is calling for is a special world fund for these countries so that stepped-up population control measures could be undertaken. But Fornos is enough of a realist to know that it is unlikely that donor countries are going to get together and create such a fund: they don't have the money to spare in this recessionary period, and even if they did I don't think Western leaders are yet sufficiently persuaded that "population" is where they should be spending more cash. I suspect, then, that what Fornos is really calling for is a renewed and increased political and moral commitment to "population" on the part of the United States that I don't think will be forthcoming, given the current political and budgetary climate.

I don't think that Werner Fornos will give up though.

Twelve

Latin America
Development Dreams, Rueful Realities

One evening in Mexico City, I'd been invited to dinner by my longtime friends, Bernd and Susan Debusmann. Bernd is a correspondent for the Reuters news agency, and we'd worked together earlier in places like Iran, Iraq, and Kenya. He is one of the all-time greats among war correspondents, having "covered" virtually every conflict in the world since Vietnam; he has scars to show from Syrian ambushes and battles in Beirut. Now he was posted to Mexico City as the Reuters chief correspondent for Central America. I was looking forward this evening to seeing him and Susan again. I took a taxi from the Hotel El Presidente in the Chapultepec area, where I was staying; the Debusmanns' tidy little apartment was no more than three miles from the hotel.

Ninety minutes after leaving the hotel, I was still in my taxi. The traffic along the Paseo de la Reforma—the broad boulevard that forms a sort of cement spine through this city—was so heavy that cars weren't even crawling: my driver, a man named Antonio, frequently shut the engine off and dozed! Since I was unfamiliar with the layout of Mexico City, I didn't dare complete the rest of the journey on foot, which would have doubtless taken me to the Debusmanns' apartment faster. Antonio and I got around to talking after a while. He was in his mid-thirties, a porcine man with a cheerful disposition. He drove taxis during the day and attended night classes in engineering, he said.

"We are slowly choking to death here," Antonio said, in pidgin English. "It is not just the pollution but also the sheer boredom of being in traffic jams all the time." There were, he said, some 3 million cars in this mile-high metropolis of 17 million people; scientists say that these automobiles—and the 35,000 factories here—retch 3 million tons of poisonous nitrous oxide into the air each year.

"This is all because of our population problem," Antonio said.

"What do you mean?" I said, wanting to hear more on this.

"All these people who keep producing children in the countryside—they all keep coming to Mexico City for jobs that aren't here," he said.

"What should they do?"

"Stay home and have smaller families."

"What about you? How many kids do you have?"

"Four," Antonio said.

"Are you planning more?"

"No, *señor!* We've made sure we won't have any more children."

"How did you do that?"

"I got myself a vasectomy."

This was highly intriguing to me. A vasectomy, in heavily Roman Catholic Mexico?

"You see, my wife went to our priest and said she was going to get herself sterilized," Antonio said. "He at once warned her not to. The Church does not permit any artificial birth control, the priest said. My wife was very upset. She was in tears. She did not know what she should do. The priest told her that Pope John Paul had again warned Catholics against artificial contraception. He told her that she should practice natural birth control. I was very angry at that priest—he doesn't have to look after my kids, I do."

The traffic was moving along just a bit now. Antonio kept talking.

"I could see that my wife was very disturbed. To insist on her getting sterilized would have caused even more problems. That was when I decided, why not get myself a vasectomy? So that was what I did."

Ten years ago, Antonio would not have been able to get himself vasectomized easily; nor would his wife have dared to discuss with her priest the business of birth control. Until 1972, in fact, Mexico followed a pronatalist policy. Then President Luis Echeverria even publicly decried family planning. "To govern is to populate," he said, employing Biblical cadences. Translation: more is better.

Then one fine day the Echeverria government discovered that it had a full-blown population problem on its hands: annual population growth had risen to more than 3.5 percent, the highest rate in a large country; Mexico City was bulging at the seams, its slums had some 5 million residents, and shanty towns were increasingly encircling the central city (these shantytowns are called *cinturons de miseria,* "belts of misery"). Unemployment edged past 10 percent. The ceaseless migration from rural areas to Mexico City and to other urban centers like Guadalajara and Monterrey was forced by a high rural birthrate, governmental neglect of agriculture, and the emphasis on industrialization. In 1972, as the Echeverria government discovered, births outstripped deaths by nearly 2 million, a gain that exceeded the combined natural increase of the population in the United States and Canada that year by 370,000! Demographers began warning that the country's population would touch 135 million by the year 2000.

Moreover, Mexico's internal economic and migratory problems had started to affect the United States as well. When Mexicans found that the perceived promise of waiting jobs in the country's cities was illusory, they kept traveling until they reached the American border. By 1972, close to a thousand Mexicans were said to be illegally crossing over every day into the United States—annually, the equivalent of Vermont's entire population!—in search of employment. The Mexicans would find menial jobs on California and Texas farms, in restaurants, at gas stations, in factories. (In an eloquent volume, *The Tarnished Door* [Times Books, 1983], John Crewdson, who won a Pulitzer Prize for his *New York Times* series on immigration problems—said it is estimated that in Mexico now one person in five depends at least partly on income earned by a relative working in the United States.)

President Echeverria decided to reverse national policy on family planning.

The government and the Church both publicly agreed that reduced population growth was a desirable thing. The Constitution was amended to include a clause that implicitly called for smaller families; a national population law was passed, establishing a national population council, which is known widely by its acronym, CONAPO. Subsequently, President Jose Lopez Portillo established specific family-planning goals, including the reduction of the annual population growth rate to 1 percent by the year 2000. Rural hospitals were built as the government's own revenues increased because of Mexico's oil production, educational programs were promoted, and voluntary sterilization projects were expanded in cities and in the countryside. It was an all-too-rare display of a government making a strong political commitment to population control and then going ahead full steam, with foreign donors like the United States pitching in with financial assistance and agencies like the United Nations contributing heavily with research and technical help.

By 1982, the annual population growth rate in Mexico had fallen to 2.5 percent. It was a stunning accomplishment by any standards, and particularly when measured against the overall population situation in Latin America.

In this region, according to Luis Olivos, who heads the Latin American section of the United Nations Fund for Population Activities, the population increased by 138 percent between 1920 and 1960. In contrast, the population of the world's developed states grew by 40 percent during this same period, while that of the developing nations as a whole increased by 70 percent. Latin American leaders generally were hostile toward family planning; some of them did not want to oppose the Church, which had reiterated its position concerning family planning in Humana Vitae, the papal encyclical that forbade Catholics to use artificial contraceptives. In Chile, Colombia, and Peru, meanwhile, the statistics of crude alleyside abortions soared alarmingly.

In Central America, the combined populations of Costa Rica, El Salvador, Guatemala, Honduras, and Nicaragua have risen in the last twenty-three years from 11.2 million to 22 million. According to World Bank projections, the population of these five states has increased at the rate of around 3 percent a year, which means that by the end of the century Central America will contain nearly 40 million people. Contributing to the growing population base in this region was the fact that infant and child mortality rates fell faster than fertility rates. For example, in the early 1960s the infant mortality rates in Central America ranged from 71 per 1,000 live births in Costa Rica to 137 per 1,000 in Honduras; by 1980, these figures had fallen to 20 per 1,000 in Costa Rica and 81 in Honduras. This meant that as fewer children died, the young population of the Central American states kept increasing. The United Nation's Economic Commission for Latin America says that in 1950 there were 886,000 Central Americans in the fifteen-to-nineteen age group, considered by social scientists as always a potentially politically explosive group. By 1980, their numbers had tripled—to almost 2.5 million. By the year 2000, there will be nearly 4 million men and women in their late teens in Central America. The Kissinger Commission recently warned: "In a region where half of the population is below the age of twenty, the combination of youth and massive unemployment is a problem of awesome—and explosive—dimensions." In the Caribbean, more than half of the total population of 32 million is under the age of twenty.

Moreover, the process of urbanization has been more severe in Latin America than almost any other region of the Third World. In 1950, the urban population of Latin America was 40 million, or 25 percent of the overall population; by 1980, the figure had climbed to 200 million, or 63 percent of the total population. Olivos says that between 1950 and 1975 the urban population in Latin America grew nearly four times faster than the rural population. If current demographic trends continue, Olivos says, then Latin America will contain 619 million people by the year 2000, of whom 466.2 million people, or 75 percent, will live in the region's already overcrowded cities.

I first traveled to Mexico City late in August 1982, which is to say that I landed in this sprawling capital in the midst of Mexico's gravest economic crisis. There was gloom and chaos everywhere, and ordinary Mexicans were wondering what had happened to their oil-rich country, which as recently as 1981 was registering the best economic growth rate in Latin America. The Mexican peso, once the most stable currency in this part of the world, had plunged in value from 20 to the American dollar to 140. Touts at the airport offered arriving American tourists almost 200 pesos for every greenback. Those Mexicans who could manage it were smuggling their dollar holdings out of the country.

Jose Lopez Portillo was still president then. Corruption charges were swirling around him and several of his political associates. The president, in an effort to stem the panic flow of hard currency out of his country, nationalized all Mexican banks. Influential newspaper columnists such as Miguel Angel Granados Chapa lamented in print that Mexico had tumbled into an economic abyss that seemed bottomless. The crisis was precipitated by the revelation that Mexico's foreign debt had soared to $81 billion, making it one of the biggest debtors in the Third World. Western bankers charged that as a result of spendthrift habits of President Lopez Portillo's government and wasteful expenditures on costly capital projects, and because its oil revenues had plummeted due to the world oil glut, by August 1982 Mexico was simply unable to make certain payments that were due on its debts. "We had never expected to find ourselves in such a mess," said Iris Lujiambo, a young Mexican who works for the United Nations.

In subsequent days, her sentiment was to be echoed by dozens of Mexicans I met across this mountainous, wonderously colorful country of 72 million people. Mexicans are generally a garrulous, exuberant people—quick to laugh, quick to praise, quick to move their feet to whatever tune that might float past their ears. They are ordinarily not a despondent people, and politically, at least, their record—in an area where governments are volatile and people are voluble—has been one of lethargy so that successive Mexican presidents have been able to fashion a tradition of near-absolute rule for the last half-century without serious resistance from the largely illiterate and impoverished population.

But now it was villain-targeting time in Mexico. President Lopez Portillo, who'd soon be vacating his office so that the newly elected Miguel de la Madrid Hurtado could take over, was being soundly criticized as the man responsible for Mexico's plight. I was told that it had become the national habit to give government servants what Mexicans called *mordida*—bribes—in order to get anything done. A number of administrative appointees were suspected of embezzling. There was a sense among many Mexicans that Lopez Portillo's handpicked successor wasn't going to be able to turn the situation around dramatically. There was the recognition among ordinary Mexicans that the country faced a bleak, belt-tightening future, where grandiose development plans were going to have to be either scrapped or trimmed radically. And there was the widespread conviction that because Western bankers and other donors had committed fresh doses of money to rescue Mexico—and to save their own investments in this country at the same time—they would impose strong fiscal requirements on Mexico.

On this visit, and on a subsequent one in 1983, the questions that intrigued me about Mexico concerned its ability to proceed with innovative population control programs at a time of severe economic distress and social turmoil. There was uncertainty in some circles about the incoming president's commitment to family planning, even though his campaign literature had included references to the need to reduce Mexico's annual population growth rate further still. I wanted to know whether the dramatic drop in the country's population growth rate had been translated into a better life for Mexico's general population? Population experts all over the Third World were praising Mexico's entertaining family-planning soap operas on television. But what about the unbroadcast daily operas of the *cinturons de miseria?* In what directions did ordinary people see their lives headed?

"There are many Mexicos today," Dr. Silvio Gomez, a representative here of the New York–based Population Council, told me. "There is the Mexico of the fabulously wealthy, the Mexico of the middle classes, the Mexico of the poor masses. These separate Mexicos do not necessarily connect with one another."

The Mexico of Salvador Casanova is a Mexico of self-made wealth. He is a diminutive man, gnomish in appearance, cultured, a chain-smoker, an industrialist whose plastics-laminates factory in Mexico City sprawls in the shadow of a giant Ford Motor Company plant. I went by to see him at the suggestion of his daughter, Maria Elena Casanova, who is the manager here of PIATA, the contraceptive research organization. Señor Casanova seemed eager to talk.

"I wish you had come to Mexico at a better time," he said, offering me a Coca Cola (Mexicans are among the biggest per capita consumers of Coke). "You have come to a Mexico where politicians have squandered billions. They have neglected agriculture, which means that they have guaranteed a river of human traffic from the farms to the cities. How can you expect our agricultural production to keep up with our population explosion?"

"What should the new president be doing?" I asked.

Señor Casanova thumped his fist on his oak desk.

"What should he be doing? For God's sake—he should first clean out government, he should restore confidence in government. He doesn't need any more advice on what he should be doing—his work is cut out for him. He thinks our population problem is over because the growth rate is declining? Well, he should visit the slums."

Maria Elena Casanova offered to take me to Netzahualcoyotl, the "lost city" of Mexico City, the largest of the *cinturons de miseria.* It was an overcast morning, as many mornings are here. Mexico City's thin air —the capital's altitude is 7,400 feet above sea level—is a factor in the photochemical smog that remains trapped in the valley in which the central city is located.

"When I was growing up, there were fields and streams around the city," Maria Elena said. "You could see Popocatepetl's snow-capped volcano on most days. Now Popocatepetl is a memory that lives only in our picture postcards."

We drove through thick traffic to Netzahualcoyotl. Accompanying us was Edith Samano, who works for Maria Elena at PIATA and who lives in the vicinity of Netzahualcoyotl. Edith told me that it takes her three hours by public bus to get to the PIATA office, which is in central

Mexico City. The streets of Netzahualcoyotl are unpaved, and when cars speed through the area they kick up huge clouds of dust. Surprisingly, the houses here are all shaded by eucalyptus trees; this is no accident. Residents plant such trees in the belief that they protect children against throat diseases. There appeared to be an extraordinarily large number of dogs in Netzahualcoyotl; this, too, was no accident. Mexicans generally are great believers in magic and spirits, and residents of these shanties believe that dogs possess the magical power to ward off evil.

We parked on a street with no name. A long line of people had formed near an open lot. Edith Samano told me that this was "sugar day," when a truck would come to the neighborhood with sugar supplies that local people could buy at relatively low cost. Sometimes the truck would come, sometimes it wouldn't. No one was sure this would be the lucky day; but the residents of Netzahualcoyotl had little choice but to wait in the line. Next to this open lot was a small shack, where a children's immunization center had been established by the government. There was hardly anyone here.

We stopped at the home of Socorro Martinez, a plump friendly woman who has two children. She lived in a brick house adjacent to a grocery store that she operated with the help of her unmarried sister, Consuela Jalisco. Here again, I was offered Coca Cola (three out of every twenty-four bottles of Coke that are produced in the world are reportedly sold in Mexico!) and cookies. Socorro's living room was spacious, with rattan sofas, linen curtains, and photographs of Pope John Paul II. There was a television set as well, a large blue refrigerator in one corner of the room, and toys strewn about.

"I don't plan to have any more children," Socorro started telling me, in Spanish that was translated by Maria Elena Casanova.

"Why?" I asked.

"Because even though I have only two children, I've had eight miscarriages. I don't think I could stand another pregnancy. Besides, how will we be able to raise any more children? My husband Angel's salary at the electronics factory he works at is not enough, and our grocery store barely pays for itself."

Did she use contraception?

"Of course," Socorro said. "I have no intention of becoming pregnant again. I use an IUD. I go to a clinic nearby. I first found out about family planning through those dramas on television."

How did she reconcile her use of artificial contraceptives to the renewed directive of her Church forbidding such methods?

Socorro Martinez smiled.

"God will understand," she said.

We moved on to another part of Netzahualcoyotl. Here the houses were packed closely together. Children ran about in tattered clothes. Rough-hewn ditches served as drainage canals. Mounds of garbage were everywhere. One block had two churches. Another block had a small schoolhouse. We walked into the home of a woman named Anna Bertha Gonsalves.

She was twenty-four years old, she said. She looked at least ten years older: lines of fatigue criss-crossed her pale face; her shoulders sagged; and her eyes were listless. She wore green slacks and a blouse that was spattered with food droppings. Her two sons, Moises, two years old, and Adam, three, played around noisily, and Anna occasionally had to reprimand them. She said she'd come with her parents to Mexico City a dozen ago from Jatesco. Her parents were peasants who could not make a decent living from their land, and they'd heard that Mexico City was where a fortune was to be made. There was, of course, no such opportunity here for Anna's parents. There was only Netzahualcoyotl.

Anna's home now consists of a three-room apartment that is squeezed into a one-story tenement. This apartment belongs to her in-laws; Anna and her husband, Fausto, cannot afford to live on their own because Fausto's salary as an assembly-line worker in a hosiery factory fetches him barely $120 a month. Fausto's parents, too, were emigres from the countryside, and their dreams had also ended up in Netzahualcoyotl. Anna can recall the days when Netzahualcoyotl was a third its size today; for her, population growth translates into chronic water shortage, sputtering electricity, indifferent sanitation services by the Mexico City municipal authorities. When she sees television programs that warn of the likelihood that the city's population will climb to 25 million by the year 2000, Anna shrugs: it couldn't get any worse in Netzahualcoyotl, they're just going to have to create new slums. President de la Madrid talks about the need to create "intermediate" townships so that rural traffic headed for Mexico City can be diverted to these new settlements. But no one has demonstrated that such proposals are economically viable or physically feasible now. And various studies have shown that even if all migration into Mexico City were to stop immediately, the capital will still grow at the rate of 2.5 percent, so that the population of 17 million will double in thirty-five years!

"One day we will move from Netzahualcoyotl," Anna Bertha Gonsalves said. But there was no confidence or conviction in her voice. Where will she and Fausto move to anyway? Another Netzahualcoyotl?

Beyond Netzahualcoyotl are the shantytowns of Ecatepec. Beyond Ecatepec is Popocatepetl, the snow-capped volcano. In the shadow of this volcano sits a small town called Amecameca, a colorful, clangorous community where the Spanish conquistadors built a formidable church hundreds of years ago. One afternoon I drove here to see what impact Mexico's family-planning programs have had in small towns. My driver was Ignatio Rodriguez, a veteran tourist guide, who kept lamenting that the sort of large-scale farming that Mexico needed was simply nonexistent. We passed small diary farms near a town called Chalco, where trees were garlanded with tiny decorations and flashing lights and where the cows seemed to be a weary, bony sort. We drove past lush corn fields near San Pedro Nexapa, stopping at a roadside kiosk to buy roasted corn on the cob. The air cleared up the more Mexico City was left behind, and I could breathe better.

It was a Saturday, and Amecameca was in a state of heightened festivity. A huge open-air bazar was laid out in the yard of the church, which itself occupied a prominent space in the middle of the town plaza. Stalls had been set up where one could buy pomegranates and *tunas,* a green cactus fruit that was sold in plastic bags. The smells of tortillas being fried stirred my palate. Mountains of cashew nuts rose from some stall counters; other stalls offered beads and silver necklaces and candy and clothes. Ignatio explained that every weekend peasants from surrounding hamlets come to Amecameca to sell their produce here and to celebrate and carouse.

"There is a desire among Mexicans to live for the moment," Ignatio, a sixty-ish man with a handlebar mustache the color of Popocatepetl's snow, said. "No peasant saves any money here. They sell their produce, and they come here and buy trinkets or drink and eat themselves into a stupor. You can't blame them, of course. After all, who knows what the future will bring?"

We stopped at a tortilla stall run by Juventina Rosas. She was a sturdy woman, about forty-eight years old, with a face that was remarkably cool and unlined. Six little boys and girls were assisting her in preparing the dough for the tortillas, frying them, and serving them on paper plates to customers. Juventina told me that she had twelve children, the oldest of them a boy thirty years old. She ran her tortilla stall on Saturdays and Sundays, she said, and during the week she helped out in her husband's carpentry shop.

"My son and his wife are about to have a second child," Juvenita said. "And I'm sure they will stop having children after this one comes along."

"How do you know that?" I asked.

"Because I have made sure that my son and his wife visit the Amecameca family-planning clinic."

"So why did you have twelve children?"

"Because the clinic wasn't there when I was producing children. Who wants twelve children in this day and age?"

Juventina's attitudes toward family size and family planning haven't been influenced only by visits to the local government family-planning clinic. She avidly watches the "population" soap operas on television and makes certain that her daughter-in-law does, too. Had Mexico started its family-planning drive two decades ago, had its leaders been enlightened and far-seeing enough instead of touting some silly notion of national-strength-through-increased-population, Mexico today would not be in such dire straits.

Officials in Mexico say that the goal is to bring down the country's annual population growth rate to 1 percent by the year 2000. While the Mexicans have demonstrated that where there is a combination of political commitment and economic resources dramatic results can indeed be achieved, I don't see how this country is going to further lower its population growth rate without a new national commitment. Mexico appears to have reached a plateau. The national population council has done little in the last five years; the national family-planning program has suffered from lackadaisical direction and from bitter internal politics. And now, with Pope John Paul II's renewed—and vigorous—call to Catholics not to accept artificial birth control, the Church hierarchy in Mexico and elsewhere in Latin America seems to be shying away from continued endorsement of even broad population-reduction goals.

For Mexico's population control to be truly successful, moreover, at least 60 percent of married women in the reproductive age group must use contraception. At present, only half of these women do so. I was told that Mexico must enroll a million new men and women each year as birth control acceptors to ensure that the population growth rate does not increase. Despite the soap operas and the media campaigns promoting family planning, the southern states of Mexico, which contain large Indian populations, are doing little to spread the message of "population" effectively. They say they have no funds for such purposes. But for a continued drop in the national population growth rate, Mexico is going to have to concentrate on some of these southern states, which still have growth rates in excess of 2.5 percent. Dr. Claudio Stern of the Collegio de Mexico, a sociologist who is an international authority on rural development and migration, told me that despite the rural emigration to the cities there still are more than 30 million people in Mexican villages and hamlets—and that their annual population growth rate remains high.

The burden on President de la Madrid is increasingly going to be how to persuade rural people to stay where they are and to improve their living standards (about 1.5 million new migrants come to Mexico City each year); his burden is also going to be to improve the living conditions of the poor of Mexico City and other urban centers while making certain somehow that better living conditions in these areas do not in turn attract more migrants from the rural regions. I just don't see how he's going to be able to do all this without changing Mexico's development strategy quite dramatically.

I went by one afternoon to see Anameli Monroy de Velasco. She is a pioneer in sex education in Latin America. "Population" experts usually talk about family-planning programs and birth control projects; few experts advocate sex education in the schools of the Third World. Since more than half the population of most Third World states is under twenty years old, these countries would be well advised to establish such educational programs—especially for teenagers. (In Mexico, 25 percent of the country's 72 million people are between ten and twenty years old!) In 1975, Dr. Monroy de Velasco set up a number of sex education centers in Mexico City; she'd received her graduate education in psychology in the United States, where she and her physician husband, Marcos, had lived for several years. Her interest in sex education began while she was a student in the United States, and eventually she received a certification from the U.S. Association of Sex Educators.

Dr. Monroy de Velasco was a tall, statuesque woman who wore a designer dress that complemented her sensational features. I found it disconcerting to interview her! It was hard to believe that she was a mother of a twenty-two-year-old daughter and two other children, for she looked no more than thirty years old. We spoke in her tiny office, whose walls were decorated by a procession of diplomas. Her sex education centers, which are run primarily for adolescent youths, were set up with the financial assistance of the U.S. Agency for International Development and Washington's Population Institute and the Population Crisis Committee, the latter two privately run nonprofit organizations. Now Dr. Monroy de Velasco also has been put in charge of the government Social Security Department's sex education program. She trains professionals not only in Mexico but also in Panama, Guatemala, and the Dominican Republic.

"I have tried to push the idea that we in Mexico, and indeed in most of Latin America, have not paid sufficient attention to the problems of our adolescents," Dr. Monroy de Velasco said. "We haven't sufficiently addressed ourselves to the fact that, as our urban populations increase, so do social problems like teenage pregnancies, drug use among adolescents, venereal disease. I got into all this when my own children started asking me questions about sex and sexual matters. I could help them in a responsible, informed fashion. But what about the ordinary Mexican kid? Who helps him or her? It is fine to talk about national family-planning programs, but why not raise the awareness level of our people while they are still in their teens?"

She has been enormously successful in setting up her clinics, and Dr. Monroy de Velasco also offers personal counseling to adolescents. She has written a dozen sex education books for teenagers and several volumes on family planning. She has been less successful in overcoming the resistance of some male colleagues, who still don't seem persuaded that a woman should be in the business of sex counseling or, for that matter, in the business of running a government program that has anything to do with family planning or social organization.

"In general, there is still quite a lot of resistance to women in high professional places," Anameli Monroy de Velasco said. "Mexican men are afraid of educated women, career women. They feel threatened. It really is a social problem in Latin America. It is very hard for women to succeed professionally, even though there are all kinds of laws about equality."

I asked Manuel Diaz-Marta about this tendency on the part of Latin males, and particularly Mexicans, to pay lip service to women's rights and not really encourage actualization. Manuel is a young executive with the Multibanco Comerex in Mexico City, a banking conglomerate; he is handsome, wears the *de rigueur* banker's "uniform" of dark three-piece suits, and can converse fluently in a half-dozen languages. We met one morning for breakfast at the coffee shop of the El Presidente Hotel; I had been earlier introduced to Manuel by his sister, Maria, who works for the United Nations in Mexico City.

"Yes, of course, Mexicans agree in principle to the idea of equal rights for females," he said. "But you will never see full social acceptance of this until you inculcate different values through education. The development of a country influences people's way of thinking—and in Mexico, with our oil boom, we've rushed ahead in a macho way assuming that social progress will automatically catch up with economic development. But we are really far behind in education: it is one thing to know how to read and write; it is entirely another matter to possess values that will truly develop our society. We in Mexico need to teach new values starting at the lowest levels of society."

Manuel had received much of his college education in the United States, and I asked him if that didn't have something to do with his views on Mexican society.

"Surely," he said. "But that's the whole point of education, isn't it—to see things differently, in a more open way? I've returned to my own country after years abroad because I wanted to be back, I wanted to contribute to Mexico's development."

We were joined at this point by Manuel's brother, Enrique. Tall, hirsute, and with flashing eyes, Enrique was an architect. He, like, Manuel, was in his late twenties and was also successful in his profession. Enrique's worry was that despite the government's claims that Mexico's population growth rate was slowing down, social tensions were on the rise around the country as the population base kept expanding. Like Manuel, Enrique felt that the emphasis had been too much on "development" and not enough on social education.

"There is very little of self-questioning at the highest levels of government here," Enrique said. "There is almost no discussion about where we are going as a nation, what we have become after two decades of 'development.' It is fashionable to talk about Mexico's debt crisis; few people want to discuss our moral and value crisis. And crisis it definitely is. Just look around you, and what do you find? Corruption, *mordida* [bribes]. We don't know what sort of society we have fashioned after all these years of oil money. Mexicans now seem to only live for the moment. But what about the next decade, the next twenty years? Are we thinking about this? We want to slow down our population growth rate, but what kind of a Mexico are we building for our future generations?"

I asked Enrique what the generation of young professionals—people like himself and Manuel—thought Mexico's future was going to be?

His response was immediate.

"We cannot help but be pessimistic," he said. "The response of the young will likely be flight, not fight. We were brought up to be ambitious, but we have grown up only to find that this is not the system we want to belong to. Do I really want to spend the rest of my professional life trying to scrape up enough money so that I can give *mordida* to the right people to get my architectural contracts?"

* * *

From Mexico it was on to Havana by a Soviet-made jet of Cubana Airlines. It was a bumpy, uncomfortable flight, but the stewardesses were cheerful and the lunch was tasty. I have seldom enjoyed flying on Soviet-built aircraft; they are okay for Socialists, who might not mind being squeezed into hard seats, but I prefer the relative comfort of capitalist-style planes—although it has lately begun to seem as though Western airlines are taking the cue from their Socialist-bloc counterparts and converting their aircraft into sardine cans. At Havana's Jose Marti Airport the formalities were not cumbersome, as such things tend to be in Third World states. Two planeloads of Western European tourists had landed just before my flight got to Havana, and the tourists were being greeted effusively by Cubans who I presumed were state officials in charge of welcoming foreigners. (After this welcome, another set of Cuban officials took over and escorted the visitors into sleek buses in which there was a third set of officials who presumably would accompany the tourists to their hotels, where perhaps there waited a fourth set of officials, and so on.) The weather was glorious, a picture postcard situation come true.

This was my second visit to Cuba. I'd first come here back in 1977 as a tourist and was struck by how pretty this Caribbean island-nation was, how pleasant its people. I was accompanied during that first visit by my friend Rahul Singh, who was then editor of the Indian edition of the *Reader's Digest.* Rahul had longtime Indian friends who worked at the time in the Indian Embassy in Havana, and these people in turn introduced us to some of their Cuban acquaintances. But as Rahul and I wandered around Havana and other areas, we soon saw that Cuba was not entirely the workers' paradise that Fidel Castro claimed it was. The shortages of food and essential consumer supplies were striking; fresh vegetables were hard to find. Toy shops were empty. People seemed healthy enough, and they smiled a lot, but their clothes were drab and shabby—a reflection of the fact that even garments were in short supply then. Cuban officials told us that the shortages were the result of the fact that Cuba's resources were being spent on providing free education, free school meals, free medical care, and old-age pensions. Some of these officials told us that such expenditures, plus the $1.27 billion Cuba spent annually on defense (an amount that represented one-fifteenth of the gross national product) meant that not enough money was available to stimulate production of consumer items.

I sought out a physician whom I'd met during my 1977 visit. He seemed delighted to see me, and he was especially pleased that I brought him a box of jams and jellies from New York. He had invited some of his friends to dinner that evening at La Bodeguita del Medio Restaurant on the Empedrado, in the heart of Old Havana, and he asked me along. La Bodeguita was one of Hemingway's hangouts in the glorious old days, and it is a popular tourist attraction. Flocks of Western tourists waited outside to get in. But my friend the physician —he asked that I refer to him only as "Jose" because in the police state he lives in it is considered undesirable to mix with foreigners and he could get into trouble if his comments about Castro's Cuba were freely quoted in a foreign publication—knew the manager and so we had no trouble being seated.

When our food arrived, it turned out to be insipid—pork, beans, a couple of fish dishes, overdone rice. The service, too, was indifferent. And when the bill came, I could see that Jose had been charged New York prices. I said this out aloud.

"But in New York at least you get some value for your money," Jose said.

Jose's friends were physicians and nurses, and they told me some fascinating things about the progress Cuba had made in health care for its 9.8 million people. When Fidel Castro and his Communists took over after the revolution of 1959, there were 6,300 doctors in the country; within three years, 3,000 of them had fled the country. But Cuba concentrated heavily on producing a new generation of physicians:

now there are more than 15,000 full-fledged doctors in the country, or 1 for every 674 Cubans. (In the Third World, the average is 1 physician for every 25,000 persons.)

Infant mortality rates fell from 60 per 1,000 live births in 1959 to 15 per 1,000 by 1983 (a figure that is as good as the infant mortality rate in the United States, and better than the rate in Washington, D.C., and in New Jersey!); in the same period, life expectancy at birth rose from sixty-two to seventy-four. Polio was eradicated in 1962, malaria in 1967, diphtheria in 1970, and tetanus of the newborn in 1973. Moreover, family planning has been an important component of general health care. Illiteracy among adults was wiped out by 1965. Cuba, I was told, has experienced one of the sharpest fertility declines in the developing world: its birthrate dropped from 35 per 1,000 in 1963 to 28 per 1,000 a decade later, to 15 per 1,000 in 1978, to just under 14 per 1,000 in 1983 (the overall Third World birthrate is 35 per 1,000). This translates into an annual population growth rate of barely 1 percent.

I wanted to know how the Cubans had achieved all this. My friend Jose told me that the one person who could provide a comprehensive answer and whom I should look up was Alvarez Lajonchere, the "father" of the Cuban health revolution. More than anyone else in this country, Lajonchere was responsible for Cuba's spectacular strides in health care. But how to reach Lajonchere? If I went through the usual bureaucratic maze, it would probably take weeks to set up an appointment.

A young man named Steve Douglas came to my assistance. Douglas was posted in Havana at the time by the United Nations Fund for Population Activities. A Canadian by birth and citizenship, Steve was fluent in Spanish; he had worked closely with the Cuban authorities and with ordinary people. He knew Lajonchere well—so well, in fact, that all it took to set up an interview with the *éminence grise* was a phone call from Steve.

Lajonchere invited me to his office. It was located in an elegant hacienda in the Miramar section of Havana, a neighborhood of leafy trees, quiet streets, and well-scrubbed sidewalks. It was plainly a neighborhood meant not for Cuba's lumpenproletariat but its elite. Mercedes and other foreign cars were parked in front of various houses; this could have been a neighborhood of Beverly Hills, it had that same veneer of wealth and style. Alvarez Lajonchere, as Cuba's most eminent physician, is entitled to all the good things of life: Fidel Castro owes him a great deal because it was Lajonchere who, after the 1959 Communist revolution, helped set up rural hospitals, polyclinics, and a system of social medicine that is probably unmatched in the Third World. At sixty-eight, he is a living legend.

Lajonchere was a bony, bespectacled man of medium height. He did not speak English very well and chose to communicate instead in his native Spanish, which was translated by his friend Monika Krause. Miss Krause was an East German who was trained as a sexologist and who brought over to Cuba and translated into Spanish much of the sex education material that is currently used in this country's schools. She was a tall, slim woman, with eyes that seemed to miss nothing; she wore jeans and a sweatshirt; she appeared at least thirty years younger than Lajonchere. Lajonchere was in shirt-sleeves. He was seated at his desk when I was brought into his office, which was a messy stable of books, papers, magazines, and cardboard cartons. Lajonchere was apparently still in the process of moving into this hacienda from a previous office in the Hospital Gonzales Coro in downtown Havana; the office had been freshly painted.

"Ah, so you are writing a book, Steve tells me," Lajonchere said, without much ceremony. "Well, in order to understand the changes in Cuba, you should know what we had here before the revolution—or rather, what we didn't have here."

Alvarez Lajonchere was one of five gynecologists who hadn't fled the country when Fidel Castro's ragged band of soldiers came down from the Sierra Maestra in December 1959 and seized power from the corrupt regime of President Fulgencio Batista y Zaldivar. There was no rural medicine network then, and virtually all of Cuba's hospital beds were to be found only in Havana and a couple of other urban communities. Infant mortality was high, especially in the countryside, as was the birthrate. Many women chose abortion as a means of controlling fertility—but most of Cuba's abortionists left the country after the 1959 revolution, and this eventually resulted in a further increase in the birthrate. In 1965, Cuba announced that abortion would be freely available to any woman above eighteen years of age on demand and without anyone's permission.

"A woman must have the choice of terminating her pregnancy if she so desires," Lajonchere said. "The principle guiding us is this: all women in every walk of life and in all economic stations of life must have the opportunity to decide for themselves if they want a child or not. I am personally convinced that, given such a choice, a woman will have fewer children."

Lajonchere then told me something quite startling. So sought after is abortion that out of every 1,000 pregnancies recorded in Cuba in 1982, 450 ended in abortions.

"I do not necessarily advocate abortion as a means of birth control," he said. "We are also heavily promoting sex education and a wider awareness and availability of family-planning techniques. Eventually, Cuban women will not have to resort to drastic measures such as abortion to prevent unwanted births. But the availability of abortion-on-demand is necessary, nevertheless. We found that maternal mortality was dramatically on the increase. Women were dying because of botched abortions done in alleyways by butchers who passed themselves off as physicians."

A number of foreign "population" specialists have told the Cubans that if the people here get too accustomed to relying on abortion as a means of birth control, this would adversely affect the application of other, less traumatic means of contraception. Such warnings do not bother Alvarez Lajonchere; he feels that if abortion were to be made illegal or were to be even restricted in Cuba, this country would find itself replicating the "Romanian experience."

"Romanian experience?" I asked.

"You know what happened in Romania, don't you? They made abortion illegal, and suddenly the birthrate practically doubled to 40 per 1,000, and maternal mortality rates rose like a rocket," Lajonchere said. "We have no intention of letting this happen in Cuba."

I asked Lajonchere what particular strategy he had used to push through health reforms during the first twenty-five years of the Cuban Revolution. In short, had he not been on the scene, would Cuba have registered these same advances in providing universal medical care for its people?

He smiled.

"My own role?" he said. "It would be facile and presumptuous if I said that the changes in Cuba have taken place only because of me. Rather, it was I who took advantage of the general social and economic changes that the revolution was bringing about to make certain suggestions. You should take into consideration that I knew very well the basic philosophy of the Marxist-Leninist founders of modern Cuba, people like Fidel. I shared this philosophy long before Fidel took over.

"I was one of those who didn't have to change his ideas after the revolution. My personal beliefs and attitudes have been consistent—I have the same ideas now as I did as a young man before the revolution.

This gave me the security that I was on the right side. Maybe this in turn influenced those who had to work with me and who were in a position to authorize decisions concerning the development of a comprehensive health care network. I was in a personal position of strength —where I could offer my opinions and suggestions in a convincing fashion. That helped a lot."

I said to Lajonchere that the political support of the Marxist Castro regime for family-planning activities was intriguing, especially in view of the fact that orthodox Communists had traditionally objected to population control programs. Such opposition has been predicated on the doctrinal ground that Lenin had denounced Malthus, arguing that it was imperialism that caused poverty and that exponential population growth was a capitalist red herring concocted to bamboozle the proletariat.

"Ah, but our family-planning programs were always in the context of maternal and child health projects," Lajonchere said. "We have never directly promoted birth control through our mass media campaigns. The emphasis has always been on general health care. We have sought only to educate people about the risks inherent in having large families. Our goals were rapid promotion of health care, and this helped bring down the birthrate."

Monika Krause, who until now had only translated Lajonchere's comments, piped in with her own thoughts.

"It is important to note the political direction of the revolution," she said. "The highest levels of leadership were very clear right from the start about the health care goals involved and the effort that would be necessary."

Alvarez Lajonchere nodded.

"And let's not minimize the role of the Cuban Women's Federation," he said, referring to a national organization that was an offshoot of a guerrilla group of women who assisted Fidel's soldiers during the struggle against Batista. The women's federation, formally founded in August 1960, has helped emancipate Cuban females to a point where there are almost as many women in the work force today as there are men, whereas back in 1959 women constituted barely 12 percent of Cuba's labor force. Half of Cuba's physicians are women; women are also strongly represented in the National Assembly. Providing economic opportunities for women and arranging vocational training programs for them are only one part of the federation's activities. Educating women about the value of small families is an equally vital function. What Cuba has demonstrated is that if women are given the right opportunities for education and employment, they will chose voluntarily to have fewer children.

Alvarez Lajonchere had spoken glowingly about the universality of health care in Cuba and of employment opportunities for women. But my friend Jose, the physician, said that in parts of Havana the situation was not quite as rosy.

One evening I was taken by one of Jose's colleagues to a neighborhood in Old Havana, where this physician paid a number of house calls. Her patients were women who worked as de facto prostitutes. The Cuban government, of course, denies that prostitution of any kind exists in the country, and I had been told by officials that the Cuban Women's Federation had rehabilitated 12,000 females who had been identified as prostitutes in various Havana localities. But the sweep had clearly not been complete; I myself was approached on a number of occasions in the lobby of the Habana Libre Hotel (once called the Hilton Hotel) and in restaurants such as the Floridita (another Hemingway hangout, this one reputedly the "home" of his favored margarita) by women who were definitely available for sex, in exchange for no more than a dress, or a bottle of foreign perfume, or a pair of jeans.

The narrow streets of Old Havana are spotless, like the streets elsewhere in this city; but here the buildings are aging, decaying structures with cantilevered arrangements, balconies with balustrades of iron, and high ceilings. This, indeed, could be an area of Madrid, for the Spanish architectural influence was strong here. Elsewhere in Havana the houses were pastel-colored, smaller and more squat. During the evening, the neighborhood "defense committees" are especially active; these committees are a Cuban version of neighborhood vigilantes, who move about in olive vans—ostensibly to prevent crime but in truth to spy on the activities and whereabouts of ordinary citizens. I was concerned that my physician friend might get into trouble for taking me along.

"Not to worry," she said. "You look Cuban. Besides, you are an Indian, and India is in favor here."

We went to the apartment of a woman named Maria. She was about thirty years old, unmarried, and the mother of three daughters. She was guaranteed a basic income (the equivalent of about thirty dollars each month), and Maria said she had no particular skills that might help her find a job.

"What do you do all day?" I asked.

Maria giggled coquettishly.

My physician friend said that Maria worked as a prostitute most evenings. Her three daughters were fathered by different men. The girls were seldom in good health, and Maria did not pay much attention to them. It was Maria's mother who looked after the girls.

"I want to leave Cuba," Maria said, all of a sudden.

"Why?" I asked.

"There is no future here."

"Where would you like to go?"

"I want to go to the United States."

"What are you doing about it?"

"I applied a long time ago for an exit visa. I used to work in a clothing factory when I applied."

"Why don't you work there anymore?"

"They asked me not to come."

"When was that?"

"The day after I applied to leave Cuba."

I was told by a number of foreign diplomats that close to 25 percent of Cubans have applied to leave the country. So much for the worker's paradise. And when people do indicate a preference for leaving, as Maria did, the state at once comes down hard on them. In a country of equals, there are those who are placed last on the ladder.

* * *

In no area of the developing world is the political influence of the Catholic church as strong as in Latin America when it comes to the business of family planning. It is not that ordinary priests vigorously oppose birth control; indeed, many young priests I met in countries like Mexico, Panama, Colombia, Ecuador, Peru, Bolivia, Chile, and Brazil seemed to feel that couples ought to decide for themselves what contraceptive technique worked best for them. Younger priests generally tended to be more understanding and more tolerant of couples' sexual customs and contraceptive needs. But in recent years, and particularly since 1982, when Pope John Paul II raised the decibel level of the birth control debate by making a series of pronouncements against artificial contraception, the Church hierarchy in many Latin American nations has been increasingly reluctant to endorse any state program or policy concerning family planning.

Strengthening the arsenal of the anti–birth control lobby in Latin America has been a new Charter of Family Rights issued not long ago by the Vatican. The 3,500-word document urges wealthy nations not to make birth control programs a condition for economic assistance to Third World countries. The charter attacks efforts to force couples to have small families. Moreover, the charter says that parents should have as many children as they want and that any attempts by governments to impose limits on family size were in truth a "grave offense against human dignity and justice." The document also says that mothers need not have to work outside their homes. According to Archbishop Edourd Gagnon of Canada, who was acting head of the Pontificial Council for the Family—the unit that technically monitors developments concerning birth control and related issues—when the charter was published, the document reflected a "spirit of service in which the Church searches to awaken in society a better respect for the laws of the Creator."

There are population experts, such as Dr. Benjamin Viel in Santiago, Chile, who contend that the most direct impact of the Vatican's position on family planning and birth control can be seen in the rising number of abortions in Latin America. Various estimates suggest that more than 3.5 million abortions are performed each year in this part of the world. These estimates also suggest that half of all maternal deaths in Latin America are abortion-related.

I stopped off in Santiago to meet Dr. Viel, who is probably Latin America's leading "population" authority. A former executive with the International Planned Parenthood Federation, he now runs an acclaimed family-planning and research center known as the Chilean Association for the Protection of the Family. The author of several books on medical subjects and on demography, Dr. Viel also lectures widely in Western countries on the question of population growth in the Third World. From accounts supplied by some people who had met him earlier, I had expected to meet a forbidding figure; Benjamin Viel instead turned out to be an amiable man, almost a grandfatherly sort.

We met in his clinic. I was struck by how European in ambiance Santiago seemed to be: its broad boulevards, stately stone buildings, handsome people in well-cut clothes. There were many parks, and the city gently rolled up the foothills of the snow-capped Andes, whose peaks are often hidden from view because of the smog over Santiago. Chile's military government does not formally support family-planning programs; military juntas in this part of the world traditionally have called for large populations—on the premise that the more people a nation has, the stronger it is. Dr. Viel's clinic was a quietly busy facility, with secretaries typing away continuously and getting up occasionally to fetch us coffee and biscuits. Dr. Viel, a tall man attired in a double-breasted blue suit, had a commanding but reassuring presence. He chain-smoked and kept apologizing for doing so.

"This whole debate about abortion absolutely revolts me," he said, in his deep, gravely voice. "Nothing to me is more saddening that the fate of an unwanted child: I'd much prefer a clean abortion, done legally. Do you know what we have in Chile, and in the rest of Latin America? We have women going to their graves because they didn't want their child and had to get an abortion in some dingy shack. Do you know that in Chile alone more than 40,000 women are hospitalized annually through septic abortions? And more than 80 percent of the women who go for abortions are already mothers of three or four children."

Benjamin Viel would like abortion to be legalized, but when I asked him what the prospects were for this, he launched into a jeremiad.

"I say to the lawmakers: 'Don't be stupid. Teenage sex and adolescent pregnancies are already going on. Let's protect these adolescents with the proper contraceptives, and let's give them proper education about sex and responsible behavior. I'd rather have abortions than unwanted children whose lives are ruined the moment they are born.' All over Latin America, women are asking for ways to protect themselves against unwanted pregnancies, but their voices in this male-dominated region lack political clout and power. If a basically conservative—and heavily Roman Catholic—state like Italy can legalize abortion, why can't we in Chile and elsewhere in this region?"

* * *

Most abortions in Latin American countries are performed in dubious clinics by physicians out to earn quick money; some abortions are done by midwives or neighborhood elderly women who use primitive methods such as abortion-inducing massage. No wonder casualties and fatality rates are so high. Population experts estimate that some 25 million abortions are performed in the world each year and that most of these are done in the countries of Latin America, Asia, and Africa, where abortion has either not been legalized or where it can be obtained legally only with much difficulty. There are very few legitimate clinics where women can go and receive proper medical attention both before and after an abortion. Physicians who may want to offer aboveboard abortion services are intimidated by the law enforcement authorities in their countries, whose actions could jeopardize medical careers. But in a few places in Latin America there are physicians who are bold enough to start clinics where women can indeed get an abortion cleanly and without fear.

I went to Colombia at the suggestion of Benjamin Viel, who thought I should see for myself one such clinic.

Colombia is an unusual country in Latin America as far as family-planning matters go; a privately financed organization called Profamilia provides more than 60 percent of all contraceptive and family-planning education services. The government does not have a formal family-planning policy, but Colombian politicians have long supported Profamilia's programs, despite opposition from powerful members of the Church hierarchy. The government itself has helped set up community-based health clinics all over the country. As a result of all these efforts, Colombia's annual population growth rate declined from 3.4 percent in 1965 to 1.9 percent last year. But half of the country's 28 million people are below the age of twenty, which means that Colombia must step up its population control programs to offset the increase in fertility that can be expected from these youngsters who are entering the childbearing period.

Profamilia's "founding father" is a large man with Bugs Bunny ears and a pleasing smile, a thoroughly affable man named Dr. Fernando Tamayo. He took me around his organization's headquarters at No. 14-52 Calle 34, in a densely packed neighborhood of Bogota, a city whose elevation is 8,800 feet above sea level and whose population is touching 5 million. Dr. Tamayo sent an office car to collect me from my hotel: he did not want me to come unescorted because Bogota had become the crime capital of the world and foreigners traveling alone in taxis had been known to be robbed and abandoned, or worse. The Profamilia building had seven stories, and it was, said Dr. Tamayo, the biggest single family-planning clinic in the world.

More than a thousand sterilizations were done each month in the brightly lit, totally sanitized rooms of this clinic, I was told. (When you count the sterilizations done at the other forty Profamilia clinics around Colombia, the figure climbs up to some 50,000 sterilizations annually. But more than 300,000 abortions also are done each year in the country, although none by Profamilia.) Nearly 4.5 million people are examined each year at Profamilia headquarters and community clinics, Dr. Tamayo said, the majority of them wishing insertion of IUDs or supplies of the pill or of condoms.

"No abortions here, however," Fernando Tamayo said.

I expressed to him some puzzlement. I had been told that Profamilia indeed performed abortions. Dr. Tamayo said that I was probably been misled: the clinic I should visit was the Unidad de Orientacion y Asistencia Materna. He suggested I should meet with its head, Dr. Jorge Villarreal, one of Colombia's leading physicians.

Dr. Villarreal's clinic was in an impressive colonial-style building that was surrounded by a large yard. Nurses in crisp white-and-blue uniforms moved about efficiently. There were armed guards on the grounds. I expected that Dr. Villarreal would be taciturn about discussing abortion. Instead, the dapper, wavy-haired doctor was surprisingly forthcoming.

"We don't believe that abortion is ideal," he said. "But a woman should be given the choice. There has to be a recognition of women's rights and the recognition that female health must have a priority in the general development of any country. It is horrible how many women die at the hands of butcher-abortionists."

As we talked, the corridors outside Dr. Villarreal's private office echoed with the traffic of patients. I asked him about how many patients the Unidad de Orientacion y Asistencia Materna got every day. The clinic performed fifty abortions a day, and 98 percent of its patients came for abortions.

"It would be difficult to enforce laws against abortion," Dr. Villarreal said. The authorities in Bogota are, of course, aware of the clinic's activities. But in a city—and country—where abortion is commonly practiced, there is at least the assurance with this clinic that the job will be done by medical experts. Dr. Villarreal insists that afterward his patients agree to using contraceptives: each year, for example, he and his associates insert more than 12,000 IUDs.

As much as the care of women who seek abortions, Dr. Villarreal is concerned with the plight of Colombia's unwanted children, the so-called *gamines*—the abandoned children who live in the streets of Bogota and other large cities like Medellin, Barranguilla, and Bucaramanga. UNICEF—the United Nations Children's Fund—estimates that in Latin America there are more than 25 million such abandoned children; they are almost always illegitimate, and they grow up to be thieves, pickpockets, drug pushers, prostitutes, and murderers. You see them in Bogota; you see them in the *favelas* of Rio de Janeiro, the hillside slums that grow like mushrooms; you see them in Sao Paulo. There is little hope in their lives, except perhaps that the next wallet they snatch will have a few more currency notes than the last one that was stolen. They grow up undernourished, illiterate, diseased. They are the product of unwanted fertility; they are the living dead, the result of stupid, shortsighted policies of governments that are too timid to liberalize their laws and legalize abortion and expand family-planning services and education.

On the way back to my hotel, I stopped to get my shoes shined at a streetside stall. A boy, perhaps no more than twelve, energetically solicited my business. As he worked on my shoes, I thought I'd ask him some questions, through a translator.

"How long have you been shining shoes?"

"All my life."

"Where do you live?"

"Everywhere."

"Do you have parents, sisters, brothers?"

"Who knows?"

"Do you have anyone who takes care of you?"

The boy, a gaunt-faced urchin, looked bewildered.

"Care? What is that?" he said.

It was perhaps no more than a five-minute walk from the shoeshine stall to my hotel. My companion, a United Nations employee, insisted on taking me there by taxi. When we got to the hotel, he reached for his wallet to pay the fare. But there was no wallet in his hip pocket; it had been stolen.

* * *

Perhaps in no country of Latin America do you see issues like rampant population growth, abortion and abandoned children more vividly played out in daily life than in Brazil. With a population of 129 million, Brazil is now the world's sixth largest country (after China, India, the Soviet Union, the United States, and Indonesia). It has half the land mass of all of South America, and it is bigger than the forty-eight contiguous states of the United States. It is a land rich in natural resources—iron ore, gold, and oil, for example. Brazil is second only to the United States as the world's biggest food producer and exporter; no country produces as much coffee as Brazil does, and Brazil is also among the world's leading sugar-growing states. Between 1970 and 1980, Brazil's population grew from 90 million to 120 million, or, looking at it another way, it added the equivalent in this decade of the entire population of neighboring Argentina; the increase was absorbed by the large cities near the Atlantic, for 70 percent of the country's population lives within 100 miles of the coast.

Brazil adds 3 million people a year, or one and a half Costa Ricas, or one Uruguay, and this means that Brazil, a country already reeling from a foreign debt of $85 billion and a domestic unemployment rate of close to 20 percent, needs to create 1.5 million new jobs each year. By the year 2000, Brazil may well have 200 million people. More than 45 percent of the country's population now is under fifteen years of age —the demographic echo of this youthful population is yet to be felt!

I was told by a man named Samuel Taylor that many experts estimate that between 1 and 2 million abortions take place in Brazil each year. Taylor, a thin, wiry man with the knotted-up face of a perpetual worrysmith, at the time worked for the U.S. Agency for International Development in Brasilia, Brazil's stylish capital city. He was a population specialist. He told me that the Church promoted the natural family-planning method but that, in an ironic way, it was adherence to this chancy method that made millions of Brazilian women pregnant each year and contributed to the abortion rate! Research had shown that a large number of women using the Church-approved natural family-planning method went for abortions, Taylor said.

Sam Taylor recounted for me a meeting between him and a Brazilian feminist leader. They'd been discussing the government's timidity in the face of Church opposition to birth control programs.

"Of course the government and the Church would never understand what family planning was all about—neither has been pregnant!" the feminist told Taylor.

The pioneer of family-planning services in Brazil is a man named Walter Rodrigues, who started a voluntary, nonprofit organization known as Bemfam back in 1965. (Bemfam is the acronyn for Sociedade Civil Bem Estar Familiar No Brasil, or the Family Planning Association of Brazil.) He has been called the Margaret Sanger of Brazil, after the American nurse who braved much opposition and set up birth control projects in the United States in the early part of this century. He has also been called a villain, and worse, by opponents; Bemfam offices in Rio de Janeiro have sometimes received bomb threats, and Bemfam workers—who are now established in eighteen of Brazil's twenty-three states—have sometimes come in for personal verbal abuse. Still, there is general agreement that Brazil's annual population growth rate would not have declined from a high of 3.2 percent to about 2.7 percent now had Dr. Rodrigues not been unintimidated and had he not persisted. I went by one day to meet with Walter Rodrigues in Rio de Janeiro.

He is a giant of a man, a man whose waistline is so large that his secretaries contend that circumambulating him is like girdling the globe. He was friendly and hospitable, offering me cup after cup of rich Brazilian coffee. His face was a battlefield, though, tired, and his eyes were sorely in need of rest. It has indeed been a twenty-year battle for him in Brazil, and this has clearly taken its toll. They say he used to be a slim man once; now he weighs more than 300 pounds, and his friends and relatives worry about his health.

"Yes, it has been rough—there are so many misunderstandings about family planning in this country, so many lies broadcast all the time," Dr. Rodrigues said, speaking in a mix of English and Portuguese, the national language of Brazil and a holdover from its colonial days. "I am optimistic nonetheless. I'm confident that one day soon we will have a national population policy and that family planning will be accepted by everyone. But I fear that it will continue to be a battle for now, and I fear that my staff will start to get discouraged. But we need to convince everybody that 'population' is not some isolated matter. It affects all of us, especially in a developing country like Brazil. Some people in government may think that because we are a huge country overcrowding is not a problem. Not a problem? Just look out of that window!"

From the window of his office, I could see a succession of small hills. Each hill was tightly packed with shacks, the so-called *favelas* of Rio de Janeiro, its slums, the breeding ground for crime and poverty. I had seen such slums in Bombay and Jakarta and Manila and Nairobi and Mexico City; and now here. It was a beautiful, bright day as I looked out of Dr. Rodrigues's window, not a cloud in the blue sky; out there was the smiling seashore, the acres of luxury apartment blocks. There were forested valleys. And above everything, as if silently blessing Brazil with outstretched arms, was the giant statue of Christ the Redeemer on the 2,300-foot peak of Mount Corcovado. But it was the *favelas* that one couldn't get away from—they were everywhere. It all seemed somehow wrong, that in a stunning place like this there should be such degradation and destitution.

"Heaven and hell on earth," Walter Rodrigues said.

* * *

I had wanted to see a remote rural area of Brazil, far away from Rio de Janeiro's glitter and gloom, and Dr. Rodrigues suggested that I visit the Natal area in the northeastern state of Rio Grande do Norte, the poorest of Brazil's provinces. It was on the way to Natal that I had stopped in Brasilia to meet with Sam Taylor of AID, and it was in Brasilia, too, that I paid the obligatory courtesy visit—"required" of all journalists who write about population matters in Brazil—to Haroldo Sanford, an influential vice-president of Brazil's 479-member Chamber of Deputies. I was taken by local contacts of Dr. Rodrigues to the futuristic Parliament building, where the dress code was so strict that the guards refused to allow me in: I was wearing my journalist-standard-issue safari suit, and the guards said I'd need to wear a jacket and tie. One of Sanford's aides intervened, and I was finally let in. Sanford was a genial, silver-haired man with thick lamb-chop sideburns and a solid gold Rolex watch that he kept bringing up to my face. He was a caricature of a politician from the Wild West.

"My main worry is that the continued high birthrate is affecting our economic development," Sanford said. He has organized an energetic committee of parliamentarians in Brazil; these parliamentarians make speeches in support of private organizations such as Bemfam and also try and prod the government into expanding rural health care programs that include family-planning services. Sanford, a widely traveled man, has also been an articulate lobbyist for the population cause not only in this country but in various parliamentary forums around the world. "It is foolish for us to think that ours is a country with unlimited land and resources. Where are all the additional people going to live? In the middle of our jungles? On the Amazon? On the beaches of Natal?"

Natal turned out to be a city of nearly 400,000 people. It was a sleepy place, warm, and with patches of vegetation that had managed to stay green despite a statewide drought that had afflicted the area for five years in a row. During World War II, the Allies had an air base here. I was nearly 2,000 miles from Rio de Janeiro, and yet the urbanization process and the spread of poverty were almost identical here. Once Natal had been a tiny community where people lazed on beaches and fished occasionally, or farmed. But the population explosion in the interior had sent people scurrying for jobs in Natal; there weren't many jobs available and so many newcomers turned to crime and violence. Only 12 percent of this city has modern sanitation, and potable water is scarce, particularly in the outlying areas.

I requested the local Bemfam representatives to take me to a village. We went by jeep to Redinha, a fishing community that sat on the shore amid coconut groves and pebbly beaches. Some of the narrow unpaved streets had lampposts that were festooned with gay buntings —there had been a spate of weddings here recently, I was told. The houses and huts had pastel walls, children played soccer in dusty fields, and women languidly carried buckets of water from the village wells to their homes. I could smell fish being fried.

I walked into the home of Maria Jose Candida Oliveira, a mother of seven children (one of whom, a six-year-old boy, had died a few days before from hepatitis). Her house had one brick wall and three walls fashioned from straw mattings. The floor was of thick sand. Hammocks hung over the floor, and a couple of children were asleep in them. A gentle breeze filtered in through the splits in the straw walls. Maria said she had no husband and that she lived with a fisherman named Francisco Guedes. Her little kids all appeared to have boils on their bodies. They looked undernourished and miserable. In these parts of Brazil, the infant mortality rate has been known to be 200 per 1,000 live births. Health care facilities are spotty. There is a listlessness, even despair, among the local people.

Maria was now expecting another child.

"Can you afford another child?" I asked Maria.

"No," she said.

"Then why are you having one?"

"I used to use the pill," she said to me through a translator. "But I stopped. The pill was giving me a lot of headaches. It made me very nervous."

"There are methods you could use for birth control."

Maria smiled weakly. There was an embarrassed pause.

"Our Church is against family planning," she said.

"But what kind of a future do your children face? What kind of a life are you giving them?"

Maria shrugged wearily.

"Maybe we will move one day to Rio or to Sao Paulo," she said.

* * *

South America is a continent of startling surprises, and for me one such surprise was in the village of Jacho, high up in the Ecuadorian Andes.

I had come to Ecuador, a country of some 9.2 million people and the size of Nevada, at the invitation of a good friend named Hugo Corvalan, a Chilean physician who headed the Quito office of the United Nations Fund for Population Activities. Corvalan and I spent several days visiting various health projects run by the Ecuadorian government. Quito, a splendid little capital city up in the mountains, is home for two internationally renowned painters who have worked with "population" themes, Eduardo Kingman and Osvaldo Guayasamin, and Corvalan, an art collector and connoisseur himself, had become friends with them and so took me along to their homes. Kingman, who lived in a rehabilitated flour mill in a Quito suburb called San Raphael, and Guayasamin, who occupied a huge estate not far away, were both friendly and garrulous. We spent hours discussing the relevance of art to modern life and the connection between modern life and art. Each of them really lived in a museum of sorts: each possessed priceless works of pre-Columbian art and artifacts, in addition to Miros and Picassos and de Koonings. Sated thus on "culture" and inclined now to return to the world of real people, Corvalan and I drove one morning a hundred miles out of Quito toward a snow-capped volcano called Cotopaxi. We thought we would visit some hamlets in the general area of Salsedo, one of the most backward regions of Ecuador.

The scenery was breathtaking. The road cut through gentle valleys where cows grazed and horses trotted about and sliced through narrow mountain passes and forests of pine, eucalyptus, willow, pimento, and apple trees. We drove through corn fields whose ripened stalks swayed as if in welcome. In the town of Salsedo, we stopped off at a large open-air market, where local Indians in colorful ponchos and capes and all wearing ridiculous black hats (even the women) were peddling clothes, roasted meat, bananas, raspberries, and dozens of varieties of potatoes. We were about 11,000 feet above sea level, and there was a slight sharpness in the mountain air. I was hungry, and Corvalan suggested we take our lunch in the open-air bazaar.

I had long ago learned my lesson about never eating food that was cooked and sold out in the open in a Third World country. But who was I to challenge Hugo Corvalan, a physician? Surely he knew all about the dangers of hepatatis and jaundice! Corvalan took me to a booth where we bought two bowls of a concoction called *yaguar locro,* a thick soup made with sheep's blood and potatoes. It was absolutely delicious. I had a second helping. Then we moved on. I had pushed my luck far enough. (My digestive tract had been toughened by my years in the developing world: the *yaguar locro* had no ill effects on me.)

We drove about at random, stopping in a hamlet here and a village there. These were desperately poor communities. Most did not even have electricity, let alone drainage and sewers. Corvalan and I stopped at a government-run health clinic, where some men and women with children were lining up for inoculation shots. We started chatting with a tough little man named Enrique Malliguinga. He had a wrinkled face, tanned from years in the sun and snow, and he wore a poorly knit sweater. He was an Indian, but he did not wear the customary black hat.

"Why don't you come and visit my village?" Malliguinga said. "I live in Jacho."

Jacho was about ten miles from Salsedo, and we had to leave the macadam road and move over a dirt path to get there. I was somewhat nervous as Corvalan drove on this narrow strip, for there were high peaks on one side and sheer drops on the other. Suddenly there was Jacho in front of us. Malliguinga gave a cry of delight.

It was a picture book community: small houses clustered together, each with a tiny garden in front and a farming plot behind. There was a schoolhouse in a little valley nearby. The children here appeared to be much healthier than those we'd seen in other hamlets in the area.

"You seem surprised," Malliguinga said, with a chuckle. "Well, let me explain."

He was the village headman, he said. For many years, Jacho shared the plight of other communities around Salsedo—poor health facilities, poor sanitation, deteriorating agriculture, high infant mortality, and high adult morbidity. Then Malliguinga was invited by the government to attend a health care seminar in Quito; the speakers included experts from AID, the United Nations, and the World Bank. They spoke not in the heavy jargon of most development specialists but in simple, easy-to-understand terms. What they suggested was that villagers undertake *minga*—the old Inca word that means volunteer work. The government would give some seed money and perhaps some more cash as incentives, but villagers should rebuild their communities and rejuvenate their agriculture.

Malliguinga said he took all this very seriously. He got together a corps of villagers, who cleared the land and cleaned Jacho village. They laid pipes for drainage, and with the assistance of government engineers, they brought in power lines to electrify the village. United Nations and AID experts were brought in to teach villagers how to plant drought-resistant, high-yield maize so that now there is a crop every four months.

Peach, apple, avocado, mango, and maraguaya—a sweet, semitropical fruit—trees were planted. Local women were invited to start hamster-breeding farms, hamsters being a delicacy around here (they were first brought here hundreds of years ago by the Incas). The villagers then built a sewage disposal unit, a water purification plant, and a recreation center for children. Within weeks of the water purification plant's inauguration, fewer children were contracting diarrhea.

"We all were really blind before," Malliguinga said. "We never realized that it was here all the time—this energy to improve our own lives by ourselves. Maybe it took some little help from the outside, but it had never even occurred to us to seek that little bit of help. And now because we did, and because we ourselves changed our own conditions, our children will have a much better life than we did in our youth."

Thirteen

Epilogue: 1984 and Beyond

ONE VERY HOT AFTERNOON in Indonesia, a man named Haryono Suyono invited me to accompany him to a rally not far from Jakarta. Suyono is a short man with tiny eyes and a goatee that gives the suggestion of villainy to his face; but villain Suyono is surely not—he is the brains behind this Asian country's remarkably successful family-planning program and a man who feels deeply that you cannot expect to lower an area's population growth rate without also improving its economy and providing decent health care for its people. We drove through the congestion of Jakarta, past rickshaws and fume-spewing automobiles and adventurous pedestrians, past slums and thickly packed tenements, and past enormous statues of mythical revolutionary workers who seemed to be fighting the polluted air with bamboo spears. The heroic statues are leftovers from the days of Sukarno, who honored the proletariat but who himself lived high on the hog and almost brought his oil-rich country to bankruptcy.

In Jakarta the trees were few, and these seemed to be choking from the pollution; but as the capital city receded from view, we drove through areas where the vegetation was lush: lots of frangipani, gay poinsettias, hibiscus, and bougainvillea. Suyono, who was attired in a smartly cut gray safari suit, talked virtually nonstop about his country's family-planning efforts, in an accent that reflected his many years as a student in the United States. He pointed out that in the last decade Indonesia had almost halved its annual birthrate, largely by emphasizing birth control, primary health care, and economic development in villages, where 87 percent of the country's 155 million people live. In many other states of the Third World, government family-planning programs have been started in the cities and then expanded to rural areas, but the Indonesians did what was the most sensible and logical thing for them to do, which was to institute family planning the other way around.

We were headed for Cibubur village in the East Jakarta region. There a reception committee was waiting for Suyono, who is as enthusiastically received in rural Indonesia as is his boss and mentor, President Suharto. A local band played several spirited numbers, and little girls danced joyously. We were taken to the home of a local leader, where we feasted on rambutan, a fruit whose red exterior is prickly but whose inside flesh is soft and scrumptious. Suyono and I were then shown around a new women's employment center, where a dozen local ladies were busily making soybean cakes or stitching tablecloths or stapling plastic shopping bags for export to cities like Jakarta. No doubt the women worked with special zeal because Suyono was inspecting their facility, but each one seemed accomplished at her art—the briskness, expertness, and ease with which the women rolled the mix for the cakes, or patterned the tablecloths, or cut plastic sheets for the shopping bags could not have been contrived.

The employment center also doubled as Cibubur's health care and family-planning clinic, and villagers could come here to weigh their babies or get their children inoculated, or collect condoms or be fitted with IUDs or get a supply of pills. It was from this center, too, that trained local volunteers set out daily to visit homes in the area and persuade people to adopt birth control. Meticulous records of these activities are kept in the center, which is one of thousands of such facilities peppered throughout Indonesia. (Superb record keeping in family planning is a special Indonesian accomplishment; I saw during my travels here that even the tiniest of hamlets had established a detailed record system. Haryono Suyono, who is deputy chairman of the national family-planning agency, told me that the record-keeping system has contributed immeasurably toward fashioning an efficient population control network.)

We walked on to the rally, which was held in a little field where local youths usually play soccer. The field was about a quarter-kilometer away from the employment center, and we could have driven in Suyono's jeep, but clearly local officials wanted me to see a bit of their village. It was less humid here than in Jakarta and, of course, less congested. Small brick houses were set back from the rough-paved streets; many houses had tiny gardens or yards. As villages go, this one seemed cleaner and neater than many I'd seen in the developing world. I mentioned this to one of my escorts.

"Ah, but you think we have given Cibubur a facelift because you were to come today, isn't it?" the official, a woman named Suyuti Budiharsono, said to me.

I acknowledged that such a thought had indeed moved through my mind.

"But it isn't like that at all," she said. "We have a year-round campaign here to keep our village clean. Our position is that how can you expect our people to have good health, to have healthy children, if they live in filth? We give out small financial bonuses to people who work especially hard in public hygiene here."

At the rally itself, Haryono Suyono was introduced with effusive praise by a local family-planning official. Then a little girl sang a song in welcome. The villagers cheered when Suyono, who was enjoying this attention, stood up to speak.

"There is no secret about family planning," Haryono Suyono told his audience of 5,000 villagers, who frequently interrupted his oratory with bursts of applause. "The facilities are here. All you need to do is to sign up. We will take care of jobs for you and better health facilities for you."

I had been told that earlier that day about 1,500 villagers from Cibubur and two nearby communities had turned up at the local family-planning center with requests ranging from tubectomies to IUD insertions. They had come not necessarily spontaneously but in response to a special appeal by local officials aimed at signing up new family-planning acceptors. Haryono Suyono makes certain that his visits to various parts of the Indonesian archipelago coincide with mass events such as these drives. The publicity that is generated through his trips stimulates other areas into launching their own drives to sign up people in family planning.

Suyono pointed to a woman who was sitting on the ground near the front of the audience.

"What is your name?" he asked.

"Asmani," the woman said, giggling shyly.

"What do you do?"

"I help my husband on his farm. I also weave baskets and sell them in the market."

"How many children do you have?"

"Three—two girls and a boy."

"Do you practice birth control?"

"Of course."

"For how long?"

"Three years."

"What do you use?"

"An IUD."

Suyono paused. Then he reached into a pocket of his safari suit and brought out a wad of Indonesian rupiah notes.

"Look, I will give you 30,000 rupiahs right now if you get up and go to the family-planning center and ask them to remove your IUD."

"No, I won't do that," the woman Asmani said.

"Why not? Don't you want this money?" (It was the equivalent of about $200 at the time.)

"Of course it would be bad to lose that money, but it would be worse for my family if I gave birth to any more children. I am now free to work on my own; I do not want to be pregnant again, and my husband agrees with me in this. And even if you or someone else ordered me to get my IUD removed, I would return to the clinic soon after and get myself a new one."

I thought the woman was being extraordinarily bold and candid.

"OK," Haryono Suyono said to the woman, with a huge smile. "I admire your attitude. I don't really want you to get your IUD removed. It was just a test. And you may have these rupiahs anyway. Put them to use on your farm."

The exchange highlighted for me the point that family planning had become, in this instance at least, a part of this woman's consciousness: It wasn't just that she'd been persuaded that family planning was a good thing generally in this fatly populated country; more significantly, she'd been convinced that it was good for her own life.

The resistance of family-planning critics in the West is sometimes explained by their perception that women are essentially subordinate to men and that if women are encouraged to control their own fertility, encouraged to be free-thinking individuals, then somehow they will be independent of men, perhaps uncontrollable and promiscuous. This is specious thinking, of course, but it is so often implicit in the positions of men who are resistant to "population" programs. I found, to the contrary, that where women are given the opportunity to control and regulate their fertility, they invariably turn out to be as responsible members of economic society as men, and often even more responsible.

My trip to Cibubur also highlighted for me the fact that one reason the Indonesians have been able to make striking gains in lowering their annual population growth rate is that they have taken their birth control programs out into the field, out to where the everyday people are. It seemed to me, after my vast travels through the Third World were completed, that one of the most important lessons concerning family planning in the last decade was this: static, clinic-based services have only a limited chance of working. To succeed, a family-planning program must have a vigorous outreach system. In too many countries—India, Kenya, Pakistan, Bangladesh, for instance—officials set up clinics at the county or provincial level and expected the masses to come to them; and in too many countries family-planning programs were set up without regard to prevailing economic conditions.

Some days after my visit to Cibubur, I was chatting with Charles Johnson, a tall, gangly man with an earnest academic manner who headed the U.S. Agency for International Development population office in Jakarta. He told me that even though Indonesia had brought down its annual population growth rate in the last decade, the fact remained that by 1990 the number of women in the reproductive age would grow from 23 million to almost 30 million. To reach Suharto's targeted birthrate of 23 per 1,000 by the end of this decade, the Indonesians would need 20 million contraceptive users—or at least 68 percent of married women in the reproductive period.

"Do you think the Indonesians will meet their goals?" I asked Johnson.

"Yes," was his immediate answer. "Because they have gone out into the villages, where the people are."

On this crowded earth of ours, there is not just one population "problem" but many. People do not live on the "globe" but in villages and towns, within the walls of their houses or shacks or tenements, and therefore, as Tarzie Vittachi puts it, there are "no global solutions to be had."

Population programs and policies must be tailored to suit a particular country, its culture, and its specific needs and conditions. In countries where there is a clearly demonstrated "problem" of too many people and too few resources—Kenya, for example—the challenge is patiently to uncover and reinforce the latent demand among everyday people for family-planning services. "What will not work is a theoretical globalism, or alarmist propaganda that goes against the grain of a people's culture and a nation's own perceptions of its conditions and priorities," Tarzie says.

I admit to being startled at how many people, particularly in the United States, still scoff at the whole notion of an overcrowded planet. They dismiss development assistance as having been a failure because of alleged waste and corruption. They naively feel that humans will take self-corrective steps to ensure there is no catastrophic population explosion, whether or not there are population assistance programs in place. Even as I write this, Germaine Greer, the celebrated Australian writer, has come out with an impassioned polemic, *Sex and Destiny: The Politics of Human Fertility,* in which she argues that the world's so-called population explosion is only a temporary phenomenon, and perhaps even a myth; she says that the Western nations have used this myth as an excuse to impose their notions of family size on the Third World. Greer, in a troubling echo of Dr. John J. Billings's views, also says that, in the traditional societies of the Third World, large families are economically vital and that they are emotionally satisfying. "I don't know how many people the earth can support, but I don't believe that anybody else does either," she writes.

> It is quite probable that the world is overpopulated and has been so for some time but getting into a tizzy about it will not prove helpful. Nothing good can come out of fear eating the soul. . . . We may be living in catastrophe now; perhaps we shall have to adapt to it, or go under. Perhaps catastrophe is the natural human environment, and even though we spend a good deal of energy trying to get away from it, we are programmed for survival amid catastrophe.

I found Greer's stance astonishingly insensitive to the everyday realities of the developing world. I do not know where exactly she went and what sort of people she interviewed, but any reporter who has been to poor countries and bothered to talk to ordinary people will testify that small, not large, families are generally desired and that when given the opportunity and means to limit family size, most people will generally do so. What I saw during my travels suggested that one of the most important functions of population assistance programs has been education—education to change attitudes concerning fertility. I saw that when it is demonstrated to people that "small is beautiful," their choice will be for small families, not large ones.

But people in the poor countries of the world need specific assistance for stimulating their own consciousness concerning family size, for educating their women, for bringing down infant mortality rates. They need assistance for comprehensive information on contraceptives—and their governments need the economic assistance to make these contraceptives widely available. More information is needed to enable people to make their choices about contraception, about which kinds of contraception have what sort of aftereffects. I am not suggesting that the Third World be blanketed with IUDs or condoms or the pill, but I do say that if people wish to regulate their fertility, then they should have the technical means to do so.

I found during my exhausting travels that in most of the Third World there simply are no safety nets such as pension and social security schemes and old-age insurance. So if people are to be persuaded to have fewer children, the general health care of the community must also be improved to ensure that the children live longer; more jobs need to be created so that women can work if they wish and not be forced to stay at home and procreate; pension programs must be established; poverty needs to be eradicated. All this takes money.

All this also takes time. There are no quick fixes, no facile, catchall solutions to the world's "population problem." While the world's overall population growth rate is slowing down, the annual decrease of the growth rate still is taking place from a very high level of numbers. It is going to take decades of patient, persistent efforts at the grass roots to educate people and to improve their health care and living conditions. My hope is that both the West and the Third World countries join hands to deal with our "population problem." It is not enough for the poor countries to rely on the magnanimity and concern of Western states to support and sustain population programs; they themselves must accelerate their domestic investment for such programs.

There is an intimate relationship between population and development, and between development and peace. Excessive population pressures make it difficult to grow enough food, create enough jobs, and train enough teachers and doctors to meet the needs of a society's expanding population base. Such population pressures exacerbate hunger, unemployment, ill health, and other social malignancies so that people become angry and resentful: throughout much of the Third World, there now exist political and social tensions that can only explode into violence. These dire possibilities should not be minimized. The world's annual population growth rate may be slowing down, but this is largely because the falloff has come for the most part in the industrialized countries of the West. Birth rates in most of the Third World continue to be frighteningly high, and the world is adding more and more people every year to its rolls because its overall population base keeps expanding. By the end of the century we may very well be adding some 100 million people to the world's population each year. In a few years more than 6 billion people will enter a new century. This figure will be larger by about a quarter than today's population; the parents of the additional billion plus people are already born. Robert S. McNamara, former president of the World Bank, says that the poorer nations will be left with massive unemployment, overflowing cities, inadequate food distribution, deteriorating environments, and a nightmare increase in "absolute poverty"—McNamara's special phrase for living conditions "so characterized by malnutrition, illiteracy and disease as to be beneath any reasonable definition of human decency." In a recent article in *Foreign Affairs,* McNamara warns that the population boom will exacerbate the global debt crisis, create new protectionist pressures, and further worsen already strained relations between have and have-not countries.

I fear that we may be on the verge of an unprecedented population crisis. I fear this especially because at a time when more resources are needed for population programs of all kinds, inflation and governmental neglect in the West particularly are undermining current population efforts. For example, under pressure from right-to-life groups in the United States who express concern about abortion programs abroad, the Reagan White House recently drafted a position paper that calls for less American aid to worldwide population programs, asserting that "population control is not a panacea" and that lack of free-market incentives is a more powerful cause of Third World poverty than overpopulation. I truly hope President Reagan does not cut back on America's traditional commitment to population concerns around the world; his own Secretary of State, George Shultz has said that excessive population growth underlies Third World poverty and undercuts opportunities for economic progress. Mr. Reagan's ambassador to the United Nations, Jeane Kirkpatrick, says that giving development assistance to poor countries without helping them lower their birth rates is like pouring water into a bucket with a hole in it. Over and over again it has been shown that population assistance has won Washington more friends than handing out developmental aid or gifting weapons. As an instrument of foreign policy, population aid has been the best investment the United States has made.

During a conversation this spring in Washington, Steve Sinding of the U.S. Agency for International Development recalled that Rafael M. Salas, the head of the United Nations Fund for Population Activities, not long ago sought to shift the dominant metaphor of population from Paul Ehrlich's "population bomb" to the image of a great wave, gathering strength and momentum as it moves across the human sea. "To extend this metaphor a bit, I see the world population movement as the effort to construct a breakwater—a structure that will stop the wave and prevent it from engulfing and sweeping away centuries of human development and civilization," Sinding said to me.

It is the dedication of people like Steve Sinding and Rafael Salas that is helping to shape the environment in dozens of societies so that family planning can be part of the general development effort and of social change. I have seen now for myself how well-designed and culturally sensitive population programs can be effective, and I have also seen how the absence of such programs can be felt profoundly in various societies. I offer no explicit models for development, no examples that any one country can emulate. To each its own, but urgently, and with commitment and compassion and, yes, caution.

Compassion and caution will win more people over to recognizing that a smaller family offers more for each of its members. When you advocate family planning, you are interfering with the most private and sensitive aspect of human relationships. You cannot, indeed must not, tread heavy-booted into people's bedrooms, however poor they might be. But you can help structure people's choices so that they make prudent and voluntary decisions concerning family size—decisions that affect not only themselves but also the societies they live in.

Glossary

The following are definitions of terms fashioned by the Population Reference Bureau and used frequently by demographers and population planners:

ABORTION RATE: The estimated number of abortions per year per 1,000 women between the ages of fifteen and forty-four years.

AGE-SPECIFIC FERTILITY RATE: Number of live births per 1,000 women in a given age group in a given year. This rate is usually calculated for five-year age groups.

CONTRACEPTIVE PREVALENCE RATE: The percentage of married women of reproductive age who are using a modern method of contraception at any given point in time.

CRUDE BIRTHRATE: Number of live births per year per every 1,000 population.

CRUDE DEATH RATE: Number of deaths per year per every 1,000 population.

INFANT MORTALITY RATE: Annual number of deaths of infants under one year of age per every 1,000 live births during that same year.

LIFE EXPECTANCY: Average number of years a child born in a given year could expect to live if mortality rates for each age-sex group remain the same.

MALTHUS: Thomas R. Malthus was born in 1766 and died in 1834. He was an English clergyman and economist who wrote the famous "Essay on the Principle of Population." In it he said that the world's population tends to increase faster than its food supply and that unless fertility is controlled, famine, vice, disease, and war will act as natural restrictions to population growth.

MATERNAL MORTALITY RATE: Number of maternal deaths per 1,000 births attributable to pregnancy, childbirth, or its complications within six weeks following childbirth.

MORBIDITY: The frequency of disease and illness in a population.

NEO-MALTHUSIAN: An advocate of restricting population growth through the use of birth control. Malthus himself did not advocate birth control.

NET REPRODUCTION RATE: The number of daughters a woman would have under prevailing fertility and mortality patterns who would survive to the average age of childbearing.

PRONATALIST POLICY: The policy of a government or a social group to increase population growth by trying to increase the number of births.

RATE OF NATURAL INCREASE: Difference between crude birthrates and crude death rates; usually expressed as a percentage.

RATE OF POPULATION GROWTH: Rate of natural increase adjusted for net migration and expressed as a percentage of the total population in a given year.

STABLE POPULATION: A population with an unchanging growth rate and an unchanging age composition because of age-specific birth and death rates having stayed constant over a sufficiently long period of time.

TOTAL FERTILITY RATE: The average number of children that would be born to a woman if she were to live to the end of her childbearing years. The total fertility rate serves as an estimate of the average number of children per family.

Author's Note

I started this book project early in the fall of 1982, after a three-year reporting assignment in Africa and the Middle East for the *New York Times.* That assignment involved incessant traveling and not enough time at my home base of Nairobi with my spouse Jayanti and our infant son Jaidev. When the idea came up for a book that would examine the population situation in different parts of the world, I balked at first because of the fresh round of globe-trotting this would necessitate.

But Jayanti was at once supportive, enthusiastic, and encouraging, even though we both knew that once again there would be long periods of separation while I was on the road. It was Jayanti who skillfully managed our thin resources during my prolonged absences. She was unintimidated by the large bills I incurred during my travels. It was Jayanti who took care of Jaidev. And when the months of reporting ended, it was Jayanti who kept after me to get on with the manuscript on those dreary days in New York City when the last thing I wanted to do was to drive my word processor. This book would never have been written without Jayanti's gallant assistance.

I am grateful to the United Nations Fund for Population Activities, which gave me financial support and a travel grant to visit all those faraway places. Rafael M. Salas, Jyoti Shankar Singh, and Edmund Kerner at the fund were also generous with their suggestions in a field that is complex and massive although they no doubt will disagree with some of my opinions and characterizations. I first met them when the *Times* assigned me to its United Nations bureau in 1977, and what started off as a professional relationship developed over the years into warm personal ties. The opinions expressed in this book are mine, and in no way should the United Nations be held responsible. My own conviction is that whatever shortcomings the United Nations population program may suffer from, had it not been in place our world would have been more crowded and more wretched.

I acknowledge my great debt to Varindra Tarzie Vittachi of UNICEF (and formerly of the United Nations Fund for Population Activities), who has been a good friend for many years. A wise and demanding journalist, Tarzie has helped many young writers not only in his native Sri Lanka but all over the world. He is an iconoclast, and his complaint about books on development often is that many of them do not sufficiently examine the impact of development programs on the daily lives of ordinary people. "Development is a matter of people," Tarzie likes to say, and I kept this in mind during my travels for this book. Tarzie's own writings are a model for writers interested in development themes because they incorporate skepticism as well as compassion, insight, vision, and hope.

My debt to A. M. Rosenthal, executive editor of the *New York Times*, must also be acknowledged. I have formally dedicated this first book of mine to him and to my spouse, Jayanti, because they have influenced my life more than perhaps they themselves realize. Abe hired me, sight unseen, to work as his news clerk when I was a timid kid fresh out of Brandeis University in 1970. Along with his friend, Arthur Gelb, then metropolitan editor of the *Times*, Abe encouraged me to start writing for the newspaper. And many years after that first coveted byline, after I had chased enough fires in the South Bronx, attended enough zoning hearings in the suburbs, and covered enough neighborhood crises in New York's five boroughs, it was Abe who gave me my first foreign assignment as the *Times* correspondent in Africa.

That assignment gave me the opportunity to see firsthand the troubles and turmoils in the Third World and to understand the aspirations of poor people in these impoverished countries to obtain a better life. Like many of my colleagues in journalism and international affairs, I think that Abe Rosenthal was one of the most extraordinary foreign correspondents of our time. I have been privileged to know him as an editor who opened the doors and vistas of journalism for me, and as a friend who cared.

I owe a special thanks to Timothy Seldes, my longtime literary agent, who has been generous with his counsel and with the facilities of his office. A warm thanks, too, to Tim's associates, Gina Maccoby and Maggie De Vechi. And at W.W. Norton special thanks to Starling Lawrence, the editor of my book, and also thanks to Nelda Freeman, Marian Schwartz, Debra Makay, and Sandy Lifland.

My thanks to Thomas Craven, the veteran filmmaker, who produced a documentary based on this book and who invited me to write the narration.

Also in New York, Bruce and Karolyn Gould, Barbara Bender, and Michael Shaffer have been long-standing supporters and ever unwavering in their encouragement. Tony Klingler, formerly with Thomas Cook, assisted greatly in my travel arrangements. Valuable advice on the manuscript was given by Alben Phillips, formerly of the *New York Times*, and Hugh O'Haire, Jr., editor of *Populi* magazine, the quarterly publication of the United Nations Fund for Population Activities. Thanks also to Ralph Buultjens, Al Moran; Gabe Cantwell of ITT; and Cally Flickinger of Citibank.

I am especially grateful to Steven W. Sinding of the U.S. Agency for International Development and Michael A. Callen of Citibank. They spent hours poring through my manuscript and offered suggestions to improve the text.

Other friends were supportive in other ways: Mohan and Nita Shah allowed me to mooch many a meal from them whenever I transited through Gotham, as did George and Marianne Vecsey, Chota Chudasama and Sudhir Pingle

Reddy, Jaswant Lalwani, and Jon and Ellen Quint. Warm thanks also to Dr. Raymond Sherman of the Cornell Medical Group at New York Hospital.

A number of journalist colleagues enthusiastically helped me during my months on this book project: at the *International Herald Tribune* in Paris, Philip Foisie, the executive editor, Walter Wells, the editor, and Bob Donahue, editor of the editorial page, published columns and dispatches I sent from different parts of the developing world, which guaranteed immense exposure for the themes and topics I believe worth writing about. At the *Reader's Digest*, valuable help was given by David L. Minter, assistant managing editor, and John "Dimi" Panitza, European editor. And at the *Atlantic Monthly*, C. Michael Curtis has always been willing to consider ideas from me. Warm thanks also to Ken Emerson of the *New York Times Magazine*.

At the Canadian Broadcasting Corporation's office in Paris, special thanks to Linda White. No one who writes about the Third World these days should neglect David Lamb's *The Africans*, a marvelous book, which I have used as reference. I must also cite *People* magazine, edited by John Rowley and published by the International Planned Parenthood Federation in London, an enormously useful journal to anyone interested in the population business. I have drawn freely on John Rowley's efforts, and I want here to say thanks to him and his staff.

At the United Nations Fund for Population Activities, my thanks to Heino Wittrin, Shigeaki Tomita, Luis Olivos, Hiro Ando, Roushdi el-Heneidi, Hans Wagener, Stephen Viederman, Jennifer Yap, Jeannie Peterson, Jack Voelpel, and Dr. T. N. Krishnan, and a special thanks to Maria Karczewski, Pat Troughton, and Jessie R. Jones, who went out of their way to respond to my often troublesome queries. James Grant, executive director of the United Nations Children's Fund (UNICEF), and Bradford Morse, administrator of the United Nations Development Programme, came forth with timely advice for my research, as did Yasushi Akashi, the United Nations's under secretary general for information; Virendra Dayal, *chef de cabinet* to Secretary General Javier Perez de Cuellar; and Jay Long, a ranking American in the United Nations Secretariat in New York.

Very special thanks to Dr. Nafis Sadik of the United Nations Fund for Population Activities and Ambassador Farooq Sobhan of Bangladesh.

During my travels, scores of people in different parts of the world were kind and generous to me, sometimes at risk to themselves. It would be impossible to name all of them, and some would prefer not to be identified because of the special political circumstances of their countries. Those whom I can name and thank include:

In Mexico, Joops Alberts, Maria Elena Casanova, Maria Luz Diaz-Marta, Iris Lujambio, of the United Nations; Bernd and Susan Debusmann of Reuters; Anameli de Velasco and Ignacio Rodriguez.

In India, Rahul Singh and B. G. Verghese of the *Indian Express;* Minhaz

Merchant of *Gentleman* magazine; Dilip Thakore of *Business World* magazine; and Vir and Malavika Sanghvi of *Imprint* magazine, who invited me to write for their publications during my travels; my parents, Balkrishna and Charusheela Gupte, and my late uncle, Keshav R. Pradhan, of Bombay; my parents-in-law, Anand and Malati Lal of Secunderabad; Pramila and Lessell David in Hyderabad; Janki Ganju, P. A. Nazareth, Pupul Jayakar, Sharada Prasad, and Ajai Lal and Indu Lal in New Delhi.

In Sri Lanka, President Junius Richard Jayewardene; Wickrema Weerasooria; Kumari Perera; Nirmala de Mel; Richard Schoonover, Kenneth Scott, and Herbert George Hagerty of the American Embassy; Nirmala Rao and Rajendra Abhyankar of the Indian High Commission; Shankar and Sujaya Menon; and Neelan and Sithie Tiruchelvam.

In Singapore, Bhavani and Kutty Narayan, Arturo and Bobbie Laguna, and Omie Kerr.

In Malaysia, Nes and Soli Talyarkhan, Bob and Jenny Bowker, Edith Russo, and M.G.G. Pillai.

In Thailand, Ambassador Ashok Gokhale and Shyamala Cowsik of the Indian Embassy; and Mechai Viravaidya.

In the Philippines, Stirling Scruggs of the United Nations Fund for Population Activities; Jose Rimon; and P.S. Hariharan of the Asian Development Bank.

In Australia, Ali Cromie, Paul Beers, Uri Themal, Fedor Mediansky, Kim Beazley, Desmond J. Ball, Katherine Betts, Frank Galbally, Dr. John Caldwell, Professor Gavin Jones, William Abeyratne, and Bruce and May Stinear. And Dr. John J. Billings.

In Chile, Sylvia Burle of the United Nations Development Programme, and Dr. Benjamin Viel.

In Ecuador, Dr. Hugo Corvalan, Alfredo Jaramillo, and Magdalena de Andrade, all of the United Nations Fund for Population Activities.

In Colombia, Maria Lucia de Gutierrez, of the United Nations office in Bogota, and Alfredo and Fina Lopez.

In Brazil, Warren Hoge and his lovely wife, Olivia. Warren was a correspondent for the *New York Times* when I visited Rio de Janeiro and has since become foreign editor of the *Times*. And, of course, Dr. Walter Rodrigues and his staff.

In Kenya, Sharad and Leena Rao; Manju and Kantic DasGupta; Geeta Manek and family; Sir Eboo and Lady Pirbhai, and their daughter Noor; High Commissioner Vinod K. Grover and his wife, Rewa, of India; Marianne Fitzgerald; and Hanson Otundo. And a special thanks to Manubhai Madhvani and the Chenni Vohra family.

In Nigeria, Alhaji Umaru Dikko; Alhaji Shehu Malami; Mohinder Singh of the Birla Group; High Commissioner Kris Srinivasan, and his wife, Brinda, of India; Zahed and Laila Baig; George and Christina Griffin of the American

Embassy; and Mikail Prest, chief of personal staff to President Shehu Shagari. President Shagari gave me several useful interviews prior to the military coup on December 31, 1983, that overthrew the civilian government. And thanks to Gen. Olesegun Obasanjo, who gave me an interview in the middle of a busy convention in Brioni, Yugoslavia.

In Morocco, Mohammed and Laila Benaissa; Bahia Bensalah Zemrani; Ambassador Joseph Verner Reed, William Marsh, and Thomas Dove of the American Embassy in Rabat; Ambassador O. N. Sheopuri and Mrs. Shanta Sheopuri at the Indian Embassy; and the indomitable Steve Hughes at Reuters.

In Tunisia, Larry Pope, Mounir Addoum, R. Ellsworth Miller, and Ahmed M. Qutub of the American Embassy.

In Egypt, Hamed Fahmy of the United Nations Fund for Population Activities, and Dr. Aziz el-Bindary.

In China, Christopher S. Wren of the *New York Times*, and Michael Weisskopf of the *Washington Post.*

In Britain, some close friends became closer during the frenetic months of the book project, offering me shelter and sustenance whenever I passed through London: Nandita and Potla Sen of the Commonwealth Secretariat; Ray and Jenepher Moseley of the *Chicago Tribune;* Tim Llewellyn of the British Broadcasting Corporation; and Babulal Jain, a large-hearted compatriot.

To all these friends around the world, some longtime and some newfound, my profound thanks. You all really made the book possible.

Pranay Gupte
New York City, May 1984

Bibliography

There is no dearth of literature on "population" and related topics. Much of this literature is heavily academic in nature and therefore somewhat heavy going for the ordinary reader. During my travels, nevertheless, I came across a number of publications that I found tremendously readable and useful, and I offer the following list:

Bailey, Anthony. *Along the Edge of the Forest.* New York: Random House, 1983.

Bernstein, Richard. *From the Center of the Earth.* Boston: Little, Brown, 1982.

Birrell, Robert and Tanya. *An Issue of People.* Melbourne: Longman-Cheshire, 1981.

Brandt, Willy. *Common Crisis.* London: Pan Books, 1983.

———. *Handbook of World Development.* Harlow: Longman, 1981.

———. *North-South: A Programme for Survival.* Cambridge: MIT Press, 1980.

Brown, Lester R. *In the Human Interest.* New York: Norton, 1974.

———. *The Twenty-Ninth Day.* New York: Norton, 1978.

Butterfield, Fox. *China: Alive in the Bitter Sea.* New York: Times Books, 1982.

Calder, Ritchie. *The Future of a Troubled World.* London: Heinemann, 1983.

Cetron, Marvin, and Thomas O'Toole. *Encounters with the Future.* New York: McGraw-Hill, 1983.

Christopher, Robert C. *The Japanese Mind.* New York: Linden Press, 1983.

Crewdson, John. *The Tarnished Door.* New York: Times Books, 1983.

Critchfield, Richard. *Villages.* New York: Doubleday/Anchor, 1983.

Didion, Joan. *Salvador.* London: Chatto and Windus, 1983.

Ehrlich, Dr. Paul R. *The Population Bomb.* New York: Sierra Club/Ballantine Books, 1968.

Fraser, John. *The Chinese.* London: William Collins, 1981.

Gavshon, Arthur. *Crisis in Africa.* London: Penguin, 1981.

Greer, Germaine. *Sex and Destiny: The Politics of Human Fertility.* New York: Harper & Row, 1984.

Harrison, Paul. *Inside the Third World.* London: Penguin, 1979.

———. *The Third World Tomorrow.* London: Penguin, 1980.

Horne, Donald. *The Lucky Country.* Sydney: Penguin, 1964.

Huston, Perdita. *Message from the Village.* New York: Epoch B. Foundation, 1978.

International Planned Parenthood Federation. *People* magazine. Edited by John Rowley. London.

Jones, Landon Y. *Great Expectations: America and the Baby Boom Generation.* New York: Coward, McCann and Geoghegan, 1980.

Kandell, Jonathan. *Passage Through El Dorado.* New York: Morrow, 1984.

Kaplan, Samuel. *The Dream Deferred.* New York: Seabury Press, 1976.

Lamb, David. *The Africans.* New York: Random House, 1982.

Lewis, Paul H. *The Governments of Argentina, Brazil and Mexico.* New York: Crowell, 1975.

Mathews, Jay and Linda. *One Billion.* New York: Random House, 1983.

McEvedy, Colin, and Richard Jones. *The Atlas of World Population History.* London: Penguin, 1978.

Middle East. Monthly magazine published in London.

Miro, Carmen A., and Joseph E. Potter. *Population Policy.* London: Frances Pinter, 1980.

Moraes, Dom. *A Matter of People.* New York: Praeger, 1974.

———. *Voices for Life.* New York: Praeger, 1975.

Mosher, Steven W. *Broken Earth: The Rural Chinese.* New York: Free Press, 1983.

Naipaul, Shiva. *North of South.* New York: Simon & Schuster, 1979.

Naipaul, V. S. *Among the Believers.* London: Andre Deutsch, 1981.

Nyerere, Julius K. *Freedom and Development: A Selection from Writings and Speeches 1968–1973.* New York: Oxford University Press, 1974.

Omran, Abdel-Rahim. *Population in the Arab World.* London: UNFPA/Croom Helm, 1980.

Ottaway, Marina and David. *Ethiopia.* New York: Africana, 1978.

Raban, Jonathan. *Arabia Through the Looking Glass.* London: Collins, 1979.

Rosenblum, Mort. *Coups and Earthquakes.* New York: Harper & Row, 1979.

Salas, Rafael M. *People: An International Choice.* New York: Pergamon Press, 1977.

Sauvy, Alfred. *Zero Growth?* London: Basil Blackwell, 1975.

Servan-Schreiber, Jean-Jacques. *The World Challenge.* New York: Simon & Schuster, 1980.

Shaplen, Robert. *A Turning Wheel: Thirty Years of the Asian Revolution.* London: Andre Deutsch, 1979.

Shipler, David K. *Russia: Broken Idols, Solemn Dreams.* New York: Times Books, 1983.

Simon, Julian L. *The Ultimate Resource.* Princeton: Princeton University Press, 1981.

Singh, Jyoti Shankar. *The New International Economic Order.* New York: Praeger, 1977.

Smith, Hedrick. *The Russians.* Rev. ed. New York: Times Books, 1983.

Sowell, Thomas. *The Economics and Politics of Race.* New York: Morrow, 1983.

Toffler, Alvin. *The Third Wave.* New York: Morrow, 1980.

Topping, Seymour. *Journey Between Two Chinas.* New York: Harper & Row, 1972.

Turnbull, Colin M. *The Lonely African.* New York: Simon & Schuster, 1962.

UNFPA. *State of the World Population 1984.* New York: United Nations Publications, 1984.

UNICEF. *The State of the World's Children 1984.* New York: Oxford University Press, 1984.

Viel, Benjamin. *The Demographic Explosion.* New York: Irvington, 1976.

Vittachi, Varindra Tarzie. *The Brown Sahib.* London: Andre Deutsch, 1962.

———. *The Fall of Sukarno.* New York: Praeger, 1967.

Warwick, Donald P. *Bitter Pills: Population Policies and Their Implementation in Eight Developing Countries.* New York: Cambridge University Press, 1982.

Whitaker, Jennifer Seymour. *Africa and the United States.* New York: New York University Press, 1978.

Williams, David. *President and Power in Nigeria.* London: Cass, 1982.

Wolfson, Margaret. *Changing Approaches to Population Problems.* Paris: OECD, 1978.

Index